Jump-Start

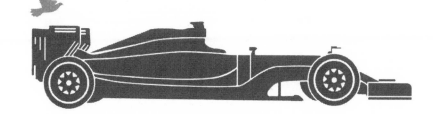

BRIDGET L. ROSE

Pitstop Series

Team Names

Velocità Rossa

Alfa

Adrenalina

GRENZENLOS

Hawke

Tempête Racing

zeitgeist racing

Klein Racing

Spark Racing

Carousel

Racing

Aerodinámica

This book is dedicated to every person who is barely keeping their head above water right now. Hold on tight to your dreams, they will raise you up high in one way or another.

CHAPTER I

Leonard

Another race. Another win. Another critic probably ready to jump on the mistake I made in the third corner during the opening lap.

I felt it in the car as soon as it happened. I didn't leave enough space for my rival, and teammate, so he went off track and lost first place. I can already see the headlines. 'Leonard Tick Only Wins Races By Cheating'. My entire life has been like this. Since I was a kid, people have attacked me and tried to tear me down. That's what happens when you're the first black race car driver in a predominantly white motorsport. I fucking love this sport, but there are so many things wrong with it. We still have a long way to go before we can truly be proud of it.

I jump out of my Formula One car, briefly appreciating the sleek black colour my team went with this year. My eyes fixate on the Grenzenlos symbol—two infinity symbols entangled—on top of the nose, a wave of nostalgia running through me. I won my first World Championship with this team and hope to win more in the future. We've come a long way over the years I've been a racer at Grenzenlos, and I couldn't be prouder of the team I have.

"Leonard!" the post-race interviewer—Jason Dirk, I believe—starts, and I stare at him with my lips pulled into a thin line.

Formula One has hardened me to the point of no return. One smile is all it takes for people to spin things out of proportion like I'm happy about the move I pulled in corner three, which inevitably led to my win. Sometimes shit like that happens,

1

it's normal in an aggressive sport like racing, but reporters don't care about that when it comes to *me* making the mistake. I'm judged a lot more harshly than other drivers.

"You drove a great race today and managed your tyres well. What a way to start the season! How do you feel coming back as a World Champion?" he asks, and I suck in an inaudible, sharp breath.

"I feel great. My team and I have worked hard and restlessly over the break, which is why it's great to see it paying off already," I say, shaking my head at his next comment.

"That incident in turn three sure did help. How do you feel about that?" *I feel like I want to punch you in the face*, I think to myself, but except for me grabbing my towel a little harder, no one would suspect how much his question bothers me. That's why it's great to have a reputation for never smiling. It allows me to hide how I truly feel.

"I will have to review the incident before I can comment on what happened. From the car, it felt like a normal racing incident," I explain, wiping away the sweat dripping down the side of my forehead.

I'm exhausted.

Today was a hot and long race, and I can't wait to get back home and spend time with my family. After test-driving the car for the past few weeks and putting every available hour into training to get ready for the start of the season, I've barely seen them. My brothers, Mum, and Dad all miss me too—they make sure to remind me every day—and I have to get back to Benz, my three-year-old pitbull. I miss her. I miss everything about my home. Even that pain in the arse, Chi—

"Well, congratulations on your win. Let's move onto our second place," Jason says, and I step over to where my performance coach, Quinn, is standing.

"Great drive, kiddo," she says before my hand slips onto her shoulder. Quinn is my best friend in the entire world. She's hardly five years older than me, but insists on keeping that nickname.

"Yeah, you liked my move in corner three?" I ask, which causes her to laugh. We both know I'm joking in the only way I do—without showing it on my face—but she's enjoying my playful attitude very much.

"I did. Now go get your trophy, kiddo. I haven't got all day," she teases, and I pinch her side in response. She laughs loudly, the sound making a wonderful warmth spread through my chest.

Before I can make my way to the cool-down room, Adrian Romana, a Formula One rookie I've only met a few times, comes up to me, still wearing his helmet. He holds out his hand for me as he calls out a 'congrats' before pulling me into an excited hug and telling me how well I drove—from what he could see as I lapped him. I don't usually show affection to people, but this barely eighteen-year-old gives me no choice, and I don't mind it as much as I thought I would. Adrian's a good kid, maybe that's why.

"I'll see you later!" he says before letting himself get weighed, just like every driver has to after a race.

I wonder what the fuck has him so happy all the time, but it's nice. Having someone positive like him in my life might be good for me. The thought is pushed away by my pessimistic side before I can linger on it.

My tired and sore feet bring me to the cool-down room, where my teammate, Jonathan Kent, is taking small sips from the bottle of water they have ready for us. There are three podium-style tables at the front of the room, and I walk toward mine, seeing the cap with the number 1 on it. I place it on my head before taking my bottle and joining the other drivers.

3

Cameron Kion, Adrian's teammate, managed to come in third, and it has him smiling so brightly, I wish I knew if he's always this fucking happy too. Whoever paired them up wanted a sunshine driver line-up. They must be quite popular with the fans.

"Nice defence in the eighth corner on the second lap, Leonard," Cameron says, and I shift my attention to his blue eyes, giving him a slight nod.

"Nice work on your start," I reply, not used to anyone making small talk with me after the race.

The other drivers mostly keep their distance from me. It's always been like this, but I can't blame them either. My facial expression doesn't communicate 'hey, I'm approachable'. It communicates 'fuck off', I've made sure of it over the years.

"My throttle was fucking stuck in the first corner," Cameron goes on, and I raise both eyebrows in response. "Yeah, it was crazy. Thank God it unstuck itself after a terrifying five seconds," he says with a slight laugh that makes his chest move. I give him a thoughtful nod, so he moves over to his water bottle.

Dreadful silence fills the room, and I'm convinced I can hear Jonathan's stomach rumble from hunger. It makes me want to kick him. We don't have the closest of relationships. He can't stand me, and I've fantasised about strangling him on many occasions. He's a spoiled, arrogant brat, and I'm too serious for him. We don't match on any level, but fans go crazy for our rivalry. Last year, we were head-to-head in the Driver's Championship, but I beat him in the second-to-last race for good. The title fell on me, and he's hated me more since. I couldn't give less of a shit. As a matter of fact, I often have to suppress a grin when he tries to talk behind my back about how I cheated to get the title. He's such a bloody sore loser, it's hilarious.

"Let's go," someone says, and I stand up from the seats at the wall to follow them toward the podium area.

First, Cameron steps onto the podium, taking his place. Then follows Jonathan, who bumps his shoulder against mine on his way out knowing full well I won't be able to trip him in front of all of these people. I would love to though. I would also very much enjoy it if he fell right on top of that nose job he had five years ago. Arsehole.

I walk onto the podium, standing on the highest spot because I'm the winner of the fucking race. I should be happy. Starting the season off like this is what every driver dreams of, but, for some reason, a numbness has spread through my chest. It's incredibly unsettling and makes me suck in a sharp breath. *What the hell?*

A frightening question crosses my thoughts a second later.

Am I falling out of love with racing?

Chapter 2
Chiara

I 'm bored. God, I never get as bored as I do at work. Art is my happy place. I could stare at a da Vinci painting for hours, finding new things about it that fascinate me. At the same time, it takes everything out of me not to rip out my eyeballs when I have to watch the same immersive show of his art for my job. It's garbage. It's so horrible, I have no idea why it's so highly praised. The quality is bad, and the music does not match da Vinci's work at all. This is what my Nonna would call a *vergogna*, a disgrace. As an art major, I can't help but agree. If I didn't need this job as much as I do, I wouldn't work here.

Graham, my best friend, and I made a deal to get as many hours in as we can. We're trying to save up to open our own immersive art gallery one day, where I get to create the shows. We're still about 498,000 pounds away from our 500,000-pound goal. We came up with this plan last year, which is why I can't help but doubt we will ever make it. Two thousand pounds a year is nothing. It's not nearly enough. Yes, we could easily get the money by asking Graham's brother—famous, smug, brooding, drop-dead gorgeous Formula One World Champion Leonard Tick—for the money, but neither one of us wants to use his wealth for our dream.

Graham and I grew up together. We met when we were four and have been inseparable since. I met him when I couldn't stop wearing pigtails and his name was still Gracie. Now we're twenty-four and don't spend a single day apart. Leonard has been in almost every memory I've had with Graham since we met. They're also inseparable, apart from Leonard traveling the world for his fancy-schmancy races.

Ugh.

I can't stand him. We're always at each other's throats. Always. I can't remember a day we didn't bicker or fight with each other. The first day we met, he tore down the sand castle I'd built in the sandbox, laughing wickedly as he did it too. I'd shoved him face-first into the remains after. Ever since then, we haven't found a way to tolerate each other. There's never been a reason for me to be nice to him, and he isn't too kind to me either. Last Halloween, he came in a costume that—according to that smug asshole—required a live snake to be around his neck for the entire duration of the evening. I hate snakes. I'm terrified of them, which is exactly why he did it. In return, I posted an unflattering photo of him mid-sneeze to social media. It was evil considering how many people know him, but I didn't care. He deserved it.

And, thinking of the devil, he walks right into the fucking room with his angel of a niece holding onto his hand. Little Ellie loves this immersive exhibition. She drags Leonard here every single weekend he's home. Ellie is Jack's daughter. Jackson Tick is Leonard's and Graham's older brother by ten years. He's been with his partner forever, and they adopted a then three-year-old Elizabeth four years ago.

"Chiara!" Ellie calls out when she sees me in the corner of the room where I have to stand in case someone has a question about the exhibition. I know, what an exciting job I have.

"Ellie," I reply and squat down to open my arms for the seven-year-old. Her face lights up because I'm the only one who calls her that. To everyone else, she's Lizzie.

"Hurry up," the little girl with strawberry blonde hair, pale skin, blue eyes, and freckles says as she tugs on Leonard's hand.

Leonard Tick. My archnemesis. The man I'd very much like to kick in the shin one day for being so irritating and gorgeous at the same time. His eyes are a deep, warm brown, just like his skin. His lips are so full and the clean, short beard he keeps on his face complements his rugged features. Tattoos peak out on his neck from under his shirt, and I suck in a sharp breath when an image of him shirtless on the beach fills my head. I shake it away. Just because I can't get along with the man doesn't mean I can't find him hot. Because he is. God, he's so fucking handsome, I can't stand to look at him for more than ten seconds without my body feeling things I do not approve of.

"Come on, Lenny," Ellie says when Leonard takes his sweet time to walk to me.

He's scowling, as usual, but it's something I don't mind about him. It's one of the few things we have in common. It's difficult for someone to get a smile out of me. Most of the time, I have what people call a resting-bitch-face, which is fine by me. I don't need to seem like the type of person who wants to be approached. I don't like most people, only the ones I've grown to love over years and years.

"Starling," Leonard greets me as soon as Ellie's arms are around my neck and mine hug her back.

"Champ," I reply, and he frowns even harder. Good. He's been calling me 'Starling' since a starling bird flew onto my head when I was six and scared the shit out of me. I've been calling him 'Champ' for about as long for no other reason than because it bothers him. It bothers him a lot.

"We came to see you," Ellie says, and I raise my eyebrow at the little girl. She's grinning so brightly, it tugs on the corners of my mouth. I let them curl up ever so slightly, sending surprise into Leonard's eyes.

"Yeah? Not to see the show?" I ask, and Ellie stares at the ground, her cheeks turning bright pink.

"Okay, maybe that too," she admits, and I give her chin a single pat with the backside of my fingers before standing upright and facing the English man I've grown to despise over the years. His eyes are on mine, thoughtful and expecting me to congratulate him at the same time. I know him too well not to realize what he wants to hear.

"Too bad about that incident in the third corner," I say since I know the sport of Formula One inside out. The man in front of me glares at me. "I wish Jonathan had kept that place," I add, causing his eyes to grow dark from irritation.

"I'm flattered you pay so much attention to my performance, Starling," he replies with his thick English accent, both of us in a stare-down at this point.

"For amusement purposes only," I spit back quietly with my Italian accent, so Ellie doesn't hear. Leonard takes a step toward me, eyes filled with heat.

"I'm surprised you still work here. Must be your great customer service skills," he says with so much sarcasm, I bite down on my bottom lip to keep from grinning because it was kind of funny. And very accurate.

"Good one," I snort, and his eyes flash me his version of a smile. "Hope you didn't burn through your last two brain cells to come up with it." It wipes the smile out of his gaze immediately.

"Demon," he whispers, and I offer him a wicked smile.

"*Stronzo*," I reply, which makes him angry. His gaze drops to my lips before he trails it back to my eyes and lets out a humming sound. My body catches on fire in response, but I decide to ignore that reaction completely as I glare back at him.

"Lenny, come, the show is about to start," Ellie says and pulls her uncle toward the bench in the middle of the room where they always sit. I screw my eyes shut and let out the breath I've been holding.

God, this man drives me crazy.

During the show, I can't keep my eyes from slipping to Leonard and Ellie, just like they always do when the two of them come to watch. It fascinates me how patient Leonard is with his niece. She keeps whispering things into his ear, and he continues to nod and whisper something back to her. If this was anyone else, it would warm my heart. When it comes to Leonard, it has a different effect. A weird one. I like seeing this side of him, but liking it immediately sends a wave of ice through me, trying to freeze any positive feelings I could ever hold for this man.

After the show, Ellie gives me one last hug. She tells me how pretty I look with my hair out of its usual French braids. It's long, reaching the top of my ass in wavy brown strands. I even added a little makeup today to highlight my bright green eyes. The more I think about it, the more I realize how much effort I put into my appearance today. I'm wearing my nicest pair of sneakers, which doesn't mean much since I'm broke, and even added my finest jewelry. It may turn my skin green if I wear it for too long, but I like the rose-gold color of the necklace, earrings, and rings. I don't know what made me decide to pay extra attention to my outfit today, but it was most certainly not because I had a feeling I'd see Leonard. That'd be absurd.

"Try not to set any retirement homes on fire when you walk past them on your way home, little demon," Leonard says, and I let out a humorless snort. My eyes swiftly skip to Ellie, but she's looking around the room, not paying attention to us.

"Ellie seems to like it when you take her here. It'd be a shame if she couldn't do that anymore if your ego grows too massive for this room. Try not to let it," I say, and he rolls his eyes at my words.

"I'll buy a bigger building if it comes to that," he replies and takes his niece's hand again, leaving me alone to roll my eyes at his words.

"Ready to go?" Graham's deep voice with his heavy accent fills my ears a minute later, and I turn around to face my best friend. It's finally the end of our shift.

"One million percent," I reply, and he takes my hand, leading me to the staff room where we keep our stuff. Lucky for us, we usually get scheduled to work together. "You just missed your brother and Ellie, by the way," I add as we pack up our things. Graham lets out a hurt scoff.

"And they didn't say 'hello' to me? That's bloody rude," he replies, and I shake my head with a slight grin.

"I'm more interesting," I tease, causing Graham to let out a snort and a quiet 'yeah, right'. I throw my scarf at him, but he catches it with ease and throws it around his neck. "Hey," I say, but he places the straps of his grey backpack on his shoulders without acknowledging my complaint.

"Are you in the mood for Thai?" he asks, and I focus my full attention on the younger version of Leonard.

They look almost identical, except my best friend doesn't have facial hair. He says it's itchy and prefers to have a clean-shaven face. I prefer no facial hair on him too, but mostly because with it, he really does look like an identical version of Leonard.

"Why? Are *you* in the mood for Thai?" I ask as he takes my bag to carry it for me.

He's done that for years because acts of service are his love language. I've stopped telling him I'm more than capable of doing such small things myself because it makes him happy to do them for me. It's his way of saying 'I love you, let me take care of you even if it's only by a little'. Fuck, I love this man with all of my heart.

"Maybe," he says suspiciously, and I nudge his side in response.

"I want Thai, but only if we're watching Tangled too," I reply, and Graham wraps his arms around my shoulders.

"Should we invite Lulu?" I give him a side glance.

"Of course, we should invite Lulu. If we watch a Disney movie without her, she'll rip our heads off," I remind him, and my best friend laughs as we walk home, dialing our childhood friend's number at the same time.

11

CHAPTER 3
Leonard

I have a week off before the next race weekend, which is why, apart from my usual training, I'm doing my best to spend as much time with my family as I possibly can. This morning, I visited Mum and Dad. Yesterday, after I dropped Ellie off, Jack and Stu insisted I spend some time at their house. I was more than happy to oblige. I had missed them both more than I will ever admit.

Today, Benz, my happy pitbull, and I are on our way over to Graham's and Chiara's place. I don't know why I'm doing this to myself, seeing that infuriating woman twice in less than twenty-four hours, but I want to hang out with my brother. Unfortunately, those two are a package deal, especially because I'm going to their flat. At least Benz is excited. Her tail is wagging in a helicopter motion as we wait for one of them to open the door. For some inexplicable reason, she loves the little demon on the other side of the door.

Chiara.

Starling.

Demon.

Potato, potahto because that woman has been a pain in my arse since we were kids and she shoved my face into a pile of sand. The events that led up to that are unimportant, except for how red her face had grown from anger. It was hilarious. Ever since she appeared in my life, she's outdone herself in being the biggest pain in the arse. She's stubborn and moody, and I hate how similar we are in every single way. Neither of us cares much for people. We don't smile, except sometimes for Ellie, Benz, and Graham, even my mum. We hate each other's presence, and we both love Benz, who is still waiting patiently for her to open the door. I don't understand why my sweet angel is so drawn to the spawn of Satan. It makes absolutely no sense to me.

"Benzie," Chiara says as she kneels and greets my daughter. Benz licks her all over the face, earning herself a tiny smile from Starling. "Ah, and you brought your annoying daddy," she says, causing my spine to stiffen in response. "You can leave now. I will bring her back tonight," Chiara says, her Italian accent thick. She moved to England when she was four, but living with her Mamma, who has the strongest Italian accent in the world, rubbed off on her. She also went to an American-Italian International School for most of her life.

"Are you having a laugh? I'm not leaving my daughter with someone who barely knows how to take care of herself," I say and point at her sweater, which is inside out. Starling follows my gaze, rolling her eyes in response.

"I know how to take care of myself, *stronzo*," she replies, and I furrow my eyebrows at her. She just called me arsehole in Italian. Chiara's done it often enough for me to have looked it up a while ago, much like many other swear words she's thrown at my head over the years. "You're so sweet," she says to Benz and pats her stomach because my little angel has rolled onto her back to have her tummy scratched.

"Can we walk through the bloody door or must we stay out here in the hall?" I ask, a little annoyed with her now. Chiara looks up at me with a scowl.

"*You* can leave," she offers, her green eyes so bright, they knock the breath out of me for a moment. Her short frame stands upright before she slips her sweater off, leaving her in only a sports bra to highlight her breasts. Fuck me.

We may hate each other, but I can't help the way my skin catches fire from her upper body half-naked and so beautiful in front of me. This woman, with her tanned skin, curvy body, long brown hair, and eyes so green they burn into my soul, could have me on my knees if she wasn't so damn infuriating. And it isn't just because she's drop-dead gorgeous. No. She's got one of the kindest hearts I've ever seen. The way she loves Graham... I'm almost jealous I've got no one who loves me like that. Unfortunately, she doesn't offer me that side of her.

"You want to take a fucking picture to jerk off to later?" she says when my eyes are stuck on her breasts, which would fit perfectly into my big hands. *Jesus, Leonard. Focus.*

"Nah, I don't have a demon kink," I reply at the same moment she places the sweatshirt back on, this time the right way around. "Plus, you're the one who undressed in front of me," I remind her, but she walks away without responding. She truly is a demon.

"You didn't have to look, pervert," she says, but I'm the one who doesn't respond this time because she's absolutely right. I didn't have to study her sexy chest, but I couldn't help it. I'm only human, and it's been a few months since I've had sex, making my body a little too excitable.

Chiara bends over to pet Benz again, and I suck in a sharp breath when she puts her arse on display for me. This woman. I groan as I walk past her and settle down on the small, ancient couch in the living room. The blue colour is faded, but Graham refuses to take any money from me to buy a new one. He also refuses to take any to move out of this safety-hazardous place, which is way too small for the brother of a Formula One World Champion.

My family had close to nothing when we were growing up. Jack, Graham, and I shared a room until we were well into our teenage years, and I finally started making some money. Not a lot, not nearly enough for my parents to stop worrying about our bills. Dad worked multiple jobs to finance my very expensive dream, but we were lucky with the people who wanted to sponsor me. I had many. I'm a talented race car driver. I know I am. Everyone does. That's what I'm famous for. Talented and grumpy as hell. Fine by me.

I earn a lot of money now. Hell, I'm a fucking millionaire. But my brother is so bloody stubborn, he doesn't accept any help. Not to mention, he'd never leave Starling, and there is no way in hell I would ever do something nice for that little demon. Nope. It's not happening. It isn't my mission to make her like me, it's never been. All I want to do is spoil my brother a little with the money he deserves. He's been working his arse off for years, and I know it's his dream to open his own immersive art gallery with Chiara one day. I just wish he'd let me help him.

"Don't think so much. It contorts your face and will give you wrinkles. You might have to start using botox soon to get rid of them, Grandpa." I frown at her. I'm only four years older than her.

"At least I can afford to get botox. With the amount of frowning you do, you'll end up a wrinkled mess in two years, begging me to pay for your procedures," I spit back, causing her eyes to narrow at me. Fuck, it tugs on the corner of my mouth to see her upset with me.

"Leonard, Chiara, are you both behaving?" Graham asks, his voice low and firm.

"No," we reply simultaneously, and I shoot her a side glance.

Chiara's on the floor with Benz now. My baby is curled up in the devil woman's lap like there's no tomorrow, and I shake my head at the image. I should have trained my dog better to detect evil-incarnate.

"You two are so annoying, but I love you both, so I would like to spend the day with the two of you. Will that work?" he asks, and I stare into my brother's dark brown eyes before giving him a slight nod.

"*I* know how to behave," Chiara chimes in, and I force myself not to stare at her and roll my eyes so violently, it'd hurt.

"Can you even hang out with us today or will you be busy torturing innocent souls with your husband Lucifer?" I ask, causing amusement to sparkle in the demon's eyes.

"Yeah, I should get your room ready down there," she replies and tilts her head as she waits for a reaction. I refuse to give her one.

"Okay, let's go. I'm in desperate need of some coffee," Graham chimes in, ignoring Starling's and my heated moment. He usually does since he has no patience for our bickering. I can't blame him either.

"Benz, heel," I say, watching my baby trotting toward me with grace and stopping right at my side. She sits like the good girl she is, waiting for me to put on her leash.

"Can I walk her?" Chiara asks after we've made our way downstairs.

"No," I reply, instinctively gripping the leash harder.

There is no doubt in my mind how well she could take care of Benz. Hell, Starling loves her almost as much as me, more than anyone else in my family, but I can be a pain in the arse too. So, I don't let her walk my daughter, and I want to smirk hard when Chiara flashes me an annoyed look.

"I want to walk her," she insists, stepping in front of me to stop me from moving. God, she's so bloody stubborn.

"No," I repeat, and she sighs. The corners of her pouty lips curl downward even more.

"You never let me take care of her when you're gone either, and I'm a dog walker. It's only fair," she says, and I furrow both of my brows. Graham lets out an annoyed sigh, but I ignore him.

"Benz is my dog!" I blurt out, getting frustrated with her relentlessness to get such a simple thing she deserves for loving Benz so fiercely. "And why the hell would I leave you in charge of her when I'm not here? I don't like you." Chiara gives me yet another eye roll.

"I don't like you either, but I love her. I love her more than anyone else does, apart from you." Yep. I just thought the same thing and it fucking bothers me how similar we think. It sends a shudder down my spine. "Please." That word knocks me backward. It also drags all of the oxygen from my lungs because damn. She's never asked me for anything before, but I like hearing her beg. I like it a lot.

"No," I say for the third time, and Starling steps out of the way again, her arse-length hair flying in response.

"*Stronzo*," she says, and Graham takes her hand as we continue to make our way toward the café down the street from their flat.

I *am* an arsehole. I could have let her take Benz. I could even let her stay with Chiara when I'm gone, but I'm petty. I don't do nice things for her, and she does none for me. It's how we've always operated, and I plan to keep it that way, except, sensing how upset Starling is, my sweet girl pulls me to the woman I'm supposed to despise. She wants to walk with Chiara, and there is no way I could deny my daughter anything. Fuck me.

"Here," I growl as I hand Starling the leash and then shove my hands into my pockets. The little demon gives me a smug smirk, a rarity that only comes out when she's won an argument. "Fuck off," I add, but Chiara's attention has already shifted to Benz's tail-wagging, happy figure.

"You're going to be pissed about that the whole day now, aren't you?" Graham asks, and I shoot him an annoyed look.

Of course I'm going to be pissed. I hate that smirk of hers. I hate that my dog chose her over me. I hate that I care so damn much about every single interaction I have with this woman, that she takes up so many of my thoughts and so much of my energy.

"She's a pain," is all I say, but Chiara and Benz are walking ahead of us now. Just to annoy me, she's skipping as if she's pure sunshine, my dog happy as fuck right by her side.

"When will you stop denying that you like her?" Graham says, and I let out a harsh snort.

"She could be the last woman on the planet, and I'd rather let humanity die out," I reply, feeling my chest tighten at my words like it does when I lie.

Yeah, I'm going to go ahead and ignore that.

CHAPTER 4
Chiara

There is nothing I dread more than going to Mamma's house. I love her more than anyone else, but her roommate of six years is... he's a horrible man. At least to me. Mamma insists he's never harassed her and mostly leaves her alone, except to discuss things regarding their flat. Me, on the other hand, he harasses every single time I go there and he decides to join my mother and me for the homemade meals she prepares. It always taints the joyful moment I try to have with her, eating my Nonna's recipes and trying to feel connected to my home again. My true home. Not England. I've never, and will never, consider this country my home. I may not remember much about Italy from when I was living there as a child, but I visit often enough. I even remember the deep-rooted feeling of safety and happiness wrapped in nostalgia I feel when I step into my Nonna's home.

So, going to Mamma's is the last thing I want to do today, especially because she let me know Tim is going to be there. She has no idea that every time I come over and he's there, he makes some sort of advance. She doesn't know he makes inappropriate comments about my body and face. I can't tell her that he's groped me once or twice over the years. Mamma relies on him to pay for more than half her rent and has been since I moved in with Graham six years ago. Tim thinks she owes him money now, and it fucking sucks. It sucks because it's my fault. If I hadn't moved out, she never would have looked for a roommate in the first place. I could have paid rent, and the person I love most in the world wouldn't have to stay with a vile man like Tim. It's all my fault for wanting to be more independent and stop relying on Mamma so much. I'm the only one to blame.

That's why I don't say anything. Mamma is in this situation because of me, and we have very limited options. She relies on him to pay. She refuses to come live with me and Graham. She doesn't get hurt or harassed by him, according to her, so that's at least a little bit of a relief for me. I don't have money to pay for her either. I wish I did. God, I want nothing more than to get her away from Tim, but I can barely pay for my rent and utilities. The saddest part about that fact is that I work four separate jobs to scrap my rent and food money together. I'm a dog walker, I work at the immersive art exhibition, I pick up some shifts at my local bookstore whenever I can, and I spend my nights bartending at a popular club downtown. My jobs are all in fields that I love, except for the bartending one, but it gets exhausting when I hardly have time to rest my eyes or go on adventures with Graham.

I snap myself out of my thoughts, blinking back the anger I know has settled in my eyes in response to the thought of seeing Tim. I fucking hate him and the way he makes me feel about myself. He's cruel, and I know it, but it doesn't make interactions with him any less bothersome. I shudder at the reminder of what happened last time. The way he'd stared at my tits and when I'd asked him what his fucking problem was, he'd replied, "Just imagining what my hands would look like on those juicy tits of yours." I'd almost thrown up and then castrated him, but Mamma walked into the room, and I had to pretend nothing happened.

I can't not go to see Mamma either. There aren't many times a month we both have a morning off at the same time, like today. Usually, I spend those with her since Graham and I squeeze some time in whenever I'm between my job shifts. He also works two jobs, but he makes more money babysitting for some famous couple I always forget the name of. They're only locally known and for something social media related.

"*Bellissima*," Mamma says as soon as she opens the door for me.

My arms wrap around her center since she's quite a bit taller than me, and hers slide across my shoulders, hugging me close to her chest. As soon as I feel her comfort seep through my skin, exhaustion consumes me. I'm so goddamn tired. I only get about four hours of sleep a night. Bartending is kicking my ass, even if I'm incredibly good at it. The men that come to see me, my regulars, love the fact that I never smile. They think it's a challenge to crack one out of me, but they're so revolting toward me, they never succeed. And they never will. The only upside is that they tip me well.

"Are you hungry?" she goes on in our mother tongue, and I flash her a look I hope says 'do you even know me?'. Mamma lets out a soft laugh before waving me into the flat. I'm on high alert, but Tim is nowhere to be seen. That forces a sigh of relief to escape me.

"How are you, Mamma?" I ask in Italian as we start working in the kitchen to get lunch ready. I lay the table and finish the salad while Mamma finishes up the gnocchi in a tomato sauce for which I am still waiting to get the recipe. It's Nonna's specialty.

"Fine, *tesoro*. How have you been?" she asks, and I share how stressful work has been for me. Mamma listens closely, asking me follow-up questions. Then, she goes straight for an uncomfortable one I've been trying to avoid for as long as possible.

"What are you going to do with that art degree, Chiara? You need to start looking for a job in your field and stop killing yourself working at places that don't pay you enough to survive on," she reminds me, and I suck in a sharp breath, feeling a stinging sensation pull through my chest.

"Graham and I are saving up for our immersive art gallery," I say, my voice sounding weak and unsure. Mamma gives me a small smile, ready to destroy my dream a little with reality.

"Okay," is all she says, and it knocks me backward a little. *She won't fight me on this?* "I believe in you, but you *are* destroying yourself trying to achieve something that is beyond difficult," she adds, and I nod in response.

I know it's hard. Fuck, it's almost impossible. Graham and I have hardly saved any money for our dream, but I never thought it'd be easy. Neither of us did. I'm struggling a bit right now, but it'll get easier. We will save enough money, I know we will. Working four separate jobs might be slowly killing me, but Mamma did the very same thing for ten years when I was younger to support us. It's also why I spent most of my time at the Tick's house and why I'm so close with Graham's mother.

"Don't worry about me, Mamma. I'm more worried about you. You're still working too hard, and the doctor said you need to slow down unless you want your heart to give out on you sooner than it should," I remind her, which was the biggest reason why I wanted to come here.

Three years ago, Mamma gave me the fright of my life when she passed out in the middle of the bookstore. I dragged her there because my favorite author's new book had come out that day. The doctor had told us she needed to slow down, which, for Mamma, was not an option. She hardly made enough money to stay here as is, and she said she couldn't afford to stop taking shifts at the local bakery. She wakes up at four in the morning, works all day, and goes to bed late because she prepares the dough for the next day already. I guess she and I aren't different at all, except I don't have her heart condition—knock on wood. She needs to take things slower, otherwise, I will lose her, and I can't afford that.

"You know I can't do that. I don't have an option," she says, and I shake my head, crossing my arms in front of my chest. I take several quiet, deep breaths to calm my racing heartbeat.

"Come live with Graham and me until we find a better solution." She snorts at my words, but I'm not even slightly amused. "I am not joking," I say, my voice firm. Mamma spins around, her heart-shaped lips pulling into a thin line.

"Actually, Chiara, there is something I've been meaning to discuss with you," she says, and my heart skips several beats.

This cannot be good. Mamma is hardly ever serious, and never to the extent she is now. After she fainted at the bookstore and came to, she started laughing and telling me that her thick head broke her fall. I could only stare at her in disbelief.

"Tell me," I reply, watching her mouth open in response before an awful tingle runs down my spine. Fuck.

"Why, hello, Chiara. I didn't know you'd come over today."

Tim's voice fills my ears, sending another terrifying shudder down my back. His hand moves onto my shoulder to give it a light squeeze, but I step away from him immediately. Lucky for him, Mamma is here, and I can't rip his arms off and throw them out the window. He's so fucking nice in front of her too, always playing the polite bastard he most certainly isn't.

Mamma is cleaning up in the dining room while I do the kitchen? He comes to me and makes inappropriate comments. Mamma goes to the washroom? He fucks me with his eyes so hard, he shifts in his seat every single time. God, that man makes me feel disgusting and cheap. He makes my skin want to rip itself off my body.

If I wasn't so fucking scared he'd kick Mamma out of the apartment, I'd have done something a long time ago. I would have fought back harder. I would have put my hands on *him* for a change, but not in a way he would have enjoyed. The coward can consider himself lucky that my mother's well-being will always come before mine for me.

"Hello, Tim," I force out through gritted teeth, causing Mamma to shoot me a confused look. *Fuck. Play nice, Chiara. Your Mamma sees right through your bullshit when you don't focus.*

"You look beautiful in that dress," he compliments me, but I don't respond. Not until Mamma makes her way into the dining room and he adds, "I could just rip it right off your body." Bile rises in my throat, but except for a small hurling noise I can't control, no words leave me.

He's not an unattractive man visually. He has short, brown hair that's fading into a timeless silver. There are faint wrinkles on his face, but not nearly enough a man his age should have. He's lean and has great style. Not to mention, he makes a shitload of money through the strip club he owns. Why he continues to live with Mamma is beyond me, but I suspect it's to be close to me. He has no other reason because money sure as hell isn't a problem. He pays for this flat almost entirely by himself nowadays.

"Come on, now, Chiara, don't give me the cold shoulder," he says as he steps toward me, but my face hardens into an emotionless expression.

My feet bring me to the stove before my fingers reach for the dial that controls the temperature. I'm about to turn it off when Tim grabs my hand. I don't think. I twist his hand and wrist until he's under my complete control. One more move and *snap*, goodbye doing anything with it for at least two months.

"Do *not* touch me," I warn.

He tries to wrestle free by using his other hand, but I take it into the same grip. He's at my complete mercy, and I would love nothing more than to use the thirteen years of kickboxing and Jiu-jitsu training in my repertoire to beat him to a pulp for everything he's ever done to me, but I let go. I let go because my stubborn Mamma doesn't want to move in with me, and I can't be the reason Tim kicks her out of the apartment. If I'm responsible, she will be so disappointed in me. I don't ever want to disappoint Mamma. I love her too much to be able to handle that.

"You've got some fire in you, little girl, but I know you're only doing it to play hard to get. Don't worry, I'm a patient man," he assures me, and my face contorts into the ugliest scowl I've ever felt on my face. All that prick does is laugh. *Would anyone miss him if I'd, I don't know, pushed him out the window?*

Luckily, Tim has a meeting over the phone, which occupies him for most of Mamma's and my lunch. We end up talking for hours about every possible topic, except for whatever she wanted to discuss earlier. I asked her about it halfway through lunch, but she brushed it off and changed the subject. When I make my way home, my stomach twists. It always does that at the thought of leaving Mamma with Tim. *He never touches her or says something inappropriate.* She's assured me that so many times with a laugh, I have started to believe it. Mamma doesn't lie to me either, she never has.

CHAPTER 5
Leonard

Graham and I are in the middle of watching our favourite football team beat our least favourite one when Chiara walks through the door. She was at her Mamma's place, according to my brother, but there is something off about her whole demeanor. Her usually angry expression is soft and upset, which twists something inside of me I have no interest in deciphering. It's probably nothing. Starling is fine. It's not completely unlike her to only pat Benz's head once before disappearing into her room. Except it is. And the feeling inside of me multiples by a thousand.

"What's up with little Ms. Sunshine?" I ask Graham, whose eyes are still on the television, just like mine should be. There is absolutely no reason for me to want to get up and check on her.

"Her mum's roommate is a creep. Chiara always comes home like this after she spends the day there. I'm pretty sure he's making vile advances toward Chiara, but except for once, she's never really shared anything about Tim with me," Graham explains, and I nod along to his words.

Okay. Whoever this Tim guy is, I'm going to kill him. He's harassing Chiara, and as much as she's a bloody pain in my arse, I won't have it. Why? I could tell myself it's because she's Graham's best friend and family to all of my relatives. I could, and I will. That's the reason for my rage toward that bastard. No other reason. I can live with that.

"Why have you never done anything to help her?" I ask, but the question is silly.

Chiara is a trained fighter and badass to her very core. Not to mention, she's stubborn and fierce as hell. She doesn't need anyone's help, but considering this man is still harassing her means there is something else going on. What I can't explain is why I feel this need deep inside of me to figure out what the hell that something is.

"Because Chiara is a grown woman, who doesn't need me to step in unless she specifically asks me to," my brother says, and I roll my eyes at him. She would never ask for help, that stubborn demon.

"Sometimes I feel like you don't know her," I blurt out before my feet bring me upright and make their way toward her bedroom door.

"Sometimes I feel like you *like* like her," Graham replies with a chuckle, but I flash him a disgusted frown.

"Not even if—" My brother cuts me off before I can finish that sentence.

"She was the last woman on Earth, yeah, yeah, you've said so before," he mutters, focusing on the television again.

Benz is already sitting in front of Chiara's door, hitting her paw at it every few minutes and booping her nose against it to get it to open. I bend down to scratch her head once and then bring my knuckles against the wood. There is a shuffling sound inside while I wait for Chiara to open the door. She doesn't. So, I knock again.

"Who is it?" she asks.

"Are you indecent?" is my response, but it earns me an annoyed sigh from her.

"Go away, Champ, I'm not in the mood," she says, using that nickname I hate more than anything in the world.

I roll my eyes before stepping inside without permission. Benz charges for Chiara, who barely manages to protect her face before my girl slobbers all over her.

"Benzie!" Chiara calls out, a soft laugh leaving her.

Woah. The sound instantly washes through me, settling somewhere deep inside my bones and weakening my knees. My fingers tighten around her doorknob to keep me upright. She's never laughed in front of me, never. She has smiled, but rarely. This laugh was so soft and innocent, it knocked the breath from my chest in a way that not even a racing incident can do. *Fuck no.* I shake my head to get rid of the thoughts and feelings.

"What's with the face? Did the kid fight back today when you tried to steal their candy?" I ask, crossing my arms in front of my chest and leaning against the doorframe. Chiara shoots me an unimpressed look.

"Ah, I see you've taken an extra dose of your asshole pills again." I narrow my eyes at her, mostly to keep myself from smiling at her witty comeback.

"So, what's wrong with you?" She cocks an eyebrow as she scratches Benz's belly, confusion slipping across her face.

"Nothing's wrong with me. Leave it be," she replies, but I can tell she's upset. Hell, I can feel it.

I've known Starling for two decades. Every little one of her tells, like the way her pouty lips are fully embracing the natural softness of her features, something they never do, lets me know everything I have to. She's upset. That Tim dude is responsible. I want to help her. *Bloody hell.* What an unsettling thought.

"Can you get out? Your presence in my room is unnerving," she says, lying down on her side and hugging Benz to her chest. I almost find this cute.

Fine, it's cute.

"Not until you tell me what has you in such a horrible mood. It's worse than normal, which is saying a lot considering you walk around with a face that says you torture people for entertainment," I say, earning me a tiny smirk from her. Warmth spreads through my chest in response and I almost stumble backward. *What the hell?*

"Not people, just you," she fires back, but I remain stern, scowling at her to the best of my ability. Meanwhile, Benz is snoring happily in Starling's arms.

"I'm just going to keep asking, so you might as well tell me." Because, as much as I hate to admit it, I'm just as stubborn and determined as her. It's why I won a championship last year and the reason why I'm so highly valued at Grenzenlos. My team.

"Leonard, I'm not in the mood, okay? I've had a long day, and I'm—" She cuts off, choking on her words.

I see tears sting her eyes, but like the absolute soldier she is, she swallows them down and clears her throat. In all the years I've known her, all the dinners, birthday parties, family events, and more, she has never shed a single tear. Never. It's frightening. Even I cried in front of her once when she smacked the ice cream out of my hand when we were five and nine. Mum had been so upset with Chiara, it had cheered me right up.

But, right now, worry fills my chest, even if I don't show it on my face. I take a step toward her then another until I'm hovering over her. I poke her arm once, twice, three times until she takes the finger I was using and pulls it into a death grip. She drags it down until I'm forced to lean forward, which is exactly what she wanted. Our faces are barely apart when she decides to tell me off.

"I don't want to fucking talk about it, asshole. Leave. Me. Alone," she spits, and my eyes drop to her lips.

Her breath is hot on my skin, and her sweet scent, peaches, fills my nose. My eyes flutter shut for the briefest second, but when she lets go of me, I know she saw. Fuck. I straighten out my back and stare down at her as I respond.

"No." That makes her groan.

"Why do you even care if I'm in a shitty mood?" Her accent is so thick, if I hadn't spent most of my life with her, I'd struggle to understand her.

"Because you live with my brother, and I don't want him to suffer," I lie. She seems to believe me because she rolls her eyes.

"Don't you have money to spend unnecessarily or something? Must you bother me?" *What?*

"Unnecessarily? What the hell is that supposed to mean?"

"Look at the car you drive, where you live, the clothes you wear. Then compare them to mine," she says, pointing at the sweatshirt on her chest, which is covered in holes. My heart sinks a little for her, but her words fucking bother me. "See, unnecessary," she says, and I feel my heart racing.

I'm very responsible with my money. Most of it is in an account where I'm saving it for my kids' futures, in case my parents ever need the money, for Graham when he decides to finally let me help him with his dream, and some for Ellie's future. Jack and Stu have their own money, they're responsible when it comes to saving, but I want to be able to give my niece everything she could ever need. After the hell my parents went through when we were kids, I have made sure to be nothing but responsible with everything that goes into my bank account. I have fancy cars, clothes, and such because of sponsorships. I don't buy any of that shit for myself, which Chiara must know. She saw how much my family struggled, but she went for a low blow. Fine. She's pissed at whatever happened at her Mamma's. I can understand that, but I will not tolerate her making wrong assumptions about the way I spend my money. Not after everything.

My fingers wrap around her wrist, dragging her upright until her face is close to mine and I'm able to grab her chin between my fingers. Tight enough to keep her in place but not so tight that it'd cause her pain. Chiara's breathing hitches as her eyes drop to my lips, and the fact that she's somewhat attracted to me, on some level, almost distracts me from what I want to say to her.

"Listen, sweetheart, there are a lot of things you get to say to me, but you don't get to comment on the way I spend my money when you've got no idea what I do with it," I say, my voice softer than I intended.

"What are you going to do about it?" she challenges, and I tilt my head a little, my eyes dropping to her mouth then running back up to hers.

"Something you're not going to like," I say and let go of her so abruptly, she falls back into the bed. I ignore the fact that all my blood has shot into a very specific place I never, ever want it to go because of Chiara as I stroll toward her bedroom door. "Benz, heel," I command, and my grey pitbull runs toward me, obeying. "Say goodbye to the little demon. You won't see her for a while," I say, and the woman on the bed stands, rushing over to us.

"You wouldn't," she snarls, and I give her half an evil smile.

"Oh, but I would. It's not forever, Starling, only until you apologise," I assure her, turning to leave when her voice, so soft and hurt, sends a wave of guilt through me.

"I'm sorry," she says and drops to her knees to have Benz run to her. My girl wastes no second to get to her best friend.

"What happened today?" I ask again, Starling's eyes fixated on my dog's bright blue ones.

"I'm sorry about bringing up money. I know it's a sensitive topic for you." Her apology sends another wave of guilt through me. Fuck, sometimes I am the biggest arsehole. "Please don't take her away from me. She's one of my three pure sources of happiness," Chiara adds, the tears from before returning to her eyes. She swallows them back down as Benz licks her cheek. I'm going to kill Tim. No one fucking tears down Starling this way.

"If you don't tell me what happened, Chiara, I can't help you," I say, keeping my tone light even though I want to physically harm a man.

"You haven't called me that in years," she points out, and I realise she's right. Bloody hell. Why did I use her actual name? I never do that. "You can't help me either way, Leonard. Whether I tell you or not, there is nothing you can do," she says and steps inside her room again, poking at the hole in her sweater. That woman needs new clothes. I don't remember a single article from her closet that isn't torn or worn way beyond it should be.

"I think you underestimate how influential I am," I remind her, and she lets out a small snort.

"Since when do you care about my life, Champ?" she asks, and I shake my head, frustrated with her now.

It's a good question. Since when is her well-being of such importance to me? We don't like each other. I can't stand being in the same room as her for more than five minutes because we always end up in a fight. Some people might call it an overload of passion, I call it two stubborn people being too much alike to make a conversation work. She's so fucking infuriating, it drives me wild.

"I don't. Like I said, I don't want my brother to suffer if you're in a shitty mood," I lie again, hating the fact that it is indeed a lie.

"Sure, if you say so," she says with a smug look, and it lets me know she'll be fine. "Now, get out. I've got to get ready for my job," she says, sending a wave of confusion through me.

"Work? At this time?" I check my watch to see it's close to ten in the evening.

"Yes, Leonard, at this time. I'm bartending at a club to pay for my bills because my other three jobs don't pay enough." *Other three jobs? Jesus fucking Christ.*

"How many times a week do you—" I cut off because the thought of her in such a dangerous occupation on top of three other jobs makes me nauseous. Why the hell does it make me nauseous?

"You want to know my schedule?" I nod, which causes her to shake her head and sigh, but I can tell this amuses her. "I work at the club six days a week, at the bookstore Monday through Friday, but mostly in the evenings. I walk dogs every day very early in the morning and then after I go straight to the gallery. They don't always have shifts for me, so it changes around a lot." I'm going to be fucking sick.

"When do you sleep?" I croak out, which seems to confuse her because her eyebrows draw together in response. I clear my throat, crossing my arms over my chest again to contain my racing heart.

"Barely," is all she says as she steps around the room to gather an outfit together.

"How many hours?" I ask, and she lets out a sigh.

"I don't like it when you decide you love to speak. You talk too much," she says, but I have no time to be bloody amused.

"How. Many. Hours?" I demand to know, and Starling turns to me, crossing her arms in front of her chest.

"Fuck. Off. It's none of your business. Now, get out. I have to change," she says, and I stare at the clothes in her hands. Something that looks a hell of a lot more like a bra than a top, a short skirt, and something with fishnets. That won't cover anything. Hell, it will show *everything*.

"It's too cold for you to wear that," I blurt out because the thought of Starling in an outfit like that, surrounded by horny men who don't know how to control themselves, makes me violent again.

"Okay, nosey man. Out. I don't know why you suddenly give a shit about me, but I still haven't learned to give one about your opinions. I don't plan on changing that either, so get out," she says, pointing at her door.

I leave without saying another word to anyone. Graham is preoccupied with watching the men on the field kick the ball around, and I have to blow off some steam. Chiara De Luca is none of my business. She hates me, I can't stand her. That's how it has always been and always will be. Whatever the hell is going on in my chest, it's unimportant. I just have to find a way to keep it from restricting my breathing, and I don't seem to be able to figure it out, not while the thought of her getting harassed by Tim and countless other men at her job floats around in my mind. *She's a trained fighter*, I keep reminding myself, but it's not nearly as soothing as I wish it was.

I need to get her out of that job, out of all four, no matter what. She's going to break herself working as hard as she is, and I can't stand by and watch it happen. It doesn't matter how we feel about each other. Starling isn't going to snap herself in half to achieve her dream. I won't let her.

I will... help her.

CHAPTER 6
Chiara

The next four weeks are strange. Leonard doesn't spend a lot of time with Graham anymore, and when he's at our place, he seems off. I know it can't be because of his job. Leonard has won all three races since the season started. He's doing incredibly well and so is his entire team. I would know. I watch every single race with my best friend. I've been to see Benz whenever he isn't home, but Rena, Leonard's mum, is also busy and doesn't have time for me to see Benz whenever I can. I miss her a lot. Usually, Leonard makes sure I get to see her when he comes over to hang out with Graham. Since he isn't spending a lot of time with his brother at the moment, I don't get to see my girl as much. I'll have to bother him about it the next time I see him.

"Chiara? Can we talk for a minute?" Graham says, and I shift my gaze to him. His black hair is short, buzz-cut, much unlike his older brother, who loves to grow out his beautiful curls.

"Sounds serious. Did I forget to flush after I peed or something?" I joke, but Graham's face is as serious as mine is most of the time.

"No, it's something you're not going to like very much," he says, and I suck in a silent, sharp breath.

"Lulu is coming over in five minutes, so if it's something serious, you might want to wait until she leaves again," I remind him, but he shakes his head, and I forget how to breathe altogether. Fuck, this can't be good at all. Graham is never this serious. God, I'm sweating.

"I'm moving to New York for half a year," he blurts out, sending a wave of shock through me. I almost burst into laughter because this must be a horrible joke.

"No, you're not," I reply, and he settles down on the coffee table to be right in front of me. I drag my legs up on the couch to give him space for his. The brown in his eyes is darker, colder today.

"I have to get out of here for a little while, Chiara. I have to. I've never traveled in my entire life, and I just got a bonus from my babysitting boss. It's good money. Enough to let me get out there, travel a bit, and clear my head." Under different circumstances, I'd be thrilled for him. But... I can't be. Not when I've been killing myself working four jobs to support myself and get a few bucks on the side to save up for *our* dream.

"What about our gallery? I thought we were in this together, Graham!" Panic floods through me, but I shove it down. I let anger consume me instead. It's a horrible decision, but I can't believe he's doing this to us.

"I feel stuck, my love. I can't keep going on like this. I'm not happy." He isn't happy. I know we don't have the easiest of lives, neither one of us does, but I find joy in his presence every single time we're even five minutes together. "I barely see you, Chiara. You're working so much, and I don't have a life outside of you and my family. I need to go find it, but I don't think I will in England. I have a friend in New York, who doesn't mind me staying with him for a while." Nausea bubbles up in my throat. I might throw up. This can't be happening. Am I dreaming?

"You're leaving me," I whisper because that fucking hurts. There is a reason why I've never been in a real relationship. It was to avoid heartbreak. Well, fuck me. Should have known the only person who could rip my heart to shreds was Graham.

"I'm not leaving you. I will be back in six months, hopefully rejuvenated and happier. I will still pay rent, don't worry, but it's time I do this. You cannot tell me you're happy with the way things are, Chiara. You can't tell me you like being in my presence when all I've been these days is an emotional wreck."

Except he didn't let me see that side of him, did he? Whenever we were together, he was his giddy and happy self. He didn't let me detect anything was off. Nothing at all. And now I feel like a horrible friend because the man I love the most in the world was struggling with his life, and I was so goddamn busy I didn't notice. Tears sting my eyes, but I blink them away. It works mostly, except the pressure behind my eyes remains.

"I'm sorry you feel this way, and you're right, you need to do this trip. If you're unhappy, you have to go, I understand. Your mental health comes first, always." I mean every single word, but it's hard not to burst into tears while saying them because I will miss him with every fiber of my being.

"Don't give me that approving bullshit, Chiara. You're mad at me, and I'm going to need you to yell." I shake my head, forcing a small smile to my lips.

"No, you need this. I understand."

I do understand. I get it. I wish I could escape this life I've built for myself too. I wish I didn't have to work four jobs to get by. I wish my bosses had given me some extra money. Then again, if they gave me a bonus, I'd invest it in our dream as soon as it hit my bank account. Graham isn't as passionate about it as I am, but that's fine. Everything will be fine. I just have to remind myself of that and not think about the fact that I've never lived by myself and it's more than a little frightening. I don't want to be alone. *No.* I don't want to be *lonely*, and I've been lonely for many years in ways I've never wanted to explore. Well, now I will get enough time to overthink it.

"Yell at me, for fuck's sake, Chiara. I know you. You aren't this quiet when you're upset about something. Leonard and you always yell at each other, and I need you to do the same with me now. Don't let me off the hook so easily. I'm being bloody selfish, and I deserve to get it thrown at my head," my best friend screams at me, and I decide to get up and away from this situation.

I will not yell at him for prioritizing his mental health. It's not who I am. Mamma struggled with depression for several years when I was younger. She taught me how important it is to put your mind first, no matter what. I haven't paid much attention to my own, so I admire what Graham is doing. If I wasn't broke and determined to achieve my dream, I'd follow him. No hesitation. No second thought or shit given.

"You're doing the right thing, Graham. I won't yell at you. I do, however, need some air," I say and grab my jacket, phone, keys, and umbrella. My hands are shaking, and I haven't quite found a way to make them stop yet. I just need to walk off this anxiety. That's all.

"Chiara, you can't leave now. Please, luv, scream. I need you to," he begs, and I let out a low growl.

"You want me to yell? Fine, I will yell. I fucking love you, okay? I'm proud of you for putting yourself first. Am I mad at myself because our little life together didn't make you happy and I didn't notice? Fuck yes, but only because I want to be a better friend. I'm not mad at you, idiot! You're my best friend, Graham, and I will always want what's best for you. All I need is to process this. Alright? Give me a fucking minute to swallow all of this," I yell, just like he wanted me to.

He stays silent as I rub my temples, ignoring the cool metal of my keys as it presses against my cheek. My lungs are burning because my breathing is unbearably uneven. Graham doesn't say another word, so I walk toward the door, ripping it open just as Lulu tries to knock.

"What the hell happened?" she asks, her gaze shifting between Graham and me.

Lulu is half-English, half-Japanese with black straight hair, and beautiful hazel eyes. She's curvy and short and straight-up gorgeous. Every time I see her, I can't help admiring her beauty, but today might be the first day I'm incapable of doing so. There is confusion pulling her eyebrows together, but I don't bother explaining. I give her a single kiss on the cheek before leaving the building.

I have no fucking clue where I'm going, but I haven't found a way to calm my breathing either. My hands tremble so aggressively, I shove them into the pockets of my jacket to get them to stop, but it's useless. It only makes my entire body shake because I'm going to be all alone. Yes, I have Mamma and Lulu, but they live far away from me. When I get home at night, I will be all alone. I won't have Graham there with me, spending time with me until it's time for my bartending shift. I won't have my best friend, roommate, and part of my family for six months. Six long months. It might not seem like a lot to other people, but I've never even been truly alone for a single day in my life, which I know makes me very fortunate. I know that, but it's also the reason why I can't stop the panic from constricting my breathing.

"What the hell?" I ask and clutch my chest, heaving as if I'd just gone on my first run in five years.

I keep walking without a destination in mind, only now realizing I didn't open my umbrella. My clothes are already halfway soaked by the time I manage to open it, but, since I have some of the worst luck on the planet during my lowest times, the wind rips the umbrella to shreds. If my body wasn't hyperventilating from fear, I might cry. I might start shedding tears, and I haven't done that in years. I curse and yell at that piece-of-shit umbrella in my hand before finding the closest garbage can and violently throwing it inside. I really can't catch a fucking break.

"Anything else you want to do to me?" I ask the universe while tilting my head back and letting the rain hit my face in a steady motion that should be calming. Instead, it pisses me off so much, I feel the urge to go punch a wall.

"Get in," I hear someone call over the rain, but I don't turn to look at that person. It can't be him. I wasn't seriously challenging the universe to throw more shit at me. I really wasn't. "Starling, get in the car before you catch a bloody cold." Leonard. I let out a breath before facing his million-dollar Grenzenlos—I'm well aware it doesn't cost that much—and crossing my arms in front of my chest.

"I'm quite content with where I am, *stronzo*," I lie, which makes him sigh from inside his car.

His beautiful eyes shift to me, his full lips so serious and inviting, I get frustrated with him for being as handsome as he is. And not just handsome. He's powerful in so many ways, from his appearance to the good he's achieving in the world. He pinches the bridge of his nose and lets out a loud sigh.

"Get in the bloody car, little demon, before I throw you over my shoulder and carry you inside. My mum would not forgive me if I let you walk around in the rain any longer," he says, and I grimace at him.

"I'd like to see you try," I challenge, somehow closer to his car now than I was when he first pulled up next to where I am on the sidewalk. When he reaches for his door and attempts to get out, more panic floods me. "Okay, for fuck's sake. I'll get in," I say, not willing to have him drag my ass into the car. Plus, I'm cold and miserable in the rain, and the thought of making his seat wet does entertain me.

"Now," he says, rushing me even though I'm already on my way to him.

"Yeah, okay, asshole. Jesus," I reply and rip his door open, settling down in the passenger seat.

As soon as I'm sitting, a tongue swipes across my cheek repeatedly. *Benz*. My heart warms before some of the panic vanishes and gets replaced by pure happiness. I turn to her, the blue eyes of the dog I love so much meeting mine.

"*Ciao, bella. Come stai?*" I ask, scratching her ears. She lets out an excited *woof*, sending another wave of warmth through me.

"Here," Leonard says, and I glance down at the jacket he's holding out for me. I hesitate. "I didn't rub it in poison if that's what you're wondering," he adds, and I cock a suspicious eyebrow.

"That's exactly what I was wondering, and just because you say it wasn't, doesn't mean I will put it on. If you were trying to kill me, that's exactly what you'd say," I reply and watch as he fights back a smile. I can tell by the way the corners of his mouth twitch.

"Put on the damn jacket, Chiara. You're not getting sick on my watch." It's stupid to fight him on this, but if I give in twice in two minutes, he's going to start believing I will do whatever he tells me to, and that's not happening.

"I'm fine in my jacket," I assure him, making him grip his steering wheel harder along with the jacket still in his other hand.

"Demon, put on the jacket or I swear to God I will make your life hell for the next three years." An empty threat, nothing more.

"And how would you do that?" I challenge while he drives onto the highway, the piece of fabric he's holding still dangling in front of me. Leonard tilts his head toward me for a moment, his eyes skipping from mine to my lips and then back up.

"I will come to your house every single day and—"

He doesn't have to finish that sentence when I snap the jacket out of his grasp. It's heavy and warm, making my body shudder from the need to have it around me. Leonard must have noticed because he reaches for the temperature dial and turns it warmer. I decide to ignore that sweet, simple gesture and peel off my jacket, my black long-sleeve so wet, it clings to my body. I notice his knuckles pushing against the skin on his hand even more. I look down to see my average-sized boobs looking bigger like this and furrow my brows at him. Did my appearance just—

"Stop staring at me," he says, and I roll my eyes. *Never mind.*

"No," I reply, sliding on the jacket while keeping my gaze firmly on him.

"I think you might be the biggest pain in the arse I've ever met," he says, which earns him a satisfied look from me.

"Just drop me at my Mamma's and then you don't have to put up with me anymore," I say because I'm not quite ready to go home yet.

"No." It's his turn for a one-word answer, but it pisses me off more than a million words could.

"What the fuck do you mean 'no'? Bring me to my Mamma's!" I say, and he shoots me a deathly glare. I snuggle into his jacket, his scent—soapy, fresh, and something that's only Leonard—filling my nose. It's a wonderful smell, only irritating me further.

"Do you *want* to go to your Mamma's?" he challenges, shutting me up for a moment.

"I don't want to go home," I admit, and he gives me another glance.

"So, Graham's told you about his plans," he says, but I'm not quite sure why anger slices through me at his words.

"You knew and didn't tell me?" As soon as I've said it, I know it sounds ridiculous. We're not friends. We don't even like each other. There is no reason for him to tell me. Instead of pointing that out to me, Leonard gives me a sympathetic look.

"It wasn't my place." It really wouldn't have been, but I'm still annoyed. I shut up and face the street, watching the rain hit the windshield with as much aggression as I can feel in my chest right now. "I'm taking you to my flat where you can dry off and stay the night if you'd like. I don't know if you're working tonight," he says, the last sentence coming out strained.

"I'm not working, it's my night off, but I'm not staying with you either," I reply, a frustrated sigh coming from him in response.

"And why not?" he asks, so I face my body toward him completely, earning myself a lick to the cheek from Benz. I scratch her chest while responding.

"Because we can't stand each other." That asshole just nods.

"So? What did my flat ever do to you?" he asks, and I close my eyes until they're merely slits.

"It's inhabited by you," I reply, and he shakes his head. His high cheekbones complement the rest of his sharp facial features, and I have to force my eyes away before they find more beautiful things about him.

"Listen, I don't like this any more than you do, but you need help, and I am a great person willing to help out." The thought of rolling down the window and throwing myself out of the car suddenly becomes very appealing.

"I don't want to go to your place," I say, my hair dripping and my legs sticking to the seat. I wiggle my ass a little to get it even wetter, making Leonard sigh again. This man and his fucking sighing are driving me crazy.

"I made my mum's famous chicken piccata," he says, and I stop arguing. That's my favorite dish Rena's ever made for me.

"Okay," is all I say as I keep scratching Benz's chest. This might be the worst idea I've had in a while, but I'm wet and miserable and have nowhere to go. Only Leonard's.

Fuck my life.

CHAPTER 7
Leonard

S tarling has been standing in the middle of my flat for several minutes, saying nothing as her face is forced into a serious look to hide the awe I see sparkling in her eyes. My flat is nice. It's clean because I can't live in filth, the furniture is light and matches the walls well. Everything is modern and big, there are windows so large, you can perfectly see the London Eye. I don't remember why I decided to move directly into the city when all of my family lives forty-five minutes outside of it, but I like the view. I like seeing people enjoying their life in the city which has always felt like home to me. I like watching the seasons change. I like everything about my life here.

"Come, Starling, let's get you into some dry clothes," I say while touching her arm once very lightly. She doesn't jerk away from my touch but leans into it a little, surprising me. Her eyes are still studying my living room when I lead her to my bedroom.

It's big, huge even. There is a king-sized bed in there for no one other than myself. I've never had a girlfriend, and my friends-with-benefits arrangement ended a while ago. Since then, no one's slept in my bed apart from me, which only bothers me when my cock starts twitching uncomfortably at the sight of Chiara's breasts getting hugged by that soaked shirt. *Nope. Go away, thought. Cock, calm down.*

"I'm not putting on your clothes," she says when I walk toward my closet.

I grab a pair of sweatpants and a shirt before opening a new box of underwear. She watches me the whole time, so I don't bother explaining the boxers are unused as I shove them into her hands.

"Would you like to walk around naked or get sick by keeping those wet clothes on?" She can't argue with me on that, which is why I decide to test my luck and grab her a towel too. "In case you want to take a shower," is all I say before pointing at my bathroom and leaving her to do what she wants.

As soon as I've created some distance from her, my skin decides to start breathing properly again and my cock relaxes. I shake my head and curse at my body for responding to such an irritating woman that way. Wanting Chiara is by far one of the worst things I could ever do. Apart from us being enemies, I have no desire to make my brother feel like I'm stealing his best friend from him. Then again, he's the one who is hurting her right now, and I've never been angrier with him.

I'm proud that he's trying to find happiness, but the way he's going about it is painful for Chiara. If I were him, I'd find a way to take her with me because that woman, more than anyone I've ever met, deserves to get away for a little. She works harder than even I do, and that's saying a lot considering I'm training, analysing data, and attending meetings with my team every chance I get.

Being a Formula One driver is a lot of hard work, something most people don't realise. They don't even think F1 is a sport sometimes, let alone that drivers have some of the most draining jobs. Yes, we earn a shit ton of money for it, but being in the spotlight on top of everything is exhausting. The media pick you apart until you're unrecognisable, even to yourself in the mirror. It's draining as hell, especially recently for me.

I've been winning races, but it hasn't meant as much to me as it used to. My love for the sport has started to crumble, and I don't have a single clue how to get it back. I also have no one to talk to because, as much as I adore her, Quinn can't help me either. It terrifies me how I feel about racing. I need to snap out of this phase as soon as possible, I just have no clue how.

Benz follows me into the kitchen where I continue cooking the food I promised Starling I was making. After finishing it, I feed my girl, watching her tail wagging from excitement at seeing the meal I've prepared for her. I recently switched her from kibble to raw, and she's been loving every single bite.

"Where is your dryer?" Chiara's heavy-accented voice flows into my ears, so soft and warm, it wraps around me for a second. I shove the feeling away as soon as it tries to settle in my chest.

"Give those to me," I say, and she furrows her brows, giving me a disapproving look.

"You're so bossy," she replies, and I lean down as I stand in front of her, our faces so close, her peachy scent fills my nose. I can't stand being close to her. My body's reactions are unforgivable.

"I have to be, otherwise your stubborn arse won't listen." She's distracted enough from shock so I can pull the wet clothes from her chest. Unfortunately, it allows me to see all of her in my clothes, and that's a sight no part of me was prepared for.

Focus! You don't like her. She drives you absolutely wild. She's irritating and stubborn and—

And gorgeous.

"Are you done ogling me or would you like me to do a spin for you, sir?" she asks like she's the most submissive woman in the world. Fuck. Me.

"Spin," I challenge her, which she wasn't expecting. Her shocked look sends a wave of contentment through me, settling in my eyes until I even feel the corners of my mouth lifting. Fuck it. I don't stop them, especially because it's only a tiny smirk.

"In your dreams, asshole," she says and walks into the kitchen where Benz is.

I smile to myself while throwing her clothes into the dryer and setting the time. When I join Starling in the kitchen, she's watching Benz enjoy her food with a soft look in her eyes. She's been wearing that expression a lot more recently, and I have an awful feeling it's because she's tired. I can't imagine how exhausted she is, but the bags under her green eyes tell me more than she ever would.

For the past four weeks, I've been keeping my distance from her because the way I felt after that night when we spoke about her job unsettled me. I've also been trying to find a way to get her to quit by offering her something safer, more stable, and with more money. So far, I've come up with nothing good, and I won't go to her with half an idea. I thought about hiring her to walk Benz and paying her a fuck ton of money, but, knowing Chiara—and I know her very well—she would never agree to it. She'd walk Benz, but she won't take my money.

My eyes fixate on her hands, watching them shake on the counter. I cock an eyebrow, worry, *fucking worry*, settling deep inside of me. I'm getting sick and tired of my head coming up with strange things, like telling me to go find out why her bloody hands are shaking and then comforting her because of it. It's not my problem. Starling is not my goddamn problem. So, where the hell are my next words coming from?

"Are you cold?" I ask, taking a step toward her. My gaze drops to her hands to signal that's why I'm asking, but Chiara shoves them into the pockets of my blue sweatpants to hide them from me.

"No."

She doesn't give me more information, but she doesn't have to. I understand why. She's anxious. Tired. Drained. Everything I am, and fuck, it feels awful to see her breaking apart slowly. *Not your problem*, I try to remind myself, but it doesn't work.

"You'll be okay," I say, Chiara's gaze fixating on the marble countertops.

"Yeah, as soon as I get to take a bite of that chicken piccata," she replies to ease the tension, but it feels wrong. I know she senses it too.

"Graham will be back in six, quick months," I assure her, and she flashes me a glare I wasn't prepared for. What did I expect? We've been at each other's throats since we met two decades ago. I've never tried to comfort her before, so she doesn't trust me or want me to do that either.

"How about we don't talk about my feelings or assume them, Champ?" she asks, and it makes a frustration like no other settle inside of me. I can't even fucking comfort that woman properly.

"Fine," I say and walk toward my pan to stir the food.

"*Fine*," she imitates me, and I turn around to grimace at her.

"How old are you? Five?" I ask, but what does she do in response? She rolls her bloody eyes and moves toward where Benz is on the floor at the entrance of the kitchen.

"You know, you didn't have to bring me here. You insisted, for some inexplicable reason, so don't let your frustration out on me. You knew we don't get along before you dragged me here," she says, and her point is so valid, it shuts me up for a very long moment.

I did know how horribly this would probably go, but when I watched her umbrella getting destroyed by the wind and then her body slumping as she stared at the sky and got soaked, I couldn't do nothing. Chiara is a pain, yes, but she also means something to—Yikes. Don't finish that thought.

"I told you. I'm a good person and for once, you get to see it too," I say, and she lets out an unamused snort.

"Yes, you're such a good person and so incredibly humble," she replies, laying on the sarcasm extra thickly just in case I was too stupid to hear it.

"Let's make a bet. I bet I can be nice to you longer than you can be nice to me," I offer because if there is one thing we both love, it's a good challenge. Chiara's face immediately shows how intrigued she is.

"What does the winner get?" she asks, and I place my hands on the countertop, thinking about her question. Her eyes immediately drift to my forearms and biceps, so I flex them a little harder. Starling swallows hard, her cheeks flushing. Not good. I was trying to tease her, but my cock hardens at the sight of her arousal on her face. Karma. It has to be.

"If I win, you have to tell me which club you're working at and let me come once," I say, causing confusion to dance onto her pouty lips. They're irritatingly beautiful, just like her eyes.

"Why would you want to do that? To make fun of me?" *No, to make sure every scenario my head has come up with about you working there is born out of paranoia and not possibility.*

"Obviously," I lie, earning myself a head shake from her. Benz whines on the floor next to Chiara because she stopped petting her.

"Fine, but if I win, I get to take care of Benz when you're gone for your next race weekend," she says, and I don't hesitate before responding.

"Under one condition." Chiara narrows her green eyes at me in response. I was thinking about leaving Benz with her next weekend anyway, but I do have that one condition. "You have to take the week off from your other jobs to give her your full attention. I will pay you, of course," I add the last sentence because Starling already started to look at me like I was insane.

"Okay," is her only reply, making me take several steps back.

"Really?" I was expecting her to fight me a little, not agree this quickly.

"Yes. I have vacation days for all of my jobs anyway, and if you pay me well, I can use them," she explains, scratching Benz's belly.

There is only pure love in Chiara's gaze as she stares at my pitbull, causing my insides to twist. Fuck, seeing those two in my apartment while I finish dinner feels uncomfortably... right. God, no. Jesus, what the hell is wrong with my head? Maybe I need to have it checked.

"Alright then, the bet's on." I walk over to her, holding my hand out. Chiara looks up at me with exasperation.

"Do I have to?" she asks, and I harden my features, feeling my jaw tick in response.

"Yes."

I wiggle my fingers, and she lets out an exaggerated sigh as she slips her fingers over my palm and shakes my hand. As soon as her skin presses against mine, electricity shoots through me. A warmth like no other sets up camp in my stomach, unsettling me. We barely ever touch. That day in her room four weeks ago when I grabbed her chin was one of those rare times, and I don't plan on doing it more now, especially because it makes me react in ways I will never admit to another human being. Maybe I will tell Benz, but she's a big fan of Chiara's touch, so she sure as hell won't judge me.

"Should I lay the table?" Starling asks after a few minutes of me working in the kitchen.

"Sure," I reply, the domesticity of this moment refreshing. We're not going to kill each other after all.

Chiara and I sit at the table in silence, but it's not even a little uncomfortable, which is a big fucking problem. It should be hell. This shouldn't feel normal, especially not the way she's inhaling my food with happy little moans leaving her. At one point, she even does a little dance in her seat because of how content she is with my cooking. It sets me on fire. *She* sets me on fire. There is so much fight and passion in her, but she's adorable when we're not fighting, and that knowledge is fucking with my head.

"How was work today?" I ask to distract myself from the cute side of her personality and the way her lips seem even fuller as she chews.

"It was good. My boss gave me some new books for free because they were a bit damaged, so unable to be up for sale," she explains, and I nod along to her words, internally cursing at the fact that Chiara struggles so much with money, she can't afford books in good condition.

"You like reading a lot," I point out, and she gives me a small nod before focusing on the plate in front of her again. "What books do you read?" This isn't me just trying to be nice. These are things I'm usually curious about too but because we don't have the type of relationship where I can ask this question, I don't. Tonight, I have the opportunity to get to know her a bit better without it turning into a fight.

"I like romance books," she says. "I'm very specific about them though. They have to meet certain criteria," she explains, and my heart flutters at the fact that she wants to share more with me by herself. *Fuck off, heart.*

"What criteria?" A little smile tugs at her lips.

"I need my female main characters not to put love before their dreams. I need the male main characters to be hopelessly obsessed with her. I need the sex scenes to be very explicit," she says, and I swallow so hard, I'm surprised my throat doesn't burn in response. Images of Chiara reading sex scenes and touching herself flood my head, so I shake it to get rid of them. Unfortunately, my erection has returned, making me shift in my seat.

"That's... interesting," I reply, swallowing once more and feeling the burn this time. That little demon fucking chuckles at my perplexed reaction. *Chuckles.* Chiara hardly ever bloody chuckles.

"Relax. You look like I just told you what my favorite sex position is." Yeah, that doesn't help my cock calm down. More visuals slip into my head. She's playing with me, she must be. There is no way she doesn't realise how bloody sexy she is when she says things like that. *Wait, sexy? God, no, Leonard, stop it.* "Jesus, snap out of it, Champ. It's just sex. Would you like me to say it again so you get more comfortable with the word? Sex, sex, sex," she repeats with a smirk, and I grip my thigh under the table. Self-control.

"Don't be such a smug pain in the arse," I say, and she lets out a *Ha!*

"Benzie, you're going to spend next weekend with Auntie Chiara," that little demon says, and I smack my forehead with the palm of my hand. Starling keeps chuckling at my reaction, and I can't help but crack a little smile too, but only once I've covered my face with my hands. I will not smile at her.

Nope.

Over my dead body.

"Thank you for letting me sleep here," she says after I've shown her the guest room. I shrug my shoulders, pretending like this isn't a big deal, even if it is.

After we finished dinner, which continued to be disgustingly pleasant, we watched a movie. We even commented on some things we liked about it throughout. So fucking unsettling. No part of me would have thought we'd have a quiet moment tonight. Instead, we barely had a loud one. It was bloody... nice, and I hate it.

"Let me get you a glass of water in case you get thirsty tonight," I blurt out when we've been staring into each other's eyes for several moments. Chiara is on the bed with Benz, that little traitor, when I return.

"I work at *Sunrise* in case you want to stop by and make fun of me anyway," she says after I've placed the glass on her bedside table. I settle down on the mattress where Benz is, scratching her head and ears until she's groaning happily in response.

"What made you tell me?" The bags under her eyes awake something protective inside of me, something I've never, ever felt before.

"You're soon to be the person I've spent the most time with in all of England apart from my Mamma," she says, causing understanding to rush into my chest.

She spends some time with Lulu, her close friend, but apart from Graham, I'm the person she sees the most. Even though I'm gone for many weeks out of the year, whenever I'm here, I spend time with my family. She happens to live and be best friends with the brother I have the closest relationship with, so she sees my face more than anyone else's. I hate how sad that makes her, and how strange I feel about it.

"That's really fucking depressing," she blurts out, and my heart breaks a little for her. I'd very much like to kick my brother's arse for making Chiara feel this way. Another unsettling thought. God, I'm tired.

"Get some sleep," I say because I need to get out of here. I need to be in my room, by myself, ignoring every single feeling she made me experience. Maybe I was onto something by staying as far away from her as possible.

"Okay," she says absentmindedly as she strokes Benz's chest. She's fast asleep, so I decide to leave her right where she is. Chiara needs her love a lot more than I do tonight.

Which is the first and last time I'm going to put that little demon before my own needs. Otherwise, I'm going to be fucked, and I can't let that happen.

CHAPTER 8
Chiara

Benz is no longer in the bed when I wake up the next morning. Rubbing my eyes, I throw the blanket off my chest and slip my legs out of bed. The scent of fresh coffee fills my room, and I trail after it to find its source. Leonard is in the kitchen, shirtless and listening to a slow R&B song over his speaker. My breathing hitches instantly at the sight of his lean but muscular chest, covered in tattoos. No one pulls them off as well as he does, and it's fucking annoying. Why can't I find him unattractive? Why does he have to be so ridiculously hot?

Ignoring the heat pooling between my legs and the tension in my chest, I bend down to pet a patiently waiting Benz. My eyes remain fixated on Leonard's backside, but it's hard not to when this is the first time I've seen him half-naked in almost five years. I'd forgotten how gorgeous he is without a shirt on.

"Morning," he grumbles, and his harsh tone surprises me so much, I look at him again.

"What's up your ass this morning?" I ask, and he rolls his eyes at me, sipping coffee from his mug.

"Didn't sleep well," he replies before his expression softens ever so slightly at Benz and me. "There is some toast and self-made jam if you're hungry. Coffee too," Leonard says, still staring at us before shaking his head and leaving the kitchen. "I'll take you home when you're ready." He leaves without waiting for a response from me. His odd behavior confuses me, but my hungry stomach growls in protest to my head trying to overthink while it remains empty.

It's a simple breakfast, but, of course, it tastes like heaven. He shouldn't have taken something as simple as jam and made my tastebuds dance from happiness in response. God, I fucking loathe him. Benz stays by my side, even when I go to the bathroom to get ready. I smile at her because it must piss Leonard off to see how much this dog loves me. It adds to the beauty of being Benz's second favorite person in the world.

I'm still clad in Leonard's clothes when I step back into the guest room to find mine folded and placed on the now-made bed. My heart flutters at the thought of him folding my underwear, but I ignore that jerk of an organ and simply get dressed. It doesn't mean anything, except maybe slight irritation for him touching my stuff. Yeah, that must be it. I'm annoyed he saw my underwear, not because it's making me feel things apart from my usual loathing.

"You ready to go?" he asks, serious as always. I give him a slight nod before following him and Benz out the door. Leonard never goes anywhere without her when he's at home.

We stay quiet for the entire forty-five minutes it takes for us to get back to my flat. For the first time in months, I feel well-rested. I have a shift at the bookstore later and work at the club tonight, but my head isn't dreading it as much. I'm not yawning every two minutes, and my eyes don't have that pressure on them from being sleep-deprived.

"What are you going to do today?" I ask, trying to be nice and make small talk. It feels wrong to be polite like this, but considering how nice he was to let me stay at his place and not make fun of my horrible state, I want to try and be better too.

"Training."

He doesn't give me more than that, so I let it go. We don't have to make conversation, no matter how normal of an evening we had yesterday. One night does not mean our entire relationship is about to change. He's infuriating, and I bother him. He's my nemesis, and I am his enemy. We're too alike to make sense to each other.

Leonard and I just don't work.

"You working tonight?" he asks when I'm saying bye to Benz and reaching for the door handle.

"Yeah, but don't come tonight. If you want to go to have fun, go tomorrow. Fridays are much busier," I say, but he shifts his body to me, one of his hands still on his steering wheel and the other between his legs on the seat.

"I wasn't going to come, I was just curious," he says, and I sense surprise trying to settle on my face, but I swallow it down.

"Okay, then. Sorry I assumed you wanted to come after you made it part of our bet yesterday," I say with a scoff, which doesn't amuse him in the slightest. His eyes are trained on mine, his knuckles pressing against his skin because he's gripping the wheel harder than necessary.

"I don't. Now, get out. I have shit to do." I don't know why I remain in his car when I have no desire to stay with him, but there is no way any part of me is going to do what he wants. Not when his tone made anger seeth into my bones.

"I think I'm going to stay right here," I blurt out, turning my body forward and ignoring the way his gaze burns into my side.

"If you do not get out, sweetheart, I'm going to take you with me everywhere I have to go, including making you work out for three hours until you pass out." This is the second time in a month he's called me that, and I hate the way a single butterfly storms around in my stomach in response.

"Fine, then I'm going to annoy you all day with uncomfortable questions. Like, why did me saying the word 'sex' yesterday bother you so much?" His jaw ticks in response, making it hard for me to keep my smile at bay.

"Has it occurred to you that it's because I have no desire to picture you naked with some loser fucking you?" I scrunch my eyebrows together, forgetting how to breathe because of his words. He doesn't want to picture me naked and having sex. That's fine. I most certainly don't want to picture him either.

"No one forced you to picture me having sex just because I said the word," I challenge, making his features harden more with frustration toward me, but, at the same time, he knows I have a point. "Maybe you do want those pictures in your head. Do you have fantasies about me, Champ?" I tease, watching his Adam's apple bob as he swallows hard.

"Yeah, fantasies of choking you," he replies, and I raise an amused eyebrow.

"Kinky," I say and his eyes widen when he realizes how I took his response. It brings a smug smirk to my lips. *The ache between my legs? Let's ignore it.* "Unfortunately for you, I'd rather throw myself in front of a moving plane than have you touch me sexually," I say, feeling how wrong those words taste.

"Why don't you go do that and get out of my bloody car?" he says, and I roll my eyes before turning to Benz one more time and flashing her a small smile.

"I know your daddy's a dick, so if you need a break from him, I will come get you," I assure her, and my baby voice earns me an excited *woof* from her.

"God give me strength," Leonard mumbles, and I chuckle under my breath as I get out.

There is something satisfying about pissing him off, getting any reaction out of him. He's the only person I'm able to let my frustrations out on, and I know he feels the same about me. Maybe we do work, in a really messed up way.

Fuck, I don't know anything anymore.

Graham was at work when I rushed around the apartment to get ready for my shift at the bookstore. We haven't spoken since I left yesterday, but I'm convinced Leonard let him know where I was. Otherwise, Graham would have blown up my phone. No matter what's going on in our lives, he'd never let me not stay the night at the apartment without at least checking in and ensuring I'm alright. We have been best friends for over two decades after all.

"You seem distracted," my manager says, and I glance up at her from the register.

"I have some family problems," I admit because Susie has also become a favorite person of mine over the past three years I've been working for her. The tall white woman with pale skin and blue eyes squeezes my arm to comfort me.

"You know you can always take the day off if you have to," she says, and I give her one tight nod.

"I need the shift." Because I need the money.

I don't tell her that. I don't tell anyone that, except Graham, and Leonard who somehow pulled it out of me. Susie simply smiles at me and then goes back to walking around the store to check for any stray books in aisles they're not supposed to be.

The door opens minutes later, my heart stopping and shrinking from fear when I see who stepped into the shop. *No.*

"Chiara," he says, and I think about running into the backroom for a moment.

"Hello, how can I help you?" Susie says instead, shifting Tim's attention away from me. She shoots me a look, but I'm frozen in place. *He's coming to my place of work now?* I shudder at the thought, at the entire situation.

"I'm here to see Chiara," Tim informs Susie, but I take several steps away from the register.

"Chiara, would you like me to escort this man out of the store?" Susie asks, and I give her a small nod. "Sir, I'm afraid I'm going to have to ask you to leave before I call the police," my manager says, but Tim gives her a cocky smile in response.

"I haven't done anything yet," he says, the amusement remaining on his face. *Yet.* He hasn't done anything *yet.* I'm going to be sick.

"Chiara, why don't you take a break in the back?" Susie says in Italian, her mother tongue as well, and I do exactly as I'm told without another moment's hesitation.

"I will wait for her to return," I hear Tim say, sending a tornado through my stomach.

He's at my job. Tim has never sought me out anywhere apart from Mamma's flat, but he's here. He found out where I work and came here. I can't fucking breathe.

"Chiara, *stai bene?*" Susie asks when she appears in the backroom where I've curled into a small ball in the corner, trying to slow my panic.

"*Sì,*" I lie because I'm anything but okay right now. Tim has taken his harassment and "pursuit" of me to the next level, and I have no idea what the hell I'm going to do. "*Io sto bene, molto bene,*" I add because the panic inside of me is forcing me to continue lying to ensure she believes me. Obviously, it does the opposite.

"Talk to me," she says, switching back to English. Her hands move to my arms, but I flinch at the affection. I was too deep in thought to realize she was getting closer, too distracted to notice she'd try to comfort me like this.

"Everything's fine. I apologize. Let's get back to work," I blurt out and stand up abruptly to walk back outside.

This was nothing. Everything will be fine. And if he doesn't leave me alone, I won't give a shit about Mamma's stubbornness of not wanting to live with me. I will beat Tim to a pulp and drag my mother's ass to my flat.

CHAPTER 9
Leonard

I've been fighting with myself for two days. Two bloody, goddamn days. Quinn looked at me like I was a completely different person when we hung out yesterday. I couldn't bring myself to think about anything apart from Chiara working at that damn *Sunrise* club downtown. Not that Quinn knew what was going through my head, she merely noticed I was even quieter than I normally am. Everything's been changing recently. I'm usually a very focused, business-oriented person. I think logically. I don't bullshit. I sure as hell don't think about going to a club to see if the little demon is safe there.

Yet, here I am, dressed in a button-down and dress pants, on my way to the fucking club. I'm so frustrated with myself, a groan escapes me every few minutes. Chiara can handle herself fine without me, she has for the past twenty-four years of her life. Something's changed recently, something I have no interest in addressing. The unnerving feeling can stay in my stomach, I don't care. I will not pay it any more attention than is absolutely necessary.

I park my car in one of the lots next to the club, noticing Chiara's barely functioning Honda in the spot across from mine. I had to drive that car once last year and almost crashed several times because her stick-shift-shit car kept choking and stopping abruptly. The thought sends a shiver down my spine, making me shudder violently. Chiara's safety has become irrationally important to me for some reason, but there is no way she would ever let me do anything for her. Even something as

61

simple as buying her a new sweater. She'd return it and then shove the money against my chest with an unhappy look on her face. I know her too well to pretend I could ever do anything without her suspecting I have an ulterior motive.

"Chiara is not going to like this," Jack, my oldest brother, says as we walk to the club. He had the night off since Ellie and Stu went to Stu's parents.

"Well, I don't like her working here, so we're even," I reply, earning myself a big grin from my brother. "What?" I ask the man who looks a lot like me, just a few years older.

All three of us Tick sons look similar with only a few differences in the shapes of our faces, width of our lips, and sharpness of our jaws. While I have hard features, Jack has much softer ones. Graham is a mix of both of us.

"She's been working here for a long time. How come it bothers you now?" I don't tell him I had no idea she was working here before. I don't want to, but he keeps talking. "Fine, don't tell me, I can rhyme it together myself. You care about her and you want to take care of her. It's nice," he says, still smiling.

I keep ignoring him, getting stopped on my way in to take a few photos with eager fans. Jack waits until they've stepped away before continuing his nosey behaviour.

"You could admit it, you know. It wouldn't make you any less of the brooding, serious man you are," he assures me, checking his phone as soon as a message lights up his screen in case Stu or Ellie need something. He loves his little family with all of his heart, and it sends a wave of longing through me. That's a problem for later. "It's not a bad thing to care for her. Chiara is a wonderful, beautiful woman, and I know you've always been drawn to her. You two just make sense, and—"

"You better shut up before I lose my patience," I warn him, pointing my finger at his chest. Jack, like the arse he is, only grins brighter at me.

"You're cute when you try to hide your feelings," he says, and I shake my head, pushing through the crowd of people to get to the bouncer.

I slip him a hundred-pound bill, and he lets us inside. Being famous does have its perks sometimes. I called the owner earlier today, and he was thrilled to hear I would be coming. I just wanted to ensure I'd be let in, so I could see Chiara isn't working in a shit hole where men harass her. I swallow hard at the thought.

"Why did you bring me if you're going to ignore me?" Jack asks, his hand slipping onto my shoulder. He's quite a bit taller than me, but I'm a lot stronger. And angrier most of the time too.

"Because Chiara will be too happy about seeing you to care about me being here as well," I explain, and my brother lets out a slight laugh.

"You're a little shit, aren't you?" he says, still chuckling at my words.

I'm too focused on making my way through the loud, blaring crowd to pay him too much mind. People bump into me, screaming and singing at the top of their lungs. I notice a lot of them realizing who I am, but I have no patience to take any more photos or pretend like I'm nicer than I actually am. There is a reason why I'm here, and I'm not wasting another minute in this atmosphere if I don't have to. This is like any other business situation. I will get the job done, then go home to spend time with Benz. Simple as that.

"Oh, I see her," Jack says at the same moment my eyes spot Chiara.

She's in a tiny top with her boobs almost spilling out and shorts so tight, her perfect arse is on display for everyone. I would appreciate how fucking gorgeous she looks if I didn't see seven different guys ogling her body and undressing her with their eyes. Yeah, the protective part inside of me, which has been growing bigger and bigger by the day, isn't having it. I rush over to her, but her eyes light up at the sight of Jack next to me. A little smile that sends a wave of heat through me slips across her face. She jumps over the bar and jogs up to my brother.

"Jackson Tick!" she says, and he smiles brightly before wrapping his arms around her and pulling her into the air. I'm capable of breathing for the moment he's hiding her half-naked body from the crowd. "What are you doing here?" she calls out over the music after my brother placed her back on her six-inch heels. *Good God, is she trying to break her ankles?*

"Leonard brought me," Jack replies, nodding in my direction. I force more disapproval into my gaze as Chiara's eyes shift to me. She looks annoyed and slightly pissed at the sight of me.

"Oh, you're here too?" she asks as if she hadn't fucking noticed me before. "Does hell not have a decent enough bar scene or why did you come here?" Starling challenges, crossing her arms under her tits and pushing them up so much, I feel the urge to cover her with my jacket. I wish it was only because men are eyeing her, but my body has been responding to that outfit since I first saw her, and I need to give my cock a second to breathe.

"I came here to see how many times you mess up a drink," I reply, mimicking her by crossing my arms in front of my chest too. Her eyes immediately drift to my forearms, a blush crossing her cheeks.

"I never mess up, *stronzo*," she spits back, giving Jack's arm a quick squeeze. "What can I make you?" she asks my brother, who tells her his order. She nods before starting to walk away, and I follow closely behind her.

"I would also like a drink," I say as she makes her way behind the bar again.

"And I would like to see you get your ass kicked by a kangaroo, but sometimes we don't get what we want," she replies, and I almost flash her the smug smile I feel coming onto my mouth.

"I always get what I want," I remind her, making her roll her eyes. "What if I tipped you a hundred pounds?" I offer and hold out the piece of paper, knowing full well she would never take the money... except she does. She snatches it from my fingers, shoves it between her breasts and places a beer in front of me. My favourite brand. Bloody hell.

"That'll be another fifteen pounds," she says, and I slap the money on the bar. She takes it and slips it into the register, a victorious little grin on her face. I'm baffled. Maybe she isn't as resigned to taking my money as I thought. That's good to know. Very good, actually. "Here you go, Jack, on the house," Starling says as she hands him his scotch, and I glare at her in response. The same smile from before intensifies. At least she's smiling...

Demon, I mouth as she winks at me. Jack takes a sip of his drink before I do the same with mine. My eyes stay on Chiara as she moves around the bar, flipping bottles and keeping any amusement she felt before off her lips. Men on the sides are cheering her on, causing irritation to grow in my stomach.

"Come on, babe, crack a smile for us!" one creep screams at her, but Chiara keeps moving around and making drinks without paying him any attention. Me, on the other hand, I'm trying my best not to punch out his preppy boy teeth. He looks like he just came from his elite university in that ugly brown polo and pale blue jeans.

"Relax. She can handle herself," Jack reminds me, grabbing my shoulder and turning my body around. "You need to get laid. You get all cranky when you're horny," he says, and I smack his stomach in response.

"I get cranky when my brother's best friend gets harassed," I clarify, but Jack shakes his head at me.

"I don't know what's going on with you, but these things have never bothered you before. Let it go. Chiara will ask for help if she needs it, which she doesn't seem to considering she's stronger and fiercer than both of us." She is. I know she is, but I also know her better than most.

She won't quit this job, no matter what is going on here. It seems to pay her well enough that she took it in the first place. This isn't what she wants to do for a living. Chiara wants to be in art, have her own gallery one day where she can make immersive shows that aren't as boring as the ones at her current job. This stubborn woman won't do anything to risk getting fired, which means letting those arseholes say things like 'crack a smile for us, babe'. God, I want to fucking punch that guy. And a wall. And myself for caring so damn much, but no one else seems to look out for Chiara, not even her best friend. No one gives a single shit about the situation she finds herself in because she's doing everything to keep her head above water. I can't stand by and watch her barely swim. I don't... I don't want her to drown one day.

"Come on, doll, just one smile," the same guy repeats, and my jaw clenches in response.

"How much are you going to tip me if I do?" Chiara asks in response, and that creep takes out a bundle of what I'm pretty sure is his daddy's money.

"This can all be yours for a smile and five minutes in the bathroom with me," he adds, and I let out a silent growl. Nope. I can't do it. I can't watch this unfold.

"How about you shove that up your arse and leave her alone?" I call out to Polo Dude, who turns to me. He's about to tell me to fuck off when realization dawns on his features.

"Leonard fucking Tick," he says, taking three strides toward me. "I'm a huge fan, man!"

"Yeah, I don't give a shit. Leave her alone or you and I are going to have a problem," I say, noticing Starling leaning closer to hear what I'm telling her "customer".

"Yeah?" Polo Dude asks with a cocky grin. "What are you going to do?" What a spoiled dick.

"Make another advance at her and find out," I challenge, but he senses how willing I am to knock out a few of his perfect teeth because he steps back and raises his hands in surrender.

"No bitch is worth it," he says, and I feel a violent scowl coming onto my face. Yeah, he really shouldn't have said that.

"Alright, stand down," Jack says only loud enough for me to hear.

"Nah, I'm going to break his nose," I reply, making Polo Dude turn to me with a poisonous smile.

"You shouldn't have said that," he says before disappearing and then returning moments later, causing all hell to break loose.

"I cannot fucking believe you," Chiara says while pulling her long, brown hair out of the ponytail she had it in.

"This is for the best," I reply, although I've never felt this guilty in my entire life.

"*For the best?*" she spits my words back at me, turning around and pressing her finger into my left pec. "You just cost me my job by threatening my boss's son. This isn't for the best, you piece of shit. I needed this job. I can't afford my life without it!" Chiara barks, sending another wave of guilt through me.

"You shouldn't work here, Starling. We'll find you something better, somewhere you're not treated like an object," I say softly, but she's so mad, she shoves me backward. Once, but hard enough to surprise me.

"You think I liked being degraded like that every night? You think that's a fun job for a woman to have in an area like this? It's not, Leonard! It's horrible, but it was the only job where I was paid a good base pay and then got tips as well. I can't find that anywhere else, asshole. So, yeah, it may not have been the best job in the world, but it was the only one that offered enough money. You, out of all people, should understand that," she rants, and I feel like the worst person in the world.

It wasn't my intention to get Chiara fired. I didn't know who that prick was when I threatened to break his nose, but I can't deny that I'm happy Starling doesn't have to feel violated every time she's here. The way Polo Dude spoke to her made me furious. I know she doesn't want me to, but I will protect her, even if we don't like each other. It doesn't matter. I will get her into a better, more stable job. I will.

"There are other jobs. We're going to find you one. You could even work for me—"

She cuts me off, impatience lacing her words. Her green eyes are so full of anger toward me, I want nothing more than to figure out how to get rid of it. I messed up, I'm well aware, but there has to be a way to get her to forgive me.

"You've done enough. As a matter of fact, I don't want to see you again until you bring me Benz before fucking off to wherever the next race is. Meanwhile, I'm going to have to do the impossible and find another job that pays me well and goes with the rest of my schedule. Thanks very much," she says and storms off toward her car.

Chiara gets in, but I hear the rumble of her engine minutes later before watching her slam her hands against the steering wheel. She tries again, but her garbage on wheels doesn't turn on. I walk over to where she is parked, signaling to Jack that I need another minute before we can go home. He gives me a small nod, compassion all over his face.

I knock on Starling's window while her head hangs between her arms, her hands grasping the steering wheel. She doesn't respond, so I open her car door. My fingers move to her arms, and she doesn't flinch away. I put them at her sides, seeing her watch me with confusion and anger. My face is barely an inch from hers as I undo her seatbelt, her scent filling my nose and driving me absolutely crazy.

"Come, I'll drive you home," I assure her, holding out my hand for her once I've stepped back. Chiara merely glares at my palm, but I can see how tired she is. "I know you're pissed as hell, Starling, and you have every right to be, but let's get you home," I say, keeping my hand in front of her. Her fingers tremble as she reaches for her steering wheel and pushes herself out of her car. I furrow my brows from confusion and concern.

"I'm calling a taxi," she says, but the adrenalin from before has worn off now, and Chiara stumbles against the side of her car. I grab onto her arms while panic widens her eyes.

"Leonard?" she asks before her body slumps against mine, and she passes out.

Fuck!

"Chiara? Come on, Starling, don't do this to me," I beg and scoop her up into my arms, barely registering the fact that I close her door and lock her car before sprinting to mine.

"What the hell did you do?" Jack asks, and I shoot him a look I hope tells him to fuck off.

"I didn't do anything. She passed out. I think she's too exhausted and the adrenalin wearing off made her crash," I say because it's the logical explanation. Then again, a million other reasons rush through my head, and none of them are rational. None of them are what I would usually think, but my brain has a way of going against my norm when it comes to Chiara.

"I'm calling myself a taxi. You go take care of Chiara," my brother says, and I don't waste a second before obeying.

I place Chiara in my passenger seat and wipe her hair off her face. To ease my hypochondriac thoughts, I press my fingers to her pulse to reassure myself. It's there. Strong even. Good.

Thank fuck.

CHAPTER 10
Chiara

My head is pounding. I have no idea what time it is, only that these soft bed sheets don't belong to me. Mine are rough and itchy because they were cheap the day I got them. These are not cheap. They feel like someone transported clouds from the sky to the ground and then wove them into the shape of bedsheets. I know they're Leonard's. I also know they aren't the ones I slept in the last time I was here.

"How are you feeling?" his familiar voice says, and I open my heavy eyes to see him place down the guitar he must have been holding. Then, Benz comes running at me, licking my face now that I'm awake. I wish I could smile, but I'm too confused.

Why am I in Leonard's bed?

Why is he watching me like a creep from the couch he has in the corner?

What happened?

Why does my head hurt so much and my mouth feel like sandpaper?

Why the hell am I here and not in my flat?

Then it all comes crashing down on me. I lost my job. Leonard cost me my job by threatening my boss's son. I slide out of bed without another moment of hesitation, ignoring the fact that I'm wearing a shirt that isn't mine on top of the clothes I wore to work. I even ignore the soapy, fresh, and all Leonard scent hitting my nose because the rage inside of me is forcing me out the door. Unfortunately, I got up way too fast, causing my head to spin and my body to waver on my feet.

"For fuck's sake, Starling, sit down," he says, catching my forearm and pushing me back down on the bed.

"I don't want to be here," I say while he stands over me with his arms crossed and the usual frown on his face.

"You fucking fainted, Starling, what did you want me to do? Let you collapse on the ground next to your non-functional garbage bag on wheels?" A gasp leaves me.

"Watch how you speak about Delilah," I spit back, and this man has the audacity to roll his eyes.

"Let's not argue about that safety-breeching shitbox you call a car. I don't have the patience to be mad right now," he says, and I stand up again. This time, my head doesn't take a spin and I remain upright, even though my brain is pounding in complaint.

"Why the hell would you be the mad one? You cost me my goddamn job. I won't even be able to pay to fix Delilah now," I say and walk over to where he placed my shoes on the ground.

"Good," is his only response. I clench my hands into fists.

"*Good*?" I ask, the word falling from my lips with anger dripping from it.

"Yes, good." Leonard's arms remain in front of his chest as he studies me like he has no concern or worry in the world. I'm going to kill him.

"Would you like to have a fast death or a slow, torturous one?" I ask, and this asshole smirks in response. It's a small one, but it's so rare, it distracts me for a moment.

"I promised you I'd help you find a better job, and I never break my promises," he says, and I close the distance between us, wishing I wasn't as short as I am because he towers over me by at least a head.

"Can I ask you a question?" I ask, our chests almost touching now. I watch his body tense as my breasts briefly graze his upper body.

"You can, but I probably won't answer," he replies, and I trail my eyes down his body then back up to his face.

"Does it make you hard to fuck with my life?" I say, and he takes a step back, but I follow him. "Do you get off on making me angry with you?" I go on, and his body hits the wall behind him. "Are you horny for me, Champ?" He grabs my hand right as I'm about to place it on his chest, his face leaning down to mine.

"You're out of your mind if you think I feel anything but irritation for you," he replies, and I give him a cocky smile because his body is telling a completely different story. He's turned on. I can see it in his eyes and when my eyes drop to his bulge, I smirk.

"If you say so," I reply, but he's holding my wrist and keeping me so close to him, it sends heat between my legs. My clit aches in response to his body warmth and lips barely away from mine.

"You're the one trapping me against the wall with a look in your eyes that's begging me to fuck you hard, not the other way around, sweetheart," he says, making me swallow hard and heavily.

"In your dreams," I bite out, and he offers me a sigh that lingers in the air.

"Always fighting me." Leonard drops my hand, breaking the sexual tension between us as he grabs me by the shoulders, gently but firmly, and guides me backward so he can step out of our confrontation.

As soon as he's gone, heat fills my cheeks. What the hell was I thinking? Getting that close to him is a horrible, terrible idea. I wanted to tease him, piss him off a little maybe, but not the reaction our bodies had to the proximity. That's the last thing I ever wanted.

"How much sleep had you gotten before you passed out on me?" he asks while he walks out of the room, expecting me to follow him to answer his damn question.

"Screw you," I say, but the scent of food fills my nose. My stomach, growling and violently complaining, decides to do as Leonard wants, to find out what he's preparing in the kitchen.

"How many hours, Starling?" the English man insists, and I drop down on the floor so Benz can cuddle up in my lap. It's dark outside, causing panic to flood through me.

"How long was I asleep?" I ask, and his back tenses in response.

"Almost seventeen hours." *Seventeen hours?*

"Leonard! You should have woken me! I had shifts at the gallery and at the bookstore today," I say before covering my mouth and rubbing my hands over my face.

"I called your jobs and told them you're taking the day off," he says so nonchalantly, my earlier desire to kill him returns.

"That wasn't your decision to make. I need the money. How many times do I have to repeat myself until you get that through your head? I cannot afford to miss a day's work," I bark so harshly, Benz looks up at me, her blue eyes full of surprise at my tone.

"No, you know what? You bloody fainted, Starling. You have not been sleeping or resting, and your body cannot keep up with you, alright? You will kill yourself if you keep going like that. Your body needed to sleep off the exhaustion you've put it through for God knows how long, and I wasn't about to wake you so you could go out and destroy yourself further."

Speechless. I'm speechless because of how unsettlingly heartwarming it is to have him care about me to this extent. No one else gives a shit. Graham loves me, but he's so busy with his own life—and used to be all for it that I worked so much to finance my life and our dream—he doesn't pay too much attention to how tired I always am. Mamma doesn't see me often enough to be truly concerned and neither does

Lulu. But, here he is, the last person who should give a shit about me, caring that I don't break myself. Tears shoot into my eyes in response, but I shove them down, far down, before my gaze meets Leonard's soft one.

"I promise, I will find you something where you are paid better so you don't have to work as many hours," he says, and I shake my head, scratching Benz's head.

"How did you keep fighting for your dream when it seemed like things were standing still instead of moving forward?" I ask quietly, but he stops moving around in the kitchen to offer me all of his attention.

"You want that gallery?" he says, his hip pushing against the kitchen island.

"Of course I do, Sherlock." He rolls his eyes at my name-calling but refocuses soon, his brown eyes fixating on my face.

"Then we will make it happen," he adds, and I let out a snort that raises his eyebrows.

"What the fuck do you mean 'we'? You and I are not a 'we'. You and I will never be a 'we'. I hate you. We don't get along," I blurt out, seeing him tense briefly at the word 'hate'.

"Fine," is all he replies and turns back to his stove. "I will give you the money I cost you by not waking you. It's my fault, so I owe you."

"No, I don't want your money," I reply, remembering the hundred pounds I took from him at the club yesterday. When I reach for it in my bra, it's still there. I take it out, staring at it and feeling wrong about keeping it now, so I place it on his kitchen island.

"Put that hundred back between your breasts or I'm going to lose it," he says, but that sentence is so fucking weird, we both burst into laughter at the same time.

It lasts for ten seconds until both of us realize what's happening. I've never heard Leonard laugh before. He's never heard me either. The first time we decide to do it in front of one another, it's at the same time and causes our voices to collide and intertwine. The sound is surprisingly beautiful too, which only adds to my panic and shuts down the sound as it tries to leave my throat again. My lips pull into a thin line, and so do Leonard's full ones. Well, that was incredibly weird.

"I'm going to go take a shower," I blurt out because I need to get away from him as soon as possible.

"I'll put some clothes for you on the bed," he replies, earning himself a quiet and muffled 'thanks' from me.

He's not kicking me out. I'm not leaving. Instead, I'm going to take a shower at his place and after, slip on the boxers, sweatpants, and shirt I wore the last time I was here only days ago. None of this is right. I should have jumped at the opportunity to go home. He should have driven me home as soon as I woke up. Then again, he shouldn't have brought me back to his flat either.

"Where is my car?" I ask once I'm back in the kitchen, and Leonard gives me a side glance in response.

"At the mechanic," he replies, stirring the light sauce he made. My stomach grunts at the sight. "Dinner is almost ready," he adds, but there is no way I will be able to eat this.

"I'm lactose-intolerant," I say, and Leonard nods, seeming to be aware of that fact even though I never told him.

"And I'm vegan," Leonard replies and adds some salt to the sauce. "Everything is made from dairy-free products, Starling, you will be able to eat this without setting a new record for most farts in a minute," he says, biting down on his bottom lip to hide how amusing he finds his joke.

"Ha, ha," I say and decide to lay the table, just like I did a few days ago. "Then, what the hell did you feed me when you made *chicken* piccata?" I ask, and his eyes sparkle with amusement.

"Plant-based meat. You couldn't even tell the difference the way I seasoned it, could you?" I could not, but he doesn't have to hear me say how wonderful of a cook I think he is. His ego is inflated enough.

"How much do I owe you for the mechanic?" I ask instead, dreading the answer.

"She's a friend of mine and owed me a favor, so, nothing." I can hear the way his voice dropped an octave, which is a clear sign that he's lying and not even trying to cover it up.

"You're a shit liar," I reply, and Leonard turns to me, the challenge written across his face.

"That's not true. Here, I can lie easily," he starts and faces me, ready to feed me some bullshit. "I like you a lot, Starling." His voice is even and normal. He doesn't blink.

"Fine, you're a great liar. Happy now?" I ask, but he merely shrugs.

"Around you? Never," he says as he turns back to his pan. "Finish laying the table and quit looking at my back," he says, forcing heat straight back into my face because I was checking out the muscles clinging to the fabric of his shirt.

"You're unbearable. I'm going to go home," I say, and he lets out a small snort before carrying the hot pan toward the table where we'll be eating.

"First, you eat. Then I'll take you home where you can keep on hating me," he suggests, and when my stomach growls, I decide that's the better option. I'm starving.

Not to mention, there is a gross part of me that wants to remain in his presence for a little longer. I should go see a doctor and have him cut it out.

Chapter 11

Leonard

"You seem distracted," Quinn says, her blue eyes scanning my face as I get ready for Qualifying. This hour-long session determines the spots all of the drivers will start in for the race tomorrow.

"I'm not," I lie, but I've been in my head all weekend.

Chiara and I hadn't seen each other in almost a week, except when I dropped Benz at her place two days ago. She barely spoke three words to me because things have been awkward between us from the moment I drove her back to her place after dinner. She's still pissed at me for costing her that job at *Sunrise*, which I completely understand. As much as I would like to claim she's merely being stubborn for not seeing this as a great thing for her physical and mental health, it should have been her decision. I shouldn't have been the reason why, and this disgusting feeling of guilt has been resting on my chest since. It's distracting me from my job, which has never happened to me.

"If there is something you'd like to talk about, you know I'm always here to listen, kiddo," Quinn says, her dark hair bouncing around her as she gathers everything I'm going to need for the Qualifying session.

"I fucked up something last week and it's weighing heavy on my mind," I explain because there isn't a single secret in the world I'd keep from Quinn. She's my best friend, always has been.

"Is this about Chiara losing her job because you threatened the boss's son?" she asks, and I do a double-take.

"How the fuck do you know about that?"

She merely grins at my question for a moment, building tension by not telling me even though I can sense her wanting to show off how she got that information. I'm not a patient person, except when it comes to Chiara. I have to be patient with that little demon. When she pressed herself against me in the bedroom a week ago, it took every ounce of patience not to give in to my body's wishes. It would have been a horrible idea. Fucking Chiara, as good as I know it would be, would be wrong on many levels. I have to keep reminding myself of that for some reason. Maybe because it would relieve stress for both of us, and knowing she was probably dripping for me doesn't ease my horniness either. God, that fucking woman is messing with my head, and I don't even like her. Not even a little. She's infuriating and annoying and gorgeous and—

Fuck me.

"Jack told Rena, who told me during our monthly coffee date. You didn't know I was close with your mom?" Quinn says, pulling me back to reality and away from Chiara. Well, somewhat.

"I did not know you were close with Mum. Why didn't either of you tell me?" I ask, taking my balaclava out of her hand. Quinn shrugs, waiting for me to pull the fabric over my head before continuing our conversation.

"Never came up. Anyway, since when do you care about doing stupid things around Chiara? I thought that's how you two worked," she says, but I pull my balaclava off again since I shoved it on the wrong way around. Jesus, I'm not present today.

"It is, but this time, I fucked up badly. Chiara is going through enough shit at the moment with Graham moving to New York and that creep of a roommate her

Mamma lives with has been harassing her. I don't need to mess things up further. I've been trying to talk to her about getting a new job, one with better pay, but she's refusing to accept my help. She's so bloody stubborn, it drives me mad," I say, but my best friend merely smiles at me like she knows something I don't. "What? What's that face for?" I ask, adjusting my black racing suit and fireproof.

"Nothing," she lies, but I have no patience to drag the information out of her. "Isn't there anything that can be done about that roommate?" Quinn's soft features turn abnormally serious at the question.

"I've tried to get her to tell me more, but she refuses. Like I said, she's stubborn," I repeat, fastening the clasps on my shoes.

"Hmmm, what about getting her a job to work for you?" she goes on, and I let out an unamused snort.

"Over her dead body," I reply because those words are the exact ones Chiara would throw at that suggestion.

I've been trying to find something she'd find acceptable as a job for me, but I haven't figured out anything she'd agree to. At least she's letting me pay her now for taking care of Benz for the time I'm gone. It was a battle to get her to take my money, but, eventually, she caved when I said I really didn't want to pay her and only did it because I didn't want to owe her anything. It was utter rubbish, but she seemed to take it as a valid reason and stopped fighting me on it. Her face after was so cute, her pouty lips frowning like—

Wait, did I just think she was cute? No! God, no, Leonard, get a fucking grip.

"You have to go. Let's continue this conversation later," Quinn says, and I give her one tight nod because my head is swimming with panic at the thought I just had.

Get out, get out, get out.

"Race hard, win harder," Quinn and I say in unison before I give her shoulder a quick squeeze.

After I've placed my helmet on, my team gives me the green light to get into the car. I adjust until I find the perfect position in the seat that was molded specially for my body. My heartbeat is steady, my breathing even, and my work mode is activated in my head. All my worries vanish as my team starts bombarding me with information and telling me what to get ready for.

The first tier of Qualifying, Q1, is about to start. After that, only fifteen drivers remain. Q2, the tier afterward, takes out five more drivers, and in Q3, the top ten drivers fight for pole. The one to get pole gets to start from first place tomorrow for the race. I've taken two out of three poles this season, but I plan on making it three today. I may not feel much when I win races anymore, but I'm still competitive as hell.

Just like Chiara.

I'm buying myself a new subconscious as soon as I kick my teammate's arse.

Pole was an easy win yesterday. Jonathan, my teammate, fucked up his fast lap, basically handing me the position without putting up a fight. Fine by me. The real task is winning today's race. As important as Qualifying is, anything can happen during a race. A driver can start from last place and end up first by the time they cross the finish line. Someone starting in first place can end up last because of pitstop problems, getting pushed off track during the race, or countless other reasons. Nothing is set in stone because of Qualifying. Absolutely nothing.

All the drivers are lined up to listen to the Austrian hymn when Adrian Romana comes up to me and places a hand on my shoulder. His usual smile rests on his lips, and he cocks an eyebrow at my serious face.

"It's nice to see you too. Great job yesterday, by the way. I rewatched your lap, and it was phenomenal. A beauty," he says, which makes me face him completely, a little surprised.

The other drivers don't treat me kindly. None of them. I'm the guy who won a championship last year. I'm *the* guy to beat. They have no reason to be friendly with me, but I don't try to give them one either. I don't need them to like me. The only people I do need in this sport are Quinn and my team.

"What? What did I say?" he asks, and I cock an eyebrow at him.

"Something nice. I'm not used to it," I reply honestly before facing away from him. Adrian lets out a short, awkward laugh.

"Yeah, I know what you mean, but I don't like how the other drivers treat you. You're an incredible driver, and that isn't something to be jealous about. It's something to look up to, and I do." *This kid.* I shake my head, offering him a softer look, one that hardly ever crosses my face during a race weekend, except when I'm in private.

"That's kind of you to say," is all I respond because this kid is warming a part of me that was frozen over a long time ago, and I feel the urge to run.

"Anytime. I hope you know now you do have a friend in this sport. In case you ever get lonely, you can always hang out with me. I'm phenomenal company," he says, his comment tugging on the corners of my mouth. I fight off the amusement, but he notices. "Ha, that's progress. Oh yeah. You like me too, that's good to know," he says with a happy grin, so I simply shake my head and nudge him in the side. He lets out a sharp breath in response before bursting into laughter.

"You're alright, kid, but you've got a long way to go until I start liking you," I say, earning me a cocky smirk from him.

"Haven't met a single person who didn't like me yet." And I can see why. Adrian is extremely likable. He's charming and charismatic, funny too. "You're not going to wreck my streak, mate, I won't let you." I shake my head again, fighting back a sigh because I won't be wrecking his streak. I like him. He's nice to me, and not many people are in this sport.

We listen to the Austrian hymn, and afterward, Adrian shakes my hand and wishes me good luck for the race. I'm still trying to wrap my head around his kindness when Jonathan Kent steps in front of me, ready to fight.

"Try not to push me out of the first corner again, Tick."

I push past him because I'm in no fucking mood to argue over racing incidents. I took full responsibility for what happened during the third corner of the first race after I rewatched the footage. I apologised to him, something I'm not required to do but thought would be the right thing. He's been on my arse so much, I've been regretting showing him any human decency and sportsmanship.

"Move out of my fucking way, Kent," I say when that prick steps right in front of me again.

"I know cheating is the only way you can win, but it's getting pathetic now," he replies, and since he's several centimetres shorter than me, he widens his stance to appear larger. It achieves nothing he obviously meant for it to. I'm not frightened. I'm not going to cave in. I'm not doing anything he hoped for. Instead, I get close to him, staring into his transparent eyes before slowing my words enough for him to understand.

"Let's take this onto the track. We will see who the better driver is," I say and walk past him, hitting my shoulder against his as a final warning.

By the time I get back to Quinn, she's holding out some water for me. I take several sips, trying to calm my racing heart. I hate confrontations with Jonathan. Robert Fuchs, the Grenzenlos team principal and my boss, has been on our arses to behave, and I don't like disappointing him.

"There is something you should see. It'll cheer you up," Quinn says and hands me my phone.

At first, I don't look at the screen. I'm too busy trying to decipher her happy facial expression. She doesn't let on anything, so I bring my gaze to whatever has her in a good mood. My heart stops beating altogether at the sight of Benz in my Grenzenlos team shirt and Chiara next to her, her arm around my daughter. Naturally, that hand is also holding up a middle finger and the serious look on her face is there, but Benz is smiling at the camera. She's showing me how happy she is to be spending time with her best friend, and I can't help but feel my insides turn. Not in a bad way though...

Chiara: Benz wanted to wish you good luck and remind you to be safe out there. I didn't want to, but she insisted.

Sometimes this woman can be so full of shit. It brings a slight smile to my lips, but I kill it quickly. Another message appears on the screen.

Chiara: Seriously though. Drive safe, stronzo. I still need to make fun of you for running naked through your neighborhood when you were twelve. Yeah, your mum just told me, and it's fucking hilarious. Can't wait to see you when you get back and milk the fuck out of that embarrassing story.

Maybe she isn't as mad as I thought she was. Maybe she can forgive me for what happened. Maybe I haven't fucked everything up. Chiara seems to feel better toward me. I'd much rather have her being a pain in the arse than ignore me. Her silent treatment is so much worse than when anyone else does it because that woman doesn't stay quiet. I'm pretty sure she gets that fire from her Italian heritage, and it's something I'm not ashamed to like about her.

"It's time," Quinn reminds me, and I hand her back my phone.

It is time.

Time to kick Jonathan Kent's arse.

CHAPTER 12

Chiara

E victed. Kicked out. Thrown into a lion's den. It's all the same thing really. The letter from my landlord feels unbearably heavy in my hands. Graham is standing in front of me, watching the way my hands are shaking after what I just read out loud to him. His arms wrap around me, and I fling mine around his, fighting back the tears that are trying to escape me. This isn't something to cry over. Lots of people get evicted because their landlord is selling their building to a large company that plans on tearing it down. It happens. People move on without breaking apart in response. Except, it's not only getting evicted. It's Tim appearing at the bookstore during my shift a few weeks ago. It's me losing my job at the bar. It's trying so hard to keep my head above water and reach my dream, which keeps slipping further away because of situations like this one. It's Graham leaving tomorrow for six months, and I'm going to miss him so much.

It feels like the whole world is conspiring against me, but that's ridiculous considering I'm a tiny speck in the world. Chiara de Luca is no one. So, why the hell is the universe taking its time slowly torturing me?

"We will find something else, my love, don't worry," Graham says, but I push off him. Getting comfort right now only drags me closer to the well of tears, and I will not cry. I haven't cried in almost two decades. It won't change today.

"No, you're catching that plane tomorrow, and I will pack up your things after you're gone. Your parents can keep it stored for you while I try to find a new place for us to live," I assure him, but Graham grabs my chin, forcing me to focus on him.

"I'm not leaving you when we're getting evicted," he says, but I know if he stays now, he will never go. Something will always get in the way, and I won't let him give up this shot at finding happiness out there in the world. I love him too much to let that happen.

"You're going, and that is final. We only have a few things, no furniture or anything, so moving will be easy," I reply. The flat came furnished years ago when we first started renting it. It's going to make my job a hell of a lot easier.

"Chiara—" He starts, but I cut him off. I'm in no mood to argue with him.

"Do you still want to go?" I ask, and he nods, his head hanging low. "Then, go. You have to. This is important. You can't put off taking care of yourself, and I've got this. If I'm feeling annoyed, I'll make Leonard help me." When I realize what I've just said, I freeze. I would never willingly invite Leonard to spend time with me. *Would I?*

"Okay, and if you're in need of a laugh, I can always leave my strap-ons and you can let him pack them." That gets a small laugh out of me. Proud of himself for getting that reaction, Graham grins. "We will find a new place when I get back, I promise. We have to be out of here in three months, which means you only have to find something for the other three. When I get back, we will go apartment hunting," Graham promises, and I give him a small nod.

Where the hell am I going to go for the other three months?

I can't go live with Mamma. Her apartment is too small, and Tim is there. I will not give that man a chance to be alone with me any more than I already have to. The only other place I can think of is the Ticks', but I would never ask them such a big favor. They're family, but they don't need a twenty-four-year-old moving into their guest room. I love Rena and Andrew, especially because they would take me in, in a heartbeat, but they're enjoying their empty nest now. I won't take it away from them. I can't.

"Come on, my parents are waiting for us," Graham says, and I give him a small nod, trying not to spiral into a dark hole of worst-case scenarios of what will happen in the future. That's a problem for later.

The Ticks are throwing a family lunch as an informal goodbye meal for Graham since he will be back in half a year. When we get to their place, a two-story single-detach house half an hour from our flat, there is a banner hung across the mahogany front door. Benz runs toward it as soon as I open the door for her and remove the dog seatbelt I put on her. Leonard is supposed to come back tomorrow from his race in Austria, which he, surprisingly enough, didn't win. Jonathan Kent, his teammate, drove into him, resulting in a double DNF—Did Not Finish—for the Grenzenlos team. I was so fucking mad watching it unfold, I almost threw my remote at the television. Not that I'd ever tell Leonard that. The last thing I need is for him to know I care about his race results. I don't even want myself to be aware of it.

Graham knocks on the front door, and we wait several seconds until his dad, a tall man with darker skin than his sons' but lighter eyes and hair, opens the door for us. His smile is warm and familiar as he opens his arms for me first. Always me first. It bugs Graham a lot, but I'm Andrew's warrior. He came to all of my fights as a kid when I was still competing. He made Leonard and Graham come too, which is something I appreciate now because it showed them just how dangerous I can be. No one fucks with me. One way or another, I will fight back, and they're not going to like it.

"How have you been, Chiara?" he asks before stepping to the side and enveloping his son in a hug too. "Son," he says, that same warm smile firmly set in place. I'm about to assure him that we've been fine when Graham beats me to it.

"We're getting evicted," he blurts out, leading his father inside.

Benz stays by my side until I assure her to go ahead, and she does with a happy wag of her tail. She runs to the kitchen first, finding Rena at the stove. Her light brown skin is complemented by the olive-colored blouse she put on. Her brown hair is slowly turning grey and white, and no one wears it quite like the beautiful woman in front of me I've grown to love so much. Rena is moving around, searching for God knows what when suddenly she stills, her head turning my way ever so slightly.

"Chiara?" she asks, and I shake my head.

"How do you always know?" I reply, walking toward her and placing my hand on her arm first. She smiles at me, so I wrap my arms around her, the scent of fresh flowers hitting my nose. "Do I stink? Is that it? I swear I showered before I came here," I promise as I step out of the hug. I study the sunglasses on her face, noticing that I've never seen them before. They suit her well, the round shape and small frame different from the ones she usually wears.

"Your footsteps are lighter than my husband's and sons'. I hear yours, but not as well," she explains, and I give her arm a slight squeeze.

Rena started going blind when I was fourteen. The doctor said it was a rare genetic disease and untreatable. It took a few years for her sight to disappear completely, but she told me recently she can still see the shapes of things and people.

"Can you help me find the salt? Andrew moved it from its usual spot when he cooked last, and I can't find it," she says, and I move over to the spices, not finding salt there. I look around the kitchen, spotting it next to the sink. "The sink?" Rena asks after I told her where it was. "That man," she says with a snicker.

Rena eventually *shoos* me out of her kitchen, telling me to go greet Ellie, Jack, and Stu. The second I step into the hall leading from where Rena is to the veranda where everyone else is, the front door opens, and Leonard walks through. He's wearing a loosely fitting white shirt that complements the color of his skin along with dark brown pants hugging his hips perfectly. He looks breathtaking especially with his sharp features, full lips, and trimmed beard. It's short and clean, like always, and when he cocks one of his full and flawless eyebrows, I realize he noticed me drooling over his gorgeous body. It makes me want to turn away and pretend it didn't happen, but I steel myself, ignoring the way my heart flutters as he comes closer.

"Starling," he says once he's close enough for me to hear.

"Champ," I reply, making him narrow his eyes at me. He studies my face for the briefest moment, then frowns.

"What happened?" Leonard asks, and I furrow my brows.

"What do you mean? Nothing happened," I reply and start walking away. His hand finds mine before he laces his fingers through my own. He tugs on me hard enough to bring my body back toward him. Surprise fills me from head to toe because he's never touched me like this, and I'm not sure why I'm not repulsed by it.

"Who was it? What did they do?" he asks, my chest now almost pressing against his. I take my hand back because I don't like that my body is drawn to him.

"It was you, and what you did was show up here early when you were only supposed to come tomorrow," I tease, crossing my arms in front of my chest. Leonard keeps his gaze on mine, not impressed or amused by my words.

"Tell me, Starling," he insists, and it tugs on something inside of me I'd rather ignore.

"Graham and I are getting evicted," I reply because he would have found out sooner rather than later anyway.

Leonard curses under his breath but keeps his eyes on me. They soften in response to something in my features, and I'm starting to dislike how well he knows me. He even realized something was off the second he saw me, for fuck's sake.

"How long do you have?" he asks, and I take another step back because his scent, so fresh and soapy and all him, is confusing my senses.

"Three months." Again, lying or hiding this would be useless. Graham doesn't keep such things from his family.

"Fucking hell, Chiara," he says, my name sounding foreign out of his mouth since he hardly ever uses it. Foreign, but beautiful. "Why are you getting evicted? What did the two of you do?" he asks, and I welcome back the familiar anger I feel toward him. It's a lot more settling than the other sensations my body's been feeling for him.

"We didn't do anything, *stronzo*. They kicked us out because the building was bought by some big corporation," I spit back and turn to leave. He follows closely behind me.

"I didn't mean it like that, Starling. I meant what they accused you of doing. I didn't phrase that properly," he explains, but I have no more interest in continuing this conversation.

"Yeah, no shit," I say, my feet bringing me to the veranda door.

"Fuck," is the last thing I hear him mutter before I step outside.

Benz was greeting everyone, but as soon as she sees her dad, she sprints toward him. He kneels on the ground and wraps his arms around her, looking like he's finally complete again while she jumps at him, barely able to contain her excitement.

"Chiara!" Ellie calls out, and before I can even process her words, her tiny arms are around my waist.

"Hello, miss sunshine," I say and offer her the slightest smile.

She takes my hand and pulls me to her dads, begging them to show me a video of her doing her first cartwheel. Apparently it happened earlier today, and Stu and Jack have never been prouder. This wholesome moment would be perfect if Leonard didn't almost press his body against mine from behind to look at the phone screen over my shoulder. His hot breath sends a shiver down my spine and heat between my legs. As if drawn to him, I lean back ever so slightly, my back hitting his front. He lets out a confused hum, but his finger moves to the screen so he can restart the video.

"I can't believe you did a cartwheel, Lizzie," Leonard says, and I can hear the pride in his tone clear as day. It also doesn't help that his lips are right next to my ear.

"Have you ever heard of personal space?" I ask him as I turn my head and hand Jack his phone.

Leonard's eyes are on my lips when he responds with a simple "No." I roll my eyes at him, bothered because he's so close, my body is vibrating.

"Can you back up?" His eyes sparkle with amusement.

"No." *God*.

"I hate you," I say quietly, and one of his hands briefly grazes my left hip. My body moves into his touch in response, earning me a smirk from him.

"Tell your body that," he whispers as his mouth almost brushes mine before stepping away, the loss of his heat leaving me off-balance for a moment.

My eyes shift forward again, going wide when I notice Jack and Stu with dropped jaws and shocked looks all over their faces. Their eyes are fixated on me, clearly trying to process whatever just happened between Leonard and me. *Well, shit*.

"I don't want to talk about it," I blurt out and walk over to the table to grab a glass of water.

Compared to the chaos from before, the rest of lunch goes by uneventfully. Everyone gives Graham a small gift, something to remind him of them, and then we all watch the football game together. Leonard and I are on opposite sides of the room, but his gaze burns my skin even from far away. I glare at him in response and mouth the words *Stop staring at me and watch the game.* This asshole keeps watching me, shaking his head.

For fuck's sake, is he ever not going to push all of my buttons?

CHAPTER 13
Leonard

L izzie dragged me to yet another show at the immersive gallery where Chiara works. I don't know why she's so fascinated with this exhibition since, like Starling has said many times too, it isn't very good. As a matter of fact, it's utter rubbish. The music selection doesn't fit the style at all, and it's so loud, my ears ring every single time the show is done. My niece, on the other hand, always looks around at the walls where the projectors are showing the pictures. Jack and Stu are not fans of art, so they make me take Lizzie whenever I'm home.

It's been a week since Graham left, and it's been just as long since I've seen the little demon. She's been as quiet as she always is, but it bothers me now more than it ever has in the past. With Graham gone, a big part of me wants to make sure she's okay all by herself in that flat. Fucking hell. I hate the thought of Chiara living alone.

"Can we get ice cream after the show?" Lizzie asks, and I give her hand a slight squeeze as we stand in line, waiting to be allowed inside the exhibit room.

"Sure," I reply, and she wiggles from side to side from happiness.

For the thousandth time since Stu and Jack adopted Lizzie, I realise I would do anything for her. I will protect her with my life from any harm that could come her way. I would fight monsters and beasts of all kinds. Her parents were friends with my brother and his partner for many years before they died when Lizzie was three years old. Jack and Stu didn't hesitate in their decision to take in the little infant

93

their friends had left behind. It's one of the reasons why I would do anything and everything for my niece. She deserves nothing but happiness, and if I could bottle up the sun for her, I would.

"Is Chiara working today?" Lizzie asks, and I ignore the way my heart skips a beat. Maybe I should go see the doctor. It's been happening a lot recently, and I need to make sure everything's alright.

"I think so," I reply and squeeze her hand again, this time involuntarily. *Muscle spasms?* Great.

"Can I tell you something?" She gives me a mischievous little grin, so I furrow my brows. *Uh oh, that's never a good sign.*

"You can tell me anything," I say and put my hand on her head, moving it from side to side. She lets out a giggle, but I'm still worried about whatever it is she wants to tell me. Kids are way too fucking honest, and they notice more than people give them credit for.

"I think you have a crush on Chiara," Lizzie says, and I suck in a sharp breath. Yeah, I was afraid that's where this conversation was going.

"I don't have a crush on anyone," I explain, my heart feeling like it's getting squeezed inside my chest. *That's it! I'm going to see a doctor.*

"You have a crush on her, I know it, Uncle Lenny. I see the way you look at her," she says, proud of herself for whatever reason. I'm about to fight her on this when I realise who I'm speaking to. Lizzie is seven years old. She doesn't know shit about this messy situation between Chiara and me, and I sure as hell won't tell her.

"What ice cream flavours will you get later?" I ask to change the topic. Lizzie's face lights up before she goes into a rant about not knowing what she wants yet but assuring me she will figure it out later.

When we step into the room, my eyes instantly drift to where Chiara usually stands at the side. She's speaking to an elderly man, who seems to be asking her a lot of questions. Starling is patient, but Lizzie isn't. The little girl pulls me to her friend, and the thought of my niece being so happy to see Chiara makes me feel a strange kind of content. Benz, Mum and Dad, Jack and Stu, Graham, and Lizzie, they all love this woman to bits, and I get why. Starling, while annoying the shit out of me most of the time, has the biggest heart of anyone I've ever met. When someone calls for her help, she wastes no time getting to them. She doesn't bullshit. She follows her passion. She makes everyone around her happy. I'm pretty sure if I didn't irritate her more than anyone else, she'd be nice to me too.

"Okay, hold on now, Liz," I say and hold her back before she can interrupt Chiara and the gentleman she's speaking to. "We have to wait until she's finished talking," I explain, but my niece is bouncing on her feet from excitement.

"Chiara, we're here," Lizzie says when the man in front of Starling leaves. Her green eyes warm at the sight of my niece. Then she brings her gaze to me, heat flooding it instantly.

"Hey, you two. I'm sorry, but my shift just ended. I was planning on going home," she says, but her attention is on Lizzie now.

"Can't she come with us to get ice cream later, Lenny? I don't even have to watch the show today," Lizzie says because she'd rather spend time with Starling.

"Whatever you and Chiara would like." Because I can't deny Lizzie anything.

"I wouldn't want to impose on your day," the woman in front of me says, this time addressing me.

"You're not." *Actually, I would like you to join us to figure out how you're doing without showing that I have any interest in your life.*

"Okay, let's watch the show first then," Chiara says, making my niece light up and drag her all the way to the bench where we always sit.

I take a seat next to Chiara, closer than I have to be, my knee brushing hers. Her body tenses for a brief moment before she relaxes against the wall behind her and listens to Lizzie tell her about what Benz did this morning. Meanwhile, I bring my leg flush against Starling's to see what she's going to do. At first, she does nothing. She listens patiently, asking my niece more questions. I really can't help myself when I lean my arm against hers next.

"I know you have no sense of personal space, but it's getting a bit ridiculous, Leonard," she hisses low enough to make sure Lizzie can't hear. "Stop touching me," she whispers, but I lean back and fight the smile wanting to settle on my lips.

"No." She groans in response. I smirk because it's impossible to keep on hiding it when fucking with her is so damn satisfying.

What happens next is so sudden, it knocks the air from my chest. Chiara's hand slips to my thigh, her whole body going rigid. I can feel the panic in her chest without looking at her, but one glance at her face tells me everything I need to know. She's scared. Something has frightened her, and it has me on high alert. I sit up straight, scanning the room to see who or what has her reacting like this. Her nails dig into my leg a moment later, but I let her because the source of her panic is walking this way and if she wasn't touching me, I'd lose it.

Tim Young, her mother's roommate and successful strip club owner, is walking toward where we are. I had him looked into by a PI—private investigator—friend of mine, who told me some things I'd much rather forget. Tim is shady as hell, and I don't want him anywhere near Chiara or her Mamma. A veil of red covers my vision as soon as that man with graying hair and blue eyes stops in front of us.

"Chiara, how wonderful to see you," he says with a thick English accent and low-pitch voice.

"Tim," she grinds out, removing her hand from my leg.

Not good. Without her touch to ground me, I might actually break his face for the way he's looking her up and down. I bring my arm around her shoulders without thinking. It makes her tense even more for a moment, but when she sees the confusion on Tim's face, she sinks against me.

"Who the fuck are you?" he asks, and I shoot him a glare I hope causes him to drop dead.

"I'm her boyfriend. Who the fuck are you?" I spit back, but Lizzie lets out a small giggle.

"No, you're not, you're—" I use the hand that's around Chiara to place it over my niece's mouth.

"We're pretty new, but that doesn't mean I don't know about the way you've been treating my girlfriend. I suggest you leave before I make you regret ever allowing your eyes to drift to her," I say, slow and careful. Chiara pinches my side, but I was expecting her to, so I don't even flinch. I keep glaring at the man hovering over us.

"Does your mum know about the kind of people you surround yourself with, Chiara? I don't think she'd approve of someone who threatens another guy," Tim says, and I almost lose my patience.

"Tim, I don't know why you keep showing up at the places I work, but, as you can see, I'm dating someone. I'm not interested in you, nor am I playing hard to get like you suggested last time."

There are many parts about those few sentences that are making me nauseous. 1) He's been showing up at her workplaces. 2) He thinks this is all a game and Chiara is just playing hard to get. 3) Her voice is calm and careful, letting me know she is scared of the repercussions yelling at him would have. She's thinking about her Mamma, and it makes me even angrier that Chiara ended up in a situation like this. And the fact that she hasn't shared any of this with someone means she's been dealing with it by herself probably since her Mamma and Tim moved in together. Six years ago. This shit started happening six years ago. I am definitely going to be sick, I'm just not sure when my body will decide it can't handle any more thoughts of my Starling getting treated like this.

"Don't worry, little girl, you will see who the better man is sooner or later," Tim replies before walking away. Chiara lets out the breath she was holding, and I release Lizzie's mouth.

"Did I say something wrong?" my niece asks, but I give her a soft look before shaking my head.

"No, it's alright, Liz, I just needed to deal with that man by myself, okay?" She gives me a small nod while I bring my hand to Starling's arm. A moment before my palm connects with her, she jumps out of her seat.

"Excuse me," is all I hear as she rushes out of the room. If Lizzie wasn't here with me, I'd run after Chiara to make sure she's okay. I'd probably end up making her angry with me again, but I'd rather have her angry than upset.

"Is Chiara okay?" Lizzie asks after the show ended and Starling didn't return.

"Yeah, she'll be fine," I lie because I want to reassure my niece, but I have no idea how Chiara's actually feeling.

We're walking out of the room, her small hand in mine. I spot the woman I've been worried about for the past half an hour sitting with her backpack on at one of the benches outside, her phone between her fingertips and her eyes fixated on the ground. She's deep in thought, but so on edge too that when I step in front of her, she jumps ever so slightly. The little demon never fucking flinches. I barely bite back the curse threatening to leave my throat.

"Let's go," I say to her, and she stands up, forcing a small smile at Lizzie.

Noticing how off Chiara seems, Lizzie slips her hand into hers so we're all walking together like a little family.

"I'm going to need you to tell me how bad this situation with Tim is," I say as soon as Chiara and I are alone in my apartment.

Somehow, I convinced her to have dinner with me tonight under the pretense that I had a job offer for her. Well maybe not a pretense entirely considering I do have a job I would like to offer her, but it was mostly to get her to talk to me about Tim. She'd agreed with little to no complaint, and I know it's because she's lonely in her flat. It must be weird to be there without Graham now, especially because in the six years they lived together, he was never gone for longer than two days, and neither was she.

"Can I help you make dinner?" she asks instead of answering my question.

"Don't change the subject, Chiara. This is important. How bad is the situation with Tim?" I repeat while she throws Benz's ball. My pitbull sprints after it, returning it to Starling's lap a moment later. She barks at it to encourage her best friend to keep playing fetch with her.

"He's verbally harassing me. Recently he showed up at the bookstore where I work. Today at the gallery. He doesn't understand I'm not interested in him," she explains, and the temperature of my blood starts to heat in my veins.

"And you haven't said anything because you're scared he will kick your Mamma out of the apartment," I observe, causing Starling to freeze for a moment.

"Yes," is all she says before throwing the ball for Benz again. She slips back into her thoughts, I can tell by the way her teeth capture her bottom lip.

"It can't go on like this," I say. Chiara lets out a sigh before scratching Benz's chest.

"For a guy who grew up in a family that struggled with money, you're really not understanding this situation," she says, but it irritates me. I lean against the wall in the living room, crossing my arms in front of my chest. Her gaze briefly slips to my forearms, and I wish I could focus on the blush settling on her cheeks in response.

"I don't understand because you have an option. Let me help you," I beg, *fucking beg*, because I'm getting tired of this awful feeling deep in my gut. Worry, concern, guilt for letting her go through all of this by herself.

"You make it sound so easy." There is nothing but irritation in her tone. She stands up and straightens out her blouse.

"It is easy," I reply, and it makes her freeze. Then, she curls her hands into fists.

"Nothing about this situation is easy, asshole. I have to leave Mamma with that man every single day because she's stubborn and refuses to come live with me. It wouldn't be ideal, but it's a hell of a lot better than her living with Tim," she starts, stepping toward me. "You just cost me one of my jobs, so I have no way of eating anything apart from dry toast for every meal. I even reduced the amount of toilet paper I use by half because that stuff is fucking expensive! Do you think that's fun? Do you think it's fun to have a dream and watch it slide further away because I have no money to even shower as much as I should?"

She shoves me backward out of frustration, but I set my feet firmly into the ground so it's easier for her to let out her frustration.

"Tim is coming to the places I work now, and I'm scared he will show up at my flat any day. So don't tell me any of this is easy. There is no easy answer to any of my problems, Leonard, none!"

Chiara hits my chest over and over with tears streaming down her face. Tears. Chiara is crying. She keeps hitting me too, but I let her, bringing my arms around her until her movements slow and sobs replace them. One of my hands moves to the back of her head while the other slips onto her back, caressing her tight muscles while she cries into my chest.

For the first time in over two decades, Chiara is letting herself cry, and I'm going to be here for her because I'm all she's got.

And I will protect her, no matter the costs.

CHAPTER 14

Chiara

I t takes my brain a few moments until I realize what I'm doing. I'm crying. Leonard's comforting me as one of his hands caresses the back of my head and the other glides up and down my spine. This is not natural. I shouldn't be so comfortable in his arms, but I am. These past few months, everything's been going to shit. I haven't had a second to breathe, except for this very moment. It's been a long time since anyone's held me like this, which is probably why I don't push off him at first.

"Relax, sweetheart, I've got you," he says, and I realize how tense I was. His reassurance makes me melt into him, but I keep my hands covering my face instead of wrapping them around him.

"You're not allowed to make fun of me for this afterward," I say and poke his chest. His fingers slide under my hair until he's cupping my head more firmly and able to tilt it backward so his eyes can meet my tear-stained ones. His face is hardened, but I know he's trying to hide his concern.

"How about just a little?" he teases, and the pad of his thumb wipes away one of my tears.

"Two mean comments, take it or leave it," I offer, and Leonard gives me a tiny smile that dies as soon as more tears stream down my face.

"Move in with me," he blurts out, and the spell breaks. I push off him, letting out a laugh I don't mean in the slightest.

"Are you okay? One hug and you forget that we hate each other?" I ask, but he crosses his arms in front of his chest and pulls his lips into a thin line.

"Come hate me here, where you're safe and sound. I have security. No one, not even Tim, can get into my building. Yours isn't safe." I open my mouth to argue with him, but there is nothing to say. He's right. And he's offering to ease my mind of one of the fears that's been plaguing it since I saw Tim at the bookstore.

"Living together would never work." Except the couple of times I stayed here, we managed not to kill each other, a great accomplishment for us.

"Yeah, it would," he challenges, and I groan at him.

"No, it wouldn't."

"Yes, it would."

"No. It. Wouldn't."

"Yes. It. Would."

Good God, I'm going to lose it. He's so stubborn, and it doesn't work when I already am stubborn as fuck. It's one of the million reasons why we could never live together. We would never agree on anything. We would butt heads every single time we speak. We would make each other miserable.

"Listen, little demon, I don't like spending time with you. I don't seek it out voluntarily, but that doesn't mean I want you to live alone when there is a guy potentially stalking you. Come live with me, fight with me all day long if you must, just move in with me," he says, his full lips relaxing instead of stretching into a frown for once. The urge to trail my fingers over them briefly distracts me, but I refocus quickly.

"Why would you offer this?" I ask, a little too tempted to take him up on it.

"Because I owe you." *Because I cost you a job you really needed.* "Speaking of which, I found a job that'll pay you money and it comes with opportunities to find sponsors for your art gallery." Now that makes me burst into laughter.

"And from what fantasyland did you get it?" I ask, and he takes a step toward me. I don't back away. I stand my ground and look up at him, wishing for the millionth time in my life I wasn't so short.

"Go shower, I will make something to eat. This is going to be a long conversation and I need you to have a full stomach so you're too tired to argue," he says with a small chuckle, and I slap his arm, ignoring the way the sound of his amusement goes straight into my bones.

"You're an asshole," I reply, and he spins me around to lead me to the bathroom.

"Take as long of a shower as you want. You need it," he says, and I turn around to pinch his side. He catches my wrist and lifts it over my head until my back hits the wall behind us.

"What are you doing?" I ask as his body presses against mine, his breathing heavy as it hits my cheek. Mine mimics his.

"Keeping my sides safe from your vicious pinching," he says, dragging my other wrist over my head too. Why do I let him? That's a very good question I have absolutely no answer to.

"You know I'm a trained fighter, right?" I remind him, but my body has turned into putty under his touch.

My clit's swollen and aching because his body is flush against mine and nothing's ever felt better. His lips are so close to my mouth, his eyes half-closed, I almost forget how much of a dick he is to me most of the time.

"Then pin me to the ground. If you can," he adds the last sentence with a challenging tone.

It takes me one well-placed foot to take out one of his before he loses balance and I take advantage of it, bringing him to the floor. I'm on top of him within seconds, his breathing hitching as we hit the ground.

"Bloody hell. I forget how skilled you are," he says, and I smile down at him, patting his chest once. I settle down completely on top of him, feeling his cock against my ass in response. Fuck me. Oh God. "Chiara," he breathes out with a strained voice, but I'm frozen in place. He's so hard against me, it makes my breathing hitch. "God," he groans as I move a little, sending a wave of pleasure through my core. I barely hold back my moan as I hurry off him and toward the shower.

He's gorgeous, of course he is, but this is not happening. I won't let it. I just need to take the edge off, maybe masturbate when I get home tonight. Anything to get rid of how good being on top of him felt.

To ignore the way I felt so safe in his arms when he held me.

We're staring at each other from across the table. He finished eating five minutes ago and has been watching me ever since. I place my last spoonful in my mouth two minutes after that, glaring at him like I always do. His face is as serious as it's been since the day I met him. He's taunting me with his silence when we both know he wants to discuss this wonderful job opportunity he mentioned earlier. I also expected things to be at least a little awkward after I had his huge, thick cock against my ass earlier, but we're both ignoring how good it felt. We're both too fucking stubborn and reserved toward each other to address anything.

"Talk," I demand, but he merely crosses his arms in front of his chest with amusement sparkling in his eyes.

"Nah, I'm good," he replies, his eyes still on me. I'd very much like to punch him.

"You love the sound of your own voice. Don't be shy. Say whatever it is you came up with," I encourage, my skin on fire from the way he looks at me. God, I hate him for making my body react like this.

"I hate leaving Benz here when I go on my race weekends," he starts, and I raise both eyebrows.

"Understandable, but I thought we were going to talk about me, not you," I say, causing a sigh to leave him as he shakes of his head. It also causes him to finally break eye contact and give my skin the chance to breathe.

"You are so very impatient," he complains, and I bite back a smile.

"Actually, I'm a very patient person. I've been waiting twenty years for you to say something nice to me or something intelligent, and neither has happened yet," I say, earning me the slightest of smiles from him.

"You want to hear something nice? Alright, I think you are a strong, determined woman, who deserves a shot at living her dream. I have organized investor meetings, gotten us invitations to art exhibits where we can get you connections to influential people, and I would like to offer you a job taking care of Benz while I travel the world for races. I will pay you double what you earned in all four of your jobs combined. I will pay for your tickets and hotel rooms so I can take Benz with me and don't have to miss her as much as I always do. When we're not traveling, I would like it if you lived with me, at least for the next six months until Graham returns. Is that nice enough for you?" he asks, but I'm absolutely and completely dumbfounded.

"What?" is all I manage to croak out. I reach for my glass of water, trying to lubricate my vocal cords because they're malfunctioning.

"What part of that speech was too complicated for you?" he asks, his voice teasing.

"All of it, asshole. Why would you want to spend every single second of every day with me?"

Because that is what his proposition would entail. Leonard and I spending all of our time together. Yes, he will be busy during the race weekends when I'd take care of Benz, but we'd still see each other afterward to go to the events he mentioned. We would live together. Be on top of each other for the next six months. He can't be serious. There is no way he'd voluntarily agree to any of this. We'd make each other miserable beyond belief. I don't buy it. There has to be another agenda here.

Except...

"When no one gave me a chance, when everything was against me, you were the one poking the man who became my biggest investor in the leg. You stood there, ten years old and determined as hell, and asked him how he could be stupid enough not to give me a chance. You made Ben smile so hard that day, he gave me the chance of a lifetime. I wouldn't have gotten anywhere if you hadn't been such a rude child, and I've owed a big part of my success to you since then. I'd merely like to repay the favor now," he says while nostalgia fills my chest.

I did do that, didn't I?

Ben, a tall white man with pitch-black hair and stunning blue eyes, had been at one of Leonard's karting races. He was a talent scout, at least that's what Andrew had told me, so I turned to him and started telling him how great of a racer Leonard was. I tried to convince him to give the boy I despised more than anything else a chance, and he did. It's the only nice thing I've ever done for Leonard, but it was perhaps one of the best I could have ever chosen to do.

"So, you want me to travel the world with you while you pay me to take care of Benz?" I ask, and Leonard gives me one, tight nod. "Because you owe me?"

"Among other things, yes." He's so fucking vague at times, I would love nothing more than to slap him.

"And you're going to help me find people who'd like to sponsor my idea to open a better immersive art gallery where I would create the shows?" I ask, trying to clarify this situation.

"Yes, Starling."

"*And* you want me to move in with you?" He clicks his tongue once, then stands up and collects our plates.

"Yes." It's the only answer he gives me before walking into the kitchen. I grab the rest from the table before following him.

"But you don't like me," I blurt out, and he gives me a single shrug of his shoulders.

"I don't have to like you. I have to tolerate you, which I do, on good days," Leonard says, and I let out an unamused snort.

"Then you already like me better than I do you," I say, and he shakes his head, but, even with his back toward me, I can tell there is a little smile on his face.

"Yes or no, little demon?" I place the pan with the delicious vegan meal he made next to the sink. I could get used to this, him cooking for me.

"Can I think about it, Champ?" His back tenses at my nickname for him, but if he gets to keep using the one I hate, then I get to do the same with him.

"As long as you need, but, please, give us both peace of mind and stay here tonight. I cannot stand the thought of you going home alone when Tim might be pissed at finding out you have a 'boyfriend'." The thought sends a wave of fear down my spine, forcing it to tense up in response.

"Thank you for doing that, by the way," I reply, but Leonard merely shakes his head.

"It was nothing, don't worry about it."

We don't speak much after that. Leonard puts on a movie, and I sit on the opposite end of the couch. Benz is between us, her head resting on my feet and her butt on Leonard's. He keeps petting her thigh, I do the same to her head. We're acting like this is the most normal thing in the goddamn world, and when I fall asleep halfway through the movie, I'm not even surprised that at the end, he carries me to bed and pulls the blanket all the way up to my chin. I'm awake enough to realize what's happening but too asleep to keep his name from slipping past my lips.

CHAPTER 15

Leonard

It's been a week since I made Chiara the offer to come live and travel the world with me. When we were talking, I finally understood why I'm doing all of this for her. I want to pay her back for what she did for me when we were kids. Asking her to live with me isn't part of that. No. It is, however, necessary. Her flat is in a dangerous area, and it doesn't sit right with me that there is no security whatsoever. Yes, the little demon can protect herself, but she shouldn't have to. No one should have to live in fear and unprotected.

I shake my head, focusing on my run. Today is the first day in May when it truly feels like spring. It's getting warmer, so much so that sweat is dripping down my temple. I'm making my way along the Thames with Quinn, who decided to come on a run with me today. She's my performance coach after all, so this isn't anything out of the ordinary. It does, however, allow me to vent a little about the situation with Chiara and that creep Tim. By the time we end our run, I've decided to tell her about the offer I made Starling to work for me and travel the world too. It's safe to say Quinn wasn't expecting that in the least.

"Don't you think it's a bit unprofessional to hire the woman you have feelings for?" she asks, and I flinch in response to her ridiculous words.

"Feelings for? You know I don't like her," I explain, but my best friend shakes her head and wipes her hair off her sweaty forehead. Then she takes a sip of her water and smiles at me like she knows more than I give her credit for.

"You sure are going through a lot of trouble for someone you don't like," she points out, but I'm well aware of how ridiculous all of this sounds.

I don't like Chiara, but I'm willing to do anything to protect her.

I can't stand being near her, but I asked her to move in with me, to be by my side for the rest of the season.

I can't stop thinking about her every second of the day.

"Chiara is family," is all I reply, but Quinn shakes her head at me with a grin.

"Why do you do that? Why do you close yourself off from having any feelings for someone? You've done it in the past, and successfully so too. Why do you keep doing it? Don't you think you deserve to have your shot at love?" I don't know how she got there from me talking about Chiara, but her question hits me like a bullet to the chest.

"I don't know," I admit honestly.

I've been around beautiful women my whole life. Being a Formula One driver allows you to meet people all over the world, but I've never felt a connection with anyone, at least not one that made me want to put energy into a relationship. I have enough on my plate as is. I don't have time to worry about someone else with my training and work taking up so much of my time. I haven't met anyone who just fits into my life perfectly, who could come and be near me as much as they wanted to be. Except for one person.

Fucking hell.

No, it can't be.

I don't even like her!

"Let's go. I'm buying you a coffee," I say and lead Quinn toward a café.

We spend the next hour talking about the upcoming race weekend in Monza. As much as I try to stay in the conversation, my head keeps drifting to Chiara. I know she's working at the bookstore today, the same place Tim showed up in the past already. I think about sending her a text to see if she's doing okay when my phone lights up from an incoming call. A call from Starling.

"What's wrong?" I ask as soon as I pick up. Silence fills the call for one... two... three seconds too long. "Chiara," I say firmly but gently.

"Someone broke into my flat," she says, her voice steady, calm even. Mine, on the other hand, is shaky and angry as I reply.

"I'll be there soon. Do not fucking go inside your apartment," I say and hang up.

Quinn gives me a confused look, but I squeeze her shoulder once, apologise, and then run toward my flat. Luckily, I took my car keys when I went out earlier so I make my way directly into the parking garage. My heart is racing, and I have to remind myself everything will be fine. Chiara is alright. She called me, and I'm on my way to her now. This is fine, not at all what I was worried about. Fucking hell, this is exactly why I wanted her to move in with me. She would be safe here. There are security guards stationed everywhere because of the amount of celebrities that live in this building. I pay a shit ton of money for this level of protection, too, especially after one fan followed me to my old apartment almost eight years ago.

"You better not be doing anything stupid, Starling," I mumble to myself as I drive onto the highway. *Why does her flat have to be so fucking far away from mine?*

By the time I get to her place, I'm still sweating, but for a completely different reason. I rush up the stairs to find her door open, probably because it doesn't close anymore, and Chiara rummaging around inside. I'm going to strangle her.

"Why the fuck would you step foot inside this apartment without me here?" I ask as I rip her door fully open. She goes on high alert for a moment until she realises it's me. Then, her shoulders sink in relief.

"Because I'm stronger, smarter, and faster than you when it comes to fighting," she reminds me, but I'm not satisfied with that answer. I step toward her, my hands grabbing her shoulders.

"You can't do shit like this, Chiara. If someone had been in here, you could have gotten hurt," I say, but in one swift movement, she removes my hands from her, twists one of my arms behind my back, and then shoves me against the wall. Jesus fucking Christ.

"I can protect myself," she grinds out, releasing me. I spin toward her, angry now because she's being so bloody stubborn.

"If it was ten guys, you couldn't have fucking protected yourself. Please tell me you're not stupid enough to believe you could have," I bark back, and she crosses her arms in front of her chest. Such a goddamn stubborn woman and yet, she's devastatingly beautiful when she's pissed at me.

"Of course not. I'm not a superhero from television, but this was fine. I grabbed a knife from the kitchen and went through the flat to make sure no one was here. When I was sure there wasn't, I started packing," she says and attempts to walk away, but her words confuse me so much, I grab her arm.

"Packing for what?" I ask, my heart racing now. Her green eyes stare into mine before she rolls them.

"To live with you, obviously." I let go of her and step back in surprise, a strange sort of excitement filling my chest. "Give me two minutes. Luckily, I already brought your mum all of Graham's things so none of his stuff was taken or will be. They destroyed the lock when they broke in, so I have to get all of my things," she says, her hands trembling a little as she adjusts her hair.

"What did they take?" I can't prove it was Tim, but I know it was.

"My laptop, television, and polaroid camera. Some of my jewelry too, but that was all worthless anyway. I was wearing the gold necklace my Nonna gave me, just like the ring from my Nonno," she says, pointing to both of them on her. "I know what you're thinking, but I don't think it was Tim. Mamma called me earlier and said they were having dinner tonight. Plus, he wouldn't have taken my things,"

Chiara adds, and I try to stop my hands from forming fists. I'd very much like to punch a fucking wall.

"How are you feeling?" I ask when she's been staring at my chest with her head lost in thought for a minute too long.

"Like my flat was broken into, forcing me to move in with someone who doesn't like me," she replies and walks away. I follow behind her, but sensing she doesn't want to continue this conversation, I merely help her pack.

An hour later, my trunk is not even half full, sending a wave of anger through me. Chiara has nothing. I have everything I could ever need, but she doesn't even have a suitcase full of clothes without goddamn holes. She doesn't have money for that, and after what she told me last time, I cannot keep myself from letting my heart flutter at the thought that I can take care of her now. Just because I owe her though, not because of anything else.

Benz is beyond happy when Starling walks through the front door with me. We carry her things into the guest room where she drops onto the bed with her bag, my dog jumping on it as well. I place her suitcase next to the closet in the corner. Chiara doesn't speak but neither do I, not until Benz barks, and I realise it's time to take her for a walk.

"Come, let's go for a stroll," I say and step out of the room. It takes her several minutes until she's by my side.

I place the leash on Benz, who is wagging happily. Chiara looks lost in her thoughts, but I don't force her to talk to me about her feelings. The evening sun isn't nearly as warm as it should be around this time of year, and I notice the stubborn woman next to me shiver as a breeze wraps around us. I don't think about what I do next. It just happens, and it frightens me. I unzip my sweater, slide it off my shoulders, and put it around hers because she sure as fuck wouldn't take it from me if I gave her a choice.

"Thanks," she whispers and slides her arms through the sleeves, pulling on the zipper until it's all the way up.

"Can I ask you something?" I say after a few minutes have passed in silence.

"If you must," she replies with the smallest hint of a smile playing on her face.

"Why did you stop fighting in competitions?" I remember when she was fourteen, she stopped partaking in them, but I never asked why.

"I started fighting because I was furious with the world for taking my father from me before I was even born. I stopped because I wasn't angry anymore. Plus, fighting was never what I wanted to do. Art is my calling," she says while I nod along to her words.

"You were unstoppable, Chiara, and you still are, even if it's in a different field. Your strength is something to admire," I blurt out because I don't seem to be able to control myself around this woman.

"Do you admire it?" She brings her green eyes to my face, a challenge in them. She knows when I lie, I can't hide that from her, but I sure as hell can't be honest either. So, I decide to go in a completely different direction. Changing the topic.

"What do you feel like having for dinner?" Chiara shakes her head and sighs.

"Answers to the million questions I have would be nice," she says and makes Benz sit before giving her a treat.

"Fire away, Starling," I offer, and her eyes go wide in response.

"Really?" I don't hesitate.

"Really."

She looks off into the distance with a thoughtful look. Then, Chiara turns back to me with her lips pulled into a thin line.

"How much rent do I pay per month?" she asks first, and I almost growl. She cannot be serious.

115

"None. Next," I reply, and she opens her mouth to argue, but it falls shut when she realises she doesn't have enough money to pay for half of my rent. It's one of the more luxurious apartments in London.

"Okay, how will working for you go?"

"You take care of Benz, I pay you," I say, giving her one of the most smart-ass answers I've ever given anyone. When she frowns, I almost laugh. She's in no mood to take my bullshit, but her frustration is adorable—no, not adorable. It's amusing. Yeah, amusing, that's better.

"How do we split the chores?" she asks instead of giving my asshole response any attention.

"However you want. Just keep your room clean and don't leave your shit every-where." I don't have to tell Chiara any of this. Out of Graham and her, she is the one who has been keeping everything neat and tidy in their apartment.

"Would it kill you to answer a question without being a complete ass?" she asks, and I finally smirk as I answer.

"Yes."

We keep walking for a while, talking about everything related to the apartment and the job I'm assuming she's taken now. Once we make our way back to the apartment, she takes off my sweater and hands it back to me. I spot a small hole on the shoulder of her shirt and hold back the curse bubbling up in my throat.

"Here," I say and hold out my credit card for her. She stares at it with a grimace on her features. "Your clothes are garbage. I'm not taking you to the next race weekend with these clothes. You're going to be associated with me, so you need better ones."

I won't have her walking beside me with Benz in ten-year-old clothes. I ignore my subconscious as it reminds me of my earlier thoughts about her lack of clothes and wanting to get her new ones. That's not what this is about. This is solely about my reputation. Appearances are important in Formula One.

"My clothes are not garbage, *stronzo*," she says, her accent so strong it knocks the breath from my chest for a second.

"Yes, they are. Now, take my card and tomorrow I expect you to get some new ones. This is important," I reply, but she shakes her head. Stubborn, stubborn, stubborn.

"I don't like shopping and I'm not spending more of your money." Chiara really loves to make my life hell.

"Take this," I say, closing the distance between us and placing the credit card against her sternum. "And spend a reasonable amount of money on clothes," I add before letting the plastic drop down her shirt. It's only fitting considering the last time I handed her money, she put it down her shirt too.

"I hate you," she says, and I lean my face closer to hers, my lips almost brushing over hers.

"Good. The code is 7243."

I get started on dinner, feeling smug but also really happy she's here.

That she's finally safe.

CHAPTER 16
Chiara

"You're really going to get all of that?" Lulu asks, and I cock an eyebrow.

"Yes. He shoved his credit card down my shirt for a reason, and I'm going to spend lots of his money. He was such a dick, he deserves to have his bank account take a little hit," I tell my friend, who grins proudly at me.

After placing everything at the cashier, we wait a while until the person has finished removing all the security tags and scanned the items. I bought myself everything I could possibly need for wherever it is we're going for his races. I got myself thirty new shirts, five new jeans, jackets to actually keep me warm, sweaters, dresses, and even a few skirts. When I hear the total, I almost swallow my own tongue because that's a lot of money. I would never, ever spend that much on myself, even for the amount of clothes I'm getting. I chose one of the cheapest stores in London and they even have a sale going on, but this is a lot. I shouldn't do this. It isn't reasonable, and Leonard made it clear I'm supposed to spend a *reasonable* amount only. He's going to be so pissed...

Do it.

I type in his code without giving it another thought. Just the idea of Leonard losing his shit over me spending too much of his money threatens to make me smile. So, Lulu and I grab all of my ten shopping bags—one for Lulu because I got her a blouse from Leonard's money too—and make our way back to the apartment. We hang out for the next six hours. Leonard's training, which is why Lulu and I take

Benz for a walk. We grab a coffee and by the time we're back, Leonard is standing shirtless in the kitchen.

"Lulu, Starling," is all he says as he takes a sip of his water and uses the towel around his neck to wipe away a bead of sweat going down the side of his face.

"God, he's so hot," Lulu whispers as she looks him up and down, and I hate myself for nodding along to her words because, *fuck me*, he is.

His hard upper body, covered in tattoos that I like a lot, is defined and chiseled. The ripples on his stomach stand out more today than any other time I've seen him without a shirt, and it makes my mouth drool, just a little.

"Having fun?" he asks me, snapping me back to reality. I narrow my eyes into slits and glare at him.

"I was just thinking that you should take a shower. You're getting sweat all over the counter," I say, and he rolls his eyes at me.

"You're living here for free, little demon, I'd watch my tone," he replies, forcing anger to course through my veins. Fuck no, he didn't just go there.

"I knew you'd bring that up the first chance you'd get. I didn't even want to move in here, but you insisted," I bark back, but he turns around to refill his water, ignoring me for a moment. I let out a groan, and Lulu nudges me in the side, reminding me to chill considering how much of his money I spent today.

"Okay, I'm going to go. You've got this under control," she whispers and presses a kiss to my cheek. I'm too pissed at Leonard to return the affection. Once the door falls shut, he turns back to me and tilts his head at my angry expression.

"I'm teasing you, Chiara. Please, relax. Tell me what you got," he says, and I almost stumble backward. *Stand your ground. Don't let him see how guilty you feel about spending his money.*

"The bags are at the entrance," I say, and he walks there to carry them into the dining room where he empties them on the table. Irritation flickers across his face, making an uncomfortable feeling settle in my stomach.

"This is all you got?" he asks, looking for the receipt, I assume.

"Yes, you told me to," I remind him, but he's going through my clothes, still searching for that piece of paper.

"How much did you spend?" Fuck.

"Nine hundred pounds," I say while crossing my arms in front of my chest. "I know it's a lot of money, but you should have specified reasonable." I sound confident, which is the opposite of how I feel right now. What happens next knocks the air from my lungs. Leonard chuckles. Leonard fucking Tick is *chuckling*.

"Nine hundred pounds is a lot?" I nod. He does it again, lets out that same low, sexy sound of amusement. It turns me on far more than I would like to admit. "Nine hundred pounds is a lot," he repeats, shaking his head and leaning against the table before crossing his arms, mimicking my stance. My head is getting dizzy from the fact that he's still very much shirtless. "I'm a millionaire, sweetheart. You could have spent nine thousand, and I would have been upset with you for not buying enough." I roll my eyes.

"Well, good for you. For me, that's a shit ton, but I'm glad I don't have to feel guilty," I reply and let my arms drop to my sides. Leonard watches me closely, the usual scowl returning to his features.

"I asked you to go shopping, to buy yourselves clothes for our trips. This is unacceptable. This isn't enough and too plain. These clothes are good for at home, not for race tracks and events." I'm about to say something when he adds, "Grab your bag, we're going shopping." And then he disappears into his room without giving me a chance to respond.

God, this man is aggravating beyond belief.

While Leonard is in the shower, I collect all of my new clothes and bring them to my bedroom. Benz is on my heels as I do so, but we both stop abruptly when I reach my room. There is a brand new laptop, television, and polaroid camera on the bed. I do my best to keep standing, but the sight of these things, things that were stolen from me only yesterday, weakens my knees. Leonard bought them for me.

There is even a bag from Pandora. I pull out several boxes, swallowing hard. He got me jewelry too. Leonard got me everything that was stolen from me, except fancier. I didn't have money for a MacBook. My polaroid was a knock-off, not from the real brand, and my television was older than me. My jewelry sure as hell didn't come from a fancy place like Pandora.

"Oh, wow," I blurt out after opening the first box and finding a stack of rings in them, some plain, some in the shape of the moon and stars. One of them even has a small diamond on top and another is in the shape of a knot.

I open more of the boxes, finding earrings and necklaces and bracelets. Leonard is a millionaire, yes, but he has always been careful about the way he spends his money. The fact that he would buy me all of this warms my insides. My mind still lingers on the jewelry as I open the polaroid camera and walk over to my suitcase where I keep the small album of pictures I took with my old camera. I like how old-fashioned this is, and the fact that I instantly get the photos to keep forever.

"Are you ready?" Looking at him now, even if he makes me angry most of the time, feels different. I feel my features soften ever so slightly at him, in a way I never thought they would.

"I'm not going shopping again. Look at all the money we've spent today. Your account limit must have been reached," I say, and he snorts at my comment.

"My account limit is five hundred thousand pounds. Now, would you like to walk to the car or do you need me to throw you over my shoulder?" Assuming he's kidding, I let out an unamused laugh, but when he approaches me, makes me stand up, and then throws me over his shoulder, I let out a surprised gasp.

"Okay, okay, I will walk. Jesus, just put me down," I say because the way his hands are gripping the backs of my thighs forces heat between my legs, and I refuse to get turned on by how strong he is.

"Fine," he says and drops me back onto my feet.

"You take whatever you want, whenever you want it, don't you?" I ask, and he grabs my chin so softly for a moment, bringing my attention to his face and nowhere else.

"Not everything. Not what I know will be bad for me in the long run," he replies, his voice low and seductive as his eyes trail over my face. "Not what drives me absolutely crazy most days, even though every part of me demands a taste," he says, releasing my chin. I let out the breath I've been holding without realizing when he walks away.

Did he just— No, it can't be. I almost laugh at the thought of Leonard wanting me.

"Today, Chiara," he says, holding the door open for me. I snap out of my trance and roll my eyes. There he is. Normalcy has been restored.

"Here," I say and smack his credit card against his chest. "I'm very tempted to go out and buy a Bugatti right now, so you better hold on to it," I add, and he smirks down at me.

"Good idea." I'm about to step through the door when I stop, let go of my pride a little, and look up at him.

"Thank you. For everything you put on my bed and the clothes I already bought." His face softens a little, letting me see the side of him I like a lot.

"You're welcome," he replies and gently nudges me out of the doorframe so he can close the door. "But don't start falling in love with me, Starling. I don't have time to break your heart," he says, and, this time, I actually laugh.

"The day I fall in love with you, a meteorite will strike the Earth," I say with another small laugh. He nudges me with his shoulder as we step toward the elevator, amusement sparkling in his eyes too.

Leonard brought me to Bond Street. I almost can't breathe when we walk past all the prestigious and luxurious stores this street has to offer. I tried turning on my heels and walking away when I realized where we were going, but Leonard brought his hands onto my shoulders and spun me back around.

"I need you to look like you have some money when we meet investors," he said to me to keep me from fighting him.

"Why?" I asked. Leonard gave me a look I interpreted as 'are you seriously asking me that right now', which made me slap his arm.

"Starling, rich people are all about appearance. You cannot go to an event in the clothes you bought today. They will eat you alive," he said, and I stopped talking afterward.

Now we're strolling in silence. I don't even complain when he takes my hand and leads me into one of the stores, his hand disappearing right after we walk through the door.

"Let me find Lilah. She will help you," he says before leaving me standing at the entrance. This store is huge. There are sections for clothes, purses, and shoes on different sides. I don't have long to study the space before Leonard grabs my attention by brushing his fingers over my arm.

"Yes, sorry," I say and turn to them. Lilah, a tall Black woman with her hair tied into tight braids and eyes full of warmth, smiles at me.

"Chiara, it is a pleasure to meet you," she says with a heavy French accent and then gives me two kisses, one on each cheek. "Come with me, *ma poupée*." The sweet woman links her arm through mine and then leads me through the store.

It takes hours to find ten different outfits, dresses and suits I would have never thought I'd ever wear. They're all classy and flawless, just like the shoes and purses Lilah shows me. Leonard waits in one of the chairs outside of the changing rooms. He's on his phone every single time I step out with a new outfit on, ignoring me completely. I'm not surprised, but, if I'm being honest, I would like it if he drooled a little bit over me considering these clothes highlight all of my curves.

"Okay, how about some lingerie?" Lilah asks after the last dress was a definite no. Leonard's head shoots up in response, a warning in his gaze.

"Sure," I blurt out, and Lilah grins before walking away.

"What the fuck do I have to buy you lingerie for?" he asks, and his reaction makes me so happy, I have to hide my smile.

"Maybe I will meet someone at one of those events and take him back to the hotel room with me." He's up on his feet and in my face before I know what has hit me.

"I'm not buying you lingerie another guy is going to take off you," he says, trapping me between the changing room door and his body. Everything inside of me catches fire in response.

"Why? Do *you* want to take it off me instead?" I ask, watching his jaw flex in response. His Adam's apple bobs as he swallows hard.

"Don't tempt me." Oh... *Oh!*

"Leonard—" I'm interrupted before I can finish my sentence.

"I'm sorry to interrupt, but I've brought you a few options," Lilah says, and the gorgeous man in front of me takes a step back.

"I'll buy them, but not for anyone else to see," is the only thing he says before leaving the changing room area altogether. I watch a knowing smirk cross Lilah's face but choose to ignore it and focus on the underwear she's brought.

"This one is very popular with our customer's partners," she says and holds up a blue one-piece, which does nothing to hide anything. I take it from her and disappear into the changing room.

CHAPTER 17
Leonard

Don't think about Chiara trying on lingerie right now. Don't do it. Don't think about how her body looks in the outfits you saw Lilah bring.

But I'm thinking about it. God, I'm picturing it so clearly in my head, my cock twitches as all the blood in my body rushes to it. Nope. It's not happening. She's a pain in the arse. She is one infuriating woman, and I am not attracted to her. I can't be. But I am. I'm so fucking attracted to her, I have to hide my goddamn hard-on by leaning against the cash register while I wait for Chiara to finish up in the dressing room.

"Chiara is—" Lilah starts and lets out a small chuckle. "She's a force to be reckoned with. Beautiful, strong, stubborn, all things that must be driving you wild," she goes on, and I give her a slight tilt of my head and a frown.

"She's my brother's best friend and temporary roommate. Nothing more. I don't even like her." I don't know why I keep reminding myself of that.

"Yes, sure, darling. Could you step back for a moment? I'd like to check something," Lilah says, and if she wasn't my friend of ten years with whom I have a lot of history, I'd tell her where to shove it.

"Any body reactions of mine are because you ended our arrangement. It's been a while," I say, and Lilah lets out a laugh.

"I ended our agreement because I found someone who loves me. Being friends with benefits doesn't last forever. Joane stepped into my life, and I knew she was it for me. Sex with you was great, but it's nothing compared to being with the love of my life," she says.

It sends me spiraling into deep thought. In my twenty-eight years, I've never fallen in love with anyone. I've never wanted to give my heart to another person. I've never desired to feel vulnerable, but it almost makes me sad that I haven't. Lilah and I were fucking for years, neither of us ready to commit to someone, but then, out of nowhere, she told me she met Joane, who had changed her life forever. They're married now, and I couldn't be happier for them. At the same time, I'm also jealous. Not because I have feelings for Lilah. We're great friends and I never felt anything more, but I'm jealous she has someone to call 'my wife'. I want a wife, someone to come home to after every race. I just don't want to set myself up for vulnerability. It's not something I have time for.

"You should try falling in love. It's great," Lilah adds right as my eyes shift to Chiara walking toward us with a bunch of little outfits my mind couldn't help but picture her in earlier.

Right now, on the other hand, I can't stop staring at her face. Her green eyes seem brighter somehow, her long brown hair dishevelled but gorgeous anyway. Her short, curvy body moving toward us with a sway in her step that's making me feel all sorts of things I'm going to go ahead and suppress.

"What?" she asks when she's next to me, placing the lingerie on the counter.

"Nothing," I reply, keeping my eyes on her so I don't look suspicious. I almost laugh at the irony that keeping my gaze on her makes me seem more normal to her than looking away awkwardly.

Chiara swallows hard when Lilah tells her the sum of the outfits, but I don't even blink as I give my friend my credit card and continue staring at Starling. Eventually, she turns her body to me, a serious look on her features, which makes her pouty lips even more so. I can't lie. I would love to know how it feels to kiss her. It would scratch an itch in the back of my mind, the one I haven't been able to reach for many years now.

"You know, about what you said earlier in front of the changing room?" I give her a tight nod, and she crooks her finger at me. I obey without thinking, bringing my ear next to her mouth. "You can't control who I wear those for, Champ," she says and steps away. The urge to smile and throw her back over my shoulder both threaten to take over, but I push them down to focus on entering my pin.

Lilah was right. Chiara is driving me wild. And I don't know how to stop her from getting under my skin. I may have just made the biggest mistake in my life by asking her to move in with me, hell, to travel the world with me to *take care of Benz*. I could have asked a thousand different people. But no. I asked the one woman I can't spend an afternoon with without ending up in some sort of conflict. All because I've become so overprotective of her, I can hardly breathe when she's at one of her current jobs.

"Where to now, Champ?" Chiara asks as we walk through the front door. "Oohh, is it time for my hair transformation now? That's usually what comes next in the movies," she says and wiggles her eyebrows. I stare down at her.

"Would you like to get a haircut?" I'm really hoping she'll say no because I like her hair this length.

"I'm in desperate need of one. I haven't had the money to get my hair done in years," she says, so I lead her down the street and toward my hair stylist.

"Can I ask you something?" I blurt out after we've been walking for a few minutes in comfortable silence.

"If you must." I stare down at her in response.

"Stop giving me that bullshit answer when I want to ask a question," I complain, but she crosses her arms in front of her chest. That's the exact moment I realise I'm carrying all of her bags. It makes me ask something completely different than I intended to at first. "Why the hell am I carrying all of your shit?" That infuriating woman starts chuckling.

"It only seems fair, considering you paid for all of it."

"You can be a real smart-ass, do you know that?" I ask, earning me a full-faced proud grin from her. God, I wish it didn't knock the air from my chest and send a wave of excitement through me. "Have you spoken to your Mamma recently? Is she doing alright?" The questions leave me before I can stop them. Chiara's shoulders tense for a moment, but when she sucks in a sharp breath and releases it again, she seems calmer.

"She's okay. There is something she wants to discuss with me, but I don't want to go to her flat," she explains, sending a wave of horror through me at the thought of Starling being anywhere near Tim. It's unsettling enough that her Mamma has to be near that man every single day.

"Invite her to ours. I will cook." Again, I don't think the words before they spill from my lips. *Ours*. Fuck me.

"Okay, thanks," Chiara replies as we stop in front of my hair stylist's little shop.

"Alright, take my card. Get the haircut you want, and I will be back in an hour to pick you up. Ask for Helen and say I sent you. She will clear her schedule, I assure you," I say, and Chiara crosses her arms in front of her chest with amusement on her lips.

"Someone's full of himself," she replies, and I cock an eyebrow.

"When you're as well-known and charming as me, you get to be full of yourself," I say, hand her my card, and make my way back to my car. I have some calls I need to make and don't have the patience to carry around seven bags until Chiara is finished at her appointment.

Graham sounded great when I spoke to him on the phone five minutes ago. We've made it a habit to speak at least every other day. Ever since he arrived in New York where his friend lives, he's sounded like a new person. Happier. Healthier. Hungover too. Two days ago, he called me with a massive headache. I almost laughed at how much he had to turn down the volume on his phone but then couldn't hear a bloody word I was saying. It was one of the most entertaining conversations I've ever had.

At the same time, all I could think about was not telling him Starling moved in with me yesterday. She hasn't shared anything with him yet, and I don't think it's my place to get between them, even if Graham is my brother. He's closer with Chiara than he is with me, so telling him she packed her things and will be my roommate for the next six months isn't my story to share. Nor is the fact that the little demon will be working for me this season, even if I feel guilty.

After calling my brother, I spend some time on the phone with Quinn. She and I discuss everything about the upcoming race weekend in France. We also talk about logistics concerning Chiara and Benz, and she lets me know where both of them can stay during the free practices, Qualifying, and the actual race. Knowing Quinn is helping me make all of this happen settles my worries a little.

Once I've called everyone I had to, I make my way back to Helen's. It's been an hour since I first dropped Chiara there, and I'm dying to see what she's done to her hair. A shudder runs down my spine because *I'm dying to know what she's done to her hair.* Jesus Christ, I'm so fucking screwed, I don't even know when I'm lying to myself anymore. I don't know when I'm in complete denial.

I have no clue how I really feel about Chiara, do I?

Starling is already standing outside when I get back, squatting next to a bench where something is sitting. The closer I get, the clearer it becomes. She's looking at a little starling bird, smiling like one of those little shits didn't fly on her head and scare the hell out of her when we were younger. But she's smiling. Chiara is giving the world one of her very rare smiles, and I can't help but soak it up for a moment, especially because her new hair is only shoulder-length and absolutely stunning. God. I might have to sit down.

"Leonard?" she asks and walks toward me. I look at my legs and realise I've actually collapsed onto one of the benches. Shit. "Are you alright?"

"Yeah, bloody perfect, actually," I lie, staring at her face, which is fully on display for me now. Her long hair was hiding it more from the world, but this? This cut is highlighting her soft features, her pouty lips, her sharp nose, and green eyes.

"Are you sure? You don't look well," she says and plants the back of her hand on my forehead, checking my temperature. I take her hand to remove it from my face because it's only making my head fuzzier.

"I'm fine. Let's go," I say, my tone harsh and cold.

"Okay," is all she replies, her fingers twirling a strand of her hair between her fingers.

She just made a big change to her hairstyle, and I haven't said anything nice about it. I'm a fucking idiot. I stop abruptly, holding her back too, and then grab her shoulders before opening my mouth to say something I would have never said to her half a year ago.

"You look beautiful." Her eyes go wide in response to my words, and then Chiara blushes. Her cheeks turn a deep red, and my breathing hitches in response.

"Thank you," she says and digs around in her pocket for a moment. She takes out my card and slides it into the pocket of my pants, causing me to hiss out a breath

131

as my body goes into full arousal mode. "For everything," she adds before walking away.

This woman is pure danger.

Chapter 18
Chiara

Leonard said I looked beautiful. It happened three days ago, but I haven't been able to get it out of my head. Today is my last day at the bookstore, which should be the only thing roaming around in my mind. But of course not because I can't stop thinking about the man who doesn't like me saying that I looked beautiful.

"Are you alright, *bella*? Your cheeks are a bright red," Susie says, and I lift my hands to feel the heat radiating off them.

"No, yeah, I'm fine," I blurt out and focus on shelving the new stock.

One of my favorite authors released special cover editions of my favorite series in the entire world, so I'm secretly hoping there will be a book in each of these boxes that is too broken to be sold. I would take it in a heartbeat. Along with the other hundred on my list of books I still want to read but can't afford.

"I'm going to miss you," Susie says once I've finished unpacking one box. I turn to her, the corners of my mouth pulling down.

"I will miss you, too. Thank you for all the opportunities you've given me. I don't know where I'd be without you," I admit and step toward her, bringing my hand to her arm and squeezing it.

"You're most welcome. You're not only the best employee I've ever had, but you're also my friend, and I hope we can grab coffee sometime soon," she says, wrapping her arms around me in a hug. I give in, placing my hands on her back and giving her a slight squeeze.

"I would like that."

Our moment is interrupted by the front door opening. My body goes rigid in response. It's been having the same reaction since Tim first walked into the bookstore, which is why I let out an audible sigh of relief at the sight of Leonard. *Wait. Leonard?*

"Hi," is all he says when I approach him.

"You know, we don't need to spend every second of the day with each other," I point out, and he frowns at me.

"I'm not here to spend time with you. Benz knocked over a glass on the kitchen table, and it ruined the book you're currently reading. I'm here to buy you another," he says nonchalantly, like he wouldn't have laughed at that in the past instead of going to a bookstore to buy me a new copy.

"Don't worry about it. I wasn't enjoying the plot anyway," I admit and walk away from him to hide the heat in my cheeks. Somehow, his proximity only increases the temperature.

"Alright. Let me buy you another then, something new," he says, but I shoot him a confused look.

"I think you've bought me enough this week," I remind him, but he walks away without gracing me with another word. Jesus. He must have been some sort of royal in a previous life.

I try to ignore Leonard as he starts a conversation with Susie, I really do, but I can't help the curiosity blooming in my chest at what they're talking about. He looks as serious and stoic as ever, but Susie is lighting up and blushing at him like there is no tomorrow. I get it too. Leonard is charming and charismatic. I'm convinced if he started smiling at people, they would follow behind him like lost puppies. It's not only because he's handsome either. Unfortunately not. It's his entire presence. He may pretend to be an unfeeling ass most of the time, but he's a very kind man.

Half an hour later, Leonard and Susie walk to the register with two huge stacks of books. I do my best to keep my jaw from dropping. My eyes catch the spines of the books, sending a wave of shivers through me when I notice every single one of them is on my to-be-read list. I told Susie about them in case she finds one that's a bit damaged, but these are all in great condition. It makes me suck in a sharp breath and focus on the man who's been showing me one kindness after another this week.

"No," I say, interrupting their conversation, and he furrows his brows at me.

"Don't worry, these aren't for you, little demon," he replies, trying to bring his focus back to Susie, but I'm not finished speaking to him.

"You're buying all of the books I want to read for yourself?" I challenge, crossing my arms in front of my chest. My friend shoots me a look I can only interpret as 'shut up, this will be good for my business'. My mouth almost immediately sows closed.

"Yes, I'm very interested to learn even more about women's pleasure, and what better way is there than romance novels?" he asks, shutting me up even more. A tingle runs down my spine as heat pools between my legs until my clit swells unbearably. I hate my body's reactions. And him too for making me feel this way with *words*.

"Fine," I reply and start checking out the books more aggressively than necessary.

"*Fine*," he repeats my response, soft and amused. Sometimes I wish I hadn't stopped fighting competitively. I could use a good fight to let out my frustrations right now.

After ten minutes, I've finally managed to scan all of his books, pack them in bags, and read aloud the sum that's making my stomach turn upside down. Leonard pays without blinking an eye, and I keep my eyes on the ground while he enters his pin. I don't know why I do it. I know his pin. He shared it with me days ago. Maybe I just want to give my skin a moment to breathe.

"Thank you for your visit," I say as I hand him his receipt, forcing a small smile onto his lips. His fingers linger on mine as he takes the long paper.

"Let's go home, Starling. Your shift is over," he says, and my eyes flicker to the antique clock on the wall on my left. He's right. It's time to go home and get ready for Mamma to come over for dinner.

Susie and I exchange goodbyes and promise to see each other soon while Leonard waits patiently by the door. I attempt to take one of the bags from him, but he jerks it away from me at the last second and tilts his head to the exit without a word. I let out a small groan because he's so stubborn and cute at the same time, it's messing with my head. I don't like him. Twenty years of fighting won't go away because he's showing me a completely different side of him now. A side so wonderful, it's confusing me.

Leonard places the bags in his trunk and goes to open my door before I get a chance to. I give him a dumbfounded look because that's exactly how I feel at the moment. This isn't normal. Leonard is more likely to slam a door in my face than be all chivalrous and rush over to my side of the car to open one. I scan the area, not getting in the vehicle even though he's giving me an impatient look.

"What are you searching for?" he asks, and I turn back to him, my gaze meeting his warm, brown eyes.

"The real Leonard," is all I say. I would have never expected him to reach for my sides and start... tickling me. I burst into a fit of giggles, stepping away and frowning at him for getting that reaction out of me. "That never happened," I blurt out before covering my mouth.

"But it did. Chiara de Luca just bloody giggled. Priceless," he says while shaking his head and smiling. Not half a smile, not a little one, no. A full-faced smile I drink in until it vanishes again, leaving me incomplete. Fucking incomplete. I want it back, see it again, which is ridiculous. It's a smile, nothing more.

Except, it's Leonard's smile...

"In the car, little demon. I still need to make dinner," he says, his features hardening again.

"Under one condition," I say, fighting him like I always do. He drops his head on the arm resting on the top of the car door.

"What condition?" he demands, and I chew on my bottom lip for a brief moment.

"I want to help you make dinner." His head lifts in surprise.

"But I don't let anyone in my kitchen," he says, and I nod. I knew that. He hasn't let me cook once since I moved in, and every single time I try to take a pot, he *shoos* me out of the kitchen, telling me he's already made a plan in his head about what he would like to cook.

"I know," I reply, his eyes scanning my face as uncertainty sparkles in them.

"Only if you promise to listen to me and not fight me on what I say in the kitchen," he offers, and I fight back a grin. I hold out my hand, trying to look as serious as possible.

"Deal."

He shakes my hand for a moment too long, but I revel in the warmth of his touch and the roughness of his hands. When he releases me, I get into the car without another thought of how well we're getting along.

Mamma all but licks her plate clean. Leonard and I managed to make a delicious vegan meal in his kitchen without arguing once, a win in my book. I've also been mesmerized that I don't miss meat, dairy products, or anything related to it since moving in with Leonard. He takes his diet very seriously, and I'm loving everything he's prepared so far, not that I would ever admit that to him.

Benz lies down next to me halfway through dinner, and I smile at her with my mouth full. As soon as she notices my attention is on her, her tail starts wagging from side to side. When I look up again, I find Leonard's eyes on me. Something lingers in his gaze, but I can't quite identify what it is. My first guess would be fondness, but that's impossible. He's never looked at me with any emotion even similar to that one.

"There is something I have to discuss with you, *tesoro*," Mamma says once we're all done eating. Leonard hurries to his feet immediately, collecting the plates. I attempt to help him, but he shakes his head at me, telling me to stay put.

"What's going on?" I ask, my heart now racing. Mamma smiles at me, easing some of the fear camping in my chest.

"I'm moving back to Italy to be with Nonna," she says, and I swallow hard. "It's time. I found a job there, and Nonna needs me to help her out, even if it's only a little. You know how stubborn she can be," Mamma explains, and I nod along to her words. I do know how stubborn Nonna is. She's the one who made me that way as well.

"Okay, I understand. When do you plan on moving?" I try to hide how much this bothers me, how sad it makes me. Mamma is my favorite person in the entire world, and now, she's leaving. I won't be able to go see her and be with her whenever I need it. Graham just left, not even two weeks ago. Why does she have to go now?

"I've already started packing. My flight is in a week," she replies, sending a wave of pain through me. *A week...*

"Do you need help packing?" I ask, trying to keep my voice from cracking. Mamma doesn't seem to notice what her words are doing to my heart, but I don't point it out either.

"No, no, I'm almost finished. Don't worry," she assures me, and I nod, my eyes fixated on the table. "We will still see each other. You can come visit, and I will be back," Mamma goes on, but my brain isn't processing anything anymore. It's still trying to swallow the fact that the two people I'm closest with will no longer live near me.

"Are you happy?" I ask because that's the most important thing about this whole situation.

"Yes. I miss my home. I can't keep living with Tim either. It's time. I think we both knew I'd move back sooner or later," she says, and I give her one more nod.

"I'm happy if you're happy," I reply, and Mamma gets up to give me a hug. I don't return it because if I do, I will break down in tears, and I can't make Mamma feel guilty about this. "I love you," I add, and she gives me a kiss on the top of my head.

"I love you more," she says and strokes my short hair once. "I like what you've done with it. It suits you." I force a small smile, swallowing down the tears.

It's always been Mamma and me. For most of my life, we've been a single unit, taking on the world together. She's been my other half in many ways for as long as I can remember, and the thought of her not being in the same country as me breaks my heart. I will miss her so much.

"I should go. It's getting late," she says as she lets go of me. I give her another small nod before bringing her to the door and waving her goodbye.

The second I close the door, I feel him behind me. His warmth collides with my body, and there is no use trying to hold back the tears. There is something about Leonard that tears down all of my restraints. He brings out every type of emotion inside of me. So, I lift my hands to my face to cover it and then let my feelings fall down my cheeks. A sob leaves me, which is when Leonard's hands move to my shoulders to spin me around and into his arms.

"I'm not crying *again*," I blurt out while he presses his cheek against the top of my head, cups the back of my head with his hand, and holds me close.

"Who said you were?" he asks, and I can't help but let out a little laugh. Then, another wave of sadness overcomes me until I'm sobbing and crying even harder. "I'm sorry, sweetheart," I hear him say while tightening his arms around me. "You really can't catch a break, can you?" he asks, and I shake my head. "See, that's what you get for being a major pain in the arse to me the last twenty years," Leonard teases, and I smack his chest, feeling and hearing his chuckle. "I'm just kidding, Starling. No one deserves to have all of this happen to them, not even Satan's daughter," he goes on, and I step out of the hug to smack his firm left pec. He's merely smirking at me like he's never been prouder of a joke he's made.

"You're an asshole," I blurt out, and he leans back a little, running a hand down the length of his face.

"That's deeply upsetting. I mean, to have you call me that, it's not only a surprise but also utterly hurtful," he says, scowling at me before one corner of his mouth tips upward.

"Shut up," I reply, and he squeezes me ever so slightly. "Apart from your stupid jokes, why are you being so nice to me?" I ask, and all amusement leaves his face as stares at me with nothing but comfort in his eyes. He cups my cheeks and wipes away my tears, easing the pain in my chest.

"Because it's you and me now, little demon."

CHAPTER 19
Leonard

"**C**an you please get rid of this box of shit?" I say when Chiara's car, Delilah, doesn't start. Starling lets out a hurt gasp.

"You call her that again, and I will punch you," she warns, but I'm massaging my temples with the tips of my fingers now.

"Starling, I know you love her, but this can't keep going on. This is the third time this week that Delilah won't turn on," I remind her, and she gets out of the car, putting her hand on the hood and patting it while whispering something I can't hear. "Come on, sweetheart. I will buy you a new car," I blurt out without thinking the words. Am I crazy? I already spent thousands of pounds on her. I'm going to keep spending more, and that's fine, but I cannot buy her a bloody car.

"Leonard, I do not have the patience to deal with your horrible jokes. I have to get to your mum's house to put Graham's boxes in the garage," she informs me, and I almost stumble backward.

"That's where you're going? And you didn't ask me to come and help?" I ask, and she shoots me a confused look.

"Why would I? I'm more than strong enough to carry a few boxes from one part of the house to the other." Yeah, I'm going to lose it with this woman.

"It's not about that. I know you're strong, but you don't *have to* do these things by yourself, Chiara. I'm here, I can help, especially because those are my brother's things you're carrying around my childhood home," I reply, wishing she wasn't too stubborn to ask for help.

"Well, it's basically a childhood home to me too, and Graham and I are as close to siblings as you can get without being blood-related," she says, but her words make my spine go rigid. I don't like that thought at all.

"Whatever. I still don't want you to keep driving this safety hazard on wheels. You could get hurt," I say, almost pleading with her now.

"Over the past two months, I have lost all four of my jobs, got evicted from my apartment, had my Mamma and best friend move to somewhere else in the world, got stalked by a man who cannot take no for an answer, and had to move in with someone who dislikes me. I am *not* losing this car."

Understanding washes through me, and the urge to hug her again pulls on my muscles. I fight back, resisting the need to comfort her when only a few days ago, I got to hold her while Chiara cried against my chest. A few more small moments like those between us, and I won't be able to resist anything with her anymore. She's already close to breaking through the ice layer covering my heart. That's unsettling enough.

"Okay. How about this? Let's bring it back to my mechanic, and let her fix it by doing a more thorough check than last time. Maybe she can get her to work again," I offer while Chiara drops her forehead against Delilah's hood. She's silent for a while, her arms joining her cheek on the hood, and my heart shatters into a million pieces when she tilts her head and I see her eyes are screwed shut.

"No. You're right. I need to let her go. She's an old girl and deserves to rest now." Chiara lets out a shaky breath, and I take a step toward her, holding out my hand to help her upright. She takes it and wraps her arms around herself once she's standing. "Delilah was my first car, my baby. I don't think I can watch them take her away," she admits, and something crosses my mind that hits me hard, right in the chest too.

Chiara isn't afraid to show me her vulnerable side anymore. Somewhen in the last two months, she started trusting me, and I had no idea how much it would mean. She thinks I don't like her. I keep telling myself I don't care for her to hold her at arm's length, but I'm so far in denial, acceptance is a foreign concept to me.

"Would you like me to take care of it?" I ask, and she looks up at me, those green eyes of hers stealing my breath.

"No. I've got this." Because she doesn't want to feel or look weak.

"But would you be mad if I took care of it for you before you got the chance to?" This is the only way she will let me do this for her, and I want to ease at least this part of her life. I've complicated other parts and somewhen have made it my mission to balance things out at least a little.

"No." I give her chin a small nudge when she's staring at her car again to get her attention to shift to my face. It works like a charm.

"Let me come with you to my parents' house. I'll help and then I can talk to my dad too about not having to take Benz anymore," I say, which makes Chiara's eyes go wide.

"Fuck. I haven't told Graham about us living together or me working for you this season," she blurts out, letting out a groan after. "Oh God, I don't want to have the conversation where I have to explain why I agreed to any of this. He's going to think I was abducted by extraterrestrials who programmed me to make the worst decisions. No offense," she adds, but I give her a look I hope says 'really?'.

She smiles in response, but I'm still not used to her giving one so easily, so my heart flutters uncontrollably. I even went to the doctor recently to make sure this heart thing is nothing, which he assured me it was. Then he laughed at me when I told him when my heart acts up like that, and I left his office without another word.

"You know, just because you add 'no offence' doesn't lessen the arsehole comment you make," I say, but then she leans her head against my arm and stares up at me with soft eyes and her bottom lip pushed forward. I forget everything, even my own name, because her peachy scent fills my nose, and her proximity stiffens my entire body.

"Have I upset you?" she asks in a teasing tone. Fuck me. I clear my throat a little, trying to appear more unaffected than I am right now. I wait too long to reply, so she beats me to it. "No, it's something else, isn't it? Your breathing is heavy and you've tensed up. Not to mention, your eyes have been stuck on my lips for several moments now. I turned you on, didn't I?" *Yes.*

"No," I grind out, and she grins at me.

"You're still a shit liar," she says and steps away from me, but I'm not having it. My hand snakes around her wrist, bringing her into my chest.

"What are you trying to achieve by doing stuff like that, Chiara?" Her hands shift up to my pecs while mine rest on her hips. "Hmmm? Why do you do it? Do you like the thought of my cock getting hard for you? Does it turn *you* on?" *Oh God, shut the fuck up, Leonard. Step away. Chiara is not the woman for you.*

"Yes."

I become undone by this single word. One word. It didn't take more than three letters strung together like that to rip me apart and put me back together.

"What do you want me to do about that, sweetheart?" She swallows hard as the rest of the world around us blurs away. It's just her and me in the parking lot of my building, and I'm way too tempted to pull down her panties and fuck her right here.

"Nothing, I don't like you," she whispers, her fingers gripping my shirt and keeping me close. Sure. That's not confusing at all.

"You don't have to like me for what I have in mind. You just have to be attracted to me." And she is. Chiara is so attracted to me, she continues to guide me closer until my hard bulge is firmly pressed against her stomach.

"Fuck me," she curses, and I smile.

"Is that what you want, little demon? To have me fuck you? Up against your shitty car where everyone could see you come on my cock?" God, it would solve nothing and everything at the same time, but right as she's about to answer, a car alarm goes off and sends me stumbling away from her.

"Sorry," someone calls out as the noise stops, and I cross my arms in front of my chest.

I'm an idiot. She hates me. She's my brother's best friend and vice versa. We live together. We're about to work together. Everything is moving against us, and it doesn't matter how desperate I am to taste her, to feel her in my bloodstream, it's not happening. I can't let things get out of control like this again, which is why I brush off what happened like it was nothing. I hope she doesn't interpret it as me not wanting her because, fuck, I do. I hate that I do, but I want her more than I've wanted anything in a long time.

"Let's go," I say and step toward my car.

We stay quiet for the entire ride to my parents' home while I list every single type of vegetable in my head to calm my overcharged body. It works eventually, but a strange feeling lingers in my chest. I wanted things to go further with Chiara. We've grown closer, but I have no fucking clue how I feel about her. She's sitting next to me, staring out the window and chewing on her bottom lip, and all I want to do is tilt her head to me and kiss her lips. At the same time, I feel the need to put as much distance between us as humanely possible.

My thoughts are interrupted as we arrive at my parents' home. Starling gets out of the car without a single word spoken between us, and I take a moment to collect myself before following behind her. I try to keep my eyes trained on the sky because her shorts are riding higher than my cock can handle at the moment. I'm happy it's summer, truly, but Chiara has been wearing clothes that drive me absolutely wild. Even her plain green shirt is bloody sexy, and there is nothing special about it. My gaze shifts to her backside again as we move up the stairs, sending a thrill through my body.

"Stop staring at me," she says without turning her head. "I can feel your gaze on my skin." It almost makes me smile.

"Stop swaying your arse so much," I reply to annoy her, and she shoots me a glare.

"You're impossible," she says, knocking on the front door.

There is nothing but silence for a moment. Then a weak, "Chiara" out of my mum's mouth sends me into high alert.

Starling rips the door before I have the chance to. We rush inside, but the fear in me soon multiplies by a million when I see Mum on the ground with blood seeping from her leg. The shelf that usually stands at the entrance is on top of her, and I run faster than I've ever gone to lift it off her. Sounds of pain are leaving her, but Chiara is right by Mum's side, brushing her fingers over her arm to let her know she's here.

"Call an ambulance," Starling says after I've lifted the dresser off Mum. I reach for my phone, listening to the soft voice of my roommate. "What happened, Rena?" she asks, inspecting the wound. Chiara seems to contemplate something, then rips her shirt off and in half before tying it around Mum's leg to slow the bleeding.

"I stumbled," Mum replies, her voice getting weaker. Fuck, fuck, fuck.

"Hi, yes, I need an ambulance, please. My mum hurt her leg. There's blood everywhere," I try to explain while sounding calm, but panic has consumed me. I give the emergency responder the address before hanging up and turning to my mother, brushing the hair out of her face. "Is it just your leg or something else, Mum? You've got to tell me," I beg and cup her face.

"Just the leg, darling, but it hurts. How bad is it? You know I can't see, so you have to tell me," she says, and I shoot Chiara a look, not sure if I should be honest or reassure her. I know what the right thing to do is, but it might not help Mum right now.

"Don't worry, Rena, the bleeding is slowing. You're going to be okay. All we have to do is wait for the paramedics so they can take you to the hospital, alright?" Chiara says, and I notice she's right. It's not bleeding as much anymore, not since she wrapped her shirt around Mum's leg. God, I could kiss her.

"Mum, where is Dad?" I ask, holding onto her hand as I watch Chiara staring at hers, covered in blood and shaking. She catches me staring at them, so she clenches them into fists and lowers them behind Mum's other leg to prevent me from seeing.

"He went out to get us some bread for lunch," Mum replies, and I squeeze her shoulder to acknowledge her words without replying.

My eyes remain on Chiara, who mouths 'Breathe' at me. I do as I'm told, letting the oxygen filter through my system. It helps the swirling happening in my head, so I keep repeating it.

The paramedics show up minutes later and take Mum onto a stretcher and then to the ambulance. Dad comes home in time, panic washing over his face. He starts yelling at me, demanding answers because he's freaking out, but I assure him everything will be fine, that he should ride in the ambulance with Mum. He goes without another word. I turn on my heels and walk back inside, toward the guest bathroom where Chiara is viciously scrubbing her hands. By the time I get to her, the blood is already washed off, but she keeps rubbing them together. I turn off the water and grab her hands in mine.

"It's okay. She's going to be alright," I say while she stares at our hands. The paramedic assured me her condition isn't life-threatening, but she'll probably have to get surgery and definitely needs a blood transfusion because she's lost too much. But she'll be okay. He assured me she will be.

"Sorry, I've just—I've never seen so much blood, and I usually faint at the sight of it, so it really is a miracle I'm still standing, but it might still come, who knows at this point, I could still pass out, so you might have to—" I bring my hand to her heaving chest and press down on it, cutting her off.

"You told me to breathe, now I'm going to tell you the same. Breathe, Starling. You're not going to faint because my mum needs you to be strong, okay?" She nods a few times, her face unbelievably pale. I need to get some sugar in her. "Let's go find you a shirt, and a piece of chocolate," I say and take her hand to lead her out of the bathroom.

"I'm pretty sure I'm the one who is supposed to comfort you," she blurts out when we arrive in my childhood bedroom.

"You kept me calm. Now I'm returning the favour," I reply because she really did. "I also heard the paramedic say she'll be fine, you didn't." I look through my old clothes until I find a shirt for her.

"I'm sorry," she says, and I spin around, holding the top out for her. She takes it and quickly slides it over her sports bra.

"Don't apologise. You did everything right, and I appreciate it, Chiara. Thank you."

I take her hand again and lead her to my car. We have to meet Dad at hospital. I don't want him to be alone while Mum is in surgery. God. Mum needs surgery. Maybe I'm not as calm as I was trying to convince myself of, but when Chiara squeezes my fingers to remind me she's right next to me, I feel my breathing and heart rate settle into a normal speed. It'll be okay. Chiara is here with me.

That thought never settled me more than it does in this moment.

CHAPTER 20

Chiara

Rena's surgery went well. Jack, Stu, Ellie, Andrew, Leonard, and I waited six hours in the emergency room a few days ago, but the doctor was positive about Rena making a full recovery soon. For now, she has to stay in the hospital, at least for another few days. Meanwhile, Leonard and I are halfway to France in his private jet when Benz decides to start barking at one of the flight attendants.

"Benz, quiet," I command, and because Leonard trained her so well, she listens right away. I catch him staring at me from the seat across mine—he had to sit there and not in one of the other four seats. He's been reading one of the books he bought for me, he gave them to me as soon as we got home from the bookstore, but he looks confused about something. "What?" I ask, trying to keep the amusement off my face. The plane shakes a little from turbulence, but Leonard continues watching me.

"Have you ever had someone fuck you like this?" he asks, sliding the book across the table between us. It's opened on a sex scene where the couple is doing it in a barn, him thrusting inside of her rough and hard while spanking her ass. I smile at the page, feeling my clit ache in response to the thought of getting fucked like this.

"No, because this is fiction, Leonard. Men like him don't exist in real life. He's sweet to her but rough when she needs him to be. He makes sure she's comfortable at all times and whispers the dirtiest and sexiest things into her ear too. Of course I haven't been fucked like this. The men I've dated don't even come close," I explain, unashamed and unapologetic. Leonard, on the other hand, narrows his eyes at me.

"You mean that jerk Tyler and that other idiot Ian? I would be surprised if they even knew where the clit was." Yeah, neither of them did, which is precisely why I didn't have long relationships with them. "So, you'd like that?" Leonard goes on, pointing at the book in my hand. "Having rough sex in a somewhat public space?" I don't know why he's so interested in finding out my preferences, but I try not to read too much into it.

"I will let you know if I ever experience it in real life," I reply and slide the book back toward him. He lets out a low humming sound before grabbing it and reading again.

"Jesus Christ," Leonard blurts out after a while, and I lift my eyes from my own book to see him staring at the page in front of him. I can't help but smile.

"What happened?" I ask, and he shakes his head, shock on his face.

"Have you read this?" I give him a nod, so he goes on. "The mum fucking betrayed the main characters. What the bloody hell, Chiara?" I grin at his genuine interest in a book I loved.

"It gets worse. Keep reading," I say, causing his eyes to almost pop out of their sockets.

"Worse? Nah. I'm done. Take the book back." I shake my head, so he holds it back up to his face and reimmerses himself in the story. I give Benz's head a quick pat before catching Leonard's eyes on my face again.

Things have been strange between us since the day of Rena's accident. Surprisingly enough, they haven't been strange in a bad way. We've both kept our distance from one another after what happened next to my car, but we've also been sharing wholesome moments, just like the one we had a minute ago. We're somehow figuring out how to be around each other without causing the end of the world, and it's refreshing. I've even considered the possibility of me enjoying Leonard's presence.

It's never been only the two of us. Graham was always there, so we never had the time to explore what it'd be like to sit on top of each other like we're forced to do now. It's not as bad as I thought it'd be. Not even close. We've made plans for the whole weekend. There is an event he plans on taking me to on Friday. It's an immersive exhibit of Van Gogh's 'Starry Night' where a lot of famous and influential people will be. Leonard has also given me an itinerary of his work schedule and assured me Benz and I will have our own little area from where we will get to watch the free practices, quali, and the race. To give me peace of mind, he has thought of everything I could need and planned it all out with clear instructions.

I can't help but glance up at him every once in a while, studying his sharp features and his clean-cut beard. His lips are so full, it's difficult not to imagine them wrapping around mine. I swallow hard at the visual floating into my mind, pushing it out as soon as I manage to calm the shivers running down my spine. It also doesn't help that he keeps looking up at me through those thick eyelashes of his and with the warmth of his brown eyes. There is a hunger in them, one that sends a wave of heat between my legs and makes my nipples unbearably hard.

His gaze immediately drops to my chest, and I curse myself for wearing the thinnest sports bra I own. Leonard's bottom lip slips between his teeth as he meets my eyes again, showing me how much he likes to see my body react like this. I can't blame him either. Whenever I feel his hard cock against me—which has happened a lot more than it should have—it sends a thrill like no other through me. I like turning him on, like the control I have over him. It's tempting and wrong, and I have no intention of acting on how I feel, but he's attracted to me. I love that he wants me.

I stare out of the window at the white, fluffy clouds surrounding us and wonder how his fresh scent has somehow filled the entire private jet. It rushes into my bloodstream with every breath I take, but I have no desire to keep it out either. There is no use at this point.

He's already consumed me in more ways than I can even begin to understand.

Leonard is taking me to dinner. Today is only Wednesday, which means he doesn't have as much to do as the rest of the race weekend. Tomorrow, he will be busy with press conferences and other media responsibilities. Tonight, however, he is free, and he invited me to dinner. He also asked another driver to join us, but I'm not quite sure who it is.

The grumpy man across from me hasn't said anything, merely stared at the skin-tight dress I put on and shook his head before scowling as usual. I've been staring at his all-black outfit—dress shirt and pants, and his boots—since he walked out of his room at the hotel.

"Is he always this late?" I ask when we've been sitting at our table for the past ten minutes.

"I don't know. This is the first time I'm having dinner with him," Leonard replies, causing my eyes to go wide.

"Oh," I blurt out, unable to contain my surprise. "Is he nice?" He shrugs.

"He's young and gets overly excited." I'm about to ask why he invited him when Leonard adds, "And kind. He's been very kind to me." His words are soft and vulnerable, tugging at something inside of me until my hand is inching toward him.

He meets me halfway, our fingers brushing against one another's. Electricity shoots through me at the contact until it's cursing through my veins.

"Hello, sorry I'm late. I came straight from the airport," a male's voice says, interrupting our moment and forcing us to pull our hands away. "Shit, did I interrupt something?" the tall man with blonde hair, light skin, and beautiful green and blue eyes asks, and Leonard and I both stand up to greet him. The longer I study him, the more I realize I know his name, I've seen him during race weekends, but it seems to have slipped my mind.

"Not at all. It's nice to see you," Leonard says, earning himself a bright smile from the young man whose hand he's shaking.

Adrian Romana. The name pops into my head as soon as our eyes meet. He's a rookie this year, driving alongside Cameron Kion for Spark Racing. He's also drop-dead gorgeous and a flirt. I see it the second a cocky smirk slips across his face and he lifts my hand to his mouth to press a kiss to the back of it.

"*Enchanté, mademoiselle. Tu es trés belle,*" he says, and I roll my eyes a little at his cheesy yet adorable advance.

"And you are a little young for me," I reply, and he lets go of my hand, placing his over his chest.

"I have many questions. First, you speak French?" His eyes light up, and we sit down together where I drag my glass of water toward me.

"Italian and English fluently, French only conversationally," I reply, noticing the way Leonard's jaw is hardening like he's biting down harder than he should. I furrow my brows at him, but he's glaring at Adrian.

"Wonderful. Second question, am I really too young for you?" There is an easiness to his tone, amusement all over his face, and joy clings to him.

"Yes, sorry. I usually go for guys that are older than me," I say, noticing the way the corners of Leonard's mouth curl upward.

"Alright, I think we should just be friends, *belle*. I hope this doesn't break your heart," he teases, and I almost burst into laughter. This guy is impossible. "I could eat everything on the menu, that's how hungry I am," Adrian goes on and places his hand on his stomach as he looks at the card. I can't help but smile at him a little.

"As long as I don't have to pay for it, you can order however much you want," Leonard chimes in, scanning his own menu.

"You invited me to dinner, so I didn't bring my wallet," Adrian says, and I can't help but watch their exchange with utter fascination. Leonard and I already don't make sense to me, and we have a lot more in common compared to sunshine boy and him.

"I wonder if they will let you wash dishes to pay for your meal," Leonard jokes, and I almost fall out of my seat. I wish such a little thing wouldn't send warmth through me, but it does. I like seeing him this way.

"Funny," Adrian replies with a snort. "Did you buy a pack of jokes to make a good impression for our first date?" Leonard raises a surprised eyebrow.

"How did you know?" I grin at Leonard before I'm able to stop myself. He catches me and then returns my smile for a moment before he realizes what he's doing and the corners of his mouth drop again. My own smile fades as my eyes fall to the table.

"Okay then," Adrian blurts out to try and break the awkward tension.

He goes on to ask me some questions about what I do for a living and how I know Leonard. After some very short answers he doesn't know what to do with, Adrian shifts his attention to Leonard to ask a few questions about this race weekend. Since he's still a rookie, there is a lot he has left to learn, but I can tell he doesn't want to hear it from anyone other than Leonard. Adrian looks up to him, admires him—for who he is or what he's achieved, I'm not sure—and everyone in the restaurant can sense it. I like Adrian for how kind he is to my roommate.

Leonard hasn't had the easiest career. He's often let it slip how the other drivers keep their distance from him. Hardly anyone in this sport has ever shown him any kindness. He's an incredible driver, better than the rest of them, and they hate that. So, media outlets attack him with racist comments and say he cheats to win. Anything to take away from how great of a driver he is.

"Did you enjoy yourself?" Leonard asks once we get back to the penthouse we're sharing. We have separate rooms with doors, but he insisted on us being together so that we can both spend time with Benz.

"I did. I liked Adrian. He's funny," I say and place my hand on his shoulder as I get on one foot. My fingers work with the straps of my high heels, but Leonard stops me by stepping in front of me.

"He seemed to enjoy himself too, right?" he asks as he drops onto one knee and takes my hands to place them on both of his shoulders.

"Yeah," I croak out, an ache settling between my legs when he places my foot on his thigh. He starts undoing the straps that wrap around my ankle, sending goosebumps all over my body. It's impossible for him not to notice them because they're originating from wherever he touches me.

"He liked you a lot," Leonard goes on, slipping the shoe off my foot and then briefly massaging the heel of it. I let my head fall backward as a small hum leaves me because it feels too good not to. "I didn't enjoy the way he was looking at you one bit," he says and puts my foot down, bringing the other onto his thigh now. Then, his fingers work on those straps as well, like it is the most normal thing he's ever done.

"Why not?" I hear myself ask. Leonard starts smirking in response to my question.

"Don't like people looking at you, never have." My head is spinning as he removes my shoe and then looks up at me. "At the same time, art is meant to be admired, so how could I blame him?"

His thumb presses down on a sore spot on my foot, and I let out a small, muffled whimper. I'm still trying to process his words when he bends forward to press a kiss to my shin. Everything inside of me explodes into a million pieces. My clit is begging for a release, which is why I don't think and simply slide my hands up his neck, gripping his nape. A low chuckle escapes him.

"Don't you agree, little demon? Don't you think you deserve to be admired?" Leonard presses another kiss to my shin, this time higher. I'm so turned on, if he keeps going, my arousal will start dripping down my legs.

"I do," I reply when I remember he asked me a question. Pleasure is making my mind fuzzy and clouded.

"Good. I think so too. And I also think the best way to do that is by getting you out of that tight dress," he says, and my heart skips several beats. *Oh God, yes, please.* "Would you like that, sweetheart?" he asks, his lips trailing upward as I nod eagerly.

"Leonard?" A woman's voice fills my ears before a soft knock follows it.

Leonard's full lips move off my body, leaving me cold as his hands disappear too. He curses under his breath as he walks toward the door to open it for whoever is disturbing our moment. Which is good. This is good. *I can't have sex with Leonard! What the hell am I thinking? He's my boss!* And roommate, nemesis, and my best friend's brother. Even letting him touch me like this is wrong. It felt incredible, better than most of my sex life has, but it was wrong.

Then why did it feel so fucking right?

"What's going on, Quinn?" I hear Leonard ask after he opens the door. I don't linger in the hallway. I move into my room and shut the door, leaning my forehead against it and taking several deep breaths.

So close. We keep getting so close, too fucking close. It can't happen again, I won't let it.

Which is exactly what I told myself after the first time I felt his touch.

And I have a feeling I won't listen to myself this time either.

CHAPTER 21
Leonard

I haven't been able to focus ever since Wednesday night. It's now Friday afternoon, and it's taking every ounce of my concentration to have my mind in the car with me and not in the private room with Benz and Chiara. I let myself lower my walls after we came back from dinner and have been avoiding her as much as possible since then. We've barely spoken three words because I'm too much of a fucking coward to face how I truly feel about her. I was *on my knees* for her. I've never let myself get so vulnerable for any woman, but there I was, worshipping her in a way I've always dreamt about doing with a woman. The right woman. *Not Chiara*. It can't be her.

I blink several times under my helmet to refocus, and a second later, a green light appears over my car, allowing me to join the other drivers on the track for the second free practice. I try not to notice the excitement spreading through my chest in a way I haven't felt all season. Then I do my best not to think about the fact that it decided to show up now with Chiara watching me on one of the screens I put in the room where she's entertaining Benz.

I do my laps before returning to my pit box with sweat dripping down my back. My heart skips several beats when I see Chiara chatting with Quinn at the side, Benz next to her with headphones on her ears. She's such a good girl, she's merely sitting there with them on, almost like she knows they're there to protect her ears from the loud noises. Chiara is also wearing a pair, her shoulder-length brown hair brushed

159

out of her infuriatingly beautiful face. I watch her the whole time my team pushes my car into its spot in the garage, unable to breathe properly.

Once I'm out, I make my way to her, only to see Jonathan Kent, my teammate and rival, in front of her. Whatever he's saying seems to make Chiara very unhappy because she takes a step toward him, anger in her eyes. He takes one toward her, sending a wave of panic through me. One of my mechanics tries to get my attention, but I push past her as I rip my helmet off to get to my little demon.

She has her hands on his collar before I can get to him. Fear crosses Jonathan's face, and I stop dead in my tracks. Chiara points a finger in his face, her hold on him tight and threatening. I fight back a smile, but it's one of the most difficult things I've had to do in a while, if not *the* most impossible.

Get him, sweetheart.

"You say one more bad word about Leonard, and I'll make sure he won't have to worry about you for the rest of the season. A few broken bones should do the trick, don't you think?" I hear her threaten him, sending me into motion.

My feet bring me behind her, and I wrap my arm around her stomach, lifting her away from my teammate. As amusing as it is to watch Jonathan hold in his pee, I don't want Chiara to be banned from coming to my races.

"Jesus, Leonard, she's a fucking menace," he says, and Starling fights my hold on her to get back to him.

"Damn right I am. You should be careful how you speak to me from now on if you don't want me to follow through on that threat."

That's my girl.

"Alright, relax," Jonathan says and backs away. Starling has calmed in my arms now, probably realizing that, as tough as she is, she would never hurt me. It also helps that she's much shorter than I am. "I can't believe you'd hire her, Leonard. She's very unprofessional."

One sentence and I'm ready to release Chiara and let her beat him up.

Leonard, did you see what happened to Jonathan?

Nope, didn't see a thing. Chiara and I were having coffee.

Yes, I would lie for her and give her an alibi at the same time. No hesitation.

"Get the fuck out of my box, Jonathan," I warn, keeping my hands on her stomach, which seems to calm her a little. Benz is barking next to us now, and I try my best not to chuckle when I see she directed her anger at Jonathan too. She's protecting her best friend and dad, which is the sweetest thing I've ever witnessed, along with Chiara protecting me.

My hands remain on Starling's hips until Jonathan is gone. Then, she spins around in my arms, poking my right shoulder with two of her fingers.

"Why didn't you tell me your teammate was such a—" Her eyes shift from my face to the ceiling as she searches for a good word to describe him. "Disgusting, rude, and awful person?" she finishes, and I scan her features like they could tell me why she's so upset about Jonathan's behaviour toward me.

"Because it isn't something you need to worry about." She scoffs at that answer.

"So you get to worry about every part of my life, but I don't get to concern myself with this part of yours?" she challenges, her gaze fixed on mine. Then, it shifts to my hands on her hips and she takes a step back. The loss of contact upsets me far more than it should.

"Yes, that's how it works between us," I reply, earning myself an eye roll from her.

"Says who?" Well, I have no answer to her question. "You are so frustrating, do you know that?" she asks when I don't answer, taking Benz's leash and walking away.

I let my head fall backward, noticing for the millionth time how wildly my heart is racing because of Chiara. No wonder my doctor laughed in my face. *Can you explain why my heart rate speeds up when I look at the woman I'm telling myself I don't have feelings for?* It's my fucking heart telling me it's useless to push her away. By offering her all the things I have, I tied us together for the rest of the season. There is no way I'm breaking our bond either. She needs this job and the connections I have. And I...

I need *her*.

A purple dress. Tight in all the right places. Hugging her curves unlike anything she's ever worn. It's all it took to make me utterly speechless. Chiara asked me if she looked alright as soon as she stepped out of her room at the hotel, and all I replied was a weird croaking sound. She gave me a confused frown before leaving me standing there, dumbfounded and beyond amazed by her beauty.

Now, I'm standing with an acquaintance at the gallery, watching her dance with Harry, an ex-mate of mine. The second he placed his hands on her hips, he became an *ex*-mate. I should have asked her first, but we were so immersed in our conversation with Fred, the man who put together this 'Starry Night' art experience, I didn't notice Harry walking toward her. And fuck me for being so stupid because now jealousy has consumed me. I don't want another man's hands on her body. I've never hated Fred more for including a dance area in his exhibit launch party.

"Are you alright?" he asks when I've been staring at Chiara and Harry with raging jealousy clinging to my very being.

"Why'd you have to include a bloody dance floor?" I ask, keeping my eyes on them. Chiara gives Harry a small smile, her equivalent of a fit of laughter. It gives me the desire to strangle him.

"Just go ask her to dance with you instead. If she had to choose, I'm pretty sure she'd choose you over the guy she met an hour ago."

Would she though? Chiara has no reason to. After all, she doesn't even like me. She defended me this morning with Jonathan, but that doesn't mean anything. I pissed her off a minute later, and she stormed away from me without another word. Then again, if I don't ask her, I'm going to lose it in a few minutes, especially because Harry is bringing her closer and closer to him, and I'm not having any of it. Starling isn't mine in any way, but I can't stand the sight of her flashing any other guy a smile. I want them all reserved for me.

"Excuse me," I say to Fred and make my way over to the dancing couple I've been glaring at for the past ten minutes. *Who the fuck needs to dance for so long anyway?* "Chiara, may I have this dance?" I hear myself ask, earning me a surprised look on her features.

"Why? Getting tired of glaring at us?" she challenges, and my back tenses. She noticed. Of course she fucking noticed.

"Very much," is all I say before giving my ex-mate a look that says 'back away before I remove you'. He mouths an *oh shit* before telling Chiara what a pleasure it was to meet her and then leaving the dance floor. My hands are on her hips a second later.

"You're such a pain. I was having a great time with Harry. Why did you have to interrupt?" *Because I don't want you to have a great time with another man who was clearly interested in ripping your dress off. Because I was jealous, and I've never been jealous in my entire life. Because I can't stand the thought of you wanting him too.*

"I didn't like the way he was holding you," I reply, and Chiara looks down at my hands on her body.

"You mean in the same way you're touching me right now?" She looks a little amused.

"Yes."

Chiara rolls her eyes at me but then places her hands on my neck, the tip of her index finger tracing the tattoo of the rose on the right side of it. My skin lights on fire, and I bring her flush against me, bringing a little gasp from her lips. The sound travels right through me until it sets off fireworks in my chest.

"It sounds like you're jealous, Champ," she says, my grip on her tightening a little in response to her words.

"What if I am?" Chiara stops moving but her hands remain on my neck. The way her eyes scan my face heats my skin, so I keep her close to listen to the accelerated beat of her heart.

"Then I should remind you we are roommates and I'm working for you this season," she says, and I nod, not giving a shit about either of those things.

"Does knowing I'm jealous you were dancing with another man make you uncomfortable?" She starts swaying to the music again, a little smile slipping onto her pouty lips. *God, I want to kiss her so badly.*

"No, it doesn't make me uncomfortable, but that is another problem entirely," she says with a little chuckle, and I melt into her at the sound. "But I think you need to dial it back, Leonard. Nothing will ever happen between us, and I wouldn't mind meeting someone to have a little fun with," Chiara goes on, causing everything inside of me to scream in protest. *I wouldn't mind meeting someone to have a little fun with.*

"That's not what we're here for," I remind her and spin her around once, guiding her back against my chest right after. Her green eyes meet mine, a challenge in them.

"I'm great at multitasking," she says, her hands intertwining at my nape. "And I already got a few contacts of potential investors. I might as well have some fun too." Have some fun. That's the second time she said it in two minutes, and the urge to let my frustrations out on a wall becomes extremely appealing.

"You want fun, sweetheart? I'll give you fun. I'll rip off your dress and then the lingerie I bought you before making you come so many times, you'll redefine your idea of fun." *Good God, where the hell did that come from?*

"I'm not wearing lingerie or any underwear for that matter." Fuuuck. Everything inside of me goes stiff as blood rushes to my cock and my fingers dig into her hips.

"You drive me fucking wild, Chiara," I admit, and she drops her hands down my chest.

"Which is exactly why we need to stop this. We don't make sense, Leonard, we never have, and I cannot risk my future, my dream, and my best friend by giving in to our bodies' needs." She steps back, leaving me so cold and dizzy, it irritates me.

"So, you'd rather fuck a stranger like Harry?" I tried to hold back the question, but it slipped out despite my effort, and it makes me sound like the biggest dick in the world. Chiara merely shrugs, unbothered by my words.

"Yes," she replies, and I shake my head, letting anger storm through me. I know it's rooted in jealousy, but I can't help it. I hate the thought of anyone else getting to pleasure her in the way I've been dreaming about at night.

"Well, I forbid it." By far the worst thing I could have said. Fury appears on her features.

"You *forbid* it? I'm sorry, I don't fucking belong to you," she barks, and I give her a small smile.

"I didn't say you did, but I won't have you fucking my friends for fun, Chiara." I do my best to keep my voice low, but I'm pretty sure we're making a scene. Realizing that too, she steps off the dance floor, and I follow behind her.

"Are you saying you will fire me or kick me out of your apartment if I do?" she asks, and panic floods my chest.

"No, of course not." Starling offers me a smile then.

"Then you really can't stop me, can you?" she says, and I stare at her, my jaw ticking with anger.

"Guess not." But I really fucking want to.

"Good," she adds, and I swallow down the nausea bubbling up in my throat.

"Fine," I reply.

"Fine," she mocks me, and I narrow my eyes at her.

"Good."

She leaves me standing right where I am before walking toward Harry and placing a flirtatious smile on her lips.

Yeah. I'm going to fucking lose it.

CHAPTER 22

Chiara

I didn't take Harry back to my hotel room. I wasn't interested in him when he asked me to dance nor did I become so after my fight with Leonard. To spite him, I should have had sex with Harry, especially after his bullshit 'I forbid it' comment. But I couldn't. I stood with that nice man as he asked me questions about my goals and passions in life, and all I could think about was the jealous man watching us from his spot on the other side of the room.

When we went home from the event—where I met so many people interested in the idea I have for the gallery I'd love to open in London—he didn't speak to me at all. This morning, however, he was the chattiest person in the world. I don't know what the fuck he ate that made him so talkative, but I was close to knocking him out to get a bit of silence.

Benz barks to get my attention, and I give it to her without a moment's hesitation. I pat her head, and she throws herself into my lap. I tumble over, laughing loudly as she attacks my face with kisses. My hands move to her head to try and redirect her focus to my hand, but, instead, she lies down in front of me and places her head in the crook of my neck. My smile is so bright, my cheeks burn. I should probably watch Leonard's Qualifying, but how could I move when Benz is acting so cute?

I still remember the day Leonard introduced me to her.

"You got a puppy?" I blurt out when this tiny being, its fur all soft and grey, and eyes so blue, starts running toward me.

"Yes, but don't touch her. I don't want your demon fingers anywhere near her."

"Ha, ha," I reply but I'm already meeting this little creature halfway. "What's her name?" I ask, and Leonard stares down at us. The puppy is wagging, tongue swiping across my fingers and making me let out a little giggle.

"Benz," he says, his voice low and firm. I look up at him to find a soft look in his eyes. I've never seen it before, not to this extent.

"You win your first championship, so you get yourself a dog to name Benz?" I challenge, earning me an eye roll from him.

"Yeah, Starling, that's exactly what happened. I adopted her out of the shelter just to name her something that means 'bright strength.' That's how full I am of myself." I frown at him, and he glares at me. Graham clears his throat from beside me on the floor, waiting for Benz to give him the time of day, but she's curled up in my lap now, not leaving.

"I grew up with dogs, you didn't. How is this fair? I'm a dog whisperer," my best friend complains, and I furrow my eyebrows at him.

"It surprises me too. Dogs are supposed to be great judges of character. Maybe not Benz," Leonard says, and I shoot him a smile I don't mean in the slightest.

"I hope Benz shits in all of your expensive shoes when you get home." The corner of his mouth twitches in response to my wish. Benz snaps me out of my staring contest with Leonard, and I shift my attention to the little, demanding baby in my lap. "I'm sorry

*you got stuck with that jerk over there, but, I promise, you will always have a home
with me," I say to Benz, who is still wagging from excitement.*

"Okay, give me my dog. I don't need the two of you to become best friends."

As the memory floods my mind, I realize how far we've come. Yes, we still bicker and
fight, but we also smile at each other and find ways to make the other person laugh.
That isn't something either of us has ever experienced, which is probably the real
reason we keep fighting at this point. It isn't because I don't like him anymore. It's
because I do, and it's fucking with my head. Never in my wildest dreams could I
have predicted Leonard would become someone as important to me as he is today.
Hell, I would have punched Jonathan yesterday for the way he spoke about the man
I keep telling myself I dislike.

"You're working for a talentless cheater."

One sentence out of Jonathan's mouth, and I was ready to break his nose. No one
speaks about Leonard like that, especially when he's more talented than any other
driver on the grid. He works harder than anyone else. He's always focused, and I
admire him for his determination. For him, business comes first. Even yesterday,
Leonard was introducing me to everyone, getting straight to the point of why we
were there and what our goal was. Business first, then, he danced with me. He held
me pressed against his body, and I never felt safer than I did in his arms. Well, at least
until the spell broke, and we were reminded for the hundredth time why we would
never work.

The ringing of my phone pulls me out of my trance, and I flinch when I read Graham's name. I haven't told him about anything that has happened since he left. I've been avoiding him because there is no way he will be okay with Leonard and me living together, or even me working for him. Graham is my best friend and I love him more than anyone except Mamma, but even he has limits to how cool he can be about situations. I just don't know how far his line is from what has been going on.

I guess there is only one way to find out...

"Hey," I say into the phone, and the sound of his low chuckle fills my ears, sending a wave of nostalgia through me. I miss him so much.

"Hey, stranger. Why have you been ignoring my calls?" he asks, and the nostalgia is replaced by blazing guilt. I've never kept anything from him, except the situation with Tim, but that was for his own good. I didn't want him to worry about me like... like Leonard is.

"Sorry. Things have been crazy. You wouldn't believe me if I told you," I reply, sucking in a breath I hope will give me courage.

"You mean that you moved in with Leonard and are working for him this season as Benz's dog sitter?" Alright, that works too.

"How the fuck do you know that? You are so far away!" Graham chuckles into the phone, completely unbothered by anything he just pointed out.

"I called Mum to check in this morning and she told me," he explains, and I sit up straighter.

"How's Rena?"

"She's doing well. She's in a lot of pain, but the medication she's taking seems to ease it," Graham replies, and I barely hold back a sigh of relief. After that terrifying afternoon, I tried calling Andrew a few times to check in, but we kept missing each other. "Can we get back to you not telling me about Leonard asking you to move in with him and stuff?" he asks, and I suck in a sharp breath.

"Do we have to?" He chuckles in response, so I busy myself by throwing Benz her ball.

"Yes. Why didn't you tell me?" he asks, sounding a little disappointed I would keep this from him. "Be honest, are you two hooking up?" Shock knocks the oxygen from my lungs, and I let out a shrill laugh.

"What? Don't be absurd," I blurt out, feeling guilty even though Leonard and I haven't done anything other than share a few intense moments with one another.

"I wouldn't be upset about it, you know? You and Leonard have always had a connection, even if you tried to cover it up by fighting. I figured you'd break down each other's walls one day and become more, hoped for it even. I think you'd be good together," Graham says, sending my head spiraling so far into unknown territory, I have to blink several times to process where I am.

My best friend thinks Leonard and I would be good together. He's hoping we will break down our walls and embrace the connection he believes we have. Graham wouldn't mind if Leonard and I hooked up. I thought I knew my best friend, but maybe I don't because he's made me speechless.

"You there?" he asks after a moment of silence turns into three, and I let out a short laugh I don't mean.

"Leonard and I are not hooking up," is all I manage to say. Graham lets out a thoughtful hum.

"But you have been growing closer," he states, and I stare at the ground in front of me.

"I'm finding investors for our gallery, Graham. By the time you come back, we will move in together again, and we will get our dream, I promise," I say to change the subject, but when silence fills the line again, I get a weird feeling in my chest.

"Chiara—" he starts, but I cut him off.

"You're not coming back, are you?" I don't know how I know, but I do. The realization hits me hard and deep in the chest until breathing becomes impossible.

"Not in the next five months, no. I met someone here, and she's—fuck, luv, she's everything. But I want you to keep fighting for your dream. I want you to make it happen and become successful because you deserve to be happy. Just like I am now."

His dreams have changed. He's no longer planning on opening an art gallery with me. I should have seen this coming, should have prepared myself for it, but I wasn't ready to accept I was alone in this.

"I'm happy for you," I whisper, feeling my heart shatter a little at the thought of him not coming back soon. It's been him and me for two decades. Now it's just me...

Because it's you and me now, little demon.

Leonard's words echo in my head, and I forget how to breathe once more. I'm not alone. No matter the chaos between us, Leonard is going to be here for me because it's him and me now. The two people closest to me are going their own way, but he's been trying to creep into their places without me realizing. I don't mind being alone, I know I can be. When I was working four jobs, I went through it all by myself, hardly seeing Mamma and Graham, or anyone really. But I don't want to be alone, I don't think anyone does deep down, and Leonard is making sure I don't have to be.

It's you and me now, little demon.

Because I'm starting to become his person too. It's inevitable when you spend as much time together as we do. It's inevitable when you do make sense together. Leonard and I are a lot alike. We both hate most people. We like bickering with each other because it blows off some steam we don't get to release in any other way. We love dogs and a perfect evening for us consists of eating a home-cooked meal and watching a good movie.

"I'll come visit soon, luv, alright?" Graham says, pulling me back to reality.

"Alright," I reply, my eyes shifting to the screen in Benz's and my private room to see Leonard didn't get pole, Jonathan did.

"I love you," Graham adds, and I say it back before lowering my phone, watching the rest of the coverage, and waiting for Leonard.

Two hours later, he steps into the room, sinking into the armchair at the far corner from me. His head drops against the backrest, and he briefly opens his eyes to help Benz adjust on his lap. I notice he changed into his team shirt, and something about the white color makes him even more attractive than he usually is.

"Are you okay? Do you need an ice bucket poured over your head?" I tease, earning me a small chuckle from him. The sound lights my heart on fire. His eyes flutter open and soften at the sight of me walking toward him.

"Your first Qualifying with me, and I didn't even get pole. Sorry, little demon." Frustration plays in his voice, so I kneel down next to his chair, wrapping my arms around my knees and keeping eye contact.

"Qualifying doesn't matter. The race does. You know that. Everything can change tomorrow, and I know you will win. You're a World Champion. You're currently leading this season's championship. You've got this, Leonard," I say, and he watches me with both uncertainty and surprise.

"You've got faith in me, Starling?" I roll my eyes at his question.

"Of course not," I lie, and he laughs in response.

"Oh, good. For a second, I was worried there," he replies and runs a hand down the length of his face. "I'm sorry about yesterday."

"Me, too, Leonard. I'm not going to have sex with any of your friends." Or anyone else for that matter because I want—

"Good, because I did forbid it," he says with a smile, but I don't return it. "I'm kidding." He mouths 'no, I'm not' right after, and I slap my forehead with the palm of my hand. "Come on, I'm in desperate need of sleep to recharge for tomorrow and kick Jonathan's arse."

Leonard lifts Benz off his lap and steps in front of me, holding out his hand for me. I take it, allowing him to help me up and pull me right against his chest. He smells fresh, clean, and like that special scent only Leonard has. I lean a little forward to take in more of it, my eyes threatening to shut. His index finger moves under my chin, tilting my head upward so my gaze meets his.

"You wanna tell me what's wrong?" he asks softly, the pad of his thumb caressing my cheek.

"Graham isn't coming back home like he said he would," I blurt out, almost as if his touch is sending some kind of truth serum from my skin right into my bloodstream.

"I'm going to need a bit more information, little demon." His voice is so, so soft, it sends me into a trance. I tell him exactly what Graham told me, Leonard's eyes remaining on my face the entire time. "He doesn't want to open the gallery with you anymore?" I shake my head, and Leonard curses.

"I will do it by myself. I'm already working on the show, and it will be great. Don't worry, you didn't waste your time yesterday or by organizing for me to meet more investors during the rest of the season, I promise," I assure him. Frustration dances onto his features again.

"Chiara, I invested my time because I believe in you. Nothing I do for you will ever be a waste of my time," he says and cups my cheeks. "Nothing," he repeats to make sure I hear him.

"Okay," I whisper as his thumbs caress my cheeks.

"Come, let's go to our hotel. I'm going to make us some food," he says and takes Benz's leash. I follow behind him, trying not to think about how much I'm looking forward to a quiet evening with Leonard.

CHAPTER 23
Leonard

I won. Jonathan tried everything today, but my team's strategy was better. My tyre management was better. *I* was better, defending first place ever since he was too slow to keep it at the start. I won the French Grand Prix, and fuck me, it feels fantastic. The numb feeling I felt during the first few races is entirely gone now. Only excitement, joy, and pride remain as I drive my car one more lap around the track, waving to the thousands of fans standing behind the metal fences and cheering me on. As much as I love and will forever be grateful for them, I rush back to the pit box, driving to the first place sign. My whole team is waiting for me as I get out of the car, and I can't help the way my heart somersaults when I notice Chiara standing in the second row, clapping for me with a little smile on her lips.

I work my way out of the car, standing on the nose of it and punching the air while a thrill runs through me. *I have to get to her*, is all my mind focuses on, so I jump off the car and run toward the crowd of cheering Grenzenlos team members. Pretending she isn't the one I was rushing for, I hug everyone else first, then I turn to her, helmet still on as I lean forward and close the distance between us. Chiara gives me a brighter smile as she nudges the underside of my helmet with her hand to tilt my head up before placing it on top of my heart and giving it three taps. My Formula One racing number is three.

I rip off my glove to wrap my fingers around hers, smiling harder under my helmet than I have in months. Chiara has jump-started something inside of me, reignited my love for this sport, and if she wasn't already coming to the rest of the races this season, I would beg her to do so now.

The rest of the post-race procedures go by in a blissful blur. The champagne tastes better than it has in a while on the podium. The cheers sound sweeter in my ears. The reporter doing the interview doesn't piss me off as much anymore. All I can think about is how proud I've just made that woman standing with the rest of my team.

Once I've finished all of my interviews and fulfilled my responsibilities, I look for Benz and Chiara, wanting nothing more than to get back to the hotel and celebrate by finishing the movie we started yesterday. I spot them at a table, Chiara and Quinn playing UNO. My heart warms at the sight of them, but a hand stops me from moving in their direction. *Danger*, my head screams, and I spin around to see Jonathan touching me.

"What?" I bark, and he takes a step back. Good. I would love nothing more than for him to back up so far, he stumbles into the bathroom, preferably into a toilet where someone forgot to put the seat down and flush.

"Calm down, dude," he says, and I barely hold myself back from punching out his perfectly straight and white teeth. Jonathan Kent is a privileged little brat with blue eyes, blonde hair, pale skin, and a stick so far up his arse, I think I can see it when he speaks.

"What do you want?" I grind out, and he smiles at me.

"I just wanted to let you know that if Chiara ever threatens me again, or does anything to undermine my safety, I will have to report her. I feel very unsafe with her around, and I shouldn't have to worry about my well-being during a race weekend," he says, and I feel anger heating my face instantly.

"The fuck did you just say?" He's threatening me? Fine. Chiara is not the only one who can fight.

"Hey, alright, fellas, why don't we all just chill," Adrian's now familiar voice drones into my ears, and I relax a little.

"Mind your own business, Romana. This has nothing to do with you," Jonathan barks, but the eighteen-year-old Monegasque steps between us anyway, placing a careful hand on my rival's shoulder.

"Well, you see here, it is my business because you're upsetting my friend, and I don't fucking play around when it comes to my friends." Damn. I take a surprised step away, anger leaving me completely. "Now, why don't you go crawl back to whatever hole you came out of and leave Leonard and Chiara alone before I follow through on whatever alleged threat she made." I fucking like this kid. Not just for defending me, which already is a huge thing for me to happen in this sport, but he's protecting Starling.

"You should be careful what side you're picking here, Romana. There is no going back once you've made your choice," Jonathan warns, but Adrian starts laughing at him.

"*There is no going back once you've made your choice*," he imitates Jonathan before bursting into more laughter. "Get the fuck outta here, man. Nobody likes you," Adrian adds before placing his hand on my shoulder and leading me away from my rival. "What a fucking garbage bag." I fight back a chuckle. "Seriously, what the hell is his problem? He's just pissed because you're the better driver. Petty jerk." If Quinn wasn't already my best friend, Adrian sure as hell would be working his way up there.

"He's quite the jerk, yes," I agree while Adrian leads me to where Chiara and Quinn are. I notice worry resting on my little demon's face, so I wink at her to assure her everything is fine. I didn't expect a blush to settle on her cheeks in response though.

"What did Chiara threaten to do to him anyway?" I can trust him, I know I can, but I hesitate anyway. "Sorry, I meant, what didn't she threaten to do to him?" I shift my head in his direction to see a mischievous smile spreading across his face.

"She most certainly didn't threaten to break multiple of his bones using her years of competitive fighting skills," I reply, and his face lights up from humour.

"That woman is badass," he says, and I glance her way, finally smirking a bit.

"Yeah, she is," I whisper before hardening my features and giving Adrian my attention again. He's offering me a knowing look I'd very much like to slap off his face. Nothing's going on between Chiara and me. He doesn't have to grin at me like there is. "Anyway, thanks for helping me out, I appreciate it." Because if he hadn't shown up, I would have done something that would have cost me my career in Formula One, and I just found my passion for the sport again. I don't want to give it up.

"Anytime, mate. If you need an alibi, I got you too. I've never liked Jonathan. The first time we met, he told me not to bother trying to do well because he's working on getting one of his friends to take my seat next year." My eyes widen in response. "Yeah, I don't know why he's such a dick, but, oh well. I'm already in talks with my team to keep my seat for next year, so I'm not worried, but damn, he's unbearable," Adrian says before giving my shoulder a squeeze and nodding his head in Chiara's direction. "It's none of my business, but I wouldn't wait too long if I were you. If she wants a partner, she won't have to look long. Gorgeous, badass, and a heart bigger than most isn't a combination you will find again, at least not easily."

More like never again.

"Didn't you want to leave?" I ask as I cross my arms, and he starts grinning at me.

"Not a feelings-talking kind of person. I understand, but if you change your mind, I'm a great listener. Always here for you, mate," he adds before walking away and leaving me with a small smile.

"Leonard," Chiara's soft voice fills my ears, and I briefly close my eyes as if it could help me savour the sound, allow it to keep filling my ears.

"Yes, little demon?" I ask as I turn to her, but before I know what has hit me, her arms wrap around my body in an unsure hug.

"You did amazing today, congratulations," she says, and I place my cheek on the top of her head, my arms flinging around her to return the hug and let comfort run through me. I've never been a big fan of affection, but, for some reason I can't explain, touching Chiara in any way fulfils a part of me I've been keeping locked up for too long.

"I think that's the first compliment you've ever paid me," I reply, and she steps back, smacking my chest lightly.

"Untrue. I've been calling you an asshole for years," she says, and I give her an amused look.

"And that counts as a compliment?" A challenge lingers in her eyes, and, God, I just want to kiss her. I want to plant my lips on hers and feel the way they'd fit with mine as perfectly as I know they would.

"Of course it does." She doesn't offer me an explanation, but I don't ask either. I'm fighting every instinct in my body not to close the distance between us and finally give in to what I want the most. *Bloody hell, when did I become this attached to Chiara?*

"You're a puzzle, Starling," I point out, and she grins at me. She grins, and everything else vanishes. She grins, and I become the luckiest man on the planet for seeing it when she doesn't offer it to most people.

"Yes, a puzzle you're having a fantastic time trying to solve," she replies and steps out of the hug to walk back over to Quinn. My best friend wiggles her eyebrows at me, and I glare at her. A silent laughter shakes her shoulders, so I decide to ignore her.

"Chiara, would you like to go out for dinner or rather have me cook?" I ask because, apparently, I'm only on this planet to please this woman now. Good God, I'm so fucking gone for her, it isn't even funny anymore.

"Oh, I would love a home-cooked meal from Leonard," Quinn chimes in, standing up with Benz's leash in her hand.

Starling takes it from her and leans down to kiss my daughter on the top of her head. I don't like the warmth spreading through me every time Chiara reminds me just how much she loves Benz, nor do I enjoy the way my heart flutters when my dog proves she loves my little demon the same.

"Leonard?" Quinn asks, and I remember we were talking about dinner.

"Sure, I'll cook," I say absentmindedly, still trying to collect my thoughts.

"Great."

My best friend hooks her arm through mine, and it's the first time since we've become close that I want to step away from her, but only to get to Chiara.

"Great indeed. Leonard makes the best food," Starling blurts out before realizing she paid me another compliment. I'm about to point it out when she raises a violent finger at me. "Say it, and I will deny it with my fist." I shouldn't like her ability to wrestle me to the ground as easily as putting on her socks, but, here we are.

Back at the hotel, I start preparing dinner while Quinn and Chiara sit in the dining area close to me. My best friend has decided to make me look like the greatest guy on the planet by telling the woman I most certainly don't have feelings for all the "amazing" things I've done. Quinn shares that I was the only one who gave her a chance in Formula One, that I gave her the opportunity to be the first female performance coach in this sport. Then she goes on to tell Chiara all about how nice I've been, even if I seem like the distant, grumpy kind most people don't get along with.

I think about stopping Quinn every few minutes, but I pretend not to hear them as I work in the kitchen, trying to get dinner ready for two of the most important people in my life. My ears go against my wish to ignore their conversation as they pick up every little word. It also doesn't help that Starling keeps asking my best friend to share more and more stories about me. She *wants* to hear them, probably mesmerized by the fact that I can be a nice person despite the years of bickering and fighting I've had with her.

"Did Leonard ever tell you about the time he got locked into his private room for six hours? He had to pee in—" I interrupt Quinn right then by placing the food on the table Chiara laid a few minutes ago.

"We don't need to hear the end of that story," I say with a firm voice, but Quinn completely ignores me when Chiara urges her on with a slight head nod.

"In a bucket. He had to pee in the bucket. It was so funny," Quinn says, and Starling looks up at me to reveal her smile. Of course this fucking amuses her.

"Don't give me that," I say because a full-faced smile like that is rare from her and she mostly shows it when it's regarding something embarrassing that happened to me.

"What? I'm not allowed to smile at you?" she challenges as she fills Quinn's and my plate with food.

"Not when it's your way of laughing at me," I reply, and she shakes her head, filling her own plate now. Fucking hell, I could watch her for hours and not get tired, even when she is doing something so incredibly mundane. *Especially when she's doing something so incredibly mundane.*

"What other embarrassing stories do you have about Leonard?" Starling asks, turning to my best friend. I shoot Quinn a warning glare, but she ignores me as she looks at the ceiling, searching her brain for another tale to tell.

"I forgot to bring him a towel once at the track building, so he had to walk out of the bathroom with two small towels covering his privates. Let's just say, the cloth wasn't big enough to cover all of *him*, so he turned a lot of heads that day," Quinn says with a mischievous grin, but I'm not too mad about the story she chose. From the way Chiara's cheeks go a flaming red, I can only imagine the visuals going through her head. She's picturing me naked now, and I fucking love it.

"It was a private area, there weren't a lot of people. I think only one bloke saw me," I explain, and Chiara clears her throat, taking a sip of water right after. Her face is a bright red, and I can't help smiling at her a little. "You alright there, Starling?" I ask, and she gives me an irritated look.

"Of course. I'm fine. It's funny, that's all, picturing you running around butt-ass naked," she says with a laugh that sounds more fake than anything else. I continue to smile at her, only bothering her more.

"Disappointed you weren't there to see me?" I challenge, earning me an eye roll from her. Then, her emerald stones meet my gaze again.

"Relieved, actually," she spits, and I lean back in my chair, crossing my arms in front of my chest. Quinn lets out an awkward laugh beside me, so I shift my focus to her.

"I didn't notice how late it is. I should go get some sleep. We have an early flight tomorrow," she says, and I furrow my brows. She still has half a plate remaining.

"You don't have to—" I start, but she stands up and cuts me off.

"It seems like you two need to spend some quality time together. Thank you for the meal," she says and gives my shoulder a quick squeeze before flashing Chiara a warm smile. "Good night," my best friend says, and Starling and I both say it back at the same time.

I wait until the door is shut before facing the woman next to me and saying, "You made my best friend leave." She had the spoon halfway up to her mouth but lowered it as I spoke. Now she's scowling at me.

"I didn't make your best friend leave! I like Quinn. She's a hell of a lot less moody than you," Chiara replies, and I narrow my eyes at her.

"Moody? I'm not fucking moody." She snorts at that.

"Yeah, sure." She fills her mouth with more food, giving me the opportunity to keep talking.

"Are you still picturing me naked?" I ask, and she stops chewing for a moment. She stuffed her mouth so much, I have the opportunity to add more without her being able to make her usual witty comeback. "Because I understand if you are. Many people have done so over the years. It's a nice visual, huh? You should see it in real life. It's even better." Chiara shakes her head, swallowing her bite before pushing her plate away. Heat has moved into her cheeks, painting them a deep red.

"I have no desire to *ever* see you naked." *Liar.*

"Mhmm, I'm sure." I lean forward on the table, resting my jaw on my intertwined fingers. "Tell me something, little demon, if you've got no desire to see me naked, why do I have a feeling your panties are completely soaked from picturing me without clothes?" It should be impossible, but, somehow, her face turns an even darker shade of red.

"Because you're full of yourself?" she asks, but I smirk at her knowing full well she's turned on right now.

Her breathing is uneven, goosebumps have covered her skin, and her eyes are fixated on my lips. Not to mention, her pupils are wider than usual and her bottom lip keeps slipping between her teeth when she doesn't concentrate.

"Tell me you haven't at least thought about fucking me once, and I will let it go," I offer, so Chiara stands up, closing the distance between us until I'm leaning back in my chair and her face is mere centimetres from mine.

"I've thought about it many times, Leonard. I've thought about how unsatisfying it would be. I've thought about how terribly you would fuck me. There, does that make you happy to hear?" I tilt my head to the side a little, bringing my mouth upward and toward hers.

"One kiss," I say, and she cocks an eyebrow. I decide to elaborate. "One kiss and you will be mine forever. That's all it would take," I say to her, and she starts smiling at me.

"Correction. One kiss and you will be on your knees, begging me to be yours," she replies before grabbing her plate and walking into the kitchen to start cleaning up while I stare after her, speechless.

She's right. One kiss and I'll be addicted. One touch of our lips and I will be hers in every way I could give myself to her. One connection between our mouths and I will become undone by the taste of her.

There is no doubt in my mind, which is why I have to stay the fuck away from her.

CHAPTER 24
Chiara

It's been a month since my first race weekend with Leonard. We haven't spoken about our moments in France once, but we've spent so much time together, I wish I'd be sick of him by now. Instead, we made plans today to visit his parents together. We've been growing closer too, and, at the same time, we're keeping each other at arm's length. It doesn't matter that we do almost everything together, we're still bickering like we always are; nothing's changed in that department. Not that I'd want it to either. In our own way, Leonard and I work well with each other, and I wouldn't want it to be any different. Well, maybe only in one aspect. He's been walking around half-naked in the apartment, and I'm so fucking hot all the time, not even my vibrator has been satisfying me properly.

Having sex with him is still a horrible idea, even if I now know Graham wouldn't be upset with us. Leonard is still my boss for the rest of the season, and I can't risk it for one night of fun. That's all it would be because I know he'd fuck me well, better than anyone else I've ever been with, but it could never last longer than one night. It's all we'd need to get it out of our systems too.

I try my best to focus on my feet as the damp grass in the Ticks' backyard envelops them. The summer sun is warm on my skin, and I make sure my step isn't too fast for Rena. She asked me to walk around with her for a little, which I know is taking a lot out of her. Although her leg has been healing well, it causes her pain. She winces every few minutes, but when I ask her if she'd like to sit down, she shakes her head and holds tighter onto my arm.

"Have you found any investors yet?" Rena asks after a few more minutes of silence, and I stare at the ground with sadness bubbling up in my chest.

"I've met plenty, but they all pretend to be interested when they're not. I've contacted several of them afterward to discuss business, but they've all ignored me so far," I explain, trying to keep my voice even so it doesn't reveal how upset I am.

I've been unlucky in finding someone who believes in my ability to produce a breathtaking immersive art exhibit. I've already made half of one, but I'm not ready for anyone to see it yet. Leonard tried to get me to show him what I created, but I chickened out at the last second and pretended the software crashed. He didn't believe me, and I couldn't blame him either. I acted like he'd caught me doing something incriminating.

"It's alright, darling, you will find someone. Leonard is determined to help you. Actually, I'm pretty sure if he thought you'd let him, he'd invest in your idea himself," Rena says, and I stop walking, forcing her to take a brief break too.

"I'd never let him do that," I reply, and she raises her hands in the air, looking for my face. I step into her touch, causing her lips to pull into a soft smile.

"He knows. Why do you think he's trying so desperately to find someone else for you?" she asks, and I close my eyes at the motherly warmth radiating off her. "How are you doing otherwise, luv?" she asks, and I fight back the tears.

I miss Mamma a lot. Rena is like a second mother to me. I mean, how could she not be? She has been there for me since I was four years old, but I miss my favorite person in the world. I miss her smile and happiness. We speak on the phone almost every day, but I haven't seen her in over a month. There is so much going on right now, I'd love nothing more than to have her give me a hug and assure me everything will work out the way it's supposed to.

"I'm doing alright. Your son is keeping me very busy by bossing me around," I joke, and Rena lets out a small laugh.

"Bring me to my chair, please," she says, and we walk over to where her spot is at the table. I pull it out for her, my eyes meeting Leonard's at the opposite side of the table.

The way he looks at me nowadays is so different from the way he looked at me not even six months ago. There is warmth and longing in his gaze, which makes no sense to me. Yes, we've been growing closer and might not want to strangle each other anymore, but we're far from being two people who can't live without one another. At least that's what I keep telling myself. The worst part of it all is, I'm convinced my expression has softened in the same way his has.

"Thank you," Rena says, and I force my head back into the moment.

"You're welcome," I add as I settle in the seat next to Leonard's. Ellie is across from me with Stu on one side of her and Jack on the other.

"Is there a race this weekend?" Ellie asks after a while of the family chatting about random things like politics and the new Marvel movie coming out tomorrow.

"Not this weekend, Liz," Leonard replies, and I do my best not to look at him *again*. People are going to start assuming there is something going on between us if I'm incapable of keeping my eyes off him.

"Hey, what do you think about sending me a ticket to come to the race next weekend?" Graham says, and I stare at the laptop screen where Andrew is video-calling my best friend so he can have dinner with us even from far away.

"You want to come?" Leonard asks, a hint of excitement lacing his words. He misses his brother probably as much as I miss my best friend.

"Yeah! I want to see Chiara," Graham says and I lean into the frame of the camera to blow him a kiss. He catches it and places it on his lips, bringing a small smile to mine.

"So, you wouldn't come for me?" Leonard asks, but I see nothing but amusement in his gaze.

"Of course not. The race is an excuse to see my best friend," he replies, and I shake my head.

"You do realize I'd be paying for it, right?" the Formula One champion reminds his brother, and I allow my eyes to get stuck on his handsome face for several moments too long.

Eventually, he catches me staring, but instead of frowning at me, he lifts his thumb to my cheek and briefly swipes across it.

"Eyelash," he explains because my body went tense in response to feeling his touch after almost an entire month of him not coming anywhere close to me.

"Thanks," I mumble and turn in my chair, blocking out Graham's attempt to redeem himself with Leonard by saying how much he loves and misses him and so on.

Stu and Jack keep looking between me and the infuriatingly vague man next to me, surprise and disbelief on their faces. I'm not sure if they think something is going on between Leonard and me, but I don't have the patience to feed their curiosity at the moment. Then again, I never have the patience for shit like that. If it were up to me, I'd take whatever happened between the F1 driver and me a secret. I haven't shared it with Lulu, Mamma, or even Graham. I wouldn't even know where to start since nothing actually happened between us. Except...

He dropped on one knee to take off my shoes and kissed me in ways that made my head dizzy.

He danced with me, pressing my body so close to his, my clit begged for mercy.

Most importantly, however, he *keeps* holding me when I need someone to do so the most.

He brings me comfort and safety.

"What do you say, Chiara? Ready to meet my girlfriend?" Graham asks, and my head shoots up. Fuck, I completely missed the entire conversation.

"Of course," I reply, hoping it's the right thing to say.

Leonard gives me a confused look, but I decide to ignore the worry in his eyes. I hate how he sees right through me. For some reason, every change in my emotions, he detects. It's almost as if he is a Chiara-emotion-reader, especially when it comes to sensing how upset I am at any given moment.

"Awesome. I will see you two next weekend. And the rest of my family, I love you all and miss you. Bye," Graham says and hangs up a minute later, making sure everyone got to say their goodbye before he ended the call.

"Come for a walk with me," Leonard says and gets up, grabbing Benz's leash on his way to the front door. I hesitate for a few seconds because everyone at the table is staring at me, but I follow him out the door soon enough.

We stroll along the sidewalk in the neighborhood for a while, silence thickening the air around us. It's not uncomfortable, it never is, but the unspoken words between us put me on edge nevertheless. Benz is sniffing the grass patches we walk by until she finds a spot to do her business. I'm already on my way to pick it up when Leonard places a hand on my collarbone to stop me and do it himself.

"Are you not excited to see Graham?" he asks on our way back to the house, and I turn my head toward him, tilting it back since he's quite a bit taller than me. His brown eyes are already scanning my face.

"I am excited, I just have a lot on my mind," I admit because keeping such little things from Leonard seems silly at this point in our relationship, whatever the hell it would qualify as.

"Are you upset because of how strange things have been between us?" he goes on, stopping me by placing a careful hand on my shoulder.

"You think they've been weird? I have no idea what you're talking about. Do you mean the fact that we both want to fuck each other, but it isn't a good idea, so we keep pushing one another away?" My words surprise both of us. He wasn't expecting me to be so blunt, and I can't believe I admitted I want him to fuck me. I'd very much like to be hit by a plane right now. A bus isn't big enough for my embarrassment to be dulled.

"Chiara—" he starts, his expression soft as he reaches out to touch my cheek, but I catch his hand halfway to my face to stop him.

"Pretend I didn't say that," I blurt out and try to walk away, but he has my hand trapped in his and drags me against his chest.

"I'm sorry I've been weird. It isn't because we had intimate moments, which we both know would have led to spectacular sex. It's because you're my brother's best friend, my roommate, and my employee in a way. The situation we're in is complicated enough as is, and I don't want to make it worse," he says, but his eyes are fixated on my lips, and I can tell he wants to kiss me. I can feel it. Instead, he backs away, breaking skin contact entirely.

"Plus, we don't even like each other," I say, earning myself a little smile from him.

"Yeah, I can't stand being in the same room as you," he replies, and I cross my arms in front of my chest, fighting back a grin.

"Agreed. Your very presence is mind-shatteringly irritating," I say, and he takes a step forward again. I hold my breath when he scans my face with pure arrogance. Leonard knows I enjoy no one else's company as much as his at the moment.

"And yet, I have a feeling the meteorite is getting closer to hitting the Earth," he says, and I snort. *The day I fall in love with you, a meteorite will strike the Earth* is what I told him when he warned me not to fall for him.

"In your dreams, Champ," I reply and start walking back to the house.

I will move the Earth to prevent the meteorite from ever hitting it. There is no way I'll ever let myself catch feelings for Leonard fucking Tick. It's not happening. We may have been getting along better these past few months, but we're still Starling and Champ. We annoy the hell out of one another for no other reason than our clashing personalities. He's stubborn, I'm stubborn. He irritates me, I irritate him. He's bossy, I'm bossy. Two strong-headed people like us shouldn't even be able to have a single pleasant conversation, which is why I'm a bit perplexed by the way we've been getting along. It seemed like an impossibility only recently, and to this day, whenever we share a laugh, it feels surreal.

"We have to go shopping again," Leonard says as we step through the gate of his childhood home. I almost let out a groan in response.

"Why?" I ask, and he chuckles at my exasperation.

"Because there is an art event my friend invited us to when we get to Singapore on Wednesday. It's a masquerade ball type of event, so you need a dress and a mask," he says, and I raise both of my eyebrows.

"Fine, but only if you choose the dress." The words leave me without my brain processing them, so Leonard shoots me a mischievous look.

"You trust me to do that?" he asks, shoving his hands into his pockets as Benz runs into the backyard to rejoin the family.

"I did, but that evil smile on your lips scared me a little," I say and he lets out a small laugh before wrapping his arm around my shoulders and tugging me against his side.

"Don't worry, little demon, I will choose a dress worthy of you," he replies before we reach the table again where everybody is staring at the way Leonard and I are walking together. I ignore them as I settle back into my seat, doing my best to keep the heat out of my cheeks.

If I already can't wrap my head around Leonard's and my new relationship, how could I expect them to?

CHAPTER 25

Leonard

"Why the hell do you keep choosing dresses that sit way too tight on my chest and ass?" Chiara asks while I wait outside of the changing room for her. A small smile dances onto my lips as I stare at the white door she's standing behind.

"Did I? My bad," I reply, but I was well aware of what type of dresses I was choosing.

"Yeah, I'm sure it wasn't on purpose," she says with a snort, and I grin at her changing room.

"Let me see," I reply. A moment later, the doorknob rattles, but she doesn't open it. Instead, she lets out a nervous laugh and a pained sound.

"Nope. You can't see this. Half of my boobs are spilling out of this dress," she explains, but now I want to see her even more.

"Sweetheart, let me see," I say, making sure to pronounce every word firmly. She lets out a sigh before opening the white door I've been staring at for too long.

My breath catches in my throat. My heart explodes at the sight of her. My entire being inches toward her because she's the flame, and I'm merely a moth, drawn to her even though she's dangerous for me. It isn't her breasts either, at least not primarily, it's everything about her appearance. The way the blue satin clings to her curves and her short brown hair frames the sides of her face. Her green eyes and the way they sparkle with uncertainty. Her full, pouty lips I'm having an impossible time trying not to devour with my own. I can't quite remember why the hell I'm not supposed to kiss her anyway. We both want me to, I know that now since she told me she wanted me to fuck her, and it's been driving me wild since.

"Would you stop staring at me and say something?" she says with frustration, and I swallow hard.

"I'm trying," I reply because I really am. I'm trying my bloody hardest to form words, but she's too beautiful for any of them to come out. I clear my throat and look away to ease a bit of the tension inside of my chest. "If you're not comfortable in this dress, we will find you another," I assure her, my traitorous eyes shifting back to her to make thinking an impossible task. The uncertainty I saw in her eyes before only intensifies.

"I'm not uncomfortable, but this is extravagant and *a lot*. I'm usually a quieter type of person," she says, and I nod at her words.

With most people, she doesn't show who she really is. She doesn't like them enough to be herself around, but I personally don't mind it one bit because she's always Chiara with me. She's my little demon, my Starling, but she's just Chiara too. A woman with a heart so big, I'm still getting used to the possibility of owning even a slight piece of it. Hell, if she only ever gives me a hair's width of it, I'll start considering myself the luckiest man in the world.

"But you also have a fire inside of you so large, you wear this dress like no one else ever could," I reply, and she looks up at me, then at the mirror on the right side of the changing rooms.

She stands before it, and I can't help but follow just to see myself standing with her. We look amazing together. I'm not an oblivious man. I know I'm attractive. I've been asked to model for many brands since I became a Formula One driver. It's the reason why I swallow hard at the sight of her. Chiara looks like a queen on her way to take the throne, and I look like her prince in my dress shirt and matching blue pants. I've never been happier about wearing fancy clothing to go shopping.

"Could you undo the zipper before I go back into the changing room?" Chiara asks after we've been staring at each other in the mirror for several minutes.

"Okay," I mumble because the thought of undressing her is making my cock twitch unbearably.

Starling turns her back to me, and I fumble with the zipper, trying my best to keep my hands from shaking. It takes me a few moments to get control of my fingers again before I slide down the metal and expose her bare back to me. She isn't wearing a bra, which doesn't help my body calm down either. If anything, knowing she's going to be almost naked in the changing room only brings me closer to her until my chest is flush against her back.

"What are you doing?" she whispers, and I run my fingers up and down her arms. My heart is racing harder than it does during race weekends.

"I'm trying to memorize the way you fit against me," I blurt out, and she tenses in response.

"I don't think this is the most efficient way to do that. There are still too many clothes in the way." God, this woman is testing my restraint.

"You want me to fuck you in the changing room, little demon? Is that why you tempt me?" I ask, but she takes a step back, pressing her arse right into my hard cock.

"Yes," she admits shamelessly, and I let out a string of curses. I press myself further into her until I hear a little moan slip past her lips. *Stop, do not go further,* my brain screams at me, but I have no control over it while Chiara rubs herself against me. I lead her back to the changing room when a voice stops me from going in with her.

"Excuse me, sir. I found the dress you were asking for." The sales associate from earlier steps toward me and hands me the other blue dress I wanted Chiara to try on.

"Starling, you want to try another dress?" I ask, and she peaks her head through a slight crack of her changing room door.

"Gimme," she says in an uncharacteristically silly and sweet voice, making a surprised chuckle escape me. I hand her the dress, which she snatches out of my grasp with a grin, and then locks the changing room door again.

The sales associate remains by my side, and I realise Lilah must have told him to stay here in case I needed anything else. The store is rather busy today, couples and groups of people storming in at once. I'm pissed to be receiving a babysitter, but I know my friend means it for the best. Maybe she also wants to make sure Chiara and I don't actually fool around in one of her changing rooms, but I shake away the thought as soon as it crosses my mind. No one thinks there is something going on between Chiara and me. Because there isn't. There shouldn't be. I won't remind myself of all the reasons again, but they're there, and I can't deny them. She's just confusing me with that dirty mouth, beautiful face, sexy body, and breathtaking personality. That's all it is.

"Ummm, Leonard?" she asks, and my spine goes rigid as I straighten out my back.

"Yes, Starling?" There is a shuffling noise inside her changing room before she answers.

"The zipper is stuck. I can't get out of the dress," she says, panic laced in her voice. It sends me on high alert. The sales associate next to me offers his help, but I'm not letting anyone else see her bare back.

"I'll help," I call back, knocking a little on the changing room door.

I should go search for Lilah. She's respectful and professional, and I know she wouldn't look anywhere near Chiara's body because she's happily married, but I don't want her to help. I want to be the one.

"Okay, but don't laugh," she says before opening the door and letting me in.

"Why would I laugh?" Chiara points at the zipper at the front, and I furrow my brows at her. "Isn't that supposed to be in the—" She cuts me off.

"Yeah, it's supposed to be the other way around, but I obviously wasn't paying attention, alright?" she barks at me, and I bite down on my bottom lip to keep from smiling. Sometimes she can be really adorable.

"If it's in the front, why do you need my help?" I ask, and Chiara lets out a strained breath.

"I can't get it to unzip," she mumbles, making it impossible for me not to grin down at her a little. "I said don't laugh," she repeats and smacks my arm.

"I'm not laughing!" I defend, but we both know a grin comes pretty close to a figurative laugh for me.

"Just help me. This is embarrassing enough as is without you laughing at me." A blush settles on her cheeks, and I feel every part of my amusement vanish. I don't want her to be embarrassed around me, ever. Maybe a few months ago I would have made a stupid comment, but not at this point.

"It's alright, Starling, we'll get you out of this predicament," I say and lift my hands to the zipper right at her cleavage. I hesitate for a moment, sucking in a silent breath. "May I?" Chiara gives me a nod, so I wrap my fingers around the metal once more and start tugging on it.

It doesn't budge.

"Maybe something's stuck, like part of the fabric," she says, but I've been staring at it for the past minute to spot anything like that, and there is nothing.

"It isn't stuck, but it won't slide down either," I reply, and she frowns at me.

"There has to be something there!" she says, a bit of desperation lacing her words. She wants to get this dress off without it breaking, I know her, but if everything else fails, I will tear it off her and pay for it. Without hesitation.

"There isn't, Chiara," I reply, still tugging.

"Maybe you need glasses because nothing else makes sense," she fires back, and I barely keep from rolling my eyes at her. We're on the brink of an argument I don't want to have while she's vulnerable in front of me.

"You're so stubborn. Why can't you believe me when I say there is nothing—"

I'm cut off by the zipper slipping all the way down. Surprised, I let go of the fabric, causing it to pool at her feet and leave her in only black lace panties. Her breasts are so stunning, one a little bigger than the other, but both perfect, it knocks the air out of me. When I realise I'm ogling her naked body, I screw my eyes shut and spin around.

"Sorry," I manage to croak out, my body overheating from desire and arousal. My cock is begging me to turn back around to her, but, luckily, my head is doing all the thinking.

"This is not how I pictured you seeing me naked for the first time," she says with a little laugh I can tell she doesn't mean. I drop my forehead against the door and try to calm my breathing.

"I didn't see anything," I lie in an attempt to make her feel better. My heart is thumping against my ribcage with so much force, I'm pretty sure I can hear my ribs moaning in complaint.

"Liar," she says, and I remember how well she can see through me.

"I didn't see much," I say to try and recover, but when her hands slip onto my shoulder blades, I lose all of my self-control. I spin around, my hands moving down her body until they cup her arse and lift her into the air. Her back hits the door I've become a massive fan of.

"Leonard," she moans as I grind my hips into her, a smile dancing onto her lips. My eyes drop to her beautiful breasts before shifting back to her lips.

"Tell me not to kiss you," I beg because my muscles burn from holding back. Her head drops against the door behind her as her smile becomes mischievous.

"Kiss me," she says instead, rolling her hips a little to rub herself against my hard cock. I lick my lips, my fingers digging into her arse. Having Chiara almost completely naked in my hands is a fantasy I've had for too long, and fuck, it's even better in reality.

I'm about to give in when I hear a loud gasp.

"Not in my changing room! Out, Leonard, before I drag you out by your dick," Lilah says, and I drop Chiara back onto her feet, the red colour painting her cheeks so wonderful, I can't help but press a kiss to it. My lips catch fire from the heat of her skin, but I leave her in the changing room, still almost naked, and face my friend.

"Calm down. I was only helping Chiara with her zipper," I explain, but Lilah's eyes drop to my crotch before they meet my gaze again.

"Yeah, sure," she spits back, and I narrow my eyes at her. "Anywhere but my changing rooms or I will block your number for the rest of eternity," Lilah warns, and I raise my arms in mock surrender for the briefest moment, then I cross them over my chest.

Chiara steps out of the changing room five minutes later, two dresses in her hand. She asks me which of these I prefer, so I take them both and walk toward the register. We line up because the store remains crowded, and I do my best not to think about our moment in the changing room. I saw her almost completely without clothes, had her under the control of my touch, even if it was only briefly. My eyes got a glimpse of the perfect curves of her tits, the dips of her hips, and the birthmark stretching across her left hip bone. It brought out something I'd never felt before.

I felt insatiable.

One look wasn't enough. I need more. I need to study her not only by staring at her body but by tracing it with my fingertips. The desire to find all of the spots on her that cause her eyes to roll into the back of her head is stronger than anything I've ever experienced before. *You can't have her*, I remind myself, so I keep all of these thoughts to myself.

Chiara and I don't speak about what happened, neither of us willing to let a moment of weakness destroy what we've been building for months. I don't know if we're friends, but whatever we are, we get to have intimate moments like the one in the changing room, right? It's completely normal for two roommates to know what the other looks like naked. It's inevitable, isn't it?

At least that's what I keep telling myself in an attempt to keep my lips from crashing against Chiara's and satisfying every need, curiosity, and desire I have for her.

CHAPTER 26
Chiara

"I've missed you so much," Graham says as soon as he wraps his arms around me. Warmth and pain and nostalgia all combine with happiness as I hug my best friend. *He's really here.*

"I've missed you too."

He releases me before stepping toward his brother and flinging his arms around him in a big hug. My eyes shift to Irena, Graham's girlfriend. She has a lightly tanned skin tone, hazel eyes, and an adorable smile.

"Hi, it's nice to meet you, Irena. I'm Chiara," I say and hold out my hand, doing my best to soften my features at her.

"Wow, you're even more beautiful than the pictures Graham showed me," she blurts out and shakes my hand. I can tell she wants to hug me instead, but I'm not the type of person to easily show affection to people I don't know.

"So are you," I reply, and her cheeks flush a bright red.

Her eyes scan my face for several seconds longer, and then she moves over to greet Leonard and thank him for buying her a plane ticket and bringing her here. The Formula One driver's features are hardened into a brooding look. My mind briefly drifts to the fact that he's been laughing and smiling with me for months now, and I'm the only person to see him so loose all the time.

His eyes catch mine, and I give him half a smile. It brings a warmth into his gaze, one only directed at me. Leonard is many things. A pain in the ass. A dick. Irritating as fuck. But he's also slowly becoming my favorite per—Nope. I can't even think it without shuddering.

I also can't think about how handsome he looks with his hair cut shorter at the sides and longer at the top. He had it done three days ago, and I've already had a thousand naughty thoughts about tugging on his curls while he pleasures me in every possible capacity.

I can't keep my eyes from drifting to him whenever they want to get their fill.

"Should we go out for dinner?" Graham says, but Leonard places a hand on his brother's shoulder, struggling to take his brown eyes off me. I smile even harder at the way he tilts his head first, keeping his gaze on me until he *has to* shift it to Graham.

"Chiara and I have an event to attend today. You know, for the art gallery you have no more interest in owning with her," Leonard replies, and I realize for the first time there is tension between the two of them.

"Leonard, this is none of your business. Leave it alone already," Graham replies while I do my best to keep my entire body from tensing to the point of breaking.

Already. This isn't the first time Leonard has said something, which only makes me angrier. This isn't something he's allowed to be upset over. It isn't even something I get to be angry about. Graham fell in love, and I'm happy for him. Plans change, it happens. Leonard shouldn't make his brother and my best friend feel bad about it.

"We should go to our room and get ready," I say to Leonard and cock my head in the direction of the door. We're in Graham's and Irena's room.

"Wait. You two are sharing a room?" my best friend asks with surprise on his face. Leonard glares at him in response.

"We have the penthouse suite, so we have separate rooms," he says in a slow and low tone, almost like he's warning Graham not to say anything else.

They're glaring at each other, and I'm losing my patience. I take three steps toward Leonard, grab his hand in mine, and pull him out of the room. He goes willingly, surprising me, but not enough to distract me from how angry I am with him. There is a lot I'm grateful for that he's done for me, but the second he started meddling in my relationship with my best friend, he brought me right back to the irritation I've felt for him for most of my life.

We walk down the hallway, take the elevator up in silence, and then I move toward our penthouse suite, unlocking the door to meet an excited Benz. She's wagging her tail and running around, jumping at Leonard's legs when he steps through the door. I'm about to start screaming at the Brit when he backs me against the wall, his face so close to mine, I can taste the mint from his gum on my tongue.

"I don't want to hear it," he says, his fingers wrapping around my wrists and pinning them to the wall. I'm so stunned, I let him do it, even though we both know I could easily wrestle him to the ground.

"You're going to hear it," I finally manage to croak out, his eyes fixated on my lips. He shakes his head and tightens his hold on me before stepping even closer, his chest flush against mine now.

"I don't want to." His nose nudges my jaw, causing my knees to go weak.

"I don't care," I say and swallow hard. Leonard lets out a groan, inhaling deeply when his nose brushes my neck.

"I don't want to fight with you right now," he replies. "Not when we're supposed to have a nice evening at the event."

"Then you shouldn't have gotten involved in *my* business with *my* best friend," I remind him, hating my body for the way it responds to his proximity. My clit is unbearably swollen, my skin is on fire, and my fingers tingle from the need to touch him.

"He's *my* brother, and he's being selfish. Someone had to tell him, especially because he's hurting you. No one gets to hurt you, Starling, not under my watch." He brings his legs and groin against me too, and I melt right into him, arching my back off the wall to have my breasts even more against him. Leonard groans in response.

"You always do this, Leonard. You get close to me, touch me in ways we're not supposed to but both want you to, and then you leave me worked up with no release. I won't have it again, so either fuck me against this wall right now, or leave me alone," I suggest, and he tightens his hold on my hands even further.

It doesn't hurt, but it turns me on beyond reason. I'm so aroused, I feel it drenching my panties. I like how rough he is with me, that he knows I need a firm grip. I like it so much, it drives me wild he hasn't ripped off my clothes yet.

"I can't leave you alone, Chiara. Don't you see? I try my hardest every time I'm in your presence, but you have a pull on me, little demon. You keep drawing me in, and I can't stop myself from touching you when I know you want me to," he says, placing my hands on his neck and lifting his to the sides of my body. "But I can't bring myself to give us what we both crave because I know I shouldn't. God, why shouldn't I?" he asks and leans forward, his mouth connecting with my neck. I moan in response. "Tell me to stop," he begs, but he pulls on my skin, his teeth grazing it, and more sounds of pleasure leave me.

"I don't want to, even though I'm mad at you," I remind both of us when he keeps nibbling on my soft spot.

"When aren't you mad at me?" he challenges, and I almost laugh. *Touché.*

"You can't get involved in my business, Leonard." As much as I'm enjoying the way he's touching me, I can't let him confuse my thoughts.

"You are my business, Chiara. I'm not sorry I will put your happiness before the rest of the world." Holy fucking shit. "Bloody hell. You taste like—" He cuts off and steps away, his eyes filling with panic. My head goes fuzzy at the loss of contact, my skin freezing at the loss of warmth. "We have to leave soon," Leonard adds before storming away and leaving me to bend over to catch my breath.

He's wearing an all-black suit and a blue mask to match my dress. I'm wearing all blue, but the mask he chose for me is black to match his outfit. We look like a couple, especially because he offered me his arm the second I stepped out of the car he booked, and I took it without hesitating. It doesn't matter how annoyed I am with him for the way he left things earlier. Now is not the time to cause a scene. We have people to woo and get interested in my vision for an immersive art gallery.

We reach the entrance, except there is a blue carpet and backdrop stretched across the side of the building where everyone is lining up. Leonard moves to the back of the line, my hand starting to shake as I scan the row of photographers. Alright. This is fine. No one is going to care that Leonard Tick, Formula One World Champion, is seen with a no-name. Except everyone is. They will call me his girlfriend. They will think we're dating. They will make up all sorts of stories because that is how imaginative and toxic the media is.

"Why are you nervous?" Leonard asks after we've lined up and my hand started shaking on his arm.

"People are going to assume we're dating if we walk across that carpet," I remind him, but he gives me an amused smile.

"You don't want people to assume we're dating?" I furrow my brows at him, even though it's significantly harder with the mask covering my face. *The masks!*

"Never mind. People won't be able to identify me. You, maybe, but that's your problem," I say, and he bites down on his bottom lip in response.

"I know you don't have social media because your phone is ancient and barely works, but people are already speaking about us. You've been photographed with me hundreds of times, little demon. Everyone already thinks we're dating." What the fuck?

"And you didn't think to mention that to me?" I ask in such a loud voice, he cups my cheeks and places his thumb on my bottom lip. I calm in an instant.

"Why does it matter?" he asks, removing his finger after he's made sure I won't cause a scene again. I wouldn't either way. This is an important event, not only for me but for Luna, the woman who is hosting it.

"I don't want anyone to think we're dating," I blurt out, and Leonard's face hardens into an angry scowl, his hands dropping from my face.

"I'm sorry that's such a horrible assumption for people to make," he spits back and shifts his body so he's next to me.

"Don't pretend like it doesn't bother you. You don't even like me," I say before I can stop myself. His whole body tenses beside me.

"You're absolutely right. I don't like you, I never have," he replies, sending a stinging pain through me. That hurts more than I would like to admit, than it would have a year ago. "I dislike you so much, I want to spend every single second of the day with you." *Wait, what?*

"Leonard, what are you saying?" At this point, I'm more confused than anything else.

"I'm saying you need to start listening when I tell you how I feel so you don't say dumb shit like that." God, he's such a pain in the ass.

"Is it impossible for you to not be a dick for once?" I ask, and he turns his head to me at the same moment I face him.

"Is it impossible for you to not be so irritating all the time?" he rebuttals, and I let my mouth fall open ever so slightly.

"At least I'm not the one who keeps saying confusing shit to you the whole time and touching you like I can't get enough of you!"

"That's because I can't get enough!" My mouth falls shut again, and he groans quietly beside me.

"Next," someone beside us says, and Leonard takes my hand, links it through his arm, and guides me onto the blue carpet.

His arm snakes around my waist as we stop for some photos, neither one of us smiling at the cameras. It's who we are, and, frankly, my head is swimming with his words. If it weren't so impossible for me to believe he could ever like me in the way he keeps suggesting, maybe it would be easy to swallow his words. Instead, my rational head is fighting with... with my heart, I think, and they're not agreeing in the slightest at the moment.

Leonard merely pulls me along the carpet, letting the cameras snap more and more pictures. The warmth of his hand on my left hip is heaven and calming, which doesn't help my head as it tries to deny the possibility of Leonard *liking* me.

We keep walking until we're off the carpet and on our way inside. It's completely dark, the only light coming from the projectors as they display Claude Monet's art. One wall shows his *Impression, Sunset* painting, another his *Lithograph of Landscape: the Parc Monceau*. More of his art is everywhere combined with a slow, soothing melody as the images melt into one another, change into something else completely, only to revert back to the first image. People are speaking quietly, and I take in everything with awe filling my chest. This is absolutely beautiful. It's what I envision my gallery to look like, not the aggressive show and music combination I had to watch every day at my old job.

"Here," Leonard says as he hands me a glass of champagne I take greedily. I take several sips, easing the dull ache inside my head from overthinking his words.

"Luna did a wonderful job. This is beautiful," I mumble to myself, but when I catch Leonard's gaze stuck on me as he agrees, I feel heat rush into my cheeks.

I let my eyes travel around the room, trying to study everyone's elegant outfits and masks when Luna, a stunning dark-skinned woman with braided hair, a green dress, and a silver mask greets Leonard. Next to her is a tall, muscular man with tanned skin, dressed in a velvet green suit to match Luna. His blue eyes are bright under his black mask, and his smile is specifically directed at me.

"Pleasure to meet you," the man says with a thick Italian accent and offers me his hand.

"*Sei italiano?*" I ask, and his face lights up even more.

I'm not quite sure what happens after, but we start talking, and we don't stop for an hour. Turns out, Dino and I have a lot in common, except that he's a billionaire and I'm far from it. He likes art because it captures a unique side of beauty that can't be found anywhere else. He loves immersive shows because it brings that very art to life, just like me. It's been a long time since I got to speak as much Italian as I'm able to with him, and it makes me genuinely content.

Dino shares that he invested in Luna's art gallery when she was starting out a few years ago, so I tell him about my dream. He listens closely, seeming to enjoy our conversation as much as I am. We end up standing at one of the high tables in the corner of the room while Leonard speaks to Luna. Our gazes meet eventually, but I can tell he's irritated with me. I don't think it's because I'm speaking to Dino, but I do think it's because I'm doing so without him by my side. I don't mean to upset him, but, at the same time, I also glare at him for being such an asshole and confusing my head.

"Would you like for him to join us?" Dino asks after a while of Leonard and me continuing our staring contest.

"What?" I say so stunned, I turn my head to him. He gives me a disappointed smile.

"Leonard's your boyfriend, no?" he replies, and I can't help myself. Maybe it's the champagne or the ridiculous words that just fell off his lips, but I let out a small snort turning into a fit of laughter.

"He most certainly is not," I reply in Italian, causing Dino's handsome features to brighten up again.

"Then you might be interested in what I've been meaning to do since you walked into the room," he says and steps toward me, his hand hovering over my arm as he waits for permission to touch me. I cock a challenging eyebrow at him as I step closer too, fighting my heart as it tries to force me backward.

"And what might that be?" I ask, but he leans down, bringing his lips closer to mine.

"Kiss you," he says, and I step on my tiptoes, closing the distance without thinking.

This is wrong. I know it is. Leonard's gaze is burning my skin, but I had to try something to get him out of my head. Unfortunately, the kiss, as amazing as it is, only makes me feel guilty. I step away five seconds after I kissed Dino, bringing my fingers to my lips in an attempt to keep myself from screaming at the top of my lungs because of my frustration. I have no reason to feel guilty. Leonard has pushed me away more times than I can keep count. He insinuates that he has feelings for me, but someone who does wouldn't keep pulling away every single time I'm under his control. I'm getting tired of his hot and cold with me, and I have every right to fuck another person if that is what I wanted. Except it's not. I don't want anyone else's hands on me, and it's driving me fucking wild.

"Chiara?" Leonard's voice fills my ears, and I realize I've been standing in the same spot, unresponsive to Dino's words, for several minutes. "What happened, sweetheart?" he asks, his hands moving to my arms to grab my attention. I look up at him, tears in my eyes. I have no idea where they came from, but I fight them back. Not quickly enough for Leonard to miss them. "The fuck did you do to her?" he barks at Dino, who takes a step back with his hands raised in the air.

"Nothing," he assures the angry man who is still holding onto me. A groan escapes Leonard's throat.

"What did he do? Tell me, baby, please," he begs, but I rip my arms free of his grasp and run outside and down the sidewalk into an alley where I rip my mask off and take a deep breath.

I can't kiss other people anymore? What the fuck kind of punishment is that? And what am I being punished for?

"Chiara de Luca, you can't run away like that. You had me worried sick," Leonard says when he reaches me, standing right in front of me with his arms crossed in front of his chest. Singapore has one of the warmest climates I've ever been in, but Leonard doesn't seem bothered by the heat. Me, on the other hand, I'm sweating profusely now.

"Stop worrying about me. Stop pretending you care. Just stop it, Leonard. I can't—I can't deal with it anymore. You're fucking with my head on purpose, and I'm done with it. So, please, stop," I say, but as soon as I'm done with my rant, I sneeze. My head starts to pound right after.

"*Gesundheit,*" Leonard says, disregarding my words. It's my turn to groan then.

"Can we just go back to the hotel?" I ask after another sneeze and another annoying *Gesundheit* from him.

"Chiara—" he starts, but I cut him off.

"I don't want to hear it," I say and walk past him.

He doesn't try to hold onto me, doesn't try to tell me whatever is weighing on his chest. Leonard lets me walk by him, and I hate myself for finding that even more frustrating than anything else between us.

CHAPTER 27

Leonard

C hiara has been sick for the past two days. She thinks she's hiding it well from me, but I've noticed. I've been subtly trying to take some load off her shoulders by checking in on her more and taking Benz for walks, but she's so goddamn stubborn, she's not letting me do anything. She's sneezing and coughing when she thinks no one's around, her energy levels have dropped significantly, and she keeps at least four metres distance from me at all times, probably so I don't catch whatever she has. I'm getting tired of it. Because of our fight and because I was a little pissed she kissed Dino, I've kept my distance the past few days. No more. Chiara needs help, and her stubborn arse will get it from me, whether she wants it or not.

Graham and Irena had to fly back to New York yesterday, but my brother didn't even notice his best friend getting sicker and sicker. He's in his honeymoon phase with his girlfriend, something I'm happy he's experiencing, but, at the same time, I wish he'd open his eyes and see Chiara needs and misses him. She doesn't say anything because of her ginormous heart and the love she holds for Graham, but I noticed the way she misses him, even when he was in the same room as her. I'll have to speak to him about his behaviour. Chiara will be pissed, but I hate seeing her hurting, no matter what kind of pain it is.

After my free practice sessions and a much-needed shower, I make my way toward the private room where Benz and Chiara are. I open the door and a second later, my

213

heart drops into my stomach. Starling is collapsed on the ground with a whining Benz sitting in front of her, nudging her with her nose. Fuck. Shit. Fuck.

"Chiara? Sweetheart?" I say as I kneel behind her, pressing my hand to her forehead. She's burning up. I let out a string of curses when she starts shivering and crying out with her eyes closed. "You're okay. You're going to be okay," I say to convince myself more than her because panic is flooding my chest. I call Quinn, telling her to contact the team doctor as soon as possible and get me some blankets.

"Leonard," Chiara says with a weak voice, and I lift her off the floor to get her to the small couch in the corner of the room.

"It's alright, baby. I'm going to help you feel better," I assure her, and she lets out a grunt.

"Stop calling me 'baby'. I'm not your baby," she complains, and I want to shake her for trying to fight with me right now when she needs to preserve her energy. I wipe the brown hair off her face, watching her eyes flutter a little open.

"Yes, you are, and you're in pain. Stop fighting my help, little demon."

A minute later, Bernie, the team doctor, steps into the room with his backpack on and worry all over his face. He's a kind man, caring and honest, but I need him to pick up the pace and figure out how bad her fever is. The short man places a thermometer under Chiara's tongue, the back of his hand pressing against her forehead.

"We need to help her break the fever. It's too high," Bernie says and turns to me. "Fill the tub you use for ice baths with lukewarm water. I will give her some ibuprofen, but we have to get it down now." Fuck, fuck, fuck.

Quinn and I rush around, grabbing the tub I used only this morning for my ice bath and filling it with lukewarm water, as instructed. My heart is pounding in my chest and my hands are shaking to the point where my best friend has to place hers over mine. Quinn flashes me a comforting smile, but I can tell she's worried too.

Chiara and my best friend have been growing closer since I first started taking her to my races almost two months ago.

"I've got this. Go get Chiara," she says, and I rush back upstairs where Starling is still shivering on the couch.

"Ready," I tell Bernie, and he steps out of the way to allow me to pick her up.

Chiara mumbles something I don't understand in my arms, but I'm too busy focusing on not missing any steps to ask her what she said. The tub is filled by the time I get back, so I place Chiara on her feet while Quinn holds her up. My hands move to cup her hot, burning cheeks, her green eyes fluttering open at my touch.

"I need to take off your shirt and shorts, alright? I will leave your underwear on, I promise," I assure her, and she nods along to my words.

"Leonard, I'm scared," she admits, tears slipping down her cheeks. Goddamn it.

"It's okay, I'm here. I will get in with you, okay?"

She nods again, and I start undressing myself first before taking off her clothes. It takes me about thirty seconds until we're standing in front of the tub. I get in first, Quinn still holding onto Chiara's arms. Starling's eyes are barely open, but she lets me lift her into the tub where we sink into a lying position. I bring my wet palm to her forehead, and she lets out a relieved moan in response.

"Better?" I ask, and her head falls backward against my shoulder.

"You have to get away from me, Leonard. You can't get sick before tomorrow and Sunday," she says, but I dip my hands into the water and place them on her stomach as my mouth attaches to her temple. Her skin is still burning, so I bring my palm back to her forehead.

"You need to rest, you infuriating woman, and I'm not going anywhere. Now, shut up and save your energy." She lets out a groan before doing the opposite of what I just told her she needed to do.

"If you get sick and miss the race, you will be pissed at me for years, and I don't have the patience to deal with that," she says. I hate the way her voice cracks and trembles from being sick and exhausted.

"I'm pissed at you most of the time anyway, might as well give me another reason to be," I tease, but she lets out a sigh and attempts to get out of the tub. I hold her against my chest, chuckling at her reaction. "Chiara, please, stay put. We have to make sure your fever goes down," I remind her, and she sinks back against me.

"You're such a dick sometimes," she complains, but her shivers have slowed now, which is a good sign. "But I guess it makes sense. You're overcompensating," she teases, and I chuckle once again.

"Yup, I'm overcompensating, you've finally figured it out," I reply and bring my fingers to the back of her neck, her skin on fire there too. I curse under my breath. "You should have been honest about how you're feeling. This is unacceptable, Chiara. We could have gotten you antibiotics days ago, it didn't have to get to this," I say with so much anger dripping from my words, it surprises her a little.

"You sound almost like you care," she replies, sending a wave of frustration through me.

"Of course I bloody care, Chiara! Do not tell me you are so blinded by our past that you cannot see what's happening in our present."

You're becoming my favourite person in the world. You're becoming the breath in my lungs, the beat of my heart, the essence of my existence. You're becoming the first woman I've ever felt this way about, and I don't have the strength to keep pushing you away anymore.

"And what the hell is happening in our present, huh?" she challenges, but we're interrupted by Bernie approaching us.

"I need to take your temperature again," he says to Chiara, who gives him a small nod. He places the thermometer under her tongue, but I keep her burning body against mine, cupping water into my hands and emptying them over her shoulders and neck. She melts against my chest.

The thermometer starts beeping once it's done measuring her temperature, and Bernie informs us it has already dropped a little. He also hands me a bottle of water and tells me to make sure she drinks it. Then, he gives me a rundown of the antibiotics Chiara has to take for the next week and when I'm supposed to give her more ibuprofen. Apparently, she got herself sick with the flu. I shake my head and let out a frustrated sigh. I understand that she doesn't want to admit she's not feeling well because it would make her seem vulnerable. I get it, but keeping her mouth shut about how horrible she was feeling is by far one of the worst things she could have done.

"This is why you shouldn't kiss random people, Chiara," I blurt out after a moment of silence between us. She lets out a strangled laugh.

"You think Dino made me sick?" The image of them kissing reappears in my head, sending a wave of heat and anger through me.

"Yes," I grind out, and she tilts her head so her green eyes meet my brown ones.

"Should have kissed me first instead of walking away then," she manages to get out before exhaustion forces her to collapse into me and her eyes to flutter shut.

We stay in the tub for a while longer. I measure her temperature right before I decide it's dropped enough to get out and dry us off. Chiara holds onto me as I run the towel over her body. Her panties and bra are soaked, but I don't think she's comfortable with me helping her out of them, so I don't ask if she wants me to remove them. I wrap the towel around her once I'm done, leading her back to the private room where Quinn put the fresh clothes I asked for earlier. It's time Starling and I got back to the hotel. She needs to rest, and I need to know she's comfortable in a bed.

"I'm sorry," she says when I sit her down on the couch and make my way over to the pile of clothes.

"Sorry for what, little demon?" I ask, hating the way her voice cracked. She's in pain. I know she is. I can feel it, and it hurts worse than if I were experiencing it myself.

"I'm sick. It's an inconvenience. I'm here to look after Benz, to make your life easier, not harder."

Tears fill her eyes, but she blinks them away quickly. My heart shatters into a million pieces when she wraps her arms around herself and stares at the ground. Her apology shows how sick she is. That and the way she had to fight back tears. Chiara is a strong person, a resilient woman who has more strength than anyone else I've ever met. Being sick goes against everything she is. It weakens her, stops her from working, prevents her from being stubborn because she knows she has to slow down, and it sets her up for vulnerability. Those are all things she hates, I know because I'm the same. I hate being vulnerable. It's the reason I've never seriously dated anyone. I hate slowing down because I have a million things on my schedule and no time to be sick. I hate when my body weakens my mind by clouding it. She might not want to believe how similar we are, but there is no denying it.

Chiara and I are two halves of one stubborn soul.

"You are not an inconvenience," I say and cup her face. Her eyes are bloodshot and barely open. "You're a pain in the arse, but not because you're sick," I tease, and she lets out a harsh snort. I grab her chin, forcing her to focus on me completely. "You can make my life as hard as you would like, sweetheart, because you're the one who makes it worth living."

Holy shit. Shut the fuck up, Leonard. Back away. This is dangerous territory. She doesn't even like you, at least that's what she keeps saying. She might be attracted to me, but she hasn't said once that she likes me.

"You say that, yet, you keep pushing me away. Dragging me close, then pushing me away. I'd start believing your words a hell of a lot more if they had any root in your actions." I drop my hand from her chin, my gaze fixated on her.

"What difference would it make, Starling?" She'd still distrust me when it comes to her heart, and I can't even fucking blame her.

"It would make the difference between the meteorite passing by the Earth and hitting it," she says, and I freeze in place for a moment, unable to even breathe.

Then, her eyes close from exhaustion, and I realise I'm making this situation so much worse. I pick up the clothes again, and Chiara tells me to turn around so she can take off her wet underwear. I do as I'm told, listening with a bleeding heart when she whimpers a little. The urge to turn around and help her is overwhelming, but I wait until she mumbles an 'okay'. I help her off the couch, and Chiara holds onto my hand the entire walk to the car. Benz is right beside me, her leash in my hand even though she listens so well, I know she doesn't need it. This is merely for safety reasons.

"Leonard?" Chiara says as I open the backseat for Benz to jump inside. Panic immediately floods my chest at the fear in her voice.

"What's wrong?" I ask and take her arms in case she feels dizzy.

"I don't feel well," she says and places her fingers on my forearms. "I might faint again," she says, which only makes me panic more.

"Alright, I've got you, okay? Let's get you in the car," I say, and she nods, following me toward the rental. Chiara has been a fainter from excessive pain ever since I've known her. I've witnessed her pass out from period cramps, breaking her leg, and even overexertion. It's not new, but it's terrifying nonetheless.

Luckily, we make it all the way to our hotel room where I help her into bed. Chiara is so tired, she doesn't even open her eyes as I bring the blanket up to her chin, but she grabs my hand before I can step away and out of the room. She's asking me to stay without words, and there isn't a single thing in this world I would deny her. So, I call for Benz to join us in Starling's room, take off my shoes and shirt, and slide under her covers. I check her temperature with the back of my hand once more and almost sigh when her skin isn't on fire like earlier. I will have to wake her in a few hours to make sure she drinks a lot of fluids and takes another ibuprofen, but, for now, she needs to sleep, and I need to pray that I won't get sick before tomorrow or Sunday. I won't care if I miss a race weekend as long as Chiara feels better, but my team would be pissed at me for being so careless. Then again, I really don't care.

My little demon is resting now, and I can't help but inch closer to her and close my eyes too. She'll be okay.

Me, on the other hand, I won't be because the woman who is becoming everything to me still doesn't like me, and I don't know if she ever will.

CHAPTER 28

Chiara

I t's race day. My fever finally went away two days ago, and, although I still feel like shit, I'm starting to get better. Leonard has been forcing water and food down my throat, along with my antibiotics. He's gone to work and come straight back to me for the past couple of days. He's been helping me into the shower—looking away every time I undress—and making sure I don't faint on him again. He's also been taking me to the roof of the hotel every night so I can admire the Singaporean skyline. We have a clear view of the Marina Bay Sands from up there, and it is the most beautiful building I've ever seen. Shaped like a boat on top of three pillars, I've never seen anything even remotely like it. I wish I could be at the track too, but it's already a miracle Leonard hasn't gotten sick because he's... been sleeping in my bed to make sure I'm okay. Sometimes I wake up with his hand on my chest like he's making sure my heart is still beating. Sometimes I wake up and find his eyes on me like he was studying the way I sleep. Sometimes he wakes me gently by tracing the apple of my cheek like I am the most precious thing in the world to him.

And I haven't minded it one single bit.

You can make my life as hard as you would like, sweetheart, because you're the one who makes it worth living.

He hasn't spoken to me about this sentence since he said it three days ago, but I haven't asked either. He can't have meant it. It's not possible. Not to mention, I keep getting dizzy at the sweet way he addresses me. Spending all this time together

221

can't have caused him to have feelings for me. We always fight, except lately it's mostly rooted in our sexual frustration, at least it is for me. I want him. I'm not ashamed to admit it.

I shake my head to ignore the thought before it sends me spiraling, which I have no time for. The race is about to start, and I still have to take Benz for a quick pee. My body has regained some of its usual energy, a good sign I will be healthy enough to travel on Wednesday. As nice as Singapore is, it's also very expensive, and if Leonard goes out to buy me one more book here— all I've been doing since getting sick is read and sleep, so I went through the book I brought days ago—I will do something stupid like be nice to him for no apparent reason.

The ringing of my phone tears me back into reality, and I grab it out of my pocket to see an unknown caller ID. I furrow my brows and hit answer.

"Hello?" I say, Benz wagging at me once she's done peeing. We make our way back to the elevator when the person on the phone responds.

"Chiara? *Come stai*?" Dino's voice fills my ear, and I raise both of my eyebrows. I haven't seen him since I ran out of the art gallery five days ago. Embarrassment heats up my cheeks.

"*Bene, grazie. E tu*?" The urge to tell him how sorry I am for how things went down between us is strong, but I have a feeling there's something he wants from me, so I wait for him to keep talking.

"I'm good as well. Listen, I'm sorry about that kiss, especially because I was very impressed with your goals and vision for your art gallery. I would like to invest if you agree to do a trial run and impress me with an art exhibit you create for the gallery I own in Italy. I understand Leonard and you will travel there in a little over a week for his next race," Dino says, and my already fuzzy brain crashes with the impossibility of his words.

"I'm a bit sick, so I'm going to need you to repeat that. I have a hard time processing information at the moment," I admit while sinking onto my bed again and trying to control the shaking of my hands. Dino chuckles into the phone.

"I will send you the details later if you would like," he offers, and I cover my mouth to keep from letting out a victorious sound that would most likely deafen him.

"I would like that very much. Thank you, Dino," I say, and we hang up moments later.

As soon as the call has ended, I grab my laptop and place it on my lap to finish working on my project. The app I use for my video projection mapping is still open, ready for me to tackle this new task. I love taking care of Benz and traveling the world with Leonard. I've been earning a lot of money, have gotten to see the most beautiful places, eaten the most delicious meals—mostly cooked by Leonard—and witnessed the most incredible immersive art shows in the world. From artists creating their own exhibitions with physical objects to video projecting like I'm doing, I've picked up a lot of inspiration over the past few months.

It all spills into my work. I hardly notice the race in the background as I work, smiling at my screen because it's turning out better than I could have ever hoped for. I take a break halfway through the race to call Mamma, who freaks out with me over the phone. She's happy I've gotten this opportunity and even more so because it's coming from a fellow *italiano*. I shake my head at her swooning over Dino—yes, she looked him up and is staring at pictures of him as we're speaking—wishing I would be able to do so with her, but I haven't been able to admire any other man apart from Leonard in a long time.

"How's Nonna?" I ask in Italian, my eyes focusing on the race now.

Leonard is in second place, fighting Jonathan for first. He started on pole, which is why I kind of wish I'd paid more attention. Instead of knowing why he's behind his rival, I can only get frustrated at the screen. At least he's merely a second behind Jonathan, which means he is in the DRS—drag reduction system—time requirement that gives the driver behind a speed advantage in the dedicated zones.

"She's happy I'm here with her, and, to be honest, so am I. My heart feels strong, and I haven't felt this happy in a long time," Mamma says, pulling me back into the moment. I stare at my hand.

"I'm glad to hear that, Mamma. I can't wait to see you both next week," I say, and she lets out a small sigh.

"Nonna will be so happy. She keeps talking about how much she misses you."

It's only been a year since we've last seen each other, but, for a family as close as mine, that's a long time. When I was growing up in Italy until I was four, Nonna and I were inseparable. When Mamma and I moved away, it broke both of our hearts. I cried for three days and then I didn't cry again up until a few months ago.

"Me, too. Give her a kiss from me, okay?" Mamma assures me she will before we exchange 'I love you's and hang up.

My heart aches a little as I bring my attention back to the television in time to see Leonard attempt an overtake on Jonathan. I hold my breath and clap my hands together when he overtakes his teammate. Benz jumps up on the bed to lick my cheek, and I laugh a little, holding her face in my hands to get her to stop. I only take my eyes off the television for a second, but when I turn back, I see Leonard's car flipping over and over again before landing on its head. Panic grips every cell in my body.

"No," I whisper, standing up to close the distance between me and the screen. I don't know why I do it, but it feels like I've started hallucinating from exhaustion and my flu symptoms. But no. Leonard's car is upside down, and so is my stomach now. "Oh God," I blurt out before rushing over to my purse and running out of the room. I don't wait to see what happens. I can't.

I have to get to Leonard.

I arrive at the track fifteen minutes later, my phone pressed to my ear as Quinn gives me updates on Leonard's condition. He's out of the car, awake but shaken up and bruised. She's telling me they have to take him to the hospital to do some tests, so I ignore the burning in my lungs from the exhaustion of running while I'm sick, trying to get to him before they bring him to the hospital. I need to see him, need to make sure for myself he's okay to ease the tightness in my chest. I'm freaking out. My heart is fucking pounding, and I can't get it to stop. I have to see him.

"Where is he now?" I ask Quinn, who gives me directions. The pass around my neck allows me to go everywhere, Leonard made sure of it.

"You have to hurry if you want to drive in the ambulance with him." I go faster than my feet should be able to in my condition, sweat dripping down my back, forehead, and neck.

I push through crowds of people. I run all the way to the medical tent where he's supposed to be, ignoring the voices telling me to slow down. I ignore every aching muscle in my body groaning from the exhaustion of running after days in bed and still recovering from being sick. There is no doubt in my mind I'm making my sickness worse this way, but I don't give a shit, not when I see Leonard sitting in an ambulance.

They're about to close the doors when I call out, "Wait, please."

Leonard's gaze meets mine, panic in his eyes. He will be furious with me for fucking with my health like this. He will be so mad I'm not resting, I can already see it in his eyes. Most of all, however, he's going to be upset because he made me worry. I ignore it all as I run the last few meters, the paramedic stepping out of the vehicle after Leonard said something to her and making room for me. She offers me a hand, and I take it, heaving myself into the back of the ambulance.

"You should be in bed," Leonard says, but I ignore him as I stand in front of him.

"Where are you hurt?" I demand to know, ignoring the stinging of the tears in my eyes. I swallow hard to get rid of them. Leonard's brown eyes warm at my concern.

"Nowhere, Starling. My ribs might be bruised they said, but that's why they're taking me to hospital," he explains, reaching out to touch my wrist.

"In how much pain are you?" I ask next, feeling his fingers around my wrist. The tears return to my eyes, but, this time, they drop down my face before I can hold them back.

"Come here, sweetheart," he says, tugging on my arm to get me to close the distance between us. I don't budge. I merely stand in front of him, crying because I've never felt so terrified in my entire life than when I saw his horrible crash.

"How much pain?" I repeat, trying to keep my voice firm, but it shakes uncontrollably from the emotional toll this situation has on my heart. Leonard offers me a small smirk.

"A lot of pain. So much pain, actually, I demand to have you come here right now and make me feel better," he says, tugging on my wrist again.

This time, I step toward him, and he guides me all the way onto his lap before wrapping his arms around me. I'm careful to keep my limbs away from his ribs, but he brings my chest flush against his, my arms tangling at his nape. More tears stream from my eyes, and I even let out a tiny sob.

"I'm okay," he assures me, and I slide my fingers into his curly, short hair, pulling a little on it.

"Don't do that to me again," I whisper against his neck, smelling his scent combined with a little bit of sweat and burnt rubber. Oh God, I don't want to think about why he smells like burnt rubber.

"I didn't know you cared," Leonard replies with a small chuckle, and I manage to keep the rest of the tears from slipping down my cheeks and soaking his fireproofs.

"I don't," I lie as he rubs his hands over my back. "I was just worried I had to find a new job," I go on, and the Formula One driver lets out a snort.

"Then why are you crying, sweetheart?" *Stop calling me that. I like it too much.*

"I won't get my big ass paycheck from any other employer," I explain, and Leonard leans back to cup my face in his hands and brush the pads of his thumbs over my cheeks.

"Don't cry over me, little demon. I'm not worth it," he says, and I wish I could slap him. *Yes, you are*, even if I will never admit it out loud.

"Could you please refrain from flipping your car from now on? Benz would be heartbroken if something happened to you," I say while he wipes away the remainder of my previous tears.

"Just Benz, huh?" he teases with a small smile. When I realize how close I am to him, our lips almost touching, I try to wiggle out of his arms. "Where are you going?" he asks, and I cover my mouth with the backside of my hand.

"I'm going to get you sick," I explain, but he merely places me next to him on the area of the ambulance where he's sitting, sliding one of my legs across his back and keeping the other in his lap.

"I don't care. I need you by my side and nowhere else," he admits before bringing his lips to my shoulder and placing a kiss to it. "I'm also incredibly pissed at you for running all this way to get to me. You should be resting, you stubborn, impossible woman," he says, one of his hands dropping to my thigh and running along its length.

"Well, you shouldn't have crashed," I say and rest my cheek on his shoulder.

"You can blame Jonathan for that. He crashed into my rear," Leonard explains, tracing circles on my bare leg then.

"I fucking hate that guy," I mumble, another chuckle coming from him in response.

"Me too. At least he will get a lot of shit from the team for the stunt he pulled today." It gives me a little bit of satisfaction, but not even close to how satisfying it would be to knock out a few of Jonathan's teeth.

"Mr. Tick, we have to get you to the hospital," the paramedic says, and I attempt to move off him once more, but Leonard keeps me tangled up in him.

"You don't have to leave, Chiara," he says, but his eyes are begging. *Please stay.* And I do because there is nowhere else I want to be right now than in Leonard Tick's arms.

CHAPTER 29

Leonard

C hiara is at home, still sick and recovering from the flu she made worse by coming to see me on Sunday after the crash. My head hasn't found a way to wrap around the fact that she cried for me. The strongest woman I know cried out of fear of something happening to me, which means she might not hate or dislike me anymore. At least that's what I hope it means because I don't want her to hate me, not at this point. Not ever again. Without her, my life has become so dull, but with her, I feel everything more intensely than ever before.

She's reignited my love for racing, and I race for her now, to see her joyful from my successes.

She's shown me how to use that organ in my chest in a way I've never experienced before in my life.

She's given me endless reasons to smile, and I have no intention of ever hiding them from her again.

She's blurred out the rest of the world, the haters and reporters that try to make me feel horrible about myself.

There are a million other ways she's jump-started my life, but I shake my head to force them all away. I already care enough about Chiara without overthinking my feelings until they get stronger and start terrifying me.

I knock on my brother's door, waiting for anyone to open it and tell me why the hell I had to rip myself off Chiara's side to come here. According to Jack, it was urgent, and I had to come straight away. Luckily, Starling was sleeping, so I could sneak away with the hope of returning before she wakes. I left a note in case she does, but I'm going to make this as short as possible. I love my family, but Chiara has priority.

Lizzie opens the door. She flashes me a bright smile, so I lean down to pick her up and place her on my hip. Her little arms wrap around me as she tells me how much she's missed me. I give her a squeeze before dropping her back onto her feet because, as well as they have been healing, my ribs still hurt like hell. Not that I would ever tell anyone that. The doctor cleared me for the race next weekend, a race we have to fly to Italy for on Saturday. Dino gave Chiara an amazing opportunity, so we have to be there a little early for her to familiarise herself with the gallery and rehearse her immersive show. She'll have to make sure everything works well together, but I have no doubt it will be perfect.

"Where are your dads?" I ask Lizzie, who takes my hand and leads me inside their small house.

"They're waiting in the kitchen for you." Waiting. Interesting. I have half a mind to turn on my heels and leave this house at once. Whatever they have summoned me for is about Chiara and me. I'm not stupid. I can feel it deep in my bones.

"Brilliant," I blurt out, and Lizzie giggles as she pulls on my arm. For a brief moment, I'm overcome by love for my little niece and her always happy mood.

"You're in trouble," she says to me as she tilts her head up, her freckles perfectly painted across the bridge of her nose and her cheeks.

"I know," I assure her, dreading the conversation that is about to follow. That's what I get for dodging their calls for the past week.

"I think it's about Chiara. I overheard them talking," Liz goes on, and I narrow my eyes at her.

"Are you becoming a little spy?" I ask, and she tugs on my hand.

"Don't tell my daddies," she says, and I give her my word I would never. It's good if she knows things like this so she can prepare me for what's to come.

Jack and Stu are sitting at their kitchen table, cups of tea in front of them while they both wait for me to approach them. I let out a sigh, and Lizzie lets go of my hand and leaves the room, yelling something about going to play with her dolls. I debate going with her for a moment because I'd rather play dolls than listen to whatever shit they're going to throw at my head. I have no patience for this. Chiara could wake up at any minute, and I—

"Sit," Jack says, his voice firm with a little hint of anger. Surprise pushes me forward until I'm doing what he wants me to.

"Is this the intervention bullshit people do?" I ask and grab a scone I'm sure Stu made for me with vegan products. I give him a questioning look, and he assures me of my suspicions when he gives me a small nod.

I look at both of them while taking a bite. My brother looks tired, but I'm assuming it's because he didn't sleep on the plane last night. Stu, Jack, and Lizzie just got back from a trip to India where they visited Stu's grandparents. It also allowed my brother's partner to reconnect with his roots, something he's wanted to do for a long time now. I study Stu's deep brown eyes for any signs of exhaustion, but he looks well-rested in comparison to my brother.

"It's not an intervention, but it's time we talked about you and Chiara, don't you think?" I knew it was coming, but the mention of her name still makes my heart tumble in my chest.

"I'm not sure what you mean." I'm really not. Nothing is going on between Chiara and me romantically.

Fuck, even I know that's a lie.

"What game are you playing with her, huh? You two used to hate each other, couldn't be in a room without fighting about something stupid, but now? You look at her like there is no one more important in the world," Jack says, sending me spiraling into my thoughts.

There isn't...

"Chiara and I are roommates and she works for me. We spend most of our days together. It's inevitable to grow closer in some ways," I explain, but I'm keeping so many emotions bottled up, I would very much like to take out the cork and let them spray everywhere like champagne.

"It's okay if you don't want to tell us, but we're here for you," Stu chimes in, and I give him a blink to acknowledge his words, nothing more. I hate talking about feelings. I'm horrifyingly bad at it, so unlike my dad, mom, and brothers.

"Leonard, I love you, you know I do, but Chiara is family too. She's important to all of us, and I need to know what the bloody hell you're doing. Are you playing her?" Jack says. My spine goes rigid, and I lean forward on the table, the scone in my hand crumbling into a million pieces.

"Excuse me?" His words feel foul in my ears, the way they hit my brain is almost worse.

"Are you playing mind games with Chiara?" Jack asks, and I let go of the crumbled mess in my hands, grabbing a napkin to clean them.

"You dragged me away from Chiara while she's sick to ask me if I'm playing mind games on the woman that has me wrapped around her bloody finger?" I stand up, but surprise has widened both of their facial features. "I'm leaving," I say, but Jack clears his throat and places his hand on the table, gently but as a warning.

"I'm not finished with you yet, Lenny. Sit down," he says, and I roll my eyes at his horrible nickname for my already horrible name. He's been using it since we were kids and now even Lizzie adopted it.

"You can be very happy you're older than me and that I hold a shit ton of respect for you, otherwise I would leave right now and ignore you for the next several weeks," I say, and Jack lets out a snort.

"Liar. You wouldn't last two weeks without seeing Elizabeth," he replies, and I tilt my head to the side.

"I still like Stu," I point out, and Jack frowns at me. I scowl back.

"Okay you two, enough. Leonard, it's obvious you are not playing mind games with Chiara, we never thought you were, at least not seriously," Stu says, but Jack raises his hand to weigh it from side to side and make an 'ehhhh' sound. I kick him in the shin under the table.

"Hey, ow. What the fuck?" he complains and rubs his leg. I don't pay him any attention because his partner catches all of mine again.

"We're merely a bit concerned because we love both of you so much, and you two haven't gotten along, ever. Chiara hasn't had the easiest of lives, and we want to make sure whatever is happening between you, it's happening with good intentions," Stu goes on, and I lean back in my chair, crossing my arms in front of my chest.

"Chiara and I are... friends. I think. But nothing more. There is nothing you need to be worried about." Jack snorts again. "Okay, if you don't stop, I will do far worse than kick you in the shin," I warn, and my brother covers his mouth before raising his hands in mock surrender.

"Sorry, I just would have never expected those words to come out of your mouth. It's surreal, and it sounds like a big, ginormous lie," he explains, rubbing his right arm as he considers me. His eyes scan my face before he grins to himself. "You're falling for her, and I bet she has no idea because you're way too scared to admit it even to yourself," Jack says, and I get up, ignoring him. I don't have time for this.

"Leonard," Stu begs, but I have no intention of staying. I have to get home before Chiara wakes up. She needs to take her antibiotics soon, and I haven't cooked anything yet. Bernie said she has to take her medicine with food.

"You can't run from your feelings forever, Lenny. I know you've been busy with your career, but you shouldn't deny yourself the experience of falling in love because you don't think you'll have enough time to be a good boyfriend," Jack says, and I stop dead in my tracks in the door frame of the kitchen.

How the hell does he know that's what I'm scared of? My heart jumps a little in my chest, but I don't turn around again. I don't answer him, nor do I admit he hit the nail right on the fucking head. My fears are not for anyone else. I haven't shared them with another person, but I don't plan on doing so either. People like my brother have this optimistic view of life where fears could simply vanish if you found the right person to love. I know better. I know they will never leave me. I know as soon as I enter a serious relationship, I'd find a way to fuck it up. My career combined with my family doesn't leave room for another person to fill.

Except Chiara already perfectly fits into my life.

Except Chiara *is* perfect in every impossible way for me.

Except Jack was so right about everything, it makes my head hurt.

I give Lizzie a kiss on the head before leaving the house and getting back into my expensive Grenzenlos. Stu was also right. Chiara hasn't had the easiest of lives, and neither have I, but mine has gotten significantly better when I got older. My childhood was beyond difficult, and I've felt horrible about my parents sacrificing everything to make my dream come true for as long as I can remember. I've done all I can to repay them, but they're stubborn and hardly take anything I offer them.

My eyes focus on the road ahead of me as I let my engine roar to live and make my way to the bakery near my flat where Chiara loves to go. I pick up a few things, all lactose-free for her, before making my way back home and praying Starling is fast asleep. Benz is nowhere to be seen when I open the door, probably because she's right next to Chiara where she's been for the past few days. I'm convinced my daughter can sense my little demon isn't feeling well, so I've become a second priority. I never thought I'd be so fine with a thought like that, happy even that Benz doesn't leave her alone.

I step into her bedroom after there is no response to my soft knocking, finding her still fast asleep in bed. A sigh of relief slips past my lips as I walk to my bedroom to put on some comfortable clothes before lying down next to Chiara in her bed where I've been sleeping since we returned from Singapore. She shuffles next to me, her hand reaching out to touch mine and her fingers grazing my skin. Her eyelids flutter ever so slightly, letting me know she's awake enough to realise I'm here.

"I didn't mean to wake you, Starling, I'm sorry," I say in a low tone. She adjusts her head on the pillow until she's looking up at me with the tiniest of smiles on her lips.

"How are Stu, Jack, and Ellie?" she asks, causing my heart to flutter a little. Of course she'd ask about them. Chiara loves them probably as much as I do.

"They're alright, sweetheart. Go back to sleep," I say and brush a strand of loose hair from her cheek. Her eyes close at my touch, and, for a moment, time freezes. I freeze. She freezes. Everything does, almost as if life wants to grant me this little bit of... home.

"I'm hungry," she admits, bringing a smile to my face.

"Yeah?" She nods, and I trail my fingers down her jawline until I reach her chin, grabbing it between my fingers to give it one quick squeeze and then letting go again. I'm having a hard time resisting the pull she has on me. "I'm going to make some food. Any requests?" I ask, and she takes my hand again, all sleepy and cute.

"I'm craving my Nonna's homemade pizza," she says, guiding my hand under her cheek. It makes me realise she's not all the way awake yet.

"Do you know the recipe? I can make it if you tell me how," I offer, and Chiara sits up in bed, rubbing at her eyes. The loss of her warm skin on mine frustrates me.

"I do know it, but I need to do something with myself. Do you mind if we make it together? I know the kitchen is your sacred place," she says, and, unlike last time, I don't hesitate in my answer.

"Of course. This is your home too," I blurt out, making her glance over her shoulder at me. Her gaze trails over my clothes and then to my pillows.

"How much longer are you going to sleep here?" she asks softly, letting me know she isn't trying to get rid of me. At least that's what I'm hoping.

"Until you've had enough of me," I reply and stop breathing, praying she won't tell me she's had enough since the first night.

Instead, she merely says, "Okay" and stretches her arms into the air. Cracking sounds fill the room, and I cringe in response. She lets her arms fall, reaching one of her hands backward to rub her back.

"Are you in pain?" I ask, raising my fingers to her spine.

"No," she lies, and I click my tongue, frustrated with her stubbornness for the millionth time since we've known each other.

"Come here," I say while reaching out to snake my fingers around her arm. Chiara leans toward me until I have access to her shoulders and back. I start kneading at her tense muscles. "You need to tell me when you're in pain, little demon, otherwise I can't help you," I remind her while she lets out a relieved hum.

"I don't need your help all the time," she replies right as I find a spot that makes her let out a moan. I stop everything. "Sorry," she mumbles, but I hit the same spot again, earning me another humming sound.

"I'm not."

I massage her back for a few minutes longer before squeezing her shoulders. She tells me she will take a quick shower, and I give her one small nod before stepping into the kitchen and gathering all the ingredients I think she might need. Then, I prepare Benz's dinner, a little jealous of her because she followed Chiara into the bathroom and is probably lying in front of the glass shower door right now.

Chiara joins me in the kitchen half an hour later, and I hand her the baked goodies I picked up before I came home. Her face lights up at the sight, turning her cheeks a wonderful pink. She takes one and breaks off a piece, shoving it into her mouth a moment later. I urge her to take her antibiotics since she's eating something, and, once she's done, we get to cooking.

We bump into each other so many times, I can't help but laugh at the third time, wrapping her into my arms and placing my cheek on her head. Chiara's arms slide across my back, holding me close to her for a single moment and then going back to cooking. I turn on some music too, watching her closely at the same time for any signs of overexertion. There are none. She takes it slow and lets me knead the dough. She starts laughing at me because I'm "doing it so wrong, it's making Nonnas all over the world cry". I join her amusement before trying to figure out a way to do it better while Chiara watches me with an amused smile.

I've never had so much fun cooking in my entire life.

Chapter 30
Chiara

I feel a lot better. A little tingle in my throat is the only reminder of how sick I was for almost two weeks. Leonard slept in his own bed last night, and I hate myself for waking up and reaching for him as if it's the most natural thing in the world. I distract myself by picking up the book I'm currently reading—a romance novel about two friends falling in love that Leonard got me yesterday all because I mentioned it on the flight home—and head into the kitchen. We're supposed to fly to Italy tomorrow morning, and we both still have to pack our things.

My heart sinks into my stomach when I see him standing at the coffee machine with a book in his hand, waiting for the beep to let him know his cup is done. His torso is naked and fully on display for me, tattoos all over his chest and back. My mouth starts to water at the sight of his muscular backside and the view of him completely immersed in the story he's reading. His bottom lip is tucked between his teeth, and when I make out the name of the book, I start to blush. It's one of the smuttier books he's gotten me, one not meant to be read as much for the plot as it is for the sex.

"Enjoying it?" I ask, and Leonard looks up at me, eyes filled with lust.

"Very much," he replies and places his forearms on the kitchen island, his hands clinging to the book as he studies my face with desire. "You've read this?" he asks, and I nod, both of us ignoring the beeping of the coffee machine. "You liked it?" Another blush covers my face.

"Yes," I manage to croak out. I'm not embarrassed about enjoying it, but my body is on fire from the intensity of his gaze, my clit swelling uncomfortably.

"Do you understand how difficult it is for me not to picture you when I read this?" I furrow my brows, my heart racing. "It's impossible, Chiara. It's impossible not to imagine me doing all of these things to you, and it's driving me wild." I swallow hard at his words.

"What's stopping you?" I ask, and he stands up, placing the book on the marble and closing the distance between us.

"Everything. And nothing at the same time because I'm finished, Chiara." His hands, gentle and careful, grab my arms and then slide up to cup my neck.

"Finished with what?" I say, my voice trembling. Leonard gives me a small smile.

"I'm finished convincing myself that we don't like each other," he replies before dropping his forehead to mine and sucking in a sharp breath. "I'm finished convincing myself I don't want to know what you taste like when it is all I think about," he admits, and I bring my hands up to his naked stomach. His skin is hot and his abs are hard, only making my head spin more.

"But I hate you," I try to remind myself, even if it's a lie, because we're about to cross a line we will never come back from.

"Don't lie to me before I kiss you. I don't want to taste it on my tongue," he says, his hands dropping to my waist as his mouth hovers so closely over mine, I can smell the scent of his toothpaste.

"It's not a lie," I whisper, letting out a gasp when he lifts me onto his kitchen counter and slightly presses my legs apart to stand between them.

"If you don't like me, why are your hands on the waistband of my pants? Why don't you tell me to stop? Why do you want me to kiss you?" he asks. Those are all great questions that have one simple answer.

I crave him.

"If you kiss me, you won't be able to take it back," I remind him, and he lets out a small chuckle, his fingers slipping into my hair.

"Good," he replies, pressing a kiss to my cheek and making his way toward my mouth. "I need a taste, Chiara, just a little one. Please," he begs, and I lift my hands to the sides of his face, placing my mouth on his.

Everything inside of me explodes into a million fireworks. His lips wrap around mine so perfectly, I melt into him, my chest pressing flush against his. He groans into my mouth as his arms wrap around me and his hands move to the small of my back to push me further against him. Pleasure consumes my cells, ripping them apart and putting them back together again in the best way possible. His tongue presses against my lips, and I open them for him, letting it sink into my mouth. A moan slips past my lips as the overwhelming feelings pulsing through my veins intensify.

Happiness. Pleasure. Excitement. Enthusiasm. Determination. Joy.

Leonard's fingers curl around my hair, bringing my face closer to him to explore my mouth more. Our tongues tangle with each other, and I hate the fact that this is the best kiss I've ever had. I hate the way my skin is on fire for him, the way my clit is begging me to move closer to the edge and rub against his groin. I want him so much, my limbs are vibrating to somehow get him closer.

"God," he moans as he breaks the kiss, only to suck in a breath and then claim my lips again.

I smile against his mouth, feeling goosebumps cover my skin. This feels right, like we've been supposed to do this for years. Like I will never be able to get enough of his minty taste and the way he completes me so effortlessly. Like we've been kidding each other by pretending we haven't wanted to do this for so long, it's all we've been thinking about when we're together. Like we were made for each other. The thought only makes me kiss him deeper, more demandingly. I'm greedy, sliding my tongue into his mouth and tasting him for as long as he lets me.

His fingers slip under my shirt, staying on my stomach even though we both want him to move them higher. I would complain, but his mouth is confusing me, tearing down rational thought until all that's left is the need to keep him in place, between my legs and kissing me into oblivion.

I break the kiss a few moments later to catch my breath, but he lets out a complaining grunt.

"One more," he begs, and I let out a breathless laugh. "You taste too good," he admits, his forehead against mine and his hands slipping higher until they rest on my ribs.

"What do I taste like?" I whisper because the kiss still has me dizzy.

"Like the sweetest poison."

Leonard kisses me again, and I surrender to it completely. Surrender to him. We both want more, not caring a single bit about the repercussions. All that matters is this moment, here and now, and I wish it would last forever. I wish there was no aftermath we have to clean up when we realize the heat of the moment clouded our judgment.

Most of all, I wish there wasn't a fucking knock on the front door.

"Who is it?" Leonard calls before going back to kissing me. I giggle uncontrollably, surprising him so much, he leans away with warmth on his face.

"I didn't giggle," I say firmly, but he's grinning at me, placing his mouth on mine over and over.

"It's Dad. Open the door," Andrew says, but Leonard doesn't stop kissing me, so I push him a little backward and break it.

"Go open the door," I say, but he groans and lets his head fall backward, his hands dropping to my waist and squeezing.

"If you don't mind, maybe you could open the door so I can put on a shirt and take care of—" He cuts off and lets out a soft laugh as his eyes drop to his cock, all hard and ready to bring me pleasure. No, I can't think about that right now. I need to open the door.

"Okay," I mumble, and Leonard presses a swift kiss to my forehead before disappearing into his bedroom and leaving me to my spiraling thoughts.

I can't linger on them for too long since Andrew is waiting behind the front door for someone to let him in. When I push off the marble island, my knees cave in a little from the after-effects of the kiss. Somehow I manage to make it to the door, taking a deep breath before ripping it open. Andrew is smiling brightly at me, closing the distance between us to give me a big hug. I return it for a moment before stepping back again, his hands remaining on my shoulders.

"I'm glad to see you're feeling better. May I come in? I'd love to have a cup of coffee," Andrew says, and I gesture for him to move inside.

"I will make you one," I say and walk into the kitchen at the same moment Leonard joins us in the entrance area. He greets his father with a small handshake and a firm nod, but I can tell he's irritated about his presence here.

"What can I help you with, Dad?" he asks while I disappear into the kitchen.

"Your mother was asking me to—" is the last thing I hear.

I remove the now cold cup of coffee Leonard made himself earlier and make three fresh ones. Leonard and Andrew are in the living room by the time I'm done, and I hand them both their cups. The Formula One driver's fingers linger on mine, a small smile on his lips as he thanks me. It makes my heart race, but I don't let myself stay in front of him. I simply retrieve my own cup before joining them in the living room and sipping on my warm coffee. I can feel Leonard's eyes on me, but I do my best not to look at him too. Andrew can't see that anything has changed between his son and me. He will tell Rena, Jack, Stu, and Graham, which is the last thing I want. They're all suspecting something already anyway. I don't need to give them more reasons to.

"I think Rena's had enough of me. She begged me to come and spend the day with you," Andrew says with a small laugh, and I tilt my head a bit to the side.

"How's she feeling?" The last time I spoke to her was at the beginning of the week. I should really call her.

"Much better. Her leg is healing well," Andrew replies, and I offer him a small smile before taking another sip of my coffee.

"I like spending time with you, Dad, but you know I had some plans today. We discussed them on Monday, remember?" Leonard says with a strange look he's directing at his father. Andrew furrows his brows before realization dawns on him.

"Oh, yes, of course. I'm sorry. Let me just finish my coffee and then I will go to Jack and Stu. I haven't seen them in a couple of weeks," he replies, and I look between both of the men in front of me, confused.

Instead of being nosy and asking what the hell that was about, I keep my mouth shut. It's none of my business. Andrew leaves ten minutes later, causing a nervous feeling to spread through my chest. Leonard and I are alone again. We kissed earlier, and I have no idea how to act around him now. It was the best kiss of my life. I want more, undoubtedly, but there are a million questions I'm not sure how to answer. Leonard has feelings for me. I have feelings for him. But we're still living together, I work for him, and if we fuck things up, which we definitely will, it will create chaos in every part of our lives. Fuck.

How the hell did we go from hating each other to sticking our tongues down each other's throats?

How the hell did Leonard become my favorite person in the whole world?

How the hell do I keep ignoring my feelings when I've had a glimpse of how alive he makes me feel?

There is no way we would work either. Neither one of us has ever been in a romantic relationship. We always fight and bicker about the stupidest things. There are a million reasons why we disliked each other. Then again, we shouldn't even be capable of being alone for an hour without a bomb going off, and we've achieved that too. Leonard and I shouldn't work, but we do. Fighting or not, we're always there for each other when it matters the most. God, I feel closer to Leonard than I've ever felt to another person in my entire life, even Mamma. A wave of fear takes my lungs hostage, preventing me from being able to breathe.

Leonard returns to the living room where I'm chained to the armchair by my feelings. He sits down on the couch beside the chair I'm in, studying my face with those beautiful brown eyes of his. To anyone else, they wouldn't seem like anything special. Billions of people have brown eyes, but, to me, they are the most breathtaking pair in the world. They're warm as they trace my features like a soft caress. Heat rushes into my cheeks in response, which he notices immediately. He leans forward, his elbows propped onto his knees.

"Would you like to tell me what's wrong?" he asks softly, reaching out to touch my thigh. My eyes flutter shut in response to the warmth of his touch.

"I hate overthinking," I admit because I don't want to keep my confused feelings hidden from him.

"Let me hear your concerns so I can take them away from you," he offers, and as wonderful as the thought is, it makes me feel nauseous to consider sharing my thoughts with him right now.

"That kiss, Leonard, was—" I cut off, and he gives me a serious look before answering for me.

"Everything."

It was. It really was, but I can't tell him that, can I? I can't risk the job opportunity he's given me in case we can't make whatever we have work. I can't let this continue, no matter how I feel about him. *I can't let the meteorite hit my world.* He said he doesn't have time to break my heart. We wouldn't work, we can't, it's impossible. I swallow hard to get rid of the knot forming in my throat.

"It was a mistake," I mumble, and he stares at me for a minute or so before letting his head drop and shaking it.

"I don't know why you're lying to me, but alright. If you'd like to call it a mistake, go for it. I'm not the type of person to fuck around, so I'm going to tell you something right here and right now. I'd very much like to kiss you again, kiss every part of your body until my lips are tattooed onto your skin. I'd like to fuck you in whatever way you love the most and then hold you after and tell you how beautiful you are. I'd like to cook for you, play my guitar for you, read the same books as you, and do everything else we've already been doing.

"If you don't want that, I won't pressure you, but I know you care for me. I know all this time we've been spending together has had an effect on you. If you don't want me, I understand, but don't try to tell me some shit like our kiss was a mistake. It was far from it," he says, sending me spiraling in my own head, but he rips me out of my thoughts again. "There is somewhere I'd like to take you. Please get ready. We're leaving in thirty minutes," he adds and then stands up, staring down at me for a moment. "That kiss, whatever you decide for it to mean, will not change how things are between us, I promise. You're too important to me." He leaves without giving me a chance to respond, not that I would have.

My head hurts. Leonard just described what I'd imagine a relationship between us to look like, and I didn't hate the image he was painting one bit. I simply can't wrap my head around the fact that he wants to... *date me? Is that what he'd want? Is it what I want?*

God, I should have never let him kiss me. I should have never kissed him back either. Everything is upside down now, and I feel like throwing something at the wall to release some tension.

A truth is weighing heavy on me, one I can't address without risking everything.

CHAPTER 31
Leonard

W e kissed. She kissed me. I kissed her back. I'm fucking giddy.

Apart from her lips on mine being everything I've been missing my entire life, it was simply the best kiss I've ever had. The way she tasted like something I can only describe as Chiara, so sweet and dangerous, is still making my head spin. The way she wanted me as much as I did her is doing things to me I can't even begin to understand. And the way I can feel her on my lips even as I stand in the kitchen, waiting for her, is making me smile like I'm the happiest person in the world. Then I remember her calling it a mistake, and everything implodes.

Starling doesn't want to be with me. She regrets the kiss. I feel like crawling under my covers and hiding from her until my heart stops burning from pain. It felt good for her, I know it did, but something is keeping her from being with me, and not knowing what it is only makes the ache in my chest worse. There is nothing I want more than to take her worries away, prove to her how good we'd be together, but I've hardly wrapped my own head around it.

How am I meant to convince her not to have doubts when I have a million?

I don't doubt how great we'd be together or that I have feelings for her. My doubts are all rooted in fears of fucking everything up when I've never felt this way about anyone before. I'm not a protective man with anyone but my family. Yet, here I am, ready to burn the world down for ever bringing her any sort of pain. I'm not possessive either, but I'd very much like to call her mine and tell everyone else who looks her way to fuck off. I don't laugh or cook for anyone but myself, and yet, Chiara has made me do everything with her.

We may not have had the healthiest of relationships, but we've always needed each other. Bickering let us blow off steam we never had the chance to blow off with anyone else. Instead of having everything pile up, we worked through our frustrations together, even if it was in a fucked up way. Now that we're closer, I'd very much like to use a different method for us to deal with our frustrations, but she doesn't want me like that. We've known each other for twenty years, and I'm only beginning to realise how oblivious I've been.

I always went over to Graham's and her apartment when I knew she'd be there. I always looked for any type of interaction with her. I always wanted to push her buttons so she'd be frustrated with me because any type of emotion she felt for me was better than none.

I never stopped thinking about her. I never let another woman get emotionally close to me because, deep down, I knew there was never going to be anyone as perfect for me as Starling. I never spent time alone with my feelings for her, but, if I had, I would have woken up a lot earlier to see how perfect she is for me.

We've found a good rhythm together. Things work smoothly between us now, even if we still fight occasionally. I'm surprised it isn't nearly as much as one would expect to argue with the person they're spending all of their time with. Moving in together shouldn't have gone as well as it has, and it's making me desperate to keep her in my flat. Graham leaving, turns out, was one of the best things to ever happen to me. Him not returning also helps. Instead of the six-month deadline, we haven't even addressed the possibility of her leaving again. I don't like the thought of her not having anywhere else to go, but I very much like the thought of being able to protect her here. Tim may not have shown his face in a while, but there are an endless amount of dangers out there. Here, with me, she's safe. Chiara will always be safe with me, no matter what she decides we will be.

"Okay, I'm ready," she says, dragging me back to reality while my heart remains in a trance of pain.

Looking at her now when I know what she tastes like and how well we fit together brings me more sadness than I've ever felt before. I try my best to keep my feelings off my face so she doesn't feel guilty for not reciprocating them. No matter what has happened, that's the last thing I want.

"Let's go," I reply and grab my keys out of the bowl at the entrance. I reach for Benz's leash, and she comes running with a happy tail moving from left to right at Formula One racing speed.

"Will you tell me where you're taking me?" Chiara asks as we head down the stairs and outside. I do my best not to look at her to avoid any further stabbing sensations in my chest.

"Not yet," I reply, fighting the urge to study her reaction. I've gotten so used to looking at her however much I desired that it's like fighting muscle memory at this point.

"Okay," she mumbles, and my hand twitches in her direction.

No. I can't intertwine our fingers to comfort her. I can't wrap my arm around her shoulders or touch her in any way. I've gotten used to feeling her skin pressed against mine, used to the way she melted into me. It will be hard to relearn the boundaries we had before she moved in with me.

It was raining the past three days in London, but the sun is shining again, warming and brightening up the day. I hate it. The urge to scream at the sun for making an appearance when I'm fucking miserable is strong. I wish for rain again so that I don't have to be a part of this happy day anymore. Nothing about it is happy, except for the kiss Chiara and I shared before everything went to shit.

"Are you upset with me?"

Her question stops me from walking, and I realise I've been frowning since she appeared in the kitchen. She's not used to seeing me like this around her anymore, just like I'm not used to putting up this facade with her. I like the person I am with her a lot more than the closed-off man I had to be for the last twenty-two years of my life.

"No, Chiara, I'm not upset with you." It's the truth.

No part of me blames her for pushing me away. Whether she's doing it to protect herself or because she's truly not interested in me doesn't change that she doesn't want to be with me. I will wrap my head around it sooner or later. All I need is time and... space. Space I would never take because I can't breathe properly without her near me.

I fucking hate everything that comes with having feelings for someone.

It's irritating.

"I'd understand if you're upset with me, you know?" she says, and I let my head turn her way, feeling a sharp pain strike through me at the sight of her green eyes.

"I'm not," I assure her, but she doesn't believe me.

"I feel like you are." Is she really trying to argue about *my* feelings?

"And yet, I'm not." Chiara narrows her eyes at me, crossing her arms in front of her chest a second later to appear more intimidating.

"You definitely are. I can see it in the way you're staring at me," she replies, annoyed with me and sad because of her words. It only frustrates me more.

"I'm not upset with you, Starling," I reply. Determination crosses her face, and I prepare for the fight I know we're about to have.

"You are, which is why you need to tell me what you need from me to make this better," she says, and I slap my forehead with the palm of my hand.

"*But I'm not upset with you*," I say through gritted teeth, so she throws her hands into the air, groaning at me.

"The more you keep it to yourself, the worse it will be after. We have to figure out what the hell we're going to do about this thing between us because you're not the only one who's done fighting against what they really want," she blurts out.

"What the hell are you talking about? You don't want me! You made that perfectly clear earlier," I reply, and she's about to respond when a bird lands on her head, causing me to stumble a step backward. "Don't move," I tell her and attempt to take it off her, but she raises her hands to stop me. "What are you doing? Let me help!" I say, but she glares at me for a moment, forcing my limbs to freeze in place.

Chiara reaches for the creature—which I now realise is a starling bird—and it steps into her hand, allowing her to bring it in front of her. The longer I study it, the more I realise it is purple, green, blue, and a little yellow. It simply sits on Chiara's palm, looking up at her as if it's expecting something from her. My gaze shifts to my little demon, who's smiling at the bird.

"Did I ever tell you what Mamma said to me after that starling bird flew on my head when we were kids?" she asks, but all I manage to do is shake my head. I'm mesmerized by the connection the bird and Chiara seem to have. "She told me Papa's favorite animal used to be starling birds," she explains, and I feel my knees weakening a little. "This little guy has been following me around England for years now. When you went to pick me up from the hair salon, I couldn't believe my eyes. He was right there, almost like he was waiting for me," Chiara goes on, and the bird flaps its wings a little.

"How do you know it's the same bird?" I ask, swallowing hard to get rid of the lump in my throat.

"He's missing a talon on his right side." She holds up the bird for me to see, and I notice one of the sharp nails missing from the creature. Holy shit. "I fed him a few times, which is probably the more logical explanation for why he keeps finding me, but, I don't know. I'd like to think my dad sent him to watch over me."

That's exactly what I was thinking. This coincidence is too strong to be ignorant and say it's impossible her dad has something to do with the bird showing up everywhere.

"Maybe it's stupid, sorry. I've never shared this with anyone. He usually doesn't land on my head, merely close by so I can see him."

"It's not stupid at all, Chiara."

She smiles at the bird once more before it flies onto my shoulder. I stop breathing while Chiara starts chuckling at my reaction. I don't mind birds, but this little guy is staring at me like he's trying to see if I'm good enough for the woman in front of me. He looks ready to report back to her father, who will ensure I have the worst luck in life if I'm not worthy of his daughter. I don't know if I believe any of these things, but I also know I do not *not* believe them. I don't know. My head is all confused with the fucking bird sitting on my shoulder.

"Do you want me to get him off?" she asks with amusement all over her face. Meanwhile, sweat has started dripping down my back.

"Nah, it's all good. It's just a bird," I reply, but, luckily, he flies away a second later, and I can stop pretending not to mind. Thank fuck.

"I didn't know you were scared of birds," Chiara says, and I frown at her.

"I most certainly am not. I'm scared of nothing but the snoring version of you when you're fast asleep. Scared me half to death recently. It was all quiet in the room and then all of a sudden—" She cuts me off by smacking my arm.

"*Stronzo*," she says with a playful frown, and I smile at the way she addresses me. It feels almost nostalgic to hear it again. It's been a while.

"Starling," I reply, and her face softens even more at the nickname. It carries a completely different weight for me now. "Let's go. We have to get there soon so we can go grab lunch after," I say and take her hand without thinking about it.

The first thing we're doing when we reach our destination is wash our hands in case the bird has any diseases, which is what I decide to focus on instead of lingering on what the hell just happened.

Chiara has been standing in the same spot at the art gallery an acquaintance of mine owns for the past five minutes. Her exhibit is different from the ones Chiara makes and is usually interested in. Instead of creative visual projections of already existing art, Annabeth created a work of art you can go through. The piece is called 'A Thousand Little Lives', and the balloons all over the room are meant to represent that idea. They are all red, some of them still fully blown up and others shriveling and withering away. A representation of life. This piece isn't supposed to last forever, Annabeth told me so herself. However, people are allowed to touch the balloons, something that doesn't sit right with Chiara.

"But, what if you touch them and they pop?" she asks, still standing inside of the art piece while I wait outside of the exhibit room with an impatient Benz. She doesn't like that she can see Chiara but not be right next to her.

"She said this is all about responsibility. Be careful how you treat the balloons or they will pop, just like you're meant to do with other people's lives," I explain, and Chiara's features soften at my words.

"That's beautiful," she says while making her way through the balloons. The walls are covered in mirrors, and I enjoy the fact that I get to see Chiara five different times from every different angle.

"Yeah, it is," I say, my eyes still on her because no piece of art could ever compare to her.

"I don't think I could ever make my own art like this," she says, so I cross my arms in front of my chest and lean against the door frame. Sensing we won't be entering the other room, Benz settles down next to me with a complaining grunt.

"If you wanted to, you most certainly could," I reply, and she turns to me with a surprised smile.

"You think so?" I nod immediately.

"Absolutely. You can do anything you put your mind to, Chiara. And I could help you too. I have connections to so many artists if you'd like to get some information about the process of coming up with ideas or anything else you need. I can also do some research myself, contact some other people I know. If you give me forty-eight hours, I will have a list of information ready for you," I say, and her eyes go wide in response.

Fuck. I've never shown this side of me to anyone except the people I work with. I'm great at analysing data with my team. I do research to try and help my team improve so I can improve too. I'm an analytical person. With anyone but Chiara, I always get straight to the point, I don't converse with them for longer than necessary. I get business done. It's who I am, but it isn't the type of person I've shown to her, especially not recently. The man who has hardened himself off from the world and focuses only on work isn't the one I want to show her. When I'm with Starling, I want to linger. Conversations with her aren't a task I have to get over with. I don't cut them short nor do I desire to do so. I linger because any words spoken between us, no matter what they are, are important to me.

"Leonard, it's not your job to help me all the time," she says and makes her way toward where I'm standing. Balloons move to the side as she clears a path, careful not to break any of them.

"I like to see people reach their potential, Chiara, especially those who have so much of it but haven't been given opportunities to reach their goals. I've gotten lots of help in my life, some of it even from you, and I wouldn't have made it to where I am today without it. I want to give back what I received too," I say, and while it isn't a lie, it's not the whole truth either. The reason why I do all of it for Chiara isn't only so she can reach her potential. It's mostly because I want to see her live her dream, to be happy.

"You're a good person, quite a big fact I need to wrap my head around," she teases and stops right in front of me.

Uncertainty lingers in her eyes as she stares at my chest. I tell Benz to stay before doing the one thing I really shouldn't do. I wrap my arms around her shoulders and bring her to my chest, realizing from the desperation in my bones that this is my love language. This is the way I tell her how I feel without having to say the words out loud. And by the way she sinks into me, melts against my chest and clicks into place like we were made for each other, lets me know she likes it as much as I do.

"I'm so confused," she mumbles against me, and I stroke her hair with my right hand.

"So am I," I admit, making her chuckle. I press her further against me.

"Well, that's not good. If one of us was at least certain, this would be easier," she says with a small laugh, and I pull back to cup her face in my hands.

"Nothing between us has ever been easy, but no truly good things come without hard work. We'll figure this out, sweetheart, because it's you—" She smiles as she finishes my sentence.

"And me now." I give her an agreeing nod, tracing her cheeks with the pads of my thumbs. "I want us to work, Leonard," she whispers, and I lean down to press one swift kiss to her lips and then wrap her up in my arms again. My cheek presses against the top of her head as I answer.

"So do I, Starling. So do I."

CHAPTER 32

Chiara

Leonard and I have been our normal selves for the past twenty-four hours, not once addressing the moment we had in the art gallery or even the kisses we shared yesterday morning. He's been treating me the same way he has for the past few months, and I stare after him like I've never seen a more stunning image than his backside. It also doesn't help that he keeps "forgetting" to put a shirt on.

Not talking about our feelings for a day has been helping me work through mine. Leonard has thrown my world upside down in the best way possible. Before I moved in with him, everything was bleak and empty. I worked too many jobs, barely slept, ate the blandest food because I didn't have money for something better, and my dream, even though I was working toward it, was never close to being within my reach. I was existing, but I wasn't living. Not like I am now.

Leonard has brought color to my life. He makes me food every single day, and it's so delicious, I've become addicted. He gave me a job I absolutely love, which pays me enough so I can save for my gallery—in case I don't find a sponsor—and allow me to spoil myself a little once in a while. Then again, he hasn't let me buy anything for myself in months because he always beats me to it. I say I like a shirt, the next day it appears on my bed. I tell him a book sounds interesting, the whole series shows up in my room. Leonard is using his connections to find me a sponsor and has been taking me to the most beautiful immersive art exhibits in the world. On top of that, he's been taking me to the most beautiful *places* in the world, even if it is mostly for work.

I'm genuinely happy. I don't remember a time I've been so completely and utterly happy. Despite missing Mamma, Graham, Nonna, and Lulu—I haven't seen her in months either because I've been so busy—a feeling of true joy has moved into my chest. Leonard is the cause of it. It isn't only tethered to him, there is a system of roots now, but he planted the seed and let it grow. It's a strange thought considering he should have been the last person to ever want to see me happy when he's the only one who's ever put me first.

We're almost out of the hotel door on our way to Nonna's house when my phone rings, catching Leonard's and my attention. My eyes shift to it in my hand, Graham's name flashing onto the screen. Leonard and I both scrunch our eyebrows together.

"Hello?" I ask after I answer the call.

"Hello, stranger. How are you?" he replies, and I hold the phone away from my ear to check the time.

"It's six in the morning in New York. Why are you up so early? And since when do you call me to check in without texting me three days in advance?" I tease, making my best friend chuckle into the phone.

"Well tonight is a big night, and I just—" Leonard snatches the phone out of my hand.

"Shut the fuck up," he scream-whispers at his brother, and I give him a look I hope says 'Do you want to lose that hand?'. He gives me an apologetic smile before covering his mouth over the speaker and saying something else to Graham.

"You have three seconds to give me back my Graham, or I will kick your ass," I warn, and Leonard swats my outstretched hand away.

"You don't frighten me," he says, and I let out a brief sigh before smoothly wrestling him to the ground. I end up on top of him, pressing the palm of my hand to his chest. My other one grabs the phone, pressing it to my ear while Leonard drops his head on the carpet and bites his bottom lip to hide a smile.

"What did you mean by 'tonight is a big night'?" I ask Graham, and Leonard tries to take my phone away again, but I pin his hand over his head, my tits right in his face. Lust appears in his eyes as his free fingers slip onto my hips, grabbing tightly to shift me backward a little, my clit finding his hard cock. *Oh God.*

"Never mind. I'll call you tomorrow," Graham says and hangs up, but I barely hear him.

My eyes are fixated on Leonard's as he looks from mine to my tits so close to his lips, I'm pretty sure if he tilted his head, he could pull one of my hard nipples into his mouth. I've never wanted clothes to disappear as badly as I do right now.

"You should know, it really turns me on when you throw me around like this," he says, rolling my hips until I break into a moan and my grip on his wrist loosens.

"I like the control," I admit, dropping my phone onto the ground and covering his hand on my hip with mine.

"I like surrendering it to you." I grind myself against his cock again, causing both of us to moan.

"We probably shouldn't be dry-humping on the floor," I manage to croak out, but I don't stop my movements either.

"You're right. Release my hands, and I'll carry you to bed," he offers, but I plant my mouth on his, desperate to taste him while I have the chance. "Oh God, Chiara, this isn't how I—" he starts but cuts off to devour my mouth, slipping his tongue into it. I pick up speed in my movements, chasing my orgasm because it brushed the tips of my fingers already, getting closer and closer with each rub against him.

"Please," I beg, and he flips us around, his body between my legs and his groin pressing into mine.

"This isn't the order I wanted to do this in, but I can't deny you anything." He kisses me swiftly, putting so much pressure on my clit with his cock, my back arches off the ground. "Pay attention, sweetheart, because this is only a little taste of what I'm planning on giving you after our date," he says, rubbing himself over me and sliding his tongue into my mouth before I have the chance to ask something important. *What date?*

"Leonard," I moan, and he groans against my neck. He's kissing and licking along it until I'm a mess.

"Can I slip my hand into your panties, baby? I need to feel how wet you are, need you to come around my fingers," he says between kisses he trails from my neck all the way to my mouth.

"Please," I say into his mouth, and he stops thrusting his groin against me. He lets out a small moan as he briefly cups my breast and then guides his hand all the way to the waistband of my shorts.

"Before I fuck you with my fingers, I need to admit something," he says, playing with the elastic of my pants, teasing me.

"Spit it out," I demand while he kisses my cheek. He chuckles against me and then brings his hand to my cheek, his thumb pulling down my bottom lip. My head is dizzy with pleasure and desperation.

"I've never wanted anyone as much as I want you, Chiara." His mouth is on mine a second later, his fingers disappearing into my panties.

As soon as his middle and ring finger rub over my clit, every tension in my body subsides. All my muscles manage to do is lift my arms so my hands can slip into his hair. I tug on his short coils, and he groans into my mouth again. His fingers disappear inside of me, sending a thunderstorm of pleasure through me and ripping down every wall and barrier I've ever put up with him. He slips them back out and thrusts them inside again, curling the tips until he grazes my perfect spot, the palm of his hand applying pressure to my clit.

"Fuck, oh God," I moan as I break the kiss, bringing the back of my hand to my mouth to bite down on it. The pleasure is too much, too overwhelming, and I can't breathe properly anymore.

"I'm not done kissing you," Leonard says, and I open my eyes to find him staring down at me with half-closed lids and his bottom lip slightly tucked between his teeth. His fingers keep thrusting inside of me, forcing more moans from my lips and causing my back to arch off the ground. "Give me back your mouth," he says with a little smile, and I can't help but let out a breathless laugh. I remove my hand and he gives me an approving nod. "You can be such a good girl, little demon," he says, planting his mouth back on mine as his fingers keep up a rhythm that has my toes curling.

"Please," I beg because my body is overcharging with pleasure, and I need a release. "Faster, please," I ask between kisses, and he obeys in an instant.

His fingers thrust inside of me harder and faster until I'm a panting mess. Leonard kisses me, swallowing all the sounds of pleasure leaving my lips like he wants to feel them deep inside his chest.

"Come," he demands, and there is no strength left in my body to fight against his wishes.

An orgasm ripples through me, shattering every rational thought inside of me. My cells explode into a trillion fireworks, and I scream his name without meaning to. Waves over waves of pleasure crash through me, but Leonard doesn't stop. He keeps fucking me with his fingers to let me ride out my orgasm for as long as possible, but I can't take more. I let out a complaining whine.

"No more," I say, completely out of breath.

"But I want another, sweetheart." Leonard kisses my neck. "And another after that." One more kiss to my neck. "And a million more after that."

"When will I get one from you?" I ask, wishing my voice wasn't so quiet, as if I'd never dirty-talked before. He nibbles on my bottom lip for a moment before answering.

"Whenever you want one, baby." *Now, right now.* "Except right now because we need to go," he says, giving me one last kiss before lifting me off the ground. I pout playfully, and he runs his thumb over my bottom lip.

His features soften as he studies me, slowly caressing my features.

"You and me, Starling." I step on my tiptoes to bring my mouth to his, responding with my lips on his.

"You and me, Champ."

CHAPTER 33

Leonard

Dad sends me a photo of a happy Benz sleeping next to Mum on the couch, and I lift the screen for Chiara to see the photo too. She merely grins at me while revealing my father sent her the same picture. It makes me smile from ear to ear. Her eyes linger on my lips for a moment before she drags them away and gazes out of the window.

We left Benz with my parents because Starling and I have a million things to do this coming week in Italy, and I wanted her to be able to completely focus on the opportunity Dino has given her without feeling guilty about ignoring Benz. I slide my hand across the seat, taking hers in mine. I don't look at her, simply study the fields over fields of greenery we drive by.

Images of her under me, begging and kissing me, flood my brain, and I have to take a deep breath when my cock gets inevitably hard. My mind lingers for a little on the red colour that spread across her cheeks and cleavage from pleasure. The way Chiara screamed for me. I always had a feeling she'd be loud, but I never expected her to be so noisy. It was ridiculously hot. I can still hear her moans, bringing a smile to my lips. Then, my fingers twitch as I remember the way her walls tightened around me as she fell apart, and I do my best to breathe through the way my cock twitches in my pants, begging me to find a release. I suck in another sharp breath, noticing Chiara's head turning in my direction.

"Are you okay?" she asks and squeezes my fingers. I had this wonderful thing planned for tonight, a surprise, but I let it slip out when pleasure was clouding my brain. I only hope she forgot about it because she was too busy enjoying me finger fuck her. "Is this about the whole date thing you mentioned?" she asks as if she could read my thoughts. *Damn it.*

"What date?" I ask, and she rolls her eyes at me, shaking her head a moment after.

"You're impossible." I smile at that. Yes, I most certainly am.

My eyes shift back out of the window and so do hers. We're on our way to her Nonna's house where her Mamma lives now too. Chiara wiggles a little in her seat, and I can sense how excited she is to see them both. It's been months since she saw her Mamma and a year since she saw her Nonna. She misses both of them with every piece of her, something I know even if she never told me. I can hear it in the way her voice changes when she's speaking to them in Italian on the phone. I can see it in the way she stares at the wall for several minutes after she hangs up the phone. I can feel it in the way sadness slips into her posture and features when she speaks about them.

Her Nonna and Mamma are two of the most important people in her life. I knew as soon as I asked Chiara to travel the world with me I would bring her here, no matter what. I would have never expected us to be this close when we got here, but it makes me happy to know I will be visiting the place she grew up in as her... friend, I think, and not her enemy. I fucking hate labels, but, right now, I'd love to ask her what she'd categorize me as. I'm definitely not her boyfriend. I haven't even taken her on our first date yet...

"You have to behave, okay?" Chiara says after a few moments of silence, so I turn to her with confusion.

"What do you mean?" I need more details before I make a stupid comment that will cause her to roll her eyes.

"I mean, my Nonna will smack you with a wooden spoon if you so much as breathe the wrong way in my presence. So, don't look at me weirdly or start arguing with me over something silly," she says, and I raise my pinky. "Pinky promise, really?" Chiara asks with a small smile, and I return it.

"Yeah, but not the way other people do it. You see, our pinkies should intertwine and our thumbs should touch. This way, you make a full circle that can't be broken, just like a promise should be. Unbreakable." She raises her pinky to mine and then we connect the pads of our thumbs. "I promise to be on my best behaviour," I say, causing her to lean back in her seat and groan.

"I don't like that," Starling replies, and I let go of her fingers only to start playing with a strand of her brown hair.

"My version of the pinky promise?" I ask, but she shakes her head.

"I don't like that you make me like you all the time." I smirk at her comment.

"You like me, little demon?" My voice has a hint of amusement in it, which is why she turns her head to me and glares.

"Nope, I'm immune to your charm," she replies and crosses her arms in front of her chest. I let out a small laugh, my eyes briefly darting to our driver to make sure he isn't paying any attention. He's not. So, I lean over to Chiara and grab her chin between my fingers to tilt her head my way again.

"If you're immune, your cheeks probably won't turn red if I kiss you, right?" Every single time I've planted my mouth on hers, colour jumped into her face, making it all rosy and happy.

"Definitely not," she replies. "You can try, but—" I cut her off with a kiss.

A few months ago, I warned myself one taste from her would be it. I would be undone by her, and I was right. I can't get enough. Every little piece of me is drawn to her now, even more so than before I first felt her lips on mine. The moment I had the feeling of utter and undeniable completeness in my chest from the way we fit together was the first time in my life everything started to make sense. I went twenty-eight fucking years perfectly alright with the belief of being incapable of falling in love. Then, Chiara and I kiss, and suddenly, it doesn't seem like something I can't do. It's become something I didn't want to do with anyone but her.

"*Siamo arrivati*," the driver says after minutes of Chiara and me making out in the back. I lean away to find her cheeks red and her lips perfectly pink.

"Not immune after all," I whisper, and she rolls her eyes playfully.

"Well, you stuck your tongue down my throat, what did you expect?" she replies while I hand the driver some money and get out of the car with her. Her taste lingers on my lips, and I can't help but smile like someone who just won the lottery. Because I did.

I really fucking did.

Anger courses through me, along with shock and a sliver of fear I'm trying to ignore. Tim is here. He's cooking in the kitchen with Chiara's Nonna, and I'm sick to my stomach. Part of me wants to run back to the entrance where Starling is still hugging her Mamma, another part of me is unable to move.

"What the hell are you doing here?" I say, fixating on the rage inside of me so my voice is steady and threatening. Tim smiles at me.

"Don't you know? Giulia and I are dating." *No.* "Oh, so you didn't know. That's interesting. I guess she wanted to keep us secret for a bit longer." I storm toward him.

"I'm going to give you an option here, Tim. Either you get the fuck out right now, or I will have my friends in law enforcement make your life very, very difficult." I feel something hard smack my arm and turn to see Nonna with her cooking spoon cocked in attack mode.

"You two, plates on the table, *pronto*," she says with a heavy Italian accent.

"Tim," Chiara says, her voice shaky and full of fear.

Instinct takes over, and I step away from the gross man in front of me to shield her with my body. Starling is a lot more skilled to protect me and herself, but it doesn't matter to me. All I care about is putting a buffer between Tim and my little demon.

"What's going on?" Giulia asks, and I give Chiara a look that says 'You need to tell her' because this has gone too bloody far now.

"Mamma," Chiara starts before ending the sentence in Italian. I don't manage to grasp any words, but I'm also too busy keeping my eyes trained on the creep glaring at me.

"I don't understand," Guilia says, catching Tim's attention.

"What did she say, my love?" he asks, and I feel more anger spreading through me. I don't know Guilia very well. I shouldn't care about her just because she's Chiara's Mamma, but I do. She's important to the woman I'd die for, therefore she's important to me. Simple as that.

"My options remain the same, you piece of shit. I'd suggest you leave before I break a few of your bones," I warn, but, suddenly, a wave of calm overwhelms me as Chiara slips her hand into mine.

"It's okay," she whispers and turns to her Nonna and Mamma again, saying something in Italian that makes the two women leave the kitchen. I can't explain it, but they look like the same person aged three different ages. "Tim, it's time for you to leave. Grab your things, and get out. Once I've told Mamma everything you've said and done to me, she'll never want to see you again." Chiara attempts to walk out of the room when he takes a step toward her and then another until his fingers are around her elbow. All I see is red as I cross the room to move between them again to punch him in the face. Starling beats me to it, throwing a perfect right hook into Tim's face.

"You bloody bitch," he curses, but I'm already raising my phone to show him I'm a second away from calling the police.

"Get out," I warn, and he flashes me one more glare before grabbing his keys in the entrance and then slipping out of the front door. Chiara locks it without hesitation, and I notice her hands shaking violently. "Sweetheart," I say, and she looks up at me, a serious look on her face as she tries to hide how scared she is.

"I'm fine," she lies and rubs her knuckles.

"Come here," I say and open my arms. Her green eyes study me for a brief moment before she sucks in a sharp breath.

"Really, it's fine. I should go explain to Mamma and Nonna what the hell just happened. They're probably confused and—" I close the distance between us and wrap my arms around her.

"I'm sorry. I kind of needed a hug," I tell her, and Chiara melts into me, her fingers tangling together at the small of my back.

"You don't need a hug, Leonard. You want to comfort me," she replies, and while she's half-right, she's also half-wrong. I always need a hug from her.

"I'll make some tea while you speak to your family," I say and kiss her forehead once before making my way into the kitchen and finding a kettle to place on the stove. Chiara disappears into a room I assume is the living room, and I let out a heavy breath.

Tim hadn't shown his face in months. I thought he'd finally understood Chiara was not interested in him. I would have never expected him to date her Mamma and make her fall for him. That's fucking disgusting. Tim is a vile man. Part of me is glad I can't hear everything Chiara is sharing with her family at the moment. If I were to hear what he's done to her in more detail than Chiara's shared with me in the past, I'd lose it. I'm already debating asking my PI friend to dig up enough dirt on Tim to put him behind bars for a long time. Someone like him probably has a lot of criminal activity going on.

Half an hour later, Chiara, Guilia, and Sofia, Starling's Nonna, walk into the kitchen again. They're all silent as they take the cups of tea I've prepared—it took me twenty minutes to find tea bags. My little demon looks exhausted, and I hate that her time with her family has already been tainted by what happened. I also notice redness around Guilia's eyes, causing my heart to sink a little. I can't imagine what must be going through her head. A man getting close to her because he's been stalking her daughter in a way. I'll have to speak to Chiara about potentially getting a restraining order to keep Tim as far away from her and her Nonna and Mamma as possible. I need them all safe.

"Leonard, come. I'm making vegan lasagna and need your help," Sofia says, waving me over to the stove where she is. I shoot Chiara a glance, noticing the way she's zoning out, lost in her thoughts.

"I need one minute, *per favore*," I say to Sofia, and she gives me a slight, warm smile before assuring me to take my time. I nod my head in the direction of the backyard door, and Chiara walks through it, checking to see if I'm right behind her with a tilt of her head. I place my hand between her shoulder blades to signal I'm right here.

"He's been taking Mamma on dates, visiting her in Italy, telling her he's been in love with her for years, and more things I can't even think about without getting nauseous," Chiara explains, settling down on an old lounge chair, which clearly has seen better days.

Everything about this little house is old. There are more cracks in the walls than I was able to count in the half an hour I was alone. The colour of the bricks used outside for the facade are faded. The furniture inside is well-loved and old as well, but there is something about this tiny place that screams home. A family is meant to live here, there is no doubt about it, and I'm glad Chiara's Nonna is no longer living here by herself.

"We should file for a restraining order," I say, and Starling gives an agreeing nod. I'm glad she isn't fighting me on this. It's too important.

"I should have told her years ago. I shouldn't have kept all of this to myself. I put her in danger, and I don't know what I would have done if Tim—" She cuts off abruptly, swallowing hard and blinking rapidly at the ground.

"This is not your fault, Starling," I remind her, my fingers twitching because they're desperate to reach out and run a comforting hand over her arm. I manage to contain the urge.

"Yeah, it is. But she knows now. She knows, and it will keep her safe. Tim won't do anything stupid, I know he won't. He's a well-known personality in London. He can't risk tainting his reputation," she says, but I know she's convincing herself more than me. My feet take a step toward her before I can stop them. Chiara stands and moves toward me too, just a little.

"What do you need from me?" I ask, and she finally lets go of her restraint and brings her hands to my neck. Mine shift to her hips.

"I need you to distract me. Take my mind off it," she begs, and I stare at the blue sky behind her, thinking about what I can tell her. Only one thing slips through my head.

"I'm going to take you on a date tonight," I say without giving myself another moment to hesitate. Her eyes light up a little at my words.

"Where to?" she asks, tilting her head up with a small smile.

JUMP-START

"Somewhere you'd never expect me to take you."

CHAPTER 34

Chiara

I've never gone on a date before. In my twenty-four years of life, no one's ever asked me to go out with them. It's never bothered me either if I'm being honest. Casual hookups have been my norm since I was eighteen, but I never minded because I was too busy for a boyfriend, first with uni and then with work. I've had lots of sex with guys whose names I can't remember anymore. I don't know when that information slipped from my mind.

That's a lie.

I'm lying to myself because it's easier than admitting every person I've been with was erased the moment Leonard kissed me for the first time. Once I've felt his mouth move with mine, memories of past hookups were obliterated, replaced by the feeling of undeniable fulfillment. The only face I see now when I imagine sex or anything related to it is Leonard's, which is a big problem I'm doing my best to disregard. It's bad enough I allowed my head to accept my feelings for him.

I'm supposed to be getting ready for our date, a great distraction from what the fuck happened this morning at Nonna's house. Tim started dating Mamma, most likely to get close to me. He was at the house like he was part of the family. I had to share every horrible word, touch, or feeling he's ever done or inflicted in me. To see her face, horrified and guilt written all over her features, broke my heart. I shouldn't have kept it from her, but when she was living with him, I couldn't say anything without risking her losing her place to live. After she moved out, I didn't see the need to share what he did when I visited her. I should have known keeping something like this from the person I love the most would be a horrible idea.

My eyes flutter shut for a moment before I shake my head to force all of those thoughts away. The dripping of my wet hair against the bathroom tile reminds me I should blow dry it and add some makeup. Once I'm satisfied with the way it looks, I slip on the navy blue summer dress I brought on the trip. It hugs my curves in a way I know will capture Leonard's eyes permanently, bringing a smile to my lips.

"Sweetheart? Are you almost ready? We have to go," Leonard says after a single knock. I open the door, still grinning because I'm excited to go on my first date ever, and with Leonard out of all people. It makes me giddy. "Fuck," he mutters under his breath as his eyes take in their fill of my appearance.

The same word leaves me when I notice how handsome he looks. Leonard could wear a reusable shopping bag and look stunning, but this outfit, the matching navy blue dress shirt to my outfit and black pants hugging his hips perfectly, makes him somehow even more attractive. His tattoos peek out from under his rolled-up sleeves, his short coils styled in place. It almost hurts to look at the tight line of his shoulders in the shirt, his defined collarbones visible underneath it because he left the top buttons undone. The veins on his hands stand out more today than I've ever seen them before. He's so breathtakingly stunning, I get dizzy when he places his hands on my hips to bring me flush against his upper body. An explosion goes off in my chest, setting everything inside of me on fire. It should be painful, but I welcome the heat, especially as it settles between my legs.

"That's one hell of a way to burn yourself into my brain for the rest of eternity," he says, causing a blush to spread across my cheeks, warming the tips of my ears.

"That was the goal, *prestante*," I reply, and he smirks down at me.

"Is that another word for 'asshole' or something nice for once?" he teases, and I run my hand up his hard chest, forcing desire into his gaze.

"Look it up," I offer, the smirk never leaving his lips as he fixates all of his attention onto my mouth.

"Are you ready to leave?" he asks, his mouth dropping to mine, but I press my index finger to his lips.

"Do you prefer lipstick or lipgloss?" I reply, and he kisses my finger, dragging me closer by my hips. My finger drops from his mouth so he can answer.

"Doesn't matter to me, little demon. As long as either will end up all over me later." He uses my surprise to press a kiss to the sensitive skin below my earlobe. "You shouldn't taste as sweet as you smell, Chiara," he says with a little groan.

"I also shouldn't want your mouth on me all the time. Nothing makes sense anymore," I reply. A low chuckle leaves him.

"You're right, it doesn't." Leonard steps back, his earlier smirk reappearing on his face. "We're leaving in three minutes. Hurry up," he says, dropping his hands to my ass for the briefest second before turning me around by my hips and back into the bathroom.

"Don't tell me what to do," I reply, but he mumbles something I don't understand with a little groan, and I turn to see his tense shoulders as he stares down at his phone outside of the bathroom. A wicked grin spreads across his face. "What?" I ask, and he looks up at me with satisfaction.

"You called me 'handsome'," he says, and I roll my eyes.

"Did not," I lie, and he holds up the google translator he used to find out what *prestante* means.

"You sure did. You think I'm handsome," he says with a little grin I've never seen on his face before. It's so unlike his usual gruff expression, it knocks the air out of me for a moment.

"You also think you're handsome, so it cancels out," I tease, and he huffs out a laugh.

"Go put on that lipstick I want smeared across me later," he says so nonchalantly, he could be telling me how many degrees it is right now. If you ask my skin, it's about fifty degrees celsius in here.

I decide on a dark pink lipstick that has Leonard's gaze glued to my lips for several minutes after I walk out of the bathroom. After a deep breath he probably thinks I can't see him inhale, he turns on his heel and disappears into his room of the penthouse. He returns with a polaroid camera—my polaroid camera, the one he bought me after someone broke into my apartment—and places it on the counter. Leonard adjusts it a few times before stepping back and taking my hand.

"What are you—" He cuts me off as he tucks me into his side and drapes his arm over my back, so he can place his hand on my hip.

"Making memories, now *shush* and smile," he says, and I do as I'm told before the camera clicks and the photo is taken. I step out of his embrace and glare at him.

"Did you just *shush* me?" I ask, and he gives me another grin.

"Yes. I was trying to get a nice picture," he explains as he walks over to study the little picture printed out of the camera. I cock an eyebrow at his backside.

"Why?" *Why is he doing all of this? Why are we going on a date? Why does he have feelings for me?* These are all very good questions I know I won't get an answer to, at least not from him.

"Because I'm not in your album," he mumbles, causing realization to dawn on me.

"You've looked through my album?"

It contains every little polaroid photo I've ever taken in my life. Everyone I love is in there, including a candid photo of Leonard in his GoKart when he was fourteen and I was ten. So, maybe he didn't look through it after all, otherwise he'd know he's in it, and it's one of my most treasured photos. Not that I'd ever admit it to him. I'd die before I tell him I've looked at a picture I took of him after he won the karting championship a thousand times over the years. He was just so happy that day, sweat dripping down the sides of his face, hair everywhere, a trophy in his hands.

"No, but I can put two and two together, Chiara," Leonard says, making a wave of guilt spread through me.

He thinks all I've had for him over the years has been hatred, but... that isn't true. He's been an asshole since I can remember. He's also a major pain in the ass, and we've fought more times than I could keep count, but he's always been my jerk. My life would have never been complete if he hadn't shown up. More often than not, I dreaded conversations with him, and still I wanted more because he somehow understood me in a way no one else did or does.

Which is why I let out a groan as I step into my room and grab the album I take with me everywhere. My hands shake as I bring it back outside to where a very confused Leonard is standing, watching me with curious eyes.

"When you put two and two together, was the answer four? Because I don't think so," I say as I open the album to the picture of him with his trophy.

"Chiara," he starts but swallows so hard, the rest of his sentence gets lost in the world of forgotten words.

"Yeah, you can make fun of me for having that picture of you from fourteen years ago now, but I needed to prove you wrong," I say and cross my arms in front of my chest.

Leonard's fingers pull the photo out of the plastic and trail over the old and worn material with a serious, intense look on his face. He sucks in a sharp breath and then lets it back out, his chest shaking a little as he does it. I'm about to ask him if he's okay when he places the picture back into the protective case and rests it next to the camera on the counter. He takes two strides toward me and cups my face, kissing me until my knees wobble.

There is desperation and an overwhelming amount of emotion in his kiss. It feels like he's telling me everything with the way he nibbles on my bottom lip and then wraps his lips around mine again. I don't know exactly what his feelings are—I couldn't name them even if I tried—but I can taste them.

"Do you understand?" he asks a little breathlessly, and I open my eyes to look up at him. His thumbs caress my cheekbones until heat fills them even more than his kiss did.

"Yes," I reply because I do. He was trying to tell me what his heart is experiencing, what I'm putting it through, and I'm glad to see it's the same thing mine is trying to deal with at the moment.

"Good, it's important."

His hands drop to my neck and shoulders, which he squeezes once and then steps away. His eyes remain on me for a little longer, but then he shakes his head and lets out a humorless laugh.

"Bloody hell, Chiara. My head's spinning," is all he says as he walks away toward where his keys and wallet are. Leonard grabs the camera too and then holds out his hand for me. "Come, sweetheart. I would like to make some more memories with you," he says, and I don't hesitate.

I take his hand and allow myself to let the meteorite go wherever it wants to strike.

I'm dumbfounded.

Leonard has organized a little picnic at *Parco di Monza*. When I asked him who put the basket there with the checkered, blue picnic blanket underneath, he merely shrugged. Apparently, I'm not supposed to know, and, if I'm being honest with myself, I don't really care either. I'm too mesmerized by the long stretch of green grass, the little river running through it as well as a bridge connecting the separate pieces of land. The breeze is warm and comfortable, the sky a bright blue, and people around us are laughing and walking. Leonard ignores them all as he leads me to our picnic area and holds my hand to help me settle down on the blanket.

"I know we've been eating vegan, but your Nonna told me how much you love some bread with *mortadella*," Leonard says as he settles down beside me, and I feel my heart beat unevenly for a split second.

"You got me *mortadella*?" I ask, and he flashes me a happy smile at the expression on my face.

"Yeah, sweetheart," he says and starts taking out all the food he's brought.

Grapes, apple slices, the *mortadella* bread he promised me, and a bottle of white wine. There are a few cookies I know will be vegan because they're for both of us, and I smile at him because this is absolutely perfect.

Then, reality decides to come crashing down on me.

What the hell are we doing?

I work for him! He made me come earlier, and I didn't even begin to consider what the repercussions will be. We may be getting along now, even have feelings for each other, but he's risking nothing. Meanwhile, I am putting everything on the line every single time he kisses me. This can't happen. We shouldn't be on a date.

"What? What happened?" Leonard asks, panic filling his eyes as he studies me. My breath catches in my throat.

"You have to take me back to the hotel, Leonard. We can't do this. I work for you. If we fuck this up, I'll lose everything. I'll—" *I will lose you*. I can't breathe.

"Chiara, baby, please breathe. I know you have a million worries running around in your head, so let's address them together, okay?" he offers, and I let myself slump back onto the blanket.

"Okay," I reply, and he takes my hand, his warm, brown eyes on me as he places a kiss to the back of it.

"No matter what happens between us, you will not lose your job. No one cares about Benz as much as you do, and I would never lose sight of that. You will get your paycheck, the same amount as always, and nothing will change about that either. When you work, you will be compensated. Simple as that. I will even make it over the team if it makes you feel better," he says, but I shake my head. The arrangement we have right now works, I was just worried I'd be jobless when we don't work out. "Tell me another concern."

"If I'm the one to fuck this up, you won't take me to meet investors anymore." Leonard nods for a moment to acknowledge my words instead of dismissing them with a lame 'I would never do that'. It sends a wave of calm through me.

"I've always wanted to see you succeed, Starling. Apart from that, I told you the many reasons why I've been using my connections to help you find an investor. You don't need me to repeat them. I would give anything to help you reach your potential, no matter our relationship status. Lastly, I don't think you're really worried about that. I think you're scared of losing what we've built these past few months," he says, and I hate him for seeing through me so easily. I know he'd never withhold help from me. It isn't the type of person Leonard is. Seeing the people he cares about succeed makes him happy.

"We're not meant to work," I tell him, and he gives me a sad smile, raising his hand to my cheek.

"If we aren't, then explain to me why we do," he replies, and like a metal to a magnet, my forehead moves against his.

"I like your cooking," I reply, and he starts laughing.

"Just my cooking? Nothing else?" I nod, and he continues sharing his sounds of amusement with me. I smile in response.

"I like that you saved Benz from a shelter," I add, and he brushes his nose over my cheek.

"Best thing I've ever done," he says, his attention drifting to my lips. "Getting you fired from that bartending job is the second best," he goes on, and I smack his shoulder.

"That is not funny," I reply, but he's serious as he glances all over my face.

"I wasn't kidding," he says firmly, running his thumb over my thigh in circles. "If I hadn't done that, you wouldn't have moved in with me. You'd still be working four jobs and living in that safety-hazardous apartment," he complains, and I give his shoulder another slap.

"That safety-hazardous apartment was my home for six, beautiful years, *stronzo*," I reply, but he breaks the bickering tension of the moment as he looks at me with nothing but admiration.

"You know what I like about you?" he asks, dropping his hand to my ribs and tugging until I give in and close the distance between us, careful not to throw any of the food over. "This," he says and points at my heart. "And this." His finger moves to my temple, and I shake my head.

"Well, the second one has caused you a lot of trouble over the years," I reply, and he nods in agreement.

"Why do you think I like it so much?" I can't help but snort a little.

"Yeah, all of a sudden," I blurt out, bringing a bright smile to his face. Like always, it knocks the breath from my chest. He shouldn't be as handsome as he is.

"No, Chiara, always."

His lips are on mine a moment later.

CHAPTER 35
Leonard

I could watch Chiara eat, drink, laugh, and talk for the rest of my life. The setting sun is making her tanned skin glow, her green eyes shine brightly, and her cheeks a perfectly rosy-red colour. Everything about her has my heart in a chokehold, but I do nothing to remove the grip she has on it either. One date is all I wanted. I was hoping it would go horribly so that neither one of us would speak about it again. That hope drained right into the river next to us when she stepped out of the bathroom at the hotel. Her peachy scent continues to fill my nose in waves as we sit in this massive park, watching people be happy.

For the first time in my life, I'm truly happy too. All of the wins and races, yeah, they made me momentarily happy, but the joy Chiara gives me feels permanent. She could take it away at any second, I'm aware of that, but it doesn't stop me from soaking in the feelings she's ignited within me for as long as she lets me. Any heartbreak, or whatever rubbish I'll have to endure later, will be worth it.

"I've never been stargazing," Chiara blurts out after a few moments of me silently playing with a strand of her hair and smiling like I never do anything else. Her head is tilted back, her eyes fixed on the sky above us.

The sun is almost gone now, so I pack up the remainder of the food and push the picnic basket out of the way. I lean back on the blanket, adjusting until I'm comfortable, and then open my arms for her. Chiara's been watching me since I first started shifting around, a small smile curling her lips upward. I return her amused

281

expression, keeping my hands in place even when she makes no attempt to move toward me.

"Come here," I beg with a teasing pout, and she shakes her head at me.

"You're unbelievable," she says, but a second later, she's adjusting herself against my side, placing her head on my shoulder and her hand on my chest. Heaven.

"My mum used to take me stargazing as a kid," I say because that's something she doesn't know about me.

No one but Mum and I know. It was our secret hiding spot when things at home got too difficult. I used to fight a lot with Dad about my dream to become a racer, and Mum helped diffuse our fights by taking me to calm down. By the end of every stargazing session, I felt horrible about what I said to him. He was doing everything he could to financially support me, and I was often very ungrateful. Which is something I never shared with anyone...

Except for Chiara now.

"I love your mum," she says against my chest, sending a warmth through it I have no power of stopping.

"She loves you too," I reply and kiss the top of Chiara's head. Everything's silent for a moment before Chiara sucks in a sharp breath.

"I miss my Papa," she admits in a whisper, and my heart sinks into my stomach. I press a kiss to her forehead and hold on tighter. "I know I never met him, but Mamma told me some things about him, like the way he always smelled like freshly-baked bread or the dimple in his right cheek. He may have died before I was born, but I miss him." Her fingers curl around my shirt, and I let myself sink into her vulnerability, trying to understand what that loss feels like. "He died of some kind of virus. I don't know what it was exactly. I never had the courage to ask Mamma," she explains, and I slip my finger under her chin, tilting her head up so her gaze meets mine.

"He would have been so proud of you, Starling. You're a force to be reckoned with, a fighter with the biggest heart. When I have a daughter one day, if I'm so lucky, I want her to be just like you," I say.

"Leonard Tick wants kids? What a shocker," she replies with a teasing tone, and I scrunch my eyebrows at her in confusion.

"How would you know if I want to have kids or not?" Chiara trails her fingers up my chest before resting them on the hollow between my neck and collarbone.

"I see how you are with Ellie. You love that little girl so much, probably more than you love everyone else," Chiara goes on, and my heart skips several beats. *Not everyone...*

"Do you want kids?" I ask to try and force my head in the right direction. Away from uncalled-for feelings.

"I want a big family. Kids, dogs, fish, all of it. In the future. With the right partner," she says and drops her head back onto my chest, probably listening to my racing heartbeat.

"Sounds like a plan," I reply, and she lets out a small laugh.

"You should really think about the way you phrase things," Chiara says, but I was well aware of what I was saying. "You're on your way to get another championship. Are you doing alright with the pressure?" she asks, and I stare down at her, surprise settling in my chest.

Are you doing alright with the pressure?

No one's ever asked me that before. This was the path I chose, to become a race car driver, so it was my fault. If I was stressed or pressured, it was on me. My parents are wonderful, but they always told me how difficult all of this would be. Therefore, they never checked on me either. Graham and Jack have always been busy with their own lives, and I can sense a little resentment from both of them toward me as well. My career has always been prioritised in our family. It was the reason why Jack couldn't get new football cleats or why Graham couldn't take kickboxing classes. I only found that out later, and I've been doing my best to make it up to them ever since. But that's why they never check on me. They're happy when I win and frustrated when I don't. They love me and my career is important to them, yet, none of them has ever asked me this one simple question Chiara just asked.

Are you doing alright with the pressure?

I'm doing alright with the pressure of becoming a second-time Formula One World Champion. However, I'm not doing alright with the pressure my feelings are putting on my heart whenever I'm around the woman lying in my arms.

"Yeah, Starling, I'm doing alright," I reply when she nudges the side of my face with her nose.

"You know if you weren't, you could tell me. I'm a great listener," she says and runs her nails down my stomach and then back up again. My cock instantly stiffens at the little teasing touch, which is why I wrap my fingers around her wrist to stop her from repeating the same action.

"I appreciate you looking out for me, Chiara, and I promise to come to you when I'm overwhelmed, okay?"

"Okay," she says and rests her cheek on my chest.

Starling wiggles her hand free and then resumes running her nails down my torso, then trailing her fingers over the button of my jeans. I let out a hissed breath and grab her wrist again, my cock twitching uncomfortably. Noticing my growing bulge, she looks up at me with a naughty grin. Her green eyes are full of lust, and I'm having a very hard time keeping my hands to myself.

"Keep going, sweetheart, and I'll throw you over my shoulder and take you back to the hotel room right now," I warn, releasing her hand to see what she will do.

I expect her to tilt her face up to the sky again. Instead, she slides her hand over my cock and palms me slightly, only enough to make a slight wave of pleasure pulse through me. I'm on my feet with her thrown over my shoulder a moment later. She squeals while I gather the picnic basket and blanket and make my way back to the rental car I picked up earlier. It's time I take off the dress that had me drooling since she put it on a few hours ago.

It's time it's just Chiara and me.

My hands are fisting her hair, tugging on it to lean her head back and attach my lips to her neck. I trail open-mouthed kisses along her sensitive skin, earning me a few breathless moans. Not enough. I need more, and I need her to be a lot louder.

Years. I've wanted her underneath me for years, and I won't stop until we're both sore and panting so hard, we might pass out from a lack of oxygen.

"Please, oh God," she moans, the sound going straight into my cock, forcing everything to pull tight.

"A few ground rules," I say, still leading her to my room.

Once we're inside, I spin her around, bringing her back to my chest. I grind my cock against her arse until she's whimpering with pleasure.

"Rule number one: if at any time you want to stop, you either tap me on the forehead or say stop."

She moans an 'okay' while I rip her dress upward and cup her pussy over her panties.

"Rule number two: if we do this, I won't be able to turn away again. I will belong to you inside and outside of the bedroom. You will be *mine*. Is that what you want?"

I ask, my voice shaking ever so slightly. I've stopped my movements, so her brain isn't foggy from pleasure.

Chiara spins around in my arms, grabbing my collar and pushing me toward the bed. She shoves until I'm on the mattress, removing her dress as I stare at her, turned on to the point of pain. I've never been so hot for a woman in my entire life. My body is begging me to touch her, and, at the same time, my arms feel too heavy to move.

"I want it all, Leonard. I want you to be mine, all mine, no one else's again. One little taste this morning wasn't enough."

She takes my chin between her fingers, curves and tanned skin on display for me, her tits barely contained by her bra and her panties a little crooked. I could come just by watching her stand in front of me, all bossy and sexy.

"But you should know, before you agree to this, I'm insatiable. I will want more of you all the time. Can you handle that?" she asks, and I debate asking her to marry me right here and now.

"Get on top of me and find out," I reply, bringing a smirk to her pouty lips. "You are mine, Chiara. I told you it's you and me, and I meant it. It's always going to be you and me. Now, remove your panties and bra. I need to taste you everywhere," I demand or beg, either would fit my tone and words. She obeys but gives me a serious look as she undoes her bra clasp.

"Don't start getting wrong ideas about me doing whatever you say. I only listen when I know you're going to fuck me," she reminds me while I unbutton my shirt. My eyes stay on hers until the fabric drops from her chest, grabbing all of my attention.

"Noted," I assure her before dragging her toward me by her hips and planting my mouth on her hip bone. I trail kisses along her soft skin, a groan slipping out of me.

"Is there another rule?" she asks, her hands slipping into my hair and tugging on it. I've never been so glad about cutting my hair short.

"Yes. Rule number three: be loud and vocal about what you like and what you don't like so I can learn how to pleasure you. Those romance books only taught me so much," I say, and Chiara chuckles. The sound soon turns into a moan when I kiss her clit through her panties.

"I like your rules," she whispers, tugging on my hair again.

"Last one. You always come first. No matter what. In every way. In this bedroom and outside of it." I run my finger over her covered pussy, her legs shaking in response. "I want my tongue right here," I say with my mouth pressed on the stretch marks visible above the band of her underwear. My fingers apply pressure to her swollen clit until she whimpers.

"Take everything you want. It's all yours," she says, and I don't waste a single second.

My fingers dig into her hips as I lift her into the air and place her on the mattress. I rip my shirt and pants off before curling my fingers around her panties and tugging them down. She's dripping wet, and the sight of her pretty pussy on display for me somehow stiffens my cock even more. I wrap a hand around myself to ease the pain as I lick along the length of her hot centre once.

Bloody fucking hell.

A moan slips from her lips, and I groan in response to how mouthwatering she tastes. Good God, I don't think I've ever had something so delicious on my tongue. I keep licking, sucking, and nibbling, earning myself every single sound of pleasure from her. I slip two fingers into her core, almost falling apart from how easily they slip inside and then how tightly her walls wrap around me. I want to replace my fingers with my cock, but not yet. Not fucking yet. I have the whole night with her, hell, hopefully I will have all the time in the world with her, and I will take it.

"Please, please, please," Chiara says between my licks, and I start using the tip of my tongue to play with her clit. "Fuck!" I smile into her pussy, sucking on her sensitive, little spot. The grip I have on my cock hardens until I whimper against her. I need a fucking release. Soon.

"Not yet," I reply before sucking her clit into my mouth again. Her thighs press against my ears, and I can't help but smile.

My fingers play with her G-spot until she's begging me to let her come. I love the way her back arches off the bed, the way she plays with her hard nipples as she bucks against my mouth to reach her orgasm. I simply take my time tasting her, pressing my tongue flat against her pussy and dragging it upward to play with her clit again. Her walls clench around my fingers every single time I thrust inside her.

"Please, Leonard, I need to come," she begs.

Desperate to watch her writhe in pleasure again, I pick up the speed of my thrusts and licks, and send her straight over the edge. Her entire body shakes with pleasure as she grinds herself against my mouth to ride out the orgasm for as long as possible. My name leaves her lips in a moan so loud, I wish I could soak in it for a while, but I've got other plans.

I stand up straight to see a happy smile on her lips, her hands covering her breasts as she watches me slide down my boxers. Her bottom lip disappears between her teeth once I'm completely bare in front of her. Chiara pushes herself up on the mattress before getting on her knees, her eyes on my erection.

"Hmmm, maybe you weren't overcompensating all these years after all," she says with a wicked grin, and I smile down at her. Her eyes are fixated on my cock, lust sparkling in them.

"What do you want, little demon?" I ask, and she licks her lips, shifting her gaze to my eyes.

"I want to suck your cock," Chiara replies, knocking me off-balance a little. "Come here," she instructs, and I'd do anything she wants me to at this point. "Good boy," she teases with a naughty grin, and I'm about to grab her chin and fuck her senseless when she takes me into her mouth without hesitation.

I'm a goner.

The warmth of her mouth is pure heaven. Everything inside of me tightens as she lifts her hands to my balls and kneads them while sucking me off. Maybe it's her, maybe it's the skilful way she licks and sucks me, but I've never felt anything better. My fingers sift through her hair until I'm fisting it. My eyes are fixed on the way her head bops back and forth, coating my cock in her saliva. It drives me so close to the edge in such a short time, I let out a loud groan, pull back, and claim her mouth with mine. I almost grunt at the taste of myself on her lips, but I'm too busy spreading her legs wide for me.

"I want an orgasm from you," she says when I bring my lips to her neck and suck hard.

"Soon, baby, when I'm inside of you, okay?" Chiara nods and brings her hands into my hair.

"Now. Come inside me now," she begs, and I chuckle at how sweet she is.

"I'd give you anything you want, sweetheart. All the stars in the sky and all the flowers in the world. Every blade of grass or grain of sand," I blurt out, and the way she smiles at me in response makes me glad I said it.

"You're obsessed with me," she says and wraps her hand around my cock, stroking me gently. I moan against her lips, unable to hold any sounds back. Everything she does sends me straight into paradise.

"Fuck yes, I most certainly am," I reply and grab a condom from my pants, sliding it down my cock. I suck in a sharp breath because she has me so worked up, I have to be careful not to push too hard, otherwise I will come before I'm even inside of her.

"I've fantasized about this a lot," Chiara admits as she lies down flat on her back. Her nipples hard and demanding my touch. I'm only happy to oblige.

"So have I. Every night for months." Years if I'm being honest.

My mouth wraps around her left nipple, sucking on it until she cries out. Fucking hell. I wish I could have all of her sounds on repeat forever. I push the thought aside before paying the same attention to her right nipple and earning me another moan from her. My cock pushes against her dripping core, causing my breathing to hitch and my skin to catch fire.

"Are you ready for me, sweetheart?" Chiara gives me an eager nod.

"Yes," she says, and I slam into her a second later. We both gasp and moan at the same time.

"Fuck, Chiara, shit," I grind out because she's wrapped around me like I was made to fit her, and it's driving me wild. I'm stretching her a little, but she's rolling her hips with satisfied moans.

"Move," she demands, but I'm hanging on for dear life.

"Give me a second," I say, trying to think of the most unattractive things in the world.

"Please."

I slam into her hard again. Her back arches off the bed and against me, but I hold her down, my thrusts steady and in a rhythm that has her panting against my shoulder. I'm right there with her. A string of curse words flows from my mouth along with her name, which tastes almost as sweet on my tongue as she does.

"You're so big and hard," she moans, and I let out a breathless laugh.

"You feel so good, baby, so tight and wet for me," I reply, lifting up her hips a little and driving into her with more force than before. A scream of pleasure leaves her,

her nails digging into my back until I feel her scratching me. Marking me as hers, and fuck, I'll never be anyone else's.

"More, more," she begs, and I repeat the same movement, attaching my mouth to her nipple again.

I fuck her in hard and deep strokes. Her soft body is completely under my control, and I can't help but revel in the way she surrenders it to me when control is so important to her. My lips wrap around hers before I slide my tongue into her mouth to taste the pleasure I'm bringing her. My thrusts don't slow, but I can feel my orgasm building in my cock. Chiara keeps clenching her walls around me, and there is no way I can fight it off when she feels like my own personal paradise.

"Fuck," I groan as my orgasm blindsides me.

I wrap my arms around her centre and go faster and harder as I ride out my orgasm, pushing her over the edge with me. My cock pulses as I release into the condom, shaking on top of her. She hums underneath me, and I collapse onto her, sweat on my forehead and some on her chest.

"You're annoyingly good at sex," Chiara says once we've both recovered from the high, and I let out a small snort.

"And you're beautiful," I reply, pushing myself up on the bed and kissing her again since that's all I seem to want to do.

I should have known having sex with Chiara would be my downfall, and in a way I did, but I never expected to feel so... whole. I feel fucking whole, and there is nothing in this world that could stop me from keeping whatever it is Chiara and I have. She's mine now, and I will do everything in my power so she wants to keep being mine.

"More," she says after a while of us cuddling, and I place a kiss on the top of her breast, smiling.

"You really are insatiable, little demon," I say and work my way up and all the way to her lips again.

More.

I'll always want more of her.

CHAPTER 36

Chiara

My show is starting in ten minutes. Mamma, Nonna, Dino, and Leonard are all here to watch my exhibit. After months of working on it, and the last two days adjusting everything to fit this room, I'm finally presenting my show. A few more guests are also here, but Dino said he didn't want to put too much pressure on me the first time. I'm also sure he doesn't want to risk the reputation of his gallery in case my show absolutely sucks, which is understandable. This is the first time I've created something to be displayed like this in front of people, and it has my stomach in knots. I'm nauseous.

"If your show is even half as beautiful as you, it'll be a success," Nonna says in Italian, and I let out a small laugh at her words.

"*Ti voglio bene*, Nonnina," I say, and she takes my hand, squeezing it once.

"I'm so proud of you," Mamma chimes in, and I feel my heart settle into a slower rhythm. It's close to beating normally when Leonard's hand appears on my left hip. His chest presses against my back, and I lean into him for support. He kisses the side of my head, earning him a warm smile from Mamma.

"How are you both doing with what happened yesterday?" I ask to distract myself a little further. Leonard's warmth is working wonders for my nervousness, but I'm still a bit on edge.

"Fine, honey, stop worrying about that now. Tim is out of our lives for good," she says, and I nod along to her words, hoping more than anything she is right and we will never see him again. He's caused more than enough trouble, and Mamma deserves to be happy with someone who hasn't been trying to fuck her daughter. *God, I'm going to be sick.*

"Your leg is shaking," Leonard whispers into my ear when Mamma takes Nonna's hand and walks around the room to speak to Dino. I stare down at my left leg, even though I feel it shake every time I place too much weight on it.

"I'm a bit sore," I admit with a small smile, making him squeeze my hips.

"Was I too rough last night?" he asks and nudges my cheek with his nose, his arms wrapping around me in a tight, gentle embrace.

"No, it was perfect."

Every night with him has been perfect for the past three days. We've been having sex, eating, sleeping, and having more sex. In every sort of position. Yesterday, he made me stand for twenty minutes, bend over at the waist, slamming inside of me from behind. So, yes, I'm most definitely sore, but in the best way possible.

"Tonight we'll take a break, okay?" I spin around in his arms, and his hands immediately lift to cup my cheeks.

"I don't want to take a break. You'll just have to do all the work, and I will lie there, happily watching you pleasure me," I say with a teasing grin, and Leonard lets his head fall back, a little chuckle shaking his upper body.

"I will do whatever you want me to, sweetheart," he replies, lips brushing over mine and hands finding the top of my ass. He rests them there, even though I give him a warning glare. Leonard merely smirks at me.

"You should be careful, Mr. Tick. Sooner or later I'm going to believe you can't live without me anymore," I joke, but his face turns serious in response.

"I can't," is all he says before pressing a kiss to my lips and turning me around to see Dino approaching.

"Everything is ready. You can start the show, if you'd like," the Italian man assures me.

"Alright," I reply and move over to where the light switch is.

I've arranged everything so the only thing John, a nice guy I met yesterday who works at the gallery, has to do is push the button to start the show. I triple-checked everything, but my nerves skyrocket anyway. Leonard seems to notice it because he steps toward me and grabs my hand, squeezing once to assure me he's here.

A slow song fills the room as the first images are projected onto the walls. Leonard smiles for the first few minutes before an expression of awe crosses his face. The same thing happens with Dino, Mamma, and Nonna. They're all impressed by what I've created, all drawn in by the art show I've worked on for the past few months, and it sends a wonderful warmth through me. They like it. I've made something the people I care about adore, and it almost brings tears to my eyes.

Okay, I'm close to crying, blinking rapidly to fight the tears.

"This is—" Leonard starts, but he's cut off by the music vanishing and the images changing.

A visual of Leonard and me on the picnic blanket yesterday, limbs tangled and my hand on his chest appears on the walls. Confusion settles in the room while panic fills my chest. The video plays until we see my palm grinding over Leonard's bulge and him throwing me over his shoulder and carrying me to the car. I only watch half of it, running to the room with all of the technology I used to make my show happen. A phone is plugged into the same place my laptop was in earlier, the video playing on the screen as well. I rip the phone away and thank my lucky stars it didn't get to the part of the video where Leonard and I make out in his car.

Who the fuck recorded us?

"Chiara?" Dino says, and I spin around to face him. He looks as upset as I feel. "What the fuck was that? I offer you an opportunity to show me what you can do, and this is how you thank me? What the fuck?" he asks in Italian, and I lose all my confidence.

"I—I," I stutter, panic feeling my chest.

"Dino, I suggest you calm the fuck down and step away from her," Leonard says, and I almost sigh at his presence.

"I promise, this wasn't me. I swear on my Mamma's and Nonna's life. It wasn't me," I assure Dino while Leonard closes the distance between us and steps protectively in front of me.

"Someone did this, and I know who it was. It wasn't Chiara's fault," Leonard says and snakes his arm around me from the front. He knows who it was. I know who it was.

Tim.

"I'm sorry if it wasn't you, Chiara, but this is highly unprofessional. You understand that I can't be associated with this in any way without risking my gallery and everyone else who I have invested in, right?"

He's not going to invest in my gallery. Dino was the only person interested, and now my chance is gone. Leonard and I will have to keep looking, but word will get out about what happened today. No one's going to look my way twice. Chiara de Luca makes erotic art shows without telling people in advance. It isn't true, but words get twisted, lies are woven, and rumors turn into deaths of careers. Everything was going so well... *what happened? Why did Tim do this? To get revenge because I wasn't interested in him?*

"So, if I understand this right, you didn't make sure there was enough security to prevent something like this from happening, and you're blaming Chiara for it? Are you having a laugh, mate?" Dino furrows his brows at Leonard's words. "You can't be bloody serious is what I'm trying to say. This isn't on Chiara. It's on you. But, whatever, mate. We don't need you. It's your loss after all," he says and takes my hand, grabbing my laptop before pulling me away from Dino. It's better this way too because I'm furious, and he isn't the right person to take it out on. Tim would be.

"Leonard?" I say when we're halfway to the room where Dino told me to put my stuff earlier. Tears are finally stinging my eyes, but I do my best to blink them away. Panic floods his features at my facial expression.

"I know, sweetheart, I know," he replies and wraps his arms around me. There is something about Leonard, there always has been, that makes it impossible for me to keep my feelings inside. So, they spill down my cheeks as he rubs my back. "It'll be alright, baby, I promise. We will figure it out, I know we will," he assures me, but humiliation is combining with the feeling of failure inside of me.

I can barely breathe past it.

A day later, I feel slightly better. I'm still embarrassed, but what happened isn't my fault. I've come to terms with that. The only thing I'm having a hard time with is accepting that this may have been my first and last opportunity to get an investor. I will keep trying, Leonard would never let me give up anyway, and it will happen. I know I will live my dream. I just need patience.

My head is on Nonna's chest while her arm is around my back, holding me close. I'm not usually one to crave too much affection. It's not something I seek out actively, but it's different with my Nonna. She gives me comfort and love, and I want to soak it all up for as long as I possibly can. The same goes for Leonard nowadays.

"I'm sorry about what you had to see yesterday," I finally say, and she kisses the top of my head, squeezing my arm in response.

"Don't be. It wasn't your fault," she replies and kisses my temple this time. "I liked your show before it was interrupted. It was beautiful," she adds, bringing a little smile to my lips, but it washes away almost immediately.

"I wish you could have seen the ending too," I mumble with a little sigh I swallow down. Nonna starts squeezing my arm.

"Maybe I wasn't meant to see it all last night. Maybe I'm supposed to wait until you have your own gallery," she says, and I sink further against her, letting some of the tension yesterday created wash off me. Nonna hasn't lost faith in me, no matter what happened. It offers me a little bit of relief.

Silence surrounds us after her words, so I simply stay in her embrace to enjoy the warmth radiating off her. My thoughts linger a while longer on the events I wish I could burn from my brain. Starting tomorrow, Leonard is going to have to go to the track every day, and he promised to take me with him even though I'm not watching Benz. I'm not quite sure why he wants me there, but that's probably because my head hasn't processed our new relationship status yet.

We're... dating, I think. I don't know. My heart prefers not to put a label on it apart from calling him mine. He's mine, and I'm his, which is probably something I should inform Graham of, but I have no intention of doing so over the phone.

"I cannot believe you're dating a Formula One driver," Mamma says when she appears in the living room. I look up at her, fighting back a grin.

"Jealous?" I tease, and she smacks my arm.

"Yes! He's so sweet with you and gorgeous. Of course I'm jealous," she replies with a dramatic *thump* onto the couch. "Plus, he's got a great *culo*," Mamma adds, making Nonna snort next to me.

"I think he's got the greatest *culo* I've ever seen on a man," she chimes in, and I let out a shocked laugh.

"Okay, can we stop talking about my boyfriend's ass when he's in the kitchen making us dinner?" I don't mean to say it like that, but Mamma and Nonna both raise their hands in mock surrender.

"Okay, okay, no need to get defensive," Nonna teases with a bright smile and squeezes my side. I burst into a fit of giggling, and before I know it, Mamma starts tickling me too.

"Enough," I beg, and they release me.

"Go see if Leonard needs some help," Mamma tells me, leaning back on the couch with a tired smile on her face.

I'm on my feet and playfully glaring at her before they carry me toward the kitchen. Leonard's muscular frame appears in my line of sight, and I close the distance between us until I can wrap my arms around him from behind. His scent fills my nose, warm and delicious, and the heat of his body sends a wave of calm through my system. We slept over at Nonna's house last night, which means he's wearing some of my Nonno's old clothes. I can smell a hint of him on the fabric.

"Dinner is almost ready," he assures me, but I turn him around to bring my hands to each side of his face.

"I'm happy you're here," I blurt out, and he leans down to give me a single kiss.

"So am I, Starling. Thank you for sharing this part of your life with me," he says, kissing me again and again and then one more time. I melt against him completely. "Are you hungry?" he asks, and I nod, pulling my bottom lip between my teeth. "Good. I hope your Nonna and Mamma will like what I've prepared. I know vegan food isn't everyone's thing," Leonard says and squeezes my hips to bring me closer.

"I didn't think I'd like it, but you're a decent cook," I tease, and he lets his hands drop to my ass, squeezing it until I gasp.

"You should be nicer to me, otherwise I might add a little too much salt to your plate," he replies, and I let out a mocking gasp.

"You wouldn't." Leonard leans down until his lips are against mine.

"I would," he says before biting down on my bottom lip and letting out an approving groan when he has to hold me up with his hands. "Stop distracting me. I need to finish dinner," he says and releases me. Instead of leaving the kitchen and him alone, I wrap my arms around him from behind again.

Being close to him isn't something I should give in to whenever my body demands it. I shouldn't start depending on the comfort of his touch, the warmth of his skin, or the feelings in my stomach whenever I hear him laugh, chuckle, or simply just inhale. Two decades. That's how long I've known this man. I hated him for as long, but it's right what they say. Love and hate is a fine line. I always thought it was easy to go from loving someone to hating them, but it turns out it's much easier to go from thinking you hate them to developing other feelings. More positive feelings.

God, my head is spinning. As a matter of fact, everything is spinning, and I have no idea how to ground myself when Leonard has me falling without a parachute.

"Leonard?" I say, and he places his hands over mine where they rest on his stomach.

"Yes, sweetheart?"

"I kind of like you," I admit, which is absolutely fucking terrifying.

"Chiara?" he asks in response, making me smile.

"Yes, Champ?"

"You're everything to me."

Well, fuck.

CHAPTER 37
Leonard

I'm getting sick and tired of it. Jonathan continues to play dirty, pushing me off the track whenever he feels like it, crashing into me, complaining to the team that they're favouring me, and endless more things while I am the one who suffers. I'm in third place now because he forced me off the track halfway through the race, when I was leading and he couldn't stand it. He couldn't overtake me any other way, so he fucked me over. I've been in communication with my team about it, but Jonathan won't be receiving a penalty for what he's done. Of course not. The FIA loves to favour him for some reason I will never be able to understand.

By the time the last lap comes around, I'm cooking in my anger. I will have to speak to my team immediately after the race. This can't keep happening. I'm still leading the championship by far, today's events won't change that, but if he continues this, I will lose, and I will do so unjustly. I've lost before. I don't mind it, it's part of racing. It's also a great source of growth and learning for me. But this? This is unacceptable, and I won't stand for it. Knowing my team principal, he won't either.

Robert Fuchs is the best team principal to have ever walked this earth. He won't allow Jonathan to pull this shit anymore. Sportsmanship is one of the most important things in our sport. Jonathan's behaviour is the opposite of sportsmanship. Obviously, the last conversation with him hasn't changed anything. I will say something this time, and he's not going to like it. Maybe I will bring Chiara as my

301

backup. He's scared of her, and I'd love to see him squirm. All she'll have to do is glare at him and that man will be pissing his pants.

I drive to the third place sign after the race is finished, trying to swallow down my anger and seem professional. It feels impossible until I set my eyes on Chiara standing with the rest of my team, an unfamiliar feeling spreading through my chest. I've seen other driver's girlfriends do this before, standing with the team while they wait for their boyfriends to pull off their helmets and go celebrate with them. They kiss them for the whole world to see, and the urge to do the same tugs at my soul. I try to resist as I climb out of my car, try to fight against every fibre of my being pulling me toward her, but then I realise I don't want to fight it. As a matter of fact, I haven't wanted anything as much as I want to kiss her right now, in front of everyone, to show them she's mine.

My limbs are tired and heavy as I stand next to my car. I tear my gloves off and make quick work of my helmet, moving over to where my team is. Chiara is standing in the second row, but I briefly give my team, along with Quinn, a high five, just like always, before reaching for Starling and bringing her to the very front. There's no smile on her face, like usually when she's among people, but as soon as I flash her the slightest of grins, her face lights up. I bring my hand to cup her face, unsure if she's okay with making our relationship public already, but Chiara steps onto her tiptoes for me, closing her eyes as she waits for a kiss.

I don't fucking hesitate.

My lips find hers, and a sigh of relief escapes me. This is exactly what I needed, which is why I ignore the reminder going off in my head, telling me I don't do this. I've kept my life as private as possible because the media already criticises every part I *can't* have to myself. But at this very second, I couldn't give less of a fuck. It feels too right. Having Chiara melt into me at the contact of our mouths is pure bliss.

After the shitty race I've had, it's everything I need to wash away my anger, at least for now.

"I'm still proud of you, loser," she says, and I let out a shocked laugh, poking her sides as I step back.

"Loser? I'm going to make you regret that later," I warn, and she purses her lips to hide the naughty smirk I know wants to spread over her face.

"Can't wait," she replies, and I give her one more quick peck before high-fiving a few more of my team members.

My feet, tired and sore, bring me to the little podium stand where a cap and water are waiting for me. I'm pulled to the side, reminded I have to get weighed like every driver on the grid, which I get over with quickly to get some water. I use the towel to wipe away the sweat dripping down the sides of my face, listening to Jonathan getting interviewed. I try not to listen because my heart is happy and full from my brief contact with Chiara and her lips, but his words trigger the anger inside of me again.

"I drove a clean race and won fairly, that's why I didn't get a penalty," Jonathan says, and I bring my eyes to him to see a smug smile on his stupid face.

Yeah, I'm going to lose it.

"You're Leonard's biggest rival in the championship at the moment. How do you feel about that?" the interviewer asks, and I suck in a sharp breath to try and calm my racing heart. His answer is going to enrage me, I already know it.

"I'm positive my team and I will keep improving and win the championship this year. Leonard is strong, but I think overall I'm the faster driver."

I can't help myself. I let out a horrifyingly loud snort. Heads turn in my direction, but I can't bring myself to care so I simply take a sip of my water, unbothered. Jonathan glares at me, so I wink at him, the bottle in my hand pressing against my lips. I can be disrespectful too.

"Well, congrats on the win," the interviewer adds, and then it's my turn to be interviewed.

My expression is as emotionless and cold as I can manage. I stand where Jonathan was only moments ago, clinging to the water bottle so I don't dig my nails into the palms of my hands. The woman interviewing us has an easy smile on her lips. I answer her questions about the race, doing my best not to let my rage come through in my voice. Since I've been practicing hiding my feelings for as long as I can remember, I don't let on anything in my tone or choice of words. Publicly is not the way to address this situation. Jonathan has decided to be arrogant. That's not my problem. Sooner or later, I will beat him in the championship, and I don't have to parade that fact around for everyone else. They will see what I'm capable of, and it will be enough for the rest of the world to stop underestimating me, including my teammate.

After the celebrations on the podium where Jonathan and I have to pretend to get along so fucking well, I'm sticky with champagne and ready for a shower. I'm halfway to my private room where I can wash off the celebrations when Adrian Romana appears in front of me, his happy smile firmly set in place. This man might have the biggest heart apart from Chiara I've ever witnessed in a person. We've hung out almost every race weekend at some point or another, and I'm genuinely content whenever he's in my presence. It feels like I can be myself around him, which is a nice contrast to the way I feel toward every other driver on the grid, including his best friend James. They're almost inseparable during race weekends, but I understand why. I recently found out Adrian has lost almost his entire family. Only his sister, Valentina, his Grandpa, and his aunt remain, but two of them live in L.A., which means he's far away from his sister for most of the year.

"That was a bullshit move, and everyone knows it, mate," is the first thing the rookie with blonde hair and bright eyes says to me. I furrow my brows at him in response, earning me a confused look from him. Oh good, we're both confused. "What?" he asks, and I study his face.

"No one will agree with you on that. People tend to root for whoever is up against me," I explain, and Adrian gives me a disgusted look.

"Well, that's fucked up. You're the best driver on the grid, and the only person who could beat you is me if I had a faster car," he says with a smug smile. I cross my arms in front of my chest, fighting back a smirk. Adrian is quite a bit taller than me, but I'm wider by a few centimetres, more muscular.

"You're the only one, huh?" I challenge, and Adrian gives me a self-assured look and a pat on the shoulder. I watch his hand where it touches me, a slight warning in my gaze that is meant to remind him to not do it again. He doesn't notice it, or, if he does, he gives zero fucks about my threatening eyes.

"If my sister Val was a driver, then I wouldn't be the only one. However, you still have a few years to prepare before she makes it into F1," he replies with a proud grin.

This isn't the first time Adrian has spoken to me about his sister. She was recently kicked from her F3 team, a racing league below Formula One. I've looked into the reasons why, but there weren't any tangible ones. Valentina was one of the fastest drivers on the grid, her lap times were close to perfection, she was dedicated, and a force to be reckoned with. Hell, I've never seen a more talented racer in my life.

Then, one day, they decided to drop her from the team. No other one has offered her a place in Formula Three again, and it's been bothering me to see someone go through the same thing I went through as a child. Apart from the people I love, no one knows I was kicked off a Formula Three team, and I intend to keep it that way. They forgot about me long enough so when I made a comeback, it was like I was a new person. Fine by me. It allowed me to go further than I was before. The thought of someone as talented as Valentina going through this gives me an itch on the inside of my brain I'm not sure how to scratch. It bothers me.

"She's in L.A., right?" I ask, and Adrian, still with that proud smile on his face, gives me a single nod.

"Yes, she is, but I hope to bring her to one of my races soon. She deserves to get away for a little, she works too hard," he explains and stretches his arms into the air, his upper body muscles flexing as he covers his mouth to hide his yawn. "Anyway, if you need backup for kicking Jonathan's ass, I'm your man. I'll even get James to help too. Despite what you may think, he isn't a big fan of your teammate either," he says right before giving my shoulder one last clasp and squeeze. Surprisingly enough, I don't mind it as much as before or when anyone else touches me. Well, anyone but Chiara. Her hands could be on me all day and I'd thank her.

"I'll keep that in mind," I reply, but right as Adrian is about to walk away, Jonathan appears behind him. I try to force down my anger, but seeing his arrogant face makes it almost impossible.

"Ah, gentlemen, having a nice tea party, are we?" Jonathan asks, and I'm about to respond when Adrian beats me to it.

"Yeah, and you weren't fucking invited. Get out of here, asshole. No one wants to talk to you, let alone look at your stupid face." *God, I freaking adore this kid.* Jonathan scrambles for words, but nothing audible comes out. "What? Did all that cheating kill your ability to form a proper sentence? That's too bad. I bet you had something really great to say." Adrian lets out a soft laugh and then turns to me. "Let's go, I want to say hi to Chiara," the Monegasque says, and I follow him to my private room. "God, he's such an ass," he mumbles, and I bring my hand to his back, giving him a slight pat.

"Yes, he is, but thanks for that. You didn't have to intervene," I assure him, but he flashes me a wicked grin.

"I know, but it's fun to see people squirm, especially when they deserve it, and Jonathan did." We step through my door to find Quinn and Chiara deep in conversation. They're looking at a screen, and whatever is on it has them in a heated discussion. "Chiara, how've you been?" Adrian asks, his lips pulling into a warm smile.

"Good, kid, how about you?" she replies, and he lets out an exasperated breath.

"You wound me, Chiara. 'Kid'? Really?" he says, and I give him a warning nudge. Not sensing what I'm trying to say because he's clueless, I decide to clarify.

"Back off," I say and step toward Starling, who is tilting her head up to me and puckering up her lips to get me to kiss her. I place my mouth on hers, somehow tasting her peachy scent on my tongue. "Mine," I whisper greedily, only for her to hear, and Chiara gives me a bright smile.

"Mine," she replies, and I grin down at her.

"Leonard, come. You have to shower and then we need to go through our post-race routine," Quinn interrupts, and I'm barely capable of peeling myself away from Chiara to do as I'm told.

"Alright, I'm going to head out and do the same. I'll be in England next week. Will you spare me a minute of your precious time to grab a coffee?" Adrian says, and I raise both of my brows at him.

"Depends. Will you be annoying?" Adrian flashes me another of those mischievous, cocky grins of his.

"Most definitely, but you love me, so it's okay. See you soon," he calls out and leaves, not giving me a chance to tell him I don't, which would have been useless anyway.

Adrian has got this confidence overload because he's young and talented. Lucky for him, his arrogance is charming, which may mostly be because he's a genuinely nice guy.

"You, shower. Now," Quinn reminds me, making me nod along to her words. I'm about to shut the bathroom door when my best friend's voice fills the small room outside. "Thank you," she says, and I hesitate.

"For what?" my little demon asks, and I lean my head against the door, scolding myself for my inability to stop eavesdropping.

"You've jump-started Leonard's life, Chiara. I know he probably doesn't think I've noticed, but ever since you two have become inseparable, everything has changed. The races mean more to him again. He's become more passionate about everything, cooking, going out, even celebrating life," Quinn says, earning a thoughtful hum from Chiara. "My point is, you've become the most important person in his life, and you've made it better in every way you possibly could have. You make him happy, and I'm grateful," my best friend goes on, and I can't deny anything about what she just said. Because it's exactly what I've felt for Chiara for a long time. She makes my life worth living.

My little demon. My sweetheart. My Starling.

My Chiara.

CHAPTER 38

Chiara

Leonard and I have been cuddling with Benz on the floor of his apartment for the past hour. He went to pick her up from his parents' house while I unpacked my suitcase and did my laundry. I wasn't allowed to wash his because it isn't my job to do his laundry, as he called it. When I was about to complain, he merely kissed me and told me to swallow down my complaint. All hazy from the way he makes me feel, I simply nodded and watched him walk out the door. Leonard is too hot for my body to handle sometimes.

"I've missed you," he says to Benz as she rolls onto her back, her tail wagging from side to side.

"I've missed you more," I tell her, and Leonard lets out an amused snort.

"You always have to one-up me, don't you?" he asks, our hands meeting on Benz's head where we are both petting her.

"Yes," I reply with a slight smile, and he returns it, rolling onto his back as Benz walks away to lie down in her bed next to the sofa. Apparently, she's had enough of us.

I watch Leonard's jaw flex, feeling heat settle between my legs until an uncomfortable ache appears. The same one only he can awake in me at this point. It's been a few days of chaos since we've had time alone with each other, and every fiber of my being is aware of it. My attraction for him has me constantly longing to be near him, intimate with him in ways I've never been with anyone else.

"Chiara?" he asks, and I swallow hard, my name the most beautiful sound I've ever heard when it comes out of his mouth.

"Hmm?" I reply, my gaze fixated on his full, plump lips. My eyes flutter shut at the memory of them pressed against mine. I could close the distance between us, make the fantasy a reality, but I wait for whatever he wants to say.

"Get on top of me," he instructs, and I open my eyes to see he's tilted his head in my direction, his gaze like a caress on my body.

"What?" I ask, stunned by his command.

"Get on top of me," he repeats, causing my heart to skip several beats. "I can feel your need, so come take whatever you desire. Ride my face or cock, whichever you prefer, sweetheart, just use me." *Good God.* "Come," he says and holds out his hand, and I crawl over to where he is.

Leonard sits up, dragging his hands through my hair and bringing his face centimeters from mine. He doesn't kiss me, merely hovers until the anticipation of the moment has me curling my toes. A shudder runs down the length of my spine as I follow the tilts of his face and try to bring my mouth to his. He leans away, smiling because he knows how desperate I am to take what I need, like he told me to only a moment ago. Instead, he cups my nape with one hand, massaging it until a soft moan leaves me. His other hand settles on my thigh and squeezes until I gasp.

"All these wonderful sounds, Chiara, I need them to be mine. Only mine," he says, and I tilt my head back when his lips move to my neck.

"They're yours, all of them," I croak out, pleasure starting to cloud my mind.

"Good," he mumbles against my throat. "Because I hate sharing, always have," he goes on, and I reach for his face, cupping it.

"You're mine," I say and grab his chin to force his gaze to mine. "And I don't fucking share either. So all your moans, kisses, orgasms, laughs, happy and sad

310

moments, I want them all. I want you, and I have for a very long time." If I'm being honest with myself.

"Everything in my life would be pointless without you, Starling," he says, and I kiss him fiercely, trying to taste his feelings and allow them to sink into my bloodstream until they reach my heart. "Take control, Chiara. I know you want to," Leonard says, and millions of ideas start floating into my head about what I would like to do to him. He rips his shirt over his head before claiming my lips once more.

"I want to try something before I ride you," I say between kisses, and he lets out an agreeing moan.

"Anything you want."

We move over to the couch where I push him down and spread his legs. I settle between them, my knees on the carpet and my lips curled into a smile. Leonard watches me with curiosity, clearly unsure about what I'm doing. I simply pull my dress over my head, leaving me in a set of black lace panties and a matching bra. His head drops back as a low groan leaves him, and I wish I knew what was going through his head. So, I ask.

"I'm wondering how I got so bloody lucky to have the sexiest woman in the world kneeling in front of me in a matching lace set," Leonard explains, his hand cupping my chin. "I'm wondering what I've done to deserve you," he goes on while I run my hands up his thighs, wishing away his pants and boxers. "Most of all, I'm hoping I will never lose you, ever. I wasn't lying when I said you were everything to me, Chiara. I meant every word," he says and kisses me, for a moment distracting me completely from everything I've planned to do. His tongue slips into my mouth, sending a wave of pleasure through me.

"Leonard," I pant out, trying to push him back to refocus. When he doesn't budge, I place my hand on his groin, pressing ever so slightly.

"Fuck," he moans, and I smile against his mouth.

"Lean back," I command, and he obeys when I palm him through his pants again.

"Good God, Chiara, you're torturing me," he says with a laugh, grinding himself against my hand. "Is that what you like? Teasing me? Do you want me to beg?" he asks, and I lick my lips before smiling up at him.

"Yes."

A smirk tugs on his lips as I sit up on my knees and guide his hands behind his back. I tell him to keep them there and then work on removing his pants and boxers. He lifts himself off the couch to help me, so I tug them down and then pull them off completely. Leonard's naked body is on full display for me, making my mouth water. He's perfect, and as much as I want to take him in my mouth or touch him, I don't do anything. I study his smooth, tattooed skin, watch the way his arms flex as he tries his best to keep them behind his back, and smile at the restraint it takes for him not to touch me.

"Beg," I say and lower my fingers until they disappear in my panties. He lets out a groan, his hands reaching for me. "No." Another groan leaves him.

"Chiara," he says, but I shake my head, rubbing my clit and moaning.

"Beg," I repeat, pleasure coursing through me as I grind against my fingers.

"Please. Please touch me," he pleads, and I remove my fingers from my pussy to wrap them around his cock. "God," he moans and drops his head against the back of the couch.

"Don't come until I allow you to," I say, and his eyes fly open before he stares down at me.

"I told you that you come first in every way, Chiara. I won't come until you do," he replies, and I smirk at him. That sounds almost like a challenge.

"We'll see," is all I say before guiding his cock under the front of my bra and between my tits.

"Shit," he moans as I press them together, trapping his hard length between my breasts. Then, I rub up and down in a steady motion, darting out my tongue to circle the tip of his cock every few seconds. The muscles in his arms flex again as he uses every bit of restraint not to touch me.

"You're doing so well for me," I praise, keeping my tits pressed together and moving up and down to jerk him off.

My clit is begging me to find anything to rub against because having him under my complete control is by far the hottest thing I've ever experienced. Goosebumps have covered me everywhere. Fire is licking up my spine until flames envelop me completely. I'm dripping with arousal from seeing the way Leonard's back arches and feeling him thrust himself up in perfect harmony with my movements.

"Please, ride me, Chiara. Don't make me finish this way," he begs, another moan leaving him as I let out a mean chuckle.

"But I want you to, baby. Come for me," I say, picking up my speed until he's calling out my name. His fingers appear on each side of him on the couch, digging into the material.

"Fucking hell," he says breathlessly, fighting to keep from orgasming. He lasts several moments longer, so I decide to give in and give him what he wants. After one more kiss to the head of his cock, I release him and lean back.

"Condom?" I ask, noticing his chest rising and falling abruptly.

"Jeans. Back left pocket," he says, reaching for me again.

"No touching," I remind him, and he bites down on his bottom lip to hide his smile. He likes me being in control probably as much as I enjoy it.

I roll the condom down his cock, watching him squirm a little underneath my touch. He's hot and thick, causing my insides to twist and turn from anticipation. I stand up straight, his eyes glued to my body as I close the distance between us and straddle his lap. My thighs are on either side of him, and I hover over his cock, my core tensing with need at the feel of his tip pressed against my panties.

"Stop teasing," he complains, but I press down on his shoulders, still hovering. One of my hands wraps around the base of his cock, keeping him firmly in place against my covered pussy.

"But I'm having so much fun," I reply, pulling my lips into a mocking pout. He smiles up at me, his eyes glistening with something I wish I could identify.

"Have all the fun you want, sweetheart, as long as my cock's inside of you while you have it." *How could I resist him?*

"Place one hand on my throat," I instruct, and he does so without hesitation. I almost moan from the pressure he applies, so firm and gentle at the same time.

"I can feel your heart racing," he says, his thumb caressing the side of my throat. "Are you excited about my cock?" I nod without thinking, and he uses his other hand to pull my panties to the side. One of his fingers dips inside of me, and he lets out an approving moan. "More than excited, I see," he adds and brings the same finger to my clit. I slam down on him without another word.

"Fuck," we say at the same time, the way he fills me perfectly sending me to heaven instantly. I wrap my hand around the wrist of the hand that's around my neck, smiling with pleasure.

"Bounce, sweetheart, chase your pleasure," he says, and I obey, the switch of power between us smooth and easy.

I come down hard on him, grinding so my clit rubs against him. His hold on me tightens, but I'm enjoying it. Fuck, I've never enjoyed sex as much as I do with Leonard.

"Alright, enough of this," he says when I've brought my movements to a painfully slow tempo to tease him again. He picks me up and slams me down on the couch, thrusting inside of me so hard, I scream out in pleasure.

"Oh God, yes, yes, yes," I moan as his strokes go deep and hard at a steady rhythm.

"Yeah?" he asks with a smug smile, but all I manage to do is nod. I nod and moan and whimper because he feels like heaven. Being intimate with him like this is like having found my other half and getting to feel us align with every stroke. It's everything.

"More, more," I beg, and he gives me exactly what I want.

"All your teasing, but now here you are, begging to come," he says, cupping my tits for a brief moment before his hands move to my wrists to pin them over my head. He rests them on the armrest of the couch, fucking into me with shallower strokes now. "So do it. Come all over my cock, sweetheart," he says, rubbing my clit with his thumb. Pleasure consumes me until my toes curl and my back arches.

"You first," I say, but he shakes his head and claims my mouth, sending me straight over the edge.

I come harder than I ever have before, the anticipation from earlier giving me a release so strong, everything inside of me shatters. Then, pleasure sweeps up all the pieces and puts me back together. My head floats into its personal paradise, and I faintly feel him falling apart inside of me too. Leonard collapses onto my chest, his fingers snaking behind my back and toward my bra clasp. I smile as I slide my hands into his hair.

"What are you doing?" I ask, a bead of sweat rolling down my neck.

"In a few minutes, you're going to want more, and I need you completely naked for round two," he explains, undoing the clasp and pulling the fabric off my chest. He presses a kiss to either breast, tugging on my panties and urging me to kick them off, which I do.

"Happy now?" I ask as he settles his head onto my chest, one of his hands flat against my ribs.

I can't help but admire how beautiful his dark skin covered in black ink looks against my tan, untattooed one. I can't help but drool at the way his long fingers are splayed out across my ribs, the veins in his hands sticking out. I can't help but lick my lips when he offers me one of his breathtaking smiles, his full, plump lips stretching over his straight, white teeth.

"Very," he replies, placing more kisses on my upper body. "I love being naked with you," Leonard whispers after a few moments of silence. "You're so warm and soft. You feel like my home," he says, causing tears to shoot into my eyes. "You are my home," he whispers, and they fall down my face because he's my home too.

He's my happy place.

He's where I want to be when I'm standing in a room full of people and can't catch my breath.

He's everything good and true about my life, and I don't want to lose him, ever.

"You're my home," I reply, and he looks up, panic crossing his eyes face he sees the tears falling from the corners of my eyes.

Months ago, crying because of sweet words or crying in general would have been unthinkable. Not anymore. I don't want to close myself off with Leonard when I've never felt more like myself than when I'm with him.

"You've always been my home, sweetheart. After every race weekend, your apartment was my first stop. After every win, I called Graham first because I knew you'd be with him and have lots of opinions about my performance. After every happy moment in my life, I showed up at your door because it wouldn't have been a truly joyful memory if your face wasn't in it," he says, causing more tears to escape me.

I wiggle down on the couch until I'm completely underneath him, my arms wrapping around his back until I'm tucked against his side.

"You've shown me what it means to live, Leonard. You've taught me how much the little things matter, what a single person's smile can do to another." He kisses me once, then leans his forehead against mine.

"Your smile is my favorite. If I could, I would keep them all to myself, bottle them up, and hold onto them forever," he says, and I bury my face in the crook of his neck, smiling.

"Champ?" I ask, and he snorts at the nickname.

"Yes, Starling?"

"More," I mumble against his throat, feeling the deep vibration of his chuckle move through my body.

"Insatiable," he says and slides down my body, hooking my legs over his shoulders and grinning. "Just my type," Leonard adds before placing his tongue against my pussy and making me drift into the land of pleasure again.

CHAPTER 39
Leonard

I shouldn't have done this, I know I shouldn't have, but after what happened at Dino's gallery, I won't take any more risks. The last thing I ever want to see again is the sadness on Chiara's face after all her hard work ended in humiliation and rejection. It won't happen again. I won't fucking allow it, even if she hates me after what I've done. There is the option of lying to her, but I have never been a bullshitter, and I won't start now, especially not with the most important person in my life.

A blindfold rests over Starling's beautiful green eyes as I lead her through the door of her art gallery. I've been thinking about buying this place for months, but I wanted this to be hers without my money as an influence. Unfortunately, people are fucking jerks, and as talented as Chiara is, as well thought-through as her vision is, they keep rejecting her. It doesn't matter that she has a degree in art. It doesn't matter that she also took courses in business management. It doesn't matter how stubborn she is and that she would have the most successful immersive art gallery in the world. To everyone else, she's a risk. To me, she is a certainty.

"We should keep this blindfold for sex stuff," she blurts out as I guide her into the middle of the gallery, well, part of it. This is the entrance area and there are five separate doors along the walls leading to rooms where she will be able to have different shows and exhibits.

"We're definitely keeping it for sex stuff, sweetheart," I reply, so she starts grinning like the insatiable woman she is. I'm pretty sure I've never been this sore in my entire life, and I'm a Formula One racer, so that's saying a lot.

"Where the hell are you taking me?" she asks, her Italian accent somehow thicker today than usual. I smile at the way the words feel in my ears.

"I can't believe how patient you are today. This is only the third time you've asked," I tease, and she lets out a happy laugh. God, I hope she won't hate me for what I've done. I'm already preparing for her to be angry, but I can't stand the thought of her hating me. I let out a shaky breath without meaning to.

"Are you nervous, *amore*?" she asks, causing my heart to flip at her new pet name for me.

"Please. Please don't hate me for this, okay?" I say and before she has a chance to respond, I pull the blindfold off and watch as she blinks a few times to adjust to the light. Her beautiful green eyes focus on me first, and I press one brief kiss to her lips in case she'll never want to speak to me again.

"Leonard, I don't understand. What's going on?" she asks, and I step away, letting her take in her surroundings. It's a plain gallery with white walls, ready to be painted in her image. It isn't anything special, but that's because she hasn't made it hers yet.

"Okay, here it is. A business proposal," I start, focusing on the logical and rational aspects of it to keep my heart from exploding. "I bought this art gallery, but it's not mine. It's yours. Your name is on the contract, so no matter what happens between us, this will always be yours." She attempts to talk, but I keep going. "This is me investing in your future, potential, and dream. I know you didn't want it to be me. I know you wanted to find someone else, but I can't stand the sight of you upset anymore when you are the person who least deserves to be in the world. We can make this a partnership if you'd like to take a bit of pressure off you, but you can also go solo on this. It's completely up to you, but what isn't is that this is your time now. Show the world what you can do, sweetheart. I'll be here to cheer you on from the sidelines for whatever you need." My rant finally ends, and I'm breathless. Actually fucking breathless. I can't remember the last time speaking exhausted me this much. Maybe when I was sick a few years ago.

"You bought me an art gallery?" she asks, her hands trembling as she lifts them to tug a runaway strand behind her ear. Noticing, she shoves them into her pockets and straightens out her back to look tougher.

"Yes. I'm investing," I repeat because I hope it'll make this seem less intense for her.

"I felt bad for spending your money on my clothes when you gave me your credit card. Do you honestly think I could accept an *art gallery*, even if I wanted to?" she says, and I place my arms behind my back.

"You can. I want you to. We'll draw up a contract, and you'll be the one to call all the shots. No strings attached." Oh God, her face turns redder than I've ever seen it before.

"This isn't right, and you know it. You're my employer, roommate, boyfriend, and friend without you becoming my investor and business partner as well. Don't you think this complicates everything even more?" Her voice is surprisingly calm considering how angry she looks.

"If it makes you happy, I don't care how fucking complicated it gets. We will figure it out, I promise. And if it makes you feel any better, I can fire you. You can replace the titles of boyfriend and friend with 'everything'," I suggest with a smile, but she isn't amused. Not a single bit. Sweat drips down my back in response.

"You shouldn't have made this huge decision without me, Leonard. If we're going to be partners in anything, business or life, you can't go and make decisions like this without me. It's not right," she says, causing a little bit of frustration to seep through me.

"You wanted this, you've been working toward it for years, Chiara, what is there left to discuss?" I ask. Chiara starts walking around the room, taking in her surroundings.

"What more is there to discuss? Leonard, you don't go spending hundreds of thousands of dollars on my dream without telling me! What is so hard to understand about that?" she calls out, and I wish I wouldn't feel angry, but there is no stopping it now that I'm terrified of losing her.

"This is what you wanted. I don't understand why you're upset. You would have accepted this investment from anyone but me. How is that fucking fair when all I want is to see you happy?" I challenge, and she spins around, throwing her arms into the air to show she's also frustrated with me.

"Because you *are* my everything. Because if for some reason we don't work out, I don't think I could stand being in the same room with you and have you not be mine. How would I be able to run a business with you? The answer is I wouldn't be. I wouldn't be able to walk in here and not see you everywhere. This is a huge step in our relationship based on trust and security and—" I cut her off.

"And you don't know if you feel those things with me?" I ask, my heart shattering in my chest. Her features soften and she wraps her arms around herself.

"Of course I do, Leonard. I trust you, but we've just started dating and now you threw me into this without speaking to me first. Try to understand why I'm overwhelmed," she says, but I shake my head, panic filling my chest.

"I've always done things by myself, Chiara, trusted my gut to tell me what the right choice is. Believe me when I tell you this will work. I can separate business from my personal life," I assure her, but she shakes her head and lets it drop, sucking in a sharp breath. It sends a wave of pain through me. This is how I lose her. I'm sure of it.

"*I* can't. I can't separate how I feel about you from business because I have never felt this way about anyone before. I know you mean well with this, but there is a reason I never asked you. You shouldn't be the one to risk it all on me if I turn out not to be good enough. You will hate me forever." There it is. Her real fear has finally come to the surface, and now we can have a better conversation, one where I understand her instead of getting frustrated with her.

"I love you." The words are out of my mouth before I can stop them. Her eyes go wide, but the panic in my chest is finally subsiding. "I'm so in love with you, it overwhelms me." Tears shoot into her eyes, and I feel some burning mine too. I don't care. I want her to see I mean every single word I've said and am about to add. "You are the only one I want to cook for every night. You are the only one I want to help me in my kitchen. You are the only one I want to argue with. I want everything you offer me because you're the love of my life." Her emotions drip down her face, and I close the distance between us to wipe them away. "Years, sweetheart, I've known it for years without realizing it, and I'm so sorry it took so long for me to understand how perfect you are for me. You complete me, and I want to be all the good titles in the world for you." I wipe away one of her tears, but she tilts her head away from me to hide her crying. Her hair falls into her face, so I push it away and bring her gaze back to mine. "You don't have to be scared about failing and me hating you, Chiara, because I never could, especially not for something like that. Do you understand me?" Her green eyes are glassy, and I wish my love declaration wouldn't make her so sad.

"I understand," she croaks out, wiping away her tears with the sleeve of her jacket. "Leonard?" Chiara asks, and I lean down to press my forehead to hers.

"Yes, sweetheart?"

"You just told me you love me," she whispers, and I let out a small laugh.

"I've been telling you for months. Have you not been listening?" A breathless laugh escapes her lips. "Chiara?" I ask this time, and she chuckles.

"Yes, Champ?" I bring my mouth against hers.

"Where's the meteorite, baby? Tell me it's getting closer," I beg, and she kisses me fully before pulling away again and looking up at me.

"It has struck the Earth," she whispers, and I pick her up off the ground and wrap her legs around my torso. "I love you," Chiara adds, and my heart bursts into a million butterflies swarming around in my chest and stomach. "Even if you told me you didn't have time to break my heart."

We both let out small laughs as I walk us into one of the rooms I would love for her to use to make a non-digital art exhibition. I placed a blanket in here earlier, along with a bottle of champagne and two glasses.

"I don't have the time to break your heart, Chiara, and even if I did, I couldn't. I've never been happier," I say, and she kisses my lips as I settle down on the blanket.

"I'm still a little mad at you," she says, her head falling backward when I bring my bulge to her pussy. I fucking love summer dresses.

"Yeah, I know. You have every right to be, but I'd very much like to make it up to you. Can you be mad at me while I make you come?" I ask, but she's already rubbing herself against me, searching for a release.

"I don't want to be mad while we fuck," Chiara says, stopping herself from chasing her pleasure. "How will this work?" she asks, her hands on either side of my face as her green eyes fixate on my brown ones.

"I already told you how. You make all the rules. We can draw up a contract or anything else you need to have security," I reply, and she wiggles on top of me.

"I have my own art gallery?" she asks, joy in her voice.

"Yes, you do."

"That's so cool," she says, kissing me all over the face. "Thank you, *amore*," Chiara adds, and I grin at her in response.

"Nothing to thank me for. You were the one who convinced me not only because of who you are to me, but who you are as a person," I reply, which seems to make her even happier.

"I don't think I should accept this so easily, but this is—it's everything I was hoping for when we started going to the events this season."

It's everything I've wanted for her too, and I don't give a shit that I had to be the one to give it to her. As a matter of fact, I prefer it this way. I'd never cut her funding, take back what I've given, or do anything another investor could do to her.

"You have enough savings to take the next few months and turn this gallery into what you've envisioned for years," I say, and uncertainty flashes across her face.

"Can I—" Chiara cuts off and places her hands on my cheeks. She doesn't know how to frame whatever it is she wants to ask for, but I have a feeling I already know.

"Yes, Starling, I would love for you to join me for the rest of the season." Her features brighten at my words, and I get a whiff of her peachy scent.

"Okay," she replies, capturing my lips. "But I don't want to work for you any-more. I'll watch Benz, but not as your employee. I'll watch her as your girlfriend," she says, and I decide not to fight her on this.

"Anything you want, it's yours." My money. My possessions. My life. It's all hers, every part of it.

"I want you on this blanket. Maybe have you spray some of that champagne on me," Chiara says, her eyes flickering with the naughty sparkle that always appears when she's dirty talking with me. I'm about to respond when she kisses me again and rubs herself over my bulge until all the blood rushes to my cock and makes me unbearably hard.

"Remove your dress," I instruct, and it's gone within a second. "Panties and bra too."

Chiara smiles as she stands up and removes both until her curves and tanned skin are perfectly on display for me. I reach out and bring my hands to her hip dips, tugging until she's next to me on the blanket again. Her body has me hot and hard while my heart races uncomfortably fast. I unbutton my shirt and slip it off my body, feeling her hands on me as soon as I'm shirtless.

"Lie back," I tell her even if her hands on me are everything I need right now.

Chiara does as she's told, still smiling at me as I pick up the champagne bottle and pop the top, spraying its contents around a little before pouring some of the liquid onto her chest and licking it off right after. The alcohol, bubbly and cold, runs down my throat, and I moan at the way she arches her body against my mouth. Chiara parts her lips and sticks out her tongue, telling me she'd like a bit of champagne too. I chuckle as I pour it into her mouth, one of my hands dropping to her clit so my fingers can rub against the swollen area.

"Fuck," she moans, and I take another sip from the bottle before kissing her, letting some of the liquid move into her mouth too. An approving groan leaves her as she digs her nails into my back. My body is flush against hers, burning with desire and need for her. "I don't want to use a condom today," she whispers as I grind my bulge against her clit. I freeze, my head lifting so my eyes meet hers.

"Are you sure?" We're both clear, and she's on birth control, but she said she needed a bit more time when we spoke about it recently.

"I am, Leonard. I only want you," she says, making everything inside and outside of me pull tight. God, I am at her mercy. "Do you want this too?" she asks, kissing along my jaw and bringing her hands into my hair.

"Yes," I croak out because my cock's aching to be inside of her now.

She fumbles with the button and zipper of my pants until she can pull them down and grab my cock in her hand. My arms on either side of her wobble because the pleasure is weakening my muscles. Chiara aligns me with her entrance, not wasting a moment. I claim her mouth to distract her for a second because anticipation already has me on the edge of fucking exploding. I take a few minutes to explore her mouth and rub my cock along her clit, making her squirm with pleasure underneath me.

"I love you," I say a moment before thrusting into her, sending my head straight into heaven.

"I love you, I love you, I love you," she repeats breathlessly with every thrust.

My self-control is hanging on by a thread. Feeling her like this, being inside of her without a condom is... paradise. It feels so fucking good, I'm on the brink of my orgasm within seconds. Her warmth is bliss, and I wish I could last hours like this because I never want to stop. I want us both to keep experiencing this pleasure because nothing's ever felt better. Not just for me, but also for her. I can tell by her whimpers and breathy moans, by the way Chiara begs for me but somehow isn't saying anything at all.

"Oh my God," she screams as she falls apart more easily than ever before. I let her ride out her pleasure before seizing my movements to hold off my orgasm. "More," Chiara begs a minute later, and I smile down at her, the strain of this position causing sweat to appear on my back and forehead.

"Give me a moment," I say and take her right nipple in my mouth instead. Her back arches off the ground again, making me take more of her tit into my mouth. I moan in response and so does she.

"Please," she begs, and I slide out of her completely only to flip her onto her stomach, spread her legs a little, and then slam into her from behind. My chest presses against her back as I find a rhythm I can barely keep up without spilling inside of her. "Yes, oh God, yes," she moans, gripping the blanket while I pump into her so hard, my vision blurs.

"You're doing so well, sweetheart," I praise, grabbing her perfect round arse and squeezing hard. She cries out with pleasure until her body shudders from another orgasm, sending me straight over the edge. "Fuuuuck," I moan, my cock pulsing inside of her as my cum fills her pussy in a way I've never experienced with anyone else before.

My mouth trails kisses along her back while I try to catch my breath. I give us both another moment before I pull out and gently spin her around again. A happy smile lingers on Chiara's features, and I trail my gaze from her face all the way to her pretty pussy. My cum is dripping out of her, sending a shiver of pleasure down my spine. *Fuck, why do I like the sight of this so much?*

"There is no way there is a shower here, right?" Chiara asks with a little laugh, and I cock an eyebrow at her.

"Do you honestly think I'd choose an art gallery without a bathroom with a shower? Come on now, sweetheart, you know me better than that," I say, and Starling's eyes go wide.

"No way," she replies, and I stand up, holding out my hand for her.

"Come. Let's get you cleaned up." Because I want another reason to have her naked for as long as possible, and a shower will give me exactly what I crave.

"Is there enough space in the shower to fuck again?" she asks with a little smirk, and I shake my head as I pull her against my chest.

"Of course there is." *My insatiable little demon.*

CHAPTER 40

Chiara

It's been a month since Leonard and I signed a carefully constructed contract that made us partners in my art gallery. He had it written up to give me ninety percent of the control while he took only ten, but he said it's not up for negotiation. I didn't fight him on it either. I've been too busy taking every available minute of my time to create immersive art shows. There are five rooms in my gallery. I plan on using three of them for digital ones, and the other two... well, I've been trying to come up with ideas for my own art. Something that's similar to the balloon exhibit Leonard took me to. Nothing I've come up with so far has been great, so I haven't gone through with it yet. But I've been productive.

Mamma and Nonna came to England two weeks ago to visit and see my art gallery. They stayed with Leonard and me at his apartment. Around the same time, he asked me to move all of my things into his bedroom, and it's almost annoying how easy the transition was, how natural. It's as if we were meant to share a bedroom. Like he was supposed to hold me from night until morning. Like our bodies were carved to fit into one another's. Like everything is just right now that we've stopped fighting how we feel about each other.

I haven't been this happy in... ever.

I haven't ever been this happy, and it's not only because I'm dating Leonard, who makes everything in my life better. It's also because my relationships with Mamma and Nonna, the Tick family, and even Lulu are strong. The only person who's been avoiding me and who I've been avoiding is Graham. My best friend, who half a year ago I didn't expect I'd have to spend two weeks without, let alone for however long he's going to stay in New York. It's weird, and it makes me sad, but I'm not quite sure how to tell him Leonard and I are dating.

Graham said he'd be fine with it, he was even rooting for Leonard and me, and still, I can't get myself to pick up the phone and tell him. It also doesn't help that it feels like we've become strangers, something I knew deep down would happen when he left. Long distance relationships, even friendships, are terribly hard to keep alive. Even friendships as old as Graham's and mine will break under the distance, especially when I'm hiding something from him. God, I hate how fucking complicated the once easiest bond in my life has become. It should be illegal.

"Just call him," Lulu said to me the last time we hung out, and I looked up from my laptop. I wanted to show her the exhibit I'd already put together so I invited her over to my art gallery. "He won't be upset if you tell him, but if he finds out from anyone else? He'd be angry," she added, and I let out a sigh.

"His family doesn't even know. Leonard kissed me once after the race, but it wasn't photographed. Who would tell him?"

"Just call him, Chiara. Otherwise, if he finds out from any of the hundred people on Leonard's team who know, you'll regret it." She was right. I couldn't fight her on this when I knew how hurt Graham would be or how much I'd regret it.

"Okay," I replied.

It's been two weeks since our conversation, and, yeah, I still haven't found the courage to tell him. Saying, 'Hey, Graham. Listen, I'm in love with your brother and have been dating him for weeks now' doesn't roll off the tongue easily, especially when I have to do it over the phone. Maybe I'm holding out hope I'll get a chance to see him soon and explain in person. Maybe I'm holding out hope I don't have to tell him until Leonard and I either break up or... *what? Get married?* Fuck. I need to tell Graham.

Benz is lying on my lap as we wait for Leonard to come back from wherever he left off to. He said he wants to spend the day with me since we barely had time to be together this weekend. It was another win for him. My boyfriend is currently leading the championship by fifty points, and it's fucking satisfying to see Jonathan's stupid face covered with rage because he lost to Leonard *again*.

Yesterday was filled with excitement. Leonard won the race, so his team and the two of us went to a bar in Mexico City to celebrate the win. For the first time in my life, I saw Leonard let loose and lower his barriers, but only because he stayed with me the whole time, one hand somehow always on me. I didn't mind it one single bit. We were both tipsy and happy while he told me how much he loves me and how he couldn't wait to get me out of my dress. He kissed me with his eyes half-closed and tequila on his tongue, and I melted against him because everything about him is delicious to me.

A little electric jolt travels through my body at the thought of what happened when we got back to the hotel room. He threw me on the bed while I laughed at the top of my lungs before he spread my legs and buried himself inside of me until we both fell apart. And while sex with him is incredible, it doesn't compare to the way it feels when he holds me after and whispers sweet things into my ear.

God, I love him so much, it hurts.

My phone rings on the floor next to me, and I smile when I read Rena and Andrew's names on my screen. Out of the two of them, she is more likely to talk to me than he is, but sometimes Mr. Tick will be on the phone too, simply listening while Rena and I chat. I hit the answer button with a slight smile on my face. It's strange. I'm smiling a lot these days, but I guess joy will do that to someone.

"Hello, how are you? How's your leg?" I ask as I press the speaker button on my phone.

"Hi, darling, I'm fine. My leg is doing a lot better, which is why I'm calling. When you get back to England, I'd love for you to give me a tour of your art gallery," she says, and my heart flutters from excitement. *Your art gallery*. That'll never get boring.

"Yes, of course! Will Andrew come as well?" I ask because Leonard's parents are the only ones who haven't been to the gallery yet. Rena's leg was still bothering her a few weeks ago, so she's been staying at home. That's why I'm so excited to hear she wants me to give her a tour. I make a plan on how I will describe everything to her.

"No, he's already seen it. Leonard took him along when he was trying to find a place," she explains, and my heart flutters at the visual of my boyfriend and his father moving around the city of London to find the perfect art gallery.

"Okay, no problem. We will have a nice girls' day," I reply, and we agree on a day and time before we talk about the shows I've already created.

"I'm so proud of you, Chiara. You're doing a great job and all that while still working for Leonard," she says, causing a wave of guilt to twist my stomach. I've never lied to this woman about anything. *Am I able to do so now?* There is a big difference between keeping something from her by avoiding the subject all together and straight-up lying. At least for me.

"Actually, I'm not working for him anymore. I'm watching Benz as—" I cut off because saying it out loud to anyone but Leonard isn't something I've done yet. Lulu kind of just figured it out by herself.

"I know, darling. My son is capable of many things, but he's not able to hide something that makes him as happy as being with you. Well, he tried, but then he blurted it out and let out a nervous laugh. It was a whole thing," she explains, and my cheeks start burning from the huge smile spreading across my face.

"I'm sorry I didn't tell you," I say, but a little chuckle escapes her.

"Don't worry, darling, I'm not mad. I always knew you two would end up together." I scratch Benz's head, trying to fight off my grin. It's impossible.

"So did I." His voice is low and husky, dragging my attention from the conversation with his mum to his warm brown eyes. My favorite pair in the whole world. "Hi, Mum," he says and kneels down beside me to pat Benz's head and kiss me.

"Hello, troublemaker," she says, and Leonard gives me a small smirk. "Chiara and I have made plans to have a girls' day on Wednesday. Can you manage to peel yourself off her long enough for us to spend it together?" she asks with a teasing tone, making my boyfriend smile.

"If I must," he replies, giving me another kiss. "Mum, Starling and I have to be somewhere soon. We'll call you tomorrow," he says, grabbing my phone and waiting for all of us to say our goodbyes before hanging up. Leonard's eyes drift to Benz as he scratches her belly once more. "Okay, baby, Mamma and I will be back in a few hours to take you for a nice, long walk," he says and stands up, leaving my head to spin by itself. *Mamma*. He thinks of me as Benz's Mamma. Fuck. I love it...

"Where are we going?" I croak out because my emotions are all over the place.

"I want to show you something I've also invested in," he replies and holds out his hands to help me up. I slide mine into his, and he pulls me up with ease, wrapping his arms around my back and bringing our chests flush together.

"Then maybe don't get me all worked up, otherwise we won't make it out of the hotel room." His teeth graze my bottom lip, sending a wave of electricity through me until it settles between my legs.

"Later, sweetheart. I promise. This is important to me, so I'd like to show you," he tells me, and I step out of his embrace to get my horny side under control.

"Say no more. Let's go," I say and grab my purse off the chair next to the bed.

"I tell you it's important and you don't argue with me? Good to know," he replies with a teasing tone and smile, and I playfully smack his arm. "Do that again," he challenges with a smirk, and I know if I do, he's going to bend me over on the bed and fuck me hard, which is the only reason why I hesitate. "You want to do it again, don't you?" he says with a laugh and a shake of his head.

"You know I do. You shouldn't dangle the possibility of sex in front of me when we have important places to go to," I tell him, and he grabs my face. Desire plays in his eyes, surprising me.

"Spread your legs," he instructs, and I furrow my brows at him. "We have two minutes. Spread your legs, sweetheart, and I'll give you what you want." I don't hesitate. "Good girl." One of his hands gently wraps around my neck as his other disappears into my panties.

Two minutes later, we're walking out of the door with his hand in mine, a post-orgasm smile on my lips, and a cocky grin on his. If I wasn't already in love with him, I would be now. Leonard gives me everything I want without hesitation, which is something I've never felt before. To be put first, always. To be everything he wants in the world. And fuck, if I wouldn't die for this man.

Leonard brought me to an animal sanctuary. A sanctuary that's huge and filled with animals rescued from circuses, people who thought it would be okay to raise a tiger as a pet, and hunters who injured the animals in their attempt to kill them. The woman in charge of the sanctuary is kind and, simply put, a ray of sunshine. She tells me she does her best to get the animals back into the wild as soon as they are healed, but most of them have sustained injuries so bad, they wouldn't be able to survive anymore. My heart shatters into a million pieces at the thought of innocent creatures having to go through so much pain and suffering, but the feeling is eased a little by the sight of them happily playing in the water in their large areas of the sanctuary.

"How can they afford all of this? It must cost a fortune," I whisper to Leonard as I smile at the lions lying together, sleeping.

"I invest, sometimes throw charity parties to raise more money too. Anything that helps," he replies, his hand on the small of my back to make me follow Pepa, the woman who owns the sanctuary.

"You do?"

I shouldn't be surprised. Leonard has the biggest heart of anyone I know. He invests in the people he believes in. Lilah, Pepa, me, and who knows how many other people wouldn't have gotten as far as we have without him. The best part of it all? He doesn't do it to get credit or attention afterward. He will stand at the back, cheering for the person succeeding.

"Yeah, sweetheart. I'd love for us to have one of those events at your gallery one day," he says and wraps his hand around mine.

"I would like that very much," I reply, and Leonard manages to give me a brief kiss before Pepa grabs our attention again.

"This is Leonard," she says, pointing at a beautiful lion with three legs and a mane so big, it has me mesmerized. "We named him after the man who saved him," she explains and tells me about how Leonard found him the day after his race.

Leonard, the lion, was bleeding out at the side of the road when my boyfriend found him and immediately brought him to an emergency hospital for animals. Leonard thinks he might have been thrown into the street by someone who was illegally breeding lions here but didn't want one with only three legs. He says the little creature had only been a few weeks old when he found him.

"Leonard brought him to me a few days later," Pepa finishes, and I turn to the man I love.

"Why have you never told anyone?" I ask, and he gives me a simple shrug, dragging my hair behind my shoulder. It's gotten longer again since I cut it a few months ago, but Leonard seems to like my long locks.

"I didn't do it to gloat," he replies, and before I can respond, something lands on my head.

"Ricky!" Pepa calls out, but I'm frozen in place. Leonard attempts to reach out for me, but I let out a strangled laugh and step away. "Ay, don't worry, Chiara. Ricky is harmless, just clingy," she goes on, and I reach for the creature on my head. He wraps himself around my hand and arm, and I realize it's a little monkey.

"Oh," is all I say while he jumps onto my shoulder and grabs my hair for stability. He lets out a few excited sounds and then places his face against my cheek, making me laugh.

"Okay now, Ricky, watch yourself. Chiara is mine," Leonard says with a small smile directed at me, and the little animal on my shoulder jumps onto my boyfriend's now outstretched arm. "I named him," Leonard says as Ricky hugs him around the neck, holding on tight.

"Did you find him on the side of the road too?" I ask, dreading the answer.

"No, we just bonded after I brought Leonard in." I give him a small smile.

I realize three important things right here and now.

1. Leonard is undoubtedly the love of my life.

2. He's a pain in the ass at times, but his big heart is everything to me.

3. I'm going to marry him one day.

There is no one else I have ever or will ever be able to imagine a future with, and I'm surprisingly fine with that thought. Not just fine. Happy. I'm happily picturing us old and gray with a life full of memories. I'm happily picturing us with a big family, and him coming home to me every single day, just like I will come home to him. I'm happy about it all.

"Come, sweetheart. I want to take a photo," Leonard says, holding up my polaroid, which he's been taking everywhere. I have about fifty polaroids of us doing the most random things by now—even a naughty one of each of us—which I have put into a separate album. He takes a selfie of us, along with Ricky still holding onto his neck, and I grab the photo as it gets printed out of the camera.

"I'll never get enough of the places you take me to," I whisper as I wait for the picture to appear.

"I'll never get enough of taking you everywhere."

CHAPTER 41

Leonard

"Uncle Lenny!" Liz calls out when I step through the door of Jack and Stu's home. She runs toward me until her arms can wrap around my waist.

"Hi, angel," I reply before hugging her back and nodding at my brother and his partner. They're both waiting for me near the kitchen with their arms crossed in front of their chests and impatient looks on their faces. I roll my eyes teasingly but follow them toward the table where coffee and biscuits are waiting for me.

Chiara and I came back from Mexico a few days ago. We haven't told anyone we're dating, and I know I can trust Mum not to say anything before we're ready. Part of me, the coward in me, wishes she'd told everyone so I don't have to, but Chiara and I decided it was time. Most of my team already knows. Her family knows. My family should too. I even sent Graham a ticket to get his arse back to London. We should inform him of our relationship in person, not over the phone. It wouldn't feel right to do that.

Jack and Stu sit opposite me at the table, their arms still crossed. I merely stare back at them while a happy Lizzie takes a bite of the biscuit. She scrunches her nose at the taste and turns to her dads to ask why they taste so funny. Stu tells her it's one of Uncle Lenny's special cookies, so I take the other half she won't eat and place it in my mouth, winking at her. I push the plate with the non-vegan biscuits in front of her, and she smiles brightly.

"Can I help you both?" I finally ask when they say nothing.

"Please tell us you're officially dating Chiara," Jack says, and my heart inevitably skips a beat at the mention of my girlfriend's name.

"I am."

"Shut the fuck up!" Stu says, earning himself a slap from his partner. "Sorry, it's just, that's huge! But don't repeat daddy's bad word, Lizzie. It's very, very naughty," he adds, and I can't help but smile.

"Yup, he's definitely dating her. Look at that smile," Jack says, causing my grin to vanish and a glare to replace it. "How long?" he asks, both of my brothers leaning forward on the table. I cock an eyebrow, getting ready to play dumb.

"How long what?"

It goes against my nature not to be forward and efficient, but I like to have my fun with these two sometimes. They're so fucking nosey, just like the rest of my family, Quinn, and even Adrian, who I've become strangely fond of for inexplicable reasons. The only person who understands boundaries is Chiara.

"How long have you been in love with her?" Stu explains Jack's vague question, and I lean back in my chair, watching Liz take a bite of her biscuit and stare out the windows at the garden. Then I bring my eyes back to the two men expecting an answer.

"My whole life." And fuck, I will be for the rest of it.

"Why did it take you so bloody long to figure it out?" Jack asks, and I shrug, not quite sure myself.

"I'm an idiot. She's a pain in the arse. It took me a while to figure out I'm *her* idiot and she's *my* pain in the arse," I explain with a small chuckle because I know she'd love what I just said.

I'll text it to her later.

"I saw it the day I met you two. Should have asked me," Stu chimes in with a little snort, and I glare at him.

"Me too," Liz chimes in, and I let out a breathless laugh.

"Okay now, all of you, *shush*. Or, I'll leave," I warn, but Jack merely lets out a low laugh, his brown eyes meeting mine. He looks like an older version of me with softer facial features and more laugh lines around his mouth and eyes.

"You can leave if you'd like. I got my answer to the one question that prompted my extending an invitation to you," he replies, and I feel the urge to be immature and flip him off, which I haven't done in years. I'm twenty-eight and a Formula One world champion. I can't go around showing people the middle finger whenever they piss me off.

"Can I go play outside?" Lizzie asks her dads, who tell her to be careful and have fun.

They recently installed a swing in their backyard, which their little girl absolutely loves. I can't count how many videos they sent me of Liz wanting to show me how high she can go. Chiara and I always watch them together. Fuck. I miss her. I saw her an hour ago, and I fucking miss her. Maybe I should check in on her. Then again, I don't want to interrupt her day with Mum.

"You're thinking about her right now, aren't you?" Stu asks, and I place my phone on the table, bringing my focus back to both of them.

"I'm always thinking about her," I reply simply and let out a small breath. "What's going on with the both of you?" I ask both because I'm done with the spotlight being on me and because I genuinely want to know how they're doing.

"We're good. Actually, Jack, can you get the photo album we just had done?" Stu asks, and his partner stands up, pressing a quick kiss to his lips and then disappearing out of the kitchen. "Okay, listen to me. I need your help," he says, and I sit up straight, on high alert now.

"Anything," I assure him, and he gives me a small smile.

"I'm going to propose to Jack, but can Chiara make one of her art shows but with photos of me and him?" he asks. I take out my phone and start writing ideas into my notes app.

"I can most certainly ask her, but she's very busy at the moment. If Chiara can't, I can ask a few of my other contacts, if you'd like. Either way, I will make it happen for you, don't worry," I reply, writing down some more things while I listen to Stu explain how he's going to ask my brother to marry him.

I never asked either of them why they haven't proposed or gotten married. Part of me always thought they were waiting for the right time. Another part thought they were merely happy with the way things are now, but I'm beyond excited to help Stu propose in any little detail I get to. Graham doesn't believe in the concept of marriage, so I only have one shot at being the best man for my brothers. I almost smile at the thought of everything we'll have to arrange. Quinn's sibling got married last year, and the ceremony and location were beautiful. Maybe I can contact her and ask who helped them plan their wedding.

"What did you say to him? His gears are turning so hard, steam's coming out of his ears," Jack says, and I shoot him an unappreciative glare.

"God, you're hilarious. Have you ever thought about doing stand-up comedy?" I ask, gathering my things before standing up and straightening out my back until it cracks. "Anyway, it was lovely chatting with you both, but I have to head home. Chiara and I are buddy reading a book, and she's a lot further ahead than I am," I explain, a yawn slipping past my lips, but I cover my mouth so I'm not impolite.

"You're buddy reading a book with your girlfriend?" Stu asks, shock lacing his words. I stare at him, unimpressed.

"Yes. You got a problem with that?" I challenge, but he merely raises his hands in mock surrender and smiles.

"No problem, bubba, I'm merely surprised. I thought you're more of a music man than a reader," my soon-to-be brother-in-law replies, grinning at me like never before. He's happy with this new version of me, and, honestly, I can't blame him.

In my twenty-eight years of life, I have never, ever been in a serious relationship. I didn't run my life around a person I'm in love with, not like I'm doing with Chiara now. She likes my cooking, I do so every night. She wants to help me in the kitchen, I let her in. She wants to buddy read a book with me, I'll buy two copies and start it right away. She wants the moon, the stars, the sun, the entire universe, I will lay it all at her feet. Anything and everything she desires, I arrange for until her heart and life are equally full. I've never felt so alive before, never knew how to use that organ in my chest properly, but Starling taught me. As a matter of fact, she taught me everything from the ages of eight to twenty-eight, and I'm only now understanding her lessons. Now I'm planning a future in my head where we're growing old together, where my grandmother's ring has rested on Chiara's hand for decades, and we watch our children succeed in whatever careers they choose.

A year ago, all of these thoughts wouldn't have made sense to me. I've never been someone to fall in love with another person, but maybe that's because I never had to fall. It's more like Chiara shoved me in love with her, probably around the time she shoved my face into the remains of her sandcastle when we were kids. I don't mind it one bit. I thought I had to push her away, pretend like I didn't like her because she didn't seem to reciprocate my feelings, but the way we are now, happy and together, it's everything I could have dreamt of. I'm complete because my other half is mine in the same way I am hers. Forever.

"Thank you both for having me," I say and walk outside to say goodbye to Liz before leaving their home.

It's only August, which means the summer sun is still bright and warm as I make my way toward my car. As much as I want to go home to catch up with Chiara in the book, I know if I sit on the couch, I will be watching the door, waiting for her to come home. I find myself doing that a lot, feeling lost nowadays when she isn't around to brighten up my days, but I know I can't always be around Chiara. So, I decide to pick up Benz and go for a walk with her, meeting up with Quinn for a coffee. It's been a while since my best friend and I simply hung out, mostly because I've been intoxicated with my new relationship. Quinn deserves better, and I will spend the day with her to be a better friend.

"Hey, stranger," she says when I meet her at our coffee place, Benz wagging happily at her friend. Usually, Chiara takes her to the gallery with her when she spends the day there, but she needs all of her attention on Mum today.

"Stranger? We spent twenty-two weekends out of the year together, not to mention all of the days we train together and meet up just for fun. I'll never be a stranger to you," I reply, moving over to give her a small hug.

"Fair enough, kiddo," she replies with a little grin, bending down to pat Benz's head.

We settle down in seats across from each other and spend an hour talking about everything and somehow nothing too. I can't help checking my phone when Chiara messages me, letting me know Mum and her are on the way to the gallery now. Apparently, they were having a late brunch first. I smile at my phone before refocusing on my best friend and continuing our conversation. More time passes until my phone rings in my lap again, Adrian's name flashing on my screen.

"Hold on, Quinn. I just want to make sure Adrian's alright. He's calling me, and he never does that," I explain and she assures me it isn't a problem before I hit answer. "What's up, rookie? Why are you calling me?" I ask as soon as I press the phone to my ear.

"You have to get to the gallery right fucking now, Leonard." My heart sinks into my chest.

"Why? What's wrong?" I'm already standing.

"Someone broke in and vandalized the whole place. Hurry up."

I don't ask why he's in England. I don't ask why he's at the gallery. I don't even ask why he didn't call me before going there first. I tell Quinn what happened and ask her to watch Benz for me instead.

The love of my life needs me, which means I'm already running toward the gallery.

CHAPTER 42

Leonard

Chiara is on her knees, holding a piece of her art gallery sign. She hung it a few days ago, and it used to be the name of the gallery. *Meteorite*. Now it's torn to shreds, along with the immersive art gallery she was putting together in one of the rooms. She was making her own art. She'd decided on a room full of hanging lights people could walk underneath, making them look like stars in the night sky. It would be an experience where people would get to spend a minute in the room by themselves, in complete darkness except for those lights. Starling finished painting the walls black and hung all the bulbs. Now? They have been crushed into tiny shards of glass and the word 'Bitch' is written across the wall. Anger causes the blood in my veins to boil.

But it doesn't end there.

Someone, and I know it was Tim, took a sledgehammer to the entrance walls and placed countless holes in them. All of the furniture and little things Chiara put into her gallery to make it hers and familiar and comfortable have been destroyed. There is nothing left except for broken pieces of her dream, and it takes everything out of me not to join her on the floor. This is devastating. I know we can easily afford to rebuild this place, I have more than enough money, but it will never be the same as before. All the hours Chiara put into the gallery are lost, and I know she'll never come home to me again, telling me she's falling in love with her process. Her heart won't let her get excited like that anymore, not after everything's been destroyed.

The thought sends tears into my eyes, and I do my best to blink them away because right now is not the time to cry. Chiara needs me.

My eyes drift to Adrian and Mum in the corner of the art gallery where the rookie is holding onto her arm. One of her hands has covered her mouth, and I realise he must have told her what happened in here. I can't think about that either. I can't think about how Chiara and Mum walked in here, maybe with Adrian too, who knows, and then my beautiful girlfriend had to go through this without me. It makes me sick to my stomach.

"Sweetheart?" I say so I don't startle her before placing my hand around her arm. She's staring at the broken piece of the sign. There are no tears, no emotions, nothing to tell anyone how she feels. Except for me. I can read her as easily as I breathe, and I can see her heartbreak in the way she attempts to hide all of her feelings.

"Tim did this," she whispers, her voice cracking at the words.

"I know," I reply, running the back of my fingers down the length of her cheek. Her eyes close in response to my touch, and when they open again, tears threaten to fall down her face.

"And we have no way to prove it," she adds, sounding stronger and more frustrated than before.

"We have security cameras, baby," I remind and promise her, but the tears drop down her cheeks while she shakes her head.

"He wiped the footage off the system. I already checked. There is nothing we can do. Nothing!" she yells the last word and throws the piece of her sign at the already broken wall in front of us.

"Chiara, sweetheart, it's okay. We will figure it out, I promise. Let's just go home first so I can make you tea to calm your nerves," I say, but she's pushing away from me, clutching her stomach and letting me know she's about to fall apart while I have no idea how to hold her together.

"No, Leonard. You—We—I—" Chiara cuts off, panic causing her breathing to hitch and falter. "I can't breathe," she says, more tears streaming down her face. Some fall from the corners of my eyes now too. It's been a while since I've cried, but at this very second, her pain is hitting me harder than any of my own ever has.

"What do you need? What can I give you?" I ask, trying to take a step closer, but she backs away from me.

"I don't know. But I can't stay here. This is my fault. This is all my fault, and it keeps being my fault. I can't do this," she says, sending a wave of fear through my chest until it settles deep inside my bones.

"This is not your fault, Chiara. I should have anticipated Tim would want to get his revenge. I should have protected this place better." I should have protected her better, no matter the costs. A security service may not have been something I thought necessary before. It most certainly is now. I will get someone day and night to watch over the art gallery, make sure Chiara is safe and sound here.

"No, Leonard. You can't keep saving me! Look at this mess. It's—Everything's gone to shit. My dream, our dream, it's gone. Destroyed. Because of me. Because of a man that's obsessed with me for some reason. Because I didn't think we needed more protection either. This is on me, and you cannot be the one to fix this. Not again. I can't—" She's cut off by a sob leaving her lips, but I'm too scared of what she's saying to focus on anything else.

"Are you breaking up with me?" I ask, my voice trembling.

Everything she's saying is pointing in that direction, and suddenly, I'm the one who can't breathe anymore. Please tell me she isn't breaking up with me, not because of what that wanker Tim did to the gallery. We can fix this. I know it'll never be the same, but Chiara did a wonderful job before. She'll do it again. I know she will. Chiara is the most talented and hard-working person I know.

"I love you more than anything or anyone else, Leonard. You're my other half. But I can't do this. I cannot keep using your money to live off of, support my dream. I can't do it. I won't. We didn't even have fucking insurance on the gallery yet, and I don't want to imagine how much fixing all of this would cost," she says and runs her hands through her hair. I'm about to step in when she lets out a laugh I know she doesn't mean. "No, I can't. I can't do this. You invested in me, and I lost it all. This is my fault, and I can't—Fuck, I'm so sorry, Leonard. I disappointed you. I've ruined everything," she adds, and then her feet bring her further away from me. She's going to run. Run from this disaster. Run from what she perceives as her failure. Run from *us*.

"Chiara, don't you dare leave right now," I warn, but she repeats her apology a hundred times before running out of the room. I'm on my way to chase after her when my mum's soft voice fills my ears.

"Leonard, darling?" I freeze because as much as I would love to chase after Chiara, Mum's leg is still not a hundred percent, and she can't see what's happening. My first priority needs to be getting her home. Adrian points to himself to assure me he can take her where she needs to go.

"Mum, I have to go after Chiara. Would it be okay if Adrian took you home? He's a good friend of mine," I say, and her hand reaches out, waiting for me to take it. I do as she wants.

"It'll be okay, Leonard. Chiara is overwhelmed and frightened, but she loves you. I think she has about as much desire to leave you as you have to leave her," Mum says, but at this moment, it doesn't feel that way. Chiara *literally* ran away from me.

"What the fuck happened here?" a very familiar voice asks, sending ice through my veins.

No, no, no, this is horrible timing.

I love Graham, but him being here while everything is going to shit solves nothing. If anything, it complicates the situation ten times more because no one's fucking told him Chiara and I are dating. I'm in trouble.

"I can't talk right now, Graham. I have to find Chiara," I say, but his next words stop me dead in my tracks.

"Did you do this to her gallery?" *Did I do this to her gallery?* "I know you both didn't always get along, but this is next level, Leonard. You invest in her dream just to take it away? That's not right."

He hasn't seen Chiara and me together over the last few months. He didn't see the way we became everything to each other. He never got to watch me embrace how in love with her I am. At least that's what I keep telling myself so I don't lose it.

"Graham, you don't know what you're talking about, so I'm not upset with you for the bullshit that just came out of your mouth, but do me one favour. Don't disappear for months and then come back thinking you still know what the hell is going on between Starling and me. As a matter of fact, just don't think, alright? It's not entirely your fault you're out of the loop, but it is partially, so don't come here with shitty assumptions about horrible things I'd do to the woman I love." Shit, I should have probably kept that last bit to myself, but I'm a bit angry about what he said if I'm being honest with myself.

"Are you dating my best friend?" he asks instead of addressing anything else I've just said. I let my head drop for a fraction of a second because every moment I spend here, the further Chiara can get without me there to comfort her. Fuck. I hope she needs my comfort, wants it even.

"No, Graham, I'm dating the love of my life."

Then I leave him standing there with Mum and Adrian, hoping more than anything I can find Chiara as soon as possible.

I have looked everywhere, for hours. Quinn brought Benz home an hour ago, and I've been sitting in Chiara's and my apartment since then, hoping she will come back to me. Meanwhile, I've already called a company that will do the repairs, called the police to report the vandalism, and contacted Starling's Mamma to ask her if she knows where Chiara might have gone. Unfortunately, she hasn't responded to me yet.

So, I'm sitting on the bloody floor, close to bloody tears, wishing she'd never walked away from me in the first place. There are a lot of things I can handle in this world. Failure. Poverty. Two broken legs at the same time—it happened to me when I was a teenager and I couldn't race for nearly six months—but this? Not knowing whether or not Chiara wants things to be over? It's killing me from the inside like heart failure would.

Benz lets out a little whining noise, walking to the front door and sitting down behind it as she waits for her Mamma to come home. The sight causes my feelings to run down my face, but I fight back the sob trying to slip past my lips. I'm not someone who gives up easily, and I haven't yet, but the uncertainty of her location combined with the way she left things is making an unbearable pain course through my system. I know Chiara is overwhelmed. I know she blames herself for what happened at the gallery, even though no part of me thinks it was her fault, but I wish she wouldn't. This guilt, her concept of my money isn't hers when I would give it all to her if it meant she was happy, upsets me.

Can't she see I'd sell my soul to make her smile?

I call Benz to me, but she remains in front of the door, waiting for the person she loves most in the world to get back. I move over to where she is, wiping my tears before pulling her onto my lap and staring at the door like that would make it open any sooner. This might be the most pathetic thing I've ever done in my entire life, but I don't give a single shit.

This is Chiara after all, and I'd wait naked in a blazing snowstorm for her if I had to.

CHAPTER 43
Chiara

My body is numb. There is a cut on my hand from when I picked up a shard of glass earlier, but I can't feel any pain. It's bleeding pretty badly, so I press a tissue to the split skin, wishing for anything to register in my brain. Hurt, pain, sadness, anything. Instead, I can't even sense the warm summer wind as it wraps around my body. Tears keep streaming down my face, but I don't feel the wetness either. It's as if every nerve in my body was murdered by the sight of my dreams in ruins. Because of Tim, which means it was because of me. It was my fault. All of Leonard's money and faith in me poured down the drain. One of my biggest fears was disappointing him, and I did. Even if he says I didn't, I know better. The gallery hasn't even been opened yet and it's already a disaster.

I settle down on the bench near the Thames where I like to go at night sometimes, a spot I haven't even shared with Leonard yet. Things have been so busy lately, I haven't had a chance to get away for a little. Right now, this is the one place I know no one will come looking for me while I do something I haven't done in a long time. I'm going to feel weird doing it, but I need this. I need to speak to him.

The piece of bread in my hand feels heavy, but I sit on the bench and wait for the little starling bird. I know it will find me. It's the only connection I have to him, even if some people might find it strange. I don't. *What kind of bird follows a person around the country if it wasn't sent by their dead father?* Okay, maybe it is strange, but I don't care. I miss my Papa, even if I never knew him. He's been watching over me my entire life, and part of me likes to believe he brought me to the Tick family so I could find both my best friend and my other half.

A low, trembling breath slips past my lips as I wait a bit longer, peeling off a piece of bread and watching the steady stream of the water. I do my best to stop crying, but it seems impossible as the images of my shattered gallery replay in my head. Then, Leonard's disappointed face reappears in my mind, and I cry even harder than before. I don't think he blames me. *What am I thinking?* Of course he doesn't blame me. Leonard loves me more than anything else, he's told me so repeatedly, but I still can't shake the feeling that I've failed him.

After months of depending on him for a job and a place to live, even for my happiness in some ways, I thought this gallery would finally allow me to feel more independent again. I love him and how things are between us, but I went from working four jobs and taking care of myself for years to *dependency*. It wasn't right. I knew it wasn't, but Leonard never made me feel like I had to be ashamed to take a breather and let him take care of me for a while. I was still working, taking care of Benz, so I didn't feel the lack of self-sufficiency until I saw my gallery torn to shreds today. I don't even have a car anymore, for fuck's sake. Leonard was driving me everywhere or I had to take his car. And even if my dependency on Leonard's money wasn't that big of a deal, disappointing him is.

It's the reason why I can't go home to him, even though being with him would ease the pain in my chest.

A warm breeze travels over my body again, but this time, I manage to feel it everywhere. It gives me hope that the numbness is eventually going to wear off, but I have yet to experience the pain from the cut on my hand. It's drenched one of my tissues already, so I pull out another one and press it to my palm. My eyes fall shut before I hear the flutter of wings right next to me on the bench. Without looking, I know it's the little starling bird I've grown so fond of. Without looking, I know my Papa heard me.

"Hi, Papa," I start, more tears burning my eyes as I stare at the bird next to me. I place a piece of bread on the bench in front of him, and he picks at it. "Everything's gone to shit," I go on in Italian, a laugh escaping my lips. It's humorless and dry, which is probably why it sends an awful shiver down my spine.

A couple walks by me, watching my exchange with the bird, and I let out another laugh, this one directed at myself. My dream is in ruins, and I'm speaking to a bird. Yeah, maybe not the best thing I could be doing at this moment, which is why I wait until I'm by myself again to continue my conversation. I pull my legs to my chest on the bench and wrap my arms around them, placing another piece of bread in front of the starling bird.

"You probably already know this, but I've fallen for a Formula One World Champion who is both the best parts of me and the worst." I scrunch my eyebrows together because that probably doesn't make much sense. "He's stubborn, strong-headed, and a pain in the ass, just like I am. But he's also compassionate, determined, and a fighter. He has such a big heart, Papa, bigger than anyone else in the world, even if he doesn't show it to everyone. In a way, if I'm being honest, it makes me feel special to be one of the few who gets to feel the pure, raw impact of it," I say, pressing my legs further into my chest as the waves of emotion overwhelm me to the point of pain.

It hurts to breathe.

"My whole life, I've been so, so scared of failure. Of feelings too. I stopped fighting instead of pursuing a professional career because I lost a few matches and it terrified me. I thought I wasn't good enough and because I was so obsessed with improving, getting better and stronger, I let it go entirely. At least that way it was my choice and not because I failed and got rejected," I explain out loud for the first time in my life.

The little starling bird flutters his wings at me while tears drop down my cheeks, and it almost feels like he's encouraging me to keep talking. To let go of of what's weighing on my chest.

"Leonard means *everything* to me. Disappointing him, becoming a failure in his eyes, is by far one of the worst things I could ever do, which is probably why I'm not with him right now. Even as every fiber of my existence is pulling me toward home, I'm glued to this fucking bench, talking to a bird I've convinced myself is you, Papa," I go on, shaking my head and crying even harder than before. "I didn't take well enough care of my dream, of the one thing Leonard was truly betting his money on. I lost it all now, and there is no way to punish Tim for what he's done."

I haven't felt the urge to kick someone's ass since after the meeting Leonard had with his team and Jonathan. It was the day Jonathan won and told everyone—after cheating his way to the win of the Grand Prix—that he could be the World Champion this year. Leonard told me every horrible thing his teammate said during the meeting, and I wanted to hurt the asshole for the way he's been treating the man I love. But it's been a while since I truly wanted to get into a fight, until today. Until I saw everything in pieces, and I wanted to break Tim's nose. Make his outside just as ugly as his inside is.

"How am I meant to face Leonard when Tim's obsession with me caused all of this? I can't. He's spent so much money on me, and it's all lost now. I know we're meant to be business partners on this, but how can it work when one partner invests and the other can't carry their weight? Instead, I'm the reason it was all destroyed," I say and let my head drop onto my knees while a sob slips past my lips.

I really have to find a way to stop crying.

"Please tell me you're not actually blaming yourself for this?" Graham's familiar voice comes from behind me, and I turn to see him standing there, a lazy half-smile on his handsome face.

"I'm sorry, do I know you?" I tease, and he frowns down at me, placing one of his hands on my head and gently stroking my hair for a moment.

"It wasn't your fault," Graham whispers as he brings his lips to the side of my head, one of his arms wrapping around from behind and settling across my collarbones.

"It wouldn't have happened if it weren't for me," I reply, more feelings spilling from the corners of my eyes.

"If the world ran out of oranges tomorrow, would you blame yourself for the shortage because you ate one when you were five?" he asks, and I'm not quite sure why he's bringing oranges, my least favorite fruit, into this conversation.

"No, of course not. But that's not the same thing, and you know it," I reply, but Graham merely kisses the side of my head and shoos the bird away without addressing how weirded out he must be.

"I think you know this isn't your fault, and I also think you should go home before my brother loses his shit. He's been looking for you for hours," Graham tells me, and a wave of guilt instantly travels through my chest. I take out my phone to text Leonard.

Chiara: I'm fine. Just need a bit more time.

More time to process.

More time to try and overcome the fear in my chest.

More time to find the breath in my lungs again without it hurting.

My phone vibrates a second after I hit Send on the message, Leonard's name popping up.

Leonard: Please come home to me, sweetheart.

He wants me to come home, to the apartment I know has become ours, but he's the only one paying for it. God, I need to stop thinking like this.

"Why didn't you tell me you were dating Leonard? I told you I was fine with it because I knew you'd eventually hook up. So, why? Why'd you keep this from me?" he asks, and I shake my head, tightening my arms around my legs and letting out a sigh.

"Because this had nothing to do with you. You moved to New York. You left me! I love you, but we drifted apart, and telling you while you were so goddamn far away from me seemed impossible. I know this sounds like excuses, and maybe they are, but I was so happy with Leonard and didn't want to risk anything threatening that happiness."

Meanwhile, the real threat was Tim.

Tim... *not me.*

Not my failure. Or more like my fear of failure. I should be ashamed of myself for thinking the man with the biggest heart on the planet would ever be disappointed in me. I have to go home. After I'm done speaking to Graham, I will go pick up my purse from where I left it at the gallery and go home. It's where I want to be the most anyway.

"I was a threat to your happiness?" Graham asks, sadness in his voice. My features fall in response, another wave of guilt washing through me.

"Everyone was. We haven't even told Jack and Stu yet." Well, I haven't. Leonard spent the day with them today, so I'm pretty sure they know now, but I'm not about to point that out to my best friend when he's already hurting.

"Okay, if we're already admitting things we've been keeping from each other, here is mine. Irena and I moved in together a month ago, and we got a cat," he says, and my jaw drops a little.

"Already?" I ask, and he gives me a little grin.

"You moved in with my brother before you even started dating," he rebuttals, and I smack his arm with a small laugh.

"I've known Leonard almost my whole life, and I knew things would go very wrong. You hardly know her and probably think everything will go right," I say, and he lets out a low chuckle, giving me an agreeing nod after. A wave of nostalgia hits me right in the chest as I stare at my best friend's handsome face. "I miss you so much," I say, and Graham wraps his arms around me, letting me sob into his chest.

"I can't believe you're crying. I've never fucking seen it before. It's scary," he replies, and I burst into laughter.

Even if it's only for a little while, I'm happy to have my best friend back.

Graham and I are on our way to the gallery, strolling down the sidewalks of London. It's getting a bit colder now, but my best friend has his arm around me, his body heat keeping me warm. We're talking about his life in New York, and I do my best not to think about Leonard sitting home alone, waiting for me. If my keys to the apartment weren't in my purse and I wasn't so worried someone would steal them to break in, I'd be running home right this second. But I can't. I have to make sure Tim doesn't steal them.

My eyes drift to the night sky to see the little starling bird following us to the art gallery. I smile up at it, happy to see Papa still watching over me in some way. All I need now is to have Leonard's arms wrapped around me. God, I should have gone home a lot sooner instead of wallowing in self-pity and all of my doubts.

"Can I ask something that might make you hate me?" I say when we're right in front of the gallery.

"I could never hate you, Chiara," Graham assures me, brown eyes so similar to Leonard's on my face.

"Seeing this gallery, even if it's in ruins right now, does it make you regret leaving our dream behind?" I ask, genuinely curious.

"Yeah, a little. I haven't quite figured out what to do with my life anymore, but I'll get there. This? This has always been more your dream than mine if I'm being honest. This is the way it's supposed to be. An art gallery that's only yours. I was never meant to be your partner," he says, and I feel my shoulders drop.

He's right. He wasn't and isn't meant to be my partner. Leonard is. In every part of my life.

"Can I ask you something?" Graham says after a moment of us merely staring at each other, having an unspoken conversation.

"No," I reply, and he gives my side a swift pinch. I let out a small laugh.

"Does he make you happy, truly happy?" That might be the easiest question I've ever had to answer because there isn't a doubt in my mind. There will never be, that's how sure I am about what Leonard and I have.

"Yes. He makes me happier than I've ever been."

Because exploring the world with him, looking at art, immersing myself in life the way a person is supposed to, has me feeling full in a way I've never been. Whole. I'm whole.

"Good," Graham replies as we step into the gallery.

"There you fucking are, you little bitch." Ice runs through my veins at the sound of his voice. My entire body goes into attack mode, and I let it take over.

"Hi, Tim. I'm glad you're here. We have some unfinished business to attend to," I reply and roll up my sleeves with a disgusting smile on my lips.

Confusion spreads over his face as I tell Graham to step back and let me deal with this.

Tim might be a hell of a lot bigger than me, but I'm angrier.

CHAPTER 44

Leonard

I'm running through the hospital with my heart racing in my chest. My job includes racing the fastest cars on a race track in the world, but it has never beaten at this speed. Adrenalin is coursing through me as I rush toward the front desk and ask where the hell Chiara de Luca is. Graham told me he took her here after Tim showed up at the gallery. It was right when I saw that even though he deleted the security footage at the gallery, it backed up into the cloud. So, I found his smug smile as he walked into the gallery with a sledgehammer and paint. If he's capable of that, I don't want to know what else he's capable of. Fuck. I'm going to be sick.

"Where is Chiara de Luca? Please, I need to see her," I tell the nurse at the front desk, who frowns at my frantic behaviour.

"And you are?" the nurse asks, making it my turn to frown.

"Her husband. Now, tell me where she is." I'm done playing nice.

Graham's phone must have died because when I asked what happened, the message didn't even go through. At least that's what I'm telling myself. It's an easier pill to swallow than the possibility that something worse might have happened.

"She's getting stitched up right now. You may come with me. I will bring you to her," she says, but my head is so stuck on the first sentence, I can't move my legs for a second. Chiara is getting stitches. As soon as it registers in my head, I sprint after the woman.

Horrible thoughts about what awaits me in the room where Chiara is fill my brain. I might actually throw up. Please let her be okay. I don't know what I'll do if she isn't. I might rip off Tim's head and feet it to the fish in the Thames.

Her laughter fills my ears as we stop outside of a room with a white door. Relief spreads across my chest, but it's multiplied when I step inside and see my beautiful girlfriend smiling at my brother. There is a small cut above her eyebrow taped together already, but the biggest one is down her left arm where a nurse is currently stitching the skin back together. Relief is replaced by anger, but when her green eyes drift to my face, all I feel is a panging desire to wrap her up in my arms. Place my lips on hers. Tell her how much I love her. Anything.

"Hi, *amore*," she says, and I remember I still have to breathe if I want to do any of the things I listed in my head.

"Sweetheart," I croak out, closing the distance between us. I see another small bruise on her left cheekbone, giving me the urge to punch someone in the teeth. I've seen her in worse conditions when she was younger and still fighting, but this, knowing where it came from, it makes it so much worse.

"Don't worry, he looks much worse," Graham chimes in when I attempt to lift my fingers to Chiara's cheek but fail. I can't manage to touch her while she's in pain because I'm scared I will hurt her more.

"You let this happen?" I ask and grab my brother by the collar.

"Hey, I don't get in the middle of Chiara's fights, I never have. Plus, he attacked her first, so it was self-defence. If anyone can press charges, it's her," Graham explains, and while it makes me feel a little better, I'm still furious with him for not calling me sooner.

"She's getting stitches, Graham! How could you let this happen?" I ask, and he lifts his hands to my wrists, wiggling on them to release my grip on his collar.

"Hey, Leonard, remember how I have a voice too? A brain that makes decisions and such?" Chiara interrupts, and I shoot her an upset glare.

"Well, your big brain doesn't always make the right decisions, especially because you're stubborn. What you pulled was fucking dangerous, Starling," I say, but she merely shrugs, giving me a small smile.

"He attacked me first. I defended myself, and in the process, I finally got to beat him up for everything he's ever done. It's not my fault that he underestimated how strong I am, what a skillful fighter," she replies and gives me a shrug I wish would ease my nerves. Instead, my gaze drops to where the nurse stabs at her skin, and I feel ten times worse.

"Baby, I can't fathom why you'd put yourself at risk like that. Why didn't you run? Why didn't you come home to me? I—I—" My voice breaks off, but she takes my hand and pulls me toward her.

"I'm okay. Everything's fine, and now, we'll finally be rid of Tim. We can get restraining orders and—"

"And get him locked up for vandalism. I have the footage," I say before explaining that it was backed up.

"See? It'll be fine. He will have to pay for the damages. We will be rid of him now," she says, and I finally see the hope in her eyes. "You won't have lost anything and you won't have to invest more," she says, but I shake my head at how bloody clueless she is.

"You think I give a shit about the money? Chiara, no. The only reason why I was angry was because you put so much hard work into your gallery, and he tore it all down. I was upset because you were in pain. Would you please stop worrying about money, sweetheart?" I ask, and her features soften, revealing how much she cried. Her eyes are puffy and red, eye bags underneath them.

"I didn't want to disappoint you," she replies, and I grab her face between my hands.

"You could never, baby. Never. I love you," I say and she purses her lips, asking me for a kiss without using words.

I'm only happy to oblige.

My lips meet hers until I'm whole again.

Chiara and I are finally in bed. Her arm is stitched up and wrapped in a bandage. She said she's not in any pain, but I don't believe her. It must hurt. She got eight stitches after all, but she says nothing. Her naked body is pressed against mine, but I refused to touch her while she might be in pain from her injuries. It earned me a frown from her, but after what she thinks she put me through, she didn't argue. Instead, she snuggled up against my side and started running her nails up and down my torso. It doesn't exactly help keep my cock under control because it's swelling up from her touch, but I push the desire aside. Chiara needs to rest.

"*Amore?*" she says into the quiet room after a while, and I tilt my chin down to look into her eyes.

"Yes, sweetheart?" I reply, brushing a strand of her hair behind her ear. All of my attention is on the way her lips purse but not in the way she does when she wants me to kiss her. No. This is her in deep thought.

"I need a car. I have some money saved up, enough to get myself something old," she says, and I frown at the thought of her in another safety-hazardous shitbox like Delilah, her former car.

"I know you don't want my money, but, please, let me buy you a car," I say, but, of course, she merely shakes her head. "Please," I beg, brushing the backs of my fingers against her cheek.

"No, Leonard. I'm not letting you buy me a car. This has to be mine. All mine, even if it's a shitbox, as you called it," she replies, and I remember the one time I did say it to her face and not just in my head like before. I let out a low chuckle.

"Okay, we will find something affordable I will approve of, I'm sure of it," I reply although there is no way the few thousand pounds she saved over the last few months will be enough to get a good car.

"Leonard?" she says, and I give her a kiss because of how sweet she is.

"Yes, Starling?" I reply.

"I want you to change your mind," she says and trails her fingers down my tattooed chest until she reaches the trail of hair that leads to my cock. She keeps going slowly, seeing if I would stop her, but there is no way in hell I could remove her hand as she wraps it around my hard cock. "Oh," she blurts out when she feels how horny I am for her, and then a little giggle escapes her lips. "Guess you already did."

My lips find hers instantly after she's done talking, her peachy scent filling my nose until I can taste her. And Chiara tastes amazing. Like my home.

"I love you," I say into her mouth, bringing a moan from her lips.

"I love you, Leonard."

I move on top of her and like always, our bodies click into place because we were made for one another. My cock rubs along her clit as I grind myself into her, drawing out her pleasure until she whimpers and begs for more. And I give her everything. I slide into her with ease because she's so ready for me, she's soaked. We chase our pleasure because after the day we had, feeling close to each other is what we both crave the most. I fuck her slow and steady, but she's a moaning mess beneath me, telling me to keep going at the same pace because she's close. So, so close.

"Fuck, please, please, make me come," she begs, and I groan on top of her, angling up her hips to hit her G-spot with every stroke. "Faster, harder," Chiara cries out, and I pick up speed as I slam inside of her harder. "Yes, God, just like that!" I smile on top of her, bringing my lips to hers as my orgasm builds in my cock.

"You're fucking perfect, sweetheart. And all mine." I go even harder and faster until she's breathless and moaning even louder.

"I'm coming," she says and screams as her walls clench around me, pulling me straight over the edge with her. I come inside of her and then pull us onto our sides, kissing her to taste the pleasure in her bloodstream.

"I want forever with you, Starling," I say, wiping a strand of hair off her sweaty forehead.

She gives me an easy smile, as if she'd done it her whole life, and it's the best thing in the entire world.

"You already have it, Champ."

My lips envelop hers again while I get lost in the thoughts of our future.

It's too early to ask Mum for Grandmum's ring, right?

Spoiler Alert: This Epilogue contains spoilers of my books Rush: Part One & Rush: Part Two.

Epilogue

Leonard

Six Years Later

I walk into my wife's gallery with a bright smile on my face. Chiara and I got married four years ago in a private ceremony with only our closest friends and family. No one knows publicly, and I do my best to keep it from people after what happened five years ago. The death threats she got, the hate messages, everything I received on a daily basis was directed at her too all of a sudden, so I keep her as far away from the toxic world of the media. It's been working well, even if I hate hiding that I have the hottest wife to ever walk the Earth. Then again, I also like that she's just mine. I don't have to share her with the spotlight, which I love.

"*Amore,*" Chiara says when I walk toward her with a bouquet of flowers in my hands.

I've made it a habit to bring her a fresh one every week because of how hard she's working every single minute of every day. Benz comes walking toward me slowly, the old girl not as fast as she used to be but still so excited to see me. She comes to work with her Mamma every single day.

Chiara's art gallery is a booming success. She's shifted completely from digital immersive experiences to creating her own rooms. One of them has a balloon exhibition, inspired by the one we went to years ago but with Chiara's own twist to it. Another has the lights idea she had six years ago because everyone absolutely loves

371

it. It's what her gallery is most known for. The other rooms have more exhibitions but I forget all about them when my lips meet hers and a happy sigh escapes her lips.

"Hi, sweetheart," I reply and give her another kiss. "Do you have a minute? I'd like to discuss something with you," I say, and she turns to Lulu, who is now one of her employees, to let her know she'll be right back. Then, her hand slips into mine as we walk toward her office.

"How did your meeting with Valentina go?" she asks as we settle down on the couch I bought years ago for the sole purpose of having sex on it with her when she needs a stress reliever.

"It went well. She wants to partner up with me on the academy," I reply, earning myself an excited squeal from Chiara before she wraps her arms around my neck and her legs around my waist.

It's been my dream for the last few years now to open up a driver academy for kids like Valentina and me. Racing candidates who've never been given a chance, not because they aren't talented but because they come from backgrounds where they either can't afford it or where people won't look at them twice. That means I want to open an academy for children of all ethnicities, financial backgrounds, genders, and so on. I want a driver academy that is inclusive without a doubt. Valentina Romana, Adrian Romana's sister, is going to be the first female race car driver in the history of Formula One. I've been mentoring her for months now. She's the only one I wanted to have as an equal on this project, and I'm beyond happy she's excited to get started with me. Valentina will be a perfect asset for this journey.

Graham has agreed to help me out with all of the financial things since he went back to school to get a degree in finance. Irena and he got married two years ago, right after he graduated from university... again. I admire his dedication to studying because I graduated from high school, and that was it for my school career. Racing has always been more important anyway. Graham and Irena also decided to move to London a year ago, which helps me a lot when it comes to discussing business with my brother. They seem happy too, thinking about adopting soon.

Chiara's Mamma and Nonna visit us regularly. I still remember sitting down with them before I asked Starling to marry me, telling them how much I love their daughter and granddaughter, hoping for the blessing to marry her. I wasn't looking for permission. I would have married Chiara either way, but I wanted to show respect and go to them first. They seemed to like me more for it, which made me happy. They're two of the most important people in Chiara's life, making them two of mine. They were there when I won my second and third World Championships, and even though I'm in one of the middle field teams now and no longer a true competitor for the Championship, they're always supporting me.

"Did you tell Val you actually do like her? You know how I feel about you being so cold toward her all these years," Chiara says, interrupting my thoughts, and I place my mouth on her temple as I guide her gently toward the ground, even more carefully than I usually do. I have to be. For the first time in her life, she's more fragile than usual.

"Yes, sweetheart, I told her why I've been so reserved toward her," I promise, earning myself a sweet smile from my wife. I return it, running my fingers over her stomach.

"I think this is going to be my favorite investment you have ever made," she says before adding with panic in her eyes, "Apart from my gallery, of course." I chuckle in response.

"It's the most important one. I don't want my little girl to go through what Valentina or I went through," I say as I drop to my knees to kiss Chiara's tiny, swollen belly. Her hands run through my hair as I place my ear to where my daughter is growing. We may not have it confirmed yet, but I'm certain it's a girl.

"She won't. She'll have you," Chiara says, grabbing my chin to bring my face back to hers and kissing me until I forget my own name.

The End

Chiara and Leonard Will Return in Future Pitstop Series Novels

Sneak Peak

The Inside of a Rainbow

Chapter 1

Storm

Peace. I never feel at peace except when racing down the highway on my bike. The rest of the world disappears into a blur as I find harmony in the speed of this heavy machine in my grasp, under my complete control.

I like being in control. It steadies me in the chaos of my life. *Work?* Forgotten. *Drama with my family?* Vanished. *All the fucking chores waiting for me at home?* Not important. Nothing's important except for the calmness of this moment.

Riding my bike is my happy place.

But every ride has to come to an end eventually. I have to return to my responsibilities and figure out what the hell I'm going to do about the huge bomb my dad dropped on me this morning. Maybe avoiding it for a bit longer isn't that bad. I could keep going, keep riding until... well, until I permanently escape this hell of a small town I call home.

My best friend, Elias, points two of his fingers toward the closest exit, and I give him a single nod of my head. I follow behind, slowing my speed as we reach the neighborhood area. He gestures to the drive-thru of the only fast-food place in our town, and I shake my head when I realize that's why he was so eager to get off the highway. That *idiota* is hungry.

Elias orders some food for both of us while I wait in the parking lot, inspecting my bike. Something felt a bit off earlier, and I want to make sure everything is in order. I didn't spend almost thirty grand on this Kawasaki to have it fall apart on me now.

I pull my helmet off my head and place it on my seat, bending down to check the left side, then the right, front, back, and as much of the underside as I can see. Nothing looks out of place, so I straighten out my back again and let out a sigh. I'm starting to imagine things. *Great.* Just what I needed at this point in my life.

"Here ya go. Smile for me, and I'll give you your food," Elias teases, but I pull my lips into a thin line.

"You have three seconds to hand over my burger." I don't tell him what happens if he doesn't. We both know I'd smack the back of his head the first chance I'd get.

"I'm just messing with you, Mr. Grumpy, don't worry," he says and hands me the bag with my food in it. I mumble a 'thanks' before I pop a fry into my mouth. "I do have one question I've always wanted to ask you." *Of fucking course.* Elias always has some sort of ridiculous question to ask.

"I swear, if it's something as stupid as you look, I will punch you," I say, and he bursts into laughter.

"No, no, I promise this is a genuine question," he assures me.

I lean the bag with my food against my helmet on my bike, waiting for him to ask it. My arms cross in front of my chest, my breathing even as I get ready to kick his ass.

"When you have sex with someone, do you also always look this unhappy, or do they get you to smile a little?"

A sigh slips past my lips before I make my way toward where he's standing. Like the coward he is, he runs around his bike and away from me, laughing at his own joke like it was the best one he's ever made.

"Okay, okay, I'm sorry," he says when I catch up to him. Lucky for him, he's still wearing his helmet, so the smack doesn't hurt him as much as I wish it would. "Come on, Storm, tell me what's bothering you," he pleads after I've gone back to eating my food.

Storm. A nickname he decided to call me exclusively because I guided him to safety when we were out for a ride and it started to pour down like the world was going to end. It was one of the scariest moments of my entire life. But nothing could ever compare to—

"Storm," Elias repeats, this time his voice sounding serious and sincere.

"Yeah?" I ask because I was spiraling into the black hole inside of my chest, and it usually takes a few hours for me to completely snap out of it again.

"What did your dad want this morning?"

My dad... my role model, guiding compass, and an absolute piece of shit when it comes to money. That man is the greediest person I've ever met.

"You know what, man? I'm not hungry anymore. I think I'll just head home. See you there?" I ask, but knowing my best friend, he's not going to leave me alone until he's found a way to cheer me up.

"You want to go ride for a while longer?" he says, and I suck in a quiet, sharp breath.

"Yeah," I reply because sadness is starting to creep into my chest, and the patience to deal with suppressing it doesn't exist in me today.

"Okay," Elias replies, squeezing my shoulder to comfort me. "Only if you smile at me though." Another sigh leaves me, then— "Ow, I'm not wearing my helmet anymore!" he complains.

"Stop asking questions that are none of your business."

Especially because I don't want him to know the last time I had sex with anyone was the day before my ex decided I was no longer good enough for her and fucked one of my former close friends. Yeah, he and I aren't very close anymore. All of this happened six months ago, and I've moved on since then, but I haven't been able to be that vulnerable with anyone else. I can't bring myself to open up to that level of losing control.

"Ah, right, your vow of sexual abstinence, I almost forgot," he jokes, but I'm too surprised by his words to scowl at him.

"I don't have a vow of abstinence," I blurt out, and Elias lets out another amused laugh, stuffing his burger into his mouth a second later.

"Yeah, right," he replies with a full mouth, and I shake my head. "When's the last time you even looked at a woman?" I cock an eyebrow at his question.

"I had lunch with Mamá yesterday." Elias rolls his eyes in response.

"We both know that's not what I meant," he replies with a snort, and I shake my head once again.

"I do not have a vow of abstinence, I just haven't found anyone I feel connected to recently, which by the way is, *again*, none of your fucking business."

I slide my helmet on, fasten the clasp, and then swing my leg over the true love of my life. For once, Elias stays quiet as he finishes his meal and then gets on his bike as well.

Elias gives me a honk once he's ready, earning himself yet another shake of my head. I don't know what kind of annoyance pills he took this morning but, fuck, he's bugging the hell out of me.

He zooms past me on the way back to the highway, and I smile under my helmet, something I only do for myself, right before I speed past him. Elias forgets that everything he knows, I taught him. I was the one who showed him how to even get on the bike. He doesn't stand a chance against me when it comes to riding, and he never will. This is second nature to me. It's what I want to do for a career.

Now, after what my dad has asked of me?

I have no idea what the hell I'm going to do.

Acknowledgements

I cannot believe that this is already the sixth book I have published. I am so eternally grateful for every single person that helped me get here because this is truly a dream come true. To all of my readers, thank you for supporting me and loving my stories. Thank you for cheering me on and loving Formula One just as much as I do. It has made it possible for me to keep writing these books.

For the first time, I also want to thank my characters. They have gotten me through so many hard times. I have come out the other end so much happier with myself, my trauma, my mental health struggles, and even some of my relationships. I am eternally grateful to them for letting me fall in love with their stories. I am eternally grateful to all of my female main characters for holding the kind of strength I sometimes cannot find in myself. I am eternally grateful to all of my male main characters for loving their women so wholly and fully.

About the Author

B ridget L. Rose is a half-German, half-Italian author, who was born and raised in Germany until the age of thirteen. She fell in love with books from a young age, and soon discovered her passion for writing as well. She likes to spend her free time with her family, reading a book, or writing one herself. She also adores the sport Formula One, which led her to write her Pitstop Series.

Books by Bridget L. Rose

The Pitstop Series

Jump-Start

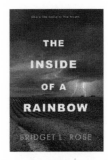

The Inside of a Rainbow

Rush: Part One & Two

Chase: Part One & Two

From Angels to Devils Series

From Devils to Angels

Made in United States
Orlando, FL
17 June 2024

48001285R00236